SPECIAL MESSAGE TO READERS

This book is published under the auspices of

THE ULVERSCROFT FOUNDATION

(registered charity No. 264873 UK)

Established in 1972 to provide funds for research, diagnosis and treatment of eye diseases. Examples of contributions made are: —

A Children's Assessment Unit at
Moorfield's Hospital, London.

•

Twin operating theatres at the
Western Ophthalmic Hospital, London.

•

A Chair of Ophthalmology at the
Royal Australian College of Ophthalmologists.

•

The Ulverscroft Children's Eye Unit at the
Great Ormond Street Hospital For Sick Children,
London.

You can help further the work of the Foundation by making a donation or leaving a legacy. Every contribution, no matter how small, is received with gratitude. Please write for details to:

**THE ULVERSCROFT FOUNDATION,
The Green, Bradgate Road, Anstey,
Leicester LE7 7FU, England.
Telephone: (0116) 236 4325**

**In Australia write to:
THE ULVERSCROFT FOUNDATION,
c/o The Royal Australian College of
Ophthalmologists,
27, Commonwealth Street, Sydney,
N.S.W. 2010.**

Sebastian Faulks is best known for his French trilogy, *The Girl at the Lion d'Or*, *Birdsong*, and *Charlotte Gray*. He has also worked extensively as a journalist, and last year wrote and presented the Channel Four series *Churchill's Secret Army*.

ON GREEN DOLPHIN STREET

America, 1959: With two young children she adores, loving parents back in London, and an admired husband, Charlie, working at the British Embassy in Washington, the world seems an effervescent place of parties, jazz and family happiness to Mary van der Linden. But the Eisenhower years are ending, and 1960 brings the presidential battle between two ambitious senators: John Kennedy and Richard Nixon. An American newspaper reporter called Frank Renzo dramatically enters the van der Lindens' lives, and through him Mary is forced to confront the terror of the Cold War that is the dark background of their carefree existence.

Books by Sebastian Faulks
Published by The House of Ulverscroft:

THE GIRL AT THE LION D'OR
CHARLOTTE GRAY

SEBASTIAN FAULKS

---------------◆---------------

ON
GREEN DOLPHIN
STREET

Complete and Unabridged

CHARNWOOD
Leicester

First published in Great Britain in 2001 by
Hutchinson
London

First Charnwood Edition
published 2002
by arrangement with
Hutchinson
The Random House Group Limited
London

The moral right of the author has been asserted

Copyright © 2001 by Sebastian Faulks
All rights reserved

British Library CIP Data

Faulks, Sebastian, *1953* –
    On Green Dolphin Street.—Large print ed.—
    Charnwood library series
    1. English—United States—Fiction
    2. United States—Politics and government—
    1953 – 1961 —Fiction
    3. Political fiction
    4. Large type books
    I. Title
    823.9'14 [F]

    ISBN 0–7089–9355–9

2838136✕
Published by
F. A. Thorpe (Publishing)
Anstey, Leicestershire

Set by Words & Graphics Ltd.
Anstey, Leicestershire
Printed and bound in Great Britain by
T. J. International Ltd., Padstow, Cornwall

This book is printed on acid-free paper

To Richard and Elizabeth Dalkeith

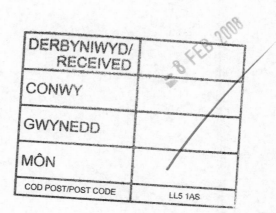

DERBYNIWYD/ RECEIVED	8 FEB 2008
CONWY	
GWYNEDD	
MÔN	
COD POST/POST CODE	LL5 1AS

1

The van der Lindens' house was distinguished from the others on the street by the creeper that covered half the front, running up to the children's rooms beneath the eaves, where at night the glow from the sidewalk lamp gave to Number 1064 the depth and shadow of a country settlement, somewhere far away from this tidy urban street. Among the row of new Cadillacs, their tail-fins glinting like a rumour of sharks, Charlie van der Linden's two-tone 1953 Kaiser Manhattan, maroon with cream roof and a dented rear fender, struck a doubtful, out-of-town note.

The house dominated its plot, the architect having sacrificed half the backyard to the status two extra rooms would bring a man. The lawn that remained was part paved, with a brick barbecue and a basketball hoop left by a previous tenant; at the end of the grass was a child's metal swing which Charlie had assembled after a summer cook-out, to the amusement of his children, who had left it to rust unused. Where its neighbours sank their near-identical roots into the earth, this house gave off an air of transience; and when at night the bedroom lights went off along the street, like candles on an old man's cake, the lamps in the van der Lindens' house would often start to blaze again as a party spilled into another room. The guests' cars were

1

parked along the street as far as Number 1082, home to the Washington correspondent of a French magazine that no one had ever seen.

In their rooms, Louisa and Richard stirred occasionally in their sleep as a shriek of mirth came up the stairs or the gesture of some exuberant raconteur sent a glass shattering on the tiled floor of the hall. If the party wore on too long, Mary would go upstairs to check on them, leaning across their beds, fussing over the blankets and tucking them in; sometimes in the morning the children had a memory of her scent, lipstick, gin, and words of love pressed into their ears and sealed with the touch of her fingers.

That December evening, the van der Lindens were having a party. It was to be their last of the decade and it marked the anniversary of their wedding eleven years earlier in London. It was a change for them to have a private pretext; it was a relief not to have to feign interest in a visiting dignitary, a national day or a harassed politician who was passing through Washington in a daze, uttering solemn pleasantries. The guests were a favoured variation of the regular diplomats and journalists; there were one or two neighbours, either the most genial or the ones who would otherwise complain; there was also Weissman, Charlie's doctor, and his Haitian bride.

'To Scottish national day,' said Charlie, flushed and off-duty as he unscrewed a bottle of scotch and poured three fingers of it over ice for Edward Renshaw, his closest ally at the British

Embassy. 'Tell me, how's your economy doing these days?'

'It's a wreck. Chin-chin.'

Mary van der Linden stood in the sitting room, her dark hair alive in the electric glow of the table lamp behind her. Her doting brown eyes returned to Charlie. Here was the fountain of her happiness, her repeated glances seemed to suggest: erratic, flawed, but, in his way, dependable. Mary's smile was not a thing anyone could predict; she was not the diplomatic wife in all circumstances. To begin with, she was too shy and found each function a trial of her resolve, but she seemed to have a resource of contentment that was stable, beyond the irritation of the day, and when her smile came from that depth, her face was lit with such serenity that people stopped for a moment to watch.

In the kitchen, Dolores, the resident Puerto Rican maid provided by the Embassy, was cutting Wisconsin cheddar into cubes, then impaling them, with olives, on to plastic cocktail sticks. With these and dishes of pretzels, nuts and clam dip with Salteen crackers, she loaded another tray and squeezed her way through the hall.

Charlie put a bossa nova record on the phonograph, took a cigarette from the pack in his shirt pocket and inhaled the smoke as he gazed upon his party. His face, though flushed by broken capillaries and patchily shaved beneath the chin, retained some youthful beauty; his rumpled hair and sagging tie gave

3

him a schoolboy look that the creeping fleshiness about his jaw had not quite dispelled. He saw Mary, now in the doorway to the hall, and smiled at her. It was a complicit smile which acknowledged the joint effort that their days consisted of — the compromises of the guest list, their shared jokes and fears about this man's wife and that man's drinking; the daily division of irksome duties, the labour of managing children and the pleasure of having despatched them, just in time, to bed. Charlie van der Linden was in trouble, not just with his health, but with his life; yet as he caught his wife's eye he felt he could postpone a reckoning indefinitely, that three more glasses of scotch, a quiet weekend in the rustic inns of the Shenandoah valley and maybe some hard thinking would see him clear.

'Who's that man talking to Mary?' Charlie felt his elbow taken by Edward Renshaw.

'He's a journalist, I think. I bumped into him this morning at the Spanish Embassy do and he claims we've met before somewhere.'

'Let's go and say hello.'

'Eddie,' said Mary, 'this is Frank Renzo. Frank's in town for a few days.'

'Good to meet you.' Frank Renzo was a tall, lean man, his cropped hair showing the first dust of grey; his accent was from the urban Midwest, perhaps Chicago.

'Do you need a drink, Frank?' said Charlie.

'No, I already have one.'

'What are you doing in town?' said Edward Renshaw politely.

4

'Just a piece for my paper. I'm based in New York.'

'Well, enjoy yourself,' said Charlie. 'Call if we can do anything to help.'

Mary watched as Charlie left the small group and went towards the bar he had set up in the corner of the room. Normally they hired a barman from the Embassy staff to stand behind the row of liquor bottles, but tonight, as a small gesture of economy, Charlie had taken the task on himself. He scooped more ice cubes into the ornamental bucket from a pail concealed beneath the tablecloth.

'They say the Kennedys are buying a new house on N Street,' said the man from the *Post*. 'Martha knows the realtor who showed them round. Apparently Jackie was crazy for it.'

'Oh yes?' Charlie poured bourbon over ice and heard it snap. 'I thought they were buying Joe Alsop's.' He felt the scotch beginning to take hold, or rather to relax his grip, as he approached the state of uncritical bonhomie he most enjoyed. He smiled to himself. It was of course an irony that only in these moments of inebriation, these instants of perfect balance, did he have the philosophical poise to see his difficulties in their true perspective and to know that he could one day banish them. For the moment he was alive, and he glowed with the pleasure of these people's company. At bad times he suspected that the fire was not renewable, that, for their delectation, he was burning away the core of himself; he feared that few of them shared his embrace of the minute, or were even momentarily diverted by his defiance of pettiness and tedium and time passing. He had never reached the lowest point of all, at which he might have wondered whether there was something morbid in his being so solitary in his flight from an unnamed terror.

Feeling as good as he did, generosity surging in his veins, tobacco unfurling in his lungs, he had no choice but to push onwards.

'We meet on Wednesdays after we've taken the kids to school,' Lauren Williams was telling Frank Renzo. 'Then for lunch Kelly makes the appetizer, Mary-Beth or I does the entrée and Katy does the dessert. She does the best desserts you ever tasted.'

'And you always have a project?'

'Sure. Sometimes we just have a book we've all read, sometimes we'll go see a show.'

'And is that all the ladies in your group?'

'Oh, no, there's more. That's just the inner circle. We're usually seven or eight. Mary comes along pretty often.'

'And what does she do?'

'You mean, like, what's her specialty? Well, she brings wine sometimes. You know, coming from Europe. I don't know.' Lauren Williams began to laugh. 'Katy, what does Mary bring to our group?'

'Mary?' Katy Renshaw, too, looking at Frank's grave face, began to laugh. 'I guess she brings culture. Isn't that right, Mary?'

'Isn't what right?' said Mary, turning from another conversation.

'In fact,' said Lauren Williams, 'Mary's writing a book.'

'Am I?'

'Charlie always says you are.'

'He has to find an explanation for me.'

Mary went with a tray out into the kitchen, where Dolores was stirring a pan.

'Happy, Dolores?'

'Yes, thank you, Mrs van der Linden. You happy?'

★ ★ ★

Mary considered, as she leaned back for a moment with her back to the stove and sipped from the glass of gin and tonic with its clashing ice. Happy . . .

When Louisa was twenty months old, she could talk with the fluency of a child of three or four, yet what was in her mind was quite unformed. On the Home Service in London she had heard the stations of the shipping forecast and talked back to them, Dogger, Fisher, German Bight, her head cocked to one side, her concentration earnest. In moments of exalted love, of rapture, Mary believed Louisa's mind was not empty, but filled with clouds of glory from a previous and purer world. She had spent many weeks in hospital with Louisa while doctors tried to discover the source of some violent allergy. When they eventually came home, they were seldom out of the same room. At bath-time, while Mary lay back in the water, the child stood hammering at her mother's raised

7

and closed knees, demanding to be let into the castle that would be formed by their parting. Once inside, she would ask questions about things that puzzled her: America, for instance: how big it was, how far, how different and then, after a long, considering pause: 'Do they have children in America?' Now, at ten years old, she had retained that unworldly grace, though she had been bruised by some encounters with the everyday that would have left no mark on others.

Richard, her brother, felt no such pain. To begin with, Mary had worried that she could not love a second child as much. He was so different from his sister that she was astounded to concede that he had eventually quarried out a comparable place in her affections for himself; by brute persistence he commandeered a territory as rare and irreplaceable as that occupied by Louisa. Perhaps it was the smell of him that first intoxicated Mary, of his neck along the hairline when she lifted him from his cot on her return from an evening out: the faint aroma of honey, calico, half-baked bread, wild strawberries, of warmth itself, was so delightful to inhale that she made excuses to 'resettle' him, though it was clear that he was already as tranquil as a sleeping child could be. His fierceness was the opposite of Louisa's detached and dream-like curiosity; he wanted the same lunch each day, the same programme on the wireless and then, at the same hour, to visit the bathroom where he would sit on the wooden seat, the cat clamped beneath his arm while, with tears rolling over his cheeks, he sang 'The Camptown Races'.

Happy, thought Mary, as she folded the apron over the back of the chair and straightened her hair in the mirror over the kitchen counter: maybe not exactly happy, not in the facile way the word itself suggested, but who in these circumstances could not at least be touched from time to time by the ridiculous joy of existing?

★ ★ ★

Back in the sitting room, beneath the simmering layer of fresh cigarette smoke, Duncan Trench was stabbing his finger at Katy Renshaw, Edward's American wife. Trench's huge, slabbed cheeks and small eyes gave him what people called a chub-face, though the colour of his complexion always reminded Mary not of fish but of undercooked beef.

'If the Negroes in North Carolina want to sit at the lunch counters all day without being served,' he was saying, 'then the storekeeper is quite entitled to use reasonable force to evict them. They're preventing him from making a living.'

Few people knew what Trench's job in Chancery entailed, but his manner was seldom diplomatic.

'Sure,' said Frank Renzo, 'and he's preventing them from having lunch.'

'There are plenty of other places they can go.'

'But they want to go to Woolworth's. They like the sixty-five cent turkey dinner. You ever try it?'

'No, but that's not the point. What I'm saying is — '

9

'You should. It needs some gravy. But, you know, it's pretty good.'

'By refusing to move they're preventing customers being served.'

'But they are the customers.'

'You know what I mean.'

Mary could see Duncan Trench's colour go from beef to bortsch as she moved swiftly into the group.

'Who'd like another drink?' she said. 'Duncan, have you met Kelly Eberstadt? She and her husband have moved into Bethesda and — '

'Did you ever hear of a young man called Emmett Till?' said Frank.

'I don't believe so,' said Trench, as Mary took his elbow and guided him away.

'You'd have liked him. Your kinda guy.' Frank Renzo watched Trench depart; Katy Renshaw stared down at her shiny shoes for a moment.

'Well,' said Katy, looking up brightly again. 'Que sera, sera.'

'Nice song.'

'Nice movie. You like Doris Day?'

'Sure I like Doris Day, though I guess I like jazz even better,' said Frank.

'Oh, so does Charlie! Let's put on a record and we can dance.'

The guests began to leave soon after one, though it took so long for them to be gone that Charlie was able to drink a half-bottle of burgundy he found in the dresser and a tumbler of Four Roses on the rocks as a nightcap. From time to time he tottered to the doorway, chastely pecking Lauren Williams on her powdered cheek, pummelling her husband, whose name always just eluded him, on the shoulder, taking the opportunity to bury his face in Katy Renshaw's fragrant hair as he squeezed her waist.

'A stoop full of kisses and goodbyes,' he murmured. 'Do you know that line?'

'What?'

'It's from Wallace Stevens.'

'Not in the *Collected* I read, Charlie,' said Edward Renshaw, as he threw a wrap round the shoulders of his wife.

'You're right, Eddie. I made it up.'

The night had grown woundingly cold with a breeze whistling down out of Canada. Charlie lit one more goodnight cigarette as he leaned against the door-frame; Mary stood beside him as the last of their guests started up their cars. An upstairs light went on opposite: it was the Chinese couple who dined on bowls of clear soup and went to bed at seven. Mary flinched. The guests had left quietly, but the rumble of Detroit machinery was enough to shake the storm-windows gently in their frames.

As Mary looked down again, she saw a tall figure making its way towards them, hunched, veering from side to side. It was Frank Renzo. He was clasping his right hand in his left, and behind him, along the snowy sidewalk, there ran a trail of blood.

'Jesus . . . goddam car door,' he was muttering.

Mary went forward anxiously. 'What happened? Come inside. It's all right, it's just tiles,'

11

said Mary as she led him, dripping, through to the kitchen.

'What happened?' said Charlie. 'Do we have a bandage or something?'

'Upstairs. In the bathroom.'

Frank's face was pale. Mary held his hand beneath the kitchen faucet and the cold water pounded on to the metal sink, swilling with its rosy flow the last of the jettisoned clam dip. Mary pushed back the shirt cuff and rolled up the sleeve of his suit with its grey nailhead pattern. The cut was deep but clean; it ran through from the base of the thumb down into the blue wiring of the wrist.

'Goddam car tool . . . '

'Maybe we should call a doctor. Perhaps it needs stitches.'

'Sutures? No, no, it's fine. As soon as it stops bleeding.'

'Is this any use?' said Charlie. He was holding a first-aid box.

'Let's have a look,' said Mary. 'You'd better keep that hand under the tap.'

'What happened?' said Charlie.

'It was an accident. Could I use your telephone?'

'I'm sure we had a bandage.'

'It's in the hall.'

'Did Louisa take it for her Barbie?'

When Frank came back into the kitchen, Mary dressed the cut with what she could find in the box.

'You sure you're all right?' said Charlie. 'Would you like a drink?'

'Maybe some scotch? Tell me, who was that guy with the red face?'

'Duncan Trench,' said Mary. 'He's at the Embassy.'

'Is he a thimble-belly?

'What?'

'Can he hold his liquor?'

'I think he was tight.'

Frank sat back with his drink. 'Thank you.' For the first time since he had been back in the house, he smiled. 'To tell the truth, I'm a little scared of blood.'

'Let's go and sit in the living room,' said Charlie, as though sensing the chance that the party might re-ignite. He poured himself a measure of Four Roses to keep Frank company and lit another cigarette as he put on 'Songs for Swingin' Lovers'. It no longer seemed polite to ask Frank exactly what had happened to his hand.

'That girl told me you like jazz,' said Frank.

'I certainly do,' said Charlie. 'We don't get to hear much in Washington. You live in New York, don't you?'

'That's right,' said Frank. 'I have an apartment loaned me by a friend who's on a foreign posting. It's in the Village.'

'How lovely,' said Mary.

'I don't like it,' said Frank, grinding out his cigarette. 'I don't like the Village.'

'Really? Why?'

'Too many bead shops and fancy bakeries.'

Mary, standing with her back to the fireplace, looked at Frank closely for the first time. It was

13

impossible to tell how serious he was being. Surely anyone below the age of fifty, particularly if he liked jazz, would want to live in Greenwich Village more than any neighbourhood in the United States of America; but Frank didn't seem to be joking. His face, with its long, narrow jaw on which the first shadows of the morning's beard were darkening, was not smiling. He looked drawn and anxious: the thin lapels of his suit, the narrow tie pulled halfway down over his cotton shirt, the long limbs folded over one another combined to suggest fragility. His pants had ridden up a little, showing where the grey woollen socks hung from his shins in slouched, concentric rings. There were dark hemispheres beneath his eyes, yet he showed no signs of wanting to leave. A drop of blood fell from the saturated dressing on to the maple parquet beside his chair.

Charlie said, 'Have you heard this fellow Ornette Coleman I keep reading about?'

'I went to see him once. At the Five Spot. I didn't really like it. That free stuff. I'm not sure it's as difficult as it looks.'

'Apparently he can play the piano and the violin and the trumpet as well.'

'Sure. But how well does he play them? That's the point. Do you like Miles Davis?'

'Quite,' said Charlie. 'But I'm pretty much lost with anything after Duke Ellington. This hard bop stuff, you know Charlie Parker and Dizzy — '

'Yeah, but Miles Davis is kind of melodic, too. Did you hear the *Kind of Blue* record?'

14

Charlie refreshed their glasses and put his feet up on the table.

'Would you two like something to eat?' said Mary. 'Those little snacks were a long time ago.'

'To tell the truth, darling,' said Charlie, 'I'm not really hungry.'

'Frank? I could make an omelette and toast. There are some potatoes I could fry up, too.'

'I guess I should head back.'

'Have a bloody omelette,' said Charlie genially. 'Here, listen to this.' He took off Frank Sinatra and began riffling through a line of long-playing records held in a red wire rack.

By four o'clock, they had sampled most of the collection and the bottle of Four Roses was empty. Mary showed Frank upstairs to the lumber room at the back of the house; he lost his footing for a moment on the uncarpeted stair. Charlie was already in bed by the time Mary got back to their room and started to undress.

'Have we got to get up early?' he said.

'Just the usual. School.'

Mary slid in beside him.

'What do you make of that chap?' said Charlie.

'Who? Frank?'

'Yes.'

'Strange,' said Mary. 'Your sort of man, though.'

'Yup. Ghastly taste in music.'

★　★　★

15

That night, for no reason she could see, Mary dreamed of David Oliver. His presence in her dreams was, naturally, unpredictable, though he always took centre stage as though nothing had gone wrong.

In the second summer of the War, having completed her studies, Mary was in London, living with her parents in their house in Regent's Park. She helped them stick tape crosses on the window panes in the corridor that ran off the first-floor landing; though London was a dangerous place to be, beneath the German bombs, her parents felt better with their only child wrapped up safe inside their house. Mary, while she set about applying to join the WAAF, was glad to be home again, and to resume the familiar routine all three of them pretended they followed only to please the other two. Before dinner they gathered in the drawing room for drinks and did the crossword in *The Times*. Mary's father, James Kirwan, read out the clues to give the women a chance to volunteer an answer; if none was forthcoming, he would fill it in himself with a propelling pencil. 'Mary, here's one for you: 'One takes a hammering, sleeping rough without security'. Twelve letters. G, two blanks C, ends P three blanks. If 'Pietà' is right, which I think it must be.'

'Glockenspiel,' said Mary. 'I don't know why.'

After dinner they would listen to the wireless, read or play cards. James often wore strangely unbecoming clothes, lumberjack shirts or tennis sweaters, after his day at the Treasury; Mary's mother, Elizabeth, was usually in a suit she had

16

worn to the surgery where she worked as a general practitioner. James was a solidly made man, patient and sardonic; Elizabeth suffered from weak eyesight, was sympathetic, untidy, with grey hair struggling to escape from a variety of restraints, and still had the clear skin and wide dark eyes that had made her beautiful. She also had a ferocious temper, which exploded without warning; although the subsequent peace-making could sometimes make the atmosphere more harmonious than before the outburst, it was a process the others both feared.

Mary had thought all children were as richly enfolded in love as she was because the child assumes the extent to which it possesses any quality is the norm, until its experience of others' lives gives it a median against which to judge. It was not until her twenties that she started to appreciate that, even among families generally termed happy, few children had enjoyed what she could now see that she had had: a triangle of affection, in which each person was fully contented only in the presence of the other two. Sometimes when it was growing dark she watched the railings at the foot of Primrose Hill from her bedroom window until she saw her father's hat and turned-up raincoat progressing towards the gloomy street lamp; though he denied it when she taxed him with it later, it was clear to her that his step unconsciously quickened to something near a run as he approached his house.

One day he brought back with him to tea a man called David Oliver, an economist who had been seconded to the Treasury from London University. He sat next to the fire with his teacup rattling in his lap; he was awkwardly polite towards Mrs Kirwan, struggling to his feet each time she came back into the room, slopping tea into the saucer, and was deferential towards her husband, occasionally slipping in a vocative 'sir'. He had round cheeks and wire-rimmed glasses; it was a face that seemed aching to be comic, and his manner suggested some hilarity suppressed, but he successfully maintained a solemn front, smiling only when he glanced across at Mary, who was sitting on the sofa, her stockinged feet beneath her, stroking the marmalade cat.

Mary Kirwan, at the age of twenty-one, had something of the feline about herself. She was smaller than either of her parents, lacking her father's solid build or her mother's height; she was small-boned, with wavy hair of a colour bordering on black, cut a little above the shoulder and held off her face with combs. Her movements were still quick and girlish, while her features were those of her mother at the same age: large, dark eyes, prone to fright, in pale, clear skin. 'It's like looking at a miniature version of myself,' Elizabeth said. 'Like looking in a mirror that slightly reduces everything.' Her sense of her daughter as someone of not quite serious adult size was integral to the way she loved her.

Mary's father often brought home people from work; he liked to think his wife and daughter would enjoy their conversation and he wanted

18

lonely colleagues to think they were free to share in his unexpected domestic happiness. A bachelor who lived in Southwark digs, where the landlady's offering was some version of stew and semolina at six o'clock, David Oliver was easily persuaded to stay to dinner. He drank gin and orange and accepted two refills.

'David's a terrific brainbox,' said Mary's father over dinner. 'People are in awe of him at work.'

'I had to make myself good at work because no one took me seriously.'

'Why was that?' said Elizabeth.

'It just happened. At school, at work, wherever I've been, it's always the same. The others always seemed to think I was a figure of fun.'

'But why?'

'I don't know.' David looked down into his wine glass; he seemed less nervous than before. 'Maybe I've just got a ridiculous face.'

A week later, Mary had a postcard from David asking if she would like to go to the pictures; there was a cinema in Bloomsbury still showing *Rebecca*, he said. Concealing the fact that she had already seen it, Mary took a bus to Russell Square and sat through the film a second time. Afterwards, they went to an ABC café, where they had tea and dry buns; David told her about his work and how little he liked it. He was in a reserved occupation, required to lend the weight of his economic expertise to the war effort; he had failed an army medical on the grounds that he was still debilitated by childhood polio.

'But it's absurd,' he said, drawing a face with his finger on the steamed window of the café.

'I'm as strong as an ox. I play squash twice a week. As soon as this job's over, I'm going to reapply.'

'I think you should,' said Mary. 'That's a good drawing, by the way.'

'What?' David rubbed his hand quickly across the pane.

'Do you do proper drawings? I mean on paper, not on glass?'

'I do go to life classes, I admit. In an awful draughty place in Battersea. We draw a little man who used to be a prize-fighter, or so he says. He's very hairy.'

Mary looked at David's face closely: his blinking eyes and plump cheeks would hardly have enthralled a Rebecca, but she felt at ease with him, flattered by his attention.

David continued to send her postcards; he seemed anxious that her parents should know that he communicated with her, that there should be nothing underhand in his approach. He invited her to watch him play squash, where he revealed an unexpectedly muscular and competitive side, whipping the small black ball from the hidden corners of the court with a powerful wrist, his plimsolls squeaking with torsion on the narrow floorboards. He took her to a pub; he took her boating on the Serpentine; he invited her back to his digs and made her toast on the gas fire in his room overlooking Trinity Church Square. At Mary's request, he showed her his sketchbooks, including charcoal drawings of the hirsute prize-fighter, and some watercolours of intense indigo and crimson.

One Sunday she arrived at David's lodgings in her WAAF uniform, free not to return until ten. The film they had agreed on was due to start at five, and David made cocktails from gin and various tins of fruit juice he had found in his landlady's cupboard. After lunch, Mary curled up on his sofa with a book, while he began to sketch, standing in the window where the light was best.

'Would you like me to pose for you?' said Mary, bored by the book.

David raised his eyebrows. 'It's rather cold.'

'David! I didn't mean — '

'Of course not. I was being silly.'

She looked at his suddenly serious face, with the light coming through behind it, and she thought how much she liked him.

Flushed by the cocktails, she said, 'I will if you like.'

David said nothing for a moment, then, 'Are you sure?'

Mary laughed and sprang from the sofa. 'You look so solemn!'

He grimaced and exhaled, as though he did not know what to do.

'You could start by lighting the gas,' said Mary.

'All right. You can undress behind that screen. There's a dressing-gown on the chair.'

As she stepped out of her skirt, Mary was aware that something more than art was happening. She had made no plans, but so great was her confidence in being loved and not betrayed that she barely hesitated, unfastening the hooks and clips of her underwear; she followed some light instinctive purpose, immune to the cautious gravity of self-questioning. Perhaps it was necessary in some way to liberate herself from the perfect triangle of her parents' pure emotion, to coarsen the texture of her life, but she felt no awareness of this thought, only a strange levity as she wrapped David's scratchy woollen dressing-gown around her.

Then, as she went back to the sofa, she changed her mind: it was only a drawing, nothing more than that. Her posing for him showed a new degree of trust and friendship — one that he had more than earned — but when she saw the prosaic details of his artistic preparations, watched him roll back the page on the pad and clip it in place, she saw she had been wrong to think this was somehow a significant moment.

'How do you want me?'

'Are you warm enough? If so, you can take the dressing-gown off.'

Apart from parents and doctors, Mary had never stood naked before anyone in her life. She had been so used to think of herself in the diminutive, her own body reflected back through the loving eyes of those who still viewed her as a child, that she had little sense of her breasts and the dark, filmy circles that spread from their centre; she was unaware of any effect the sight of her pale skin and its inverse, hidden folds might have on the clothed man standing opposite.

She held her hand for a moment across her

chest as she sat down again, then breathed deeply and put it by her side.

'Is this all right?'

'Just turn to your left a little. That's right.'

For twenty minutes, David stood scratching at the pad with short, irritable strokes, his eyes flashing back and forth behind the lenses of his spectacles. Mary knew that one thing a model was not supposed to do was ask to see the picture, and she concentrated on keeping still. Her back ached from the lack of support in the broken-springed sofa, and a nerve, which had caught in the ball of her foot where she had arched it in the hope of grace, was making her leg tremble.

Eventually, David put down his pencil and came over to where she sat.

'Can I rearrange you a little?' he said.

He lifted her elbow and resettled it.

'This isn't working at all,' he said.

'You look so worried.'

'I can't concentrate. You know why.'

'Do I?' It was the first time Mary had seen herself through the eyes of a man; and this intelligent, worldly person seemed quite disabled, reduced to helplessness, by some power of hers alone. Seeing this, she felt an exquisite trepidation.

David moved her arm again, this time allowing his hand to touch her breast. His voice was clotted. 'You're very beautiful, you know.'

'I'm not.'

'You are, you are.' He ran his hand over her abdomen, down between her legs while his other

23

hand stroked her forehead. 'With your black gypsy hair.'

'It's not black.'

'Almost.'

His hand ran slickly through her, then settled to a point of sensation that made her close her eyes as she felt her spine grow numb. The last coherent thought she had was that she still had not kissed him.

Later, although they had not actually made love, Mary felt ashamed of how easily she seemed to have found her way into this new experience; she felt awkward as she fumbled with the fastenings of her clothes behind the screen. By the next time she saw David, however, the natural poise of her temperament had reasserted itself: they went to the National Gallery and then for lunch in a café; she enjoyed being with him and was, in the end, disappointed that he did not seem to feel himself entitled to repeat his forward behaviour. She wondered if he really valued her, or if perhaps she had accommodated him too readily. She wanted to seduce him properly so that he would be forced to confront this new reality, whatever it turned out to be.

David needed no persuading, only an opportunity, which came the following weekend after a party given by a colleague. They took a taxi back to David's lodgings, slipped their shoes off at the door and crept upstairs. He put a penny in the gas meter, lit the fire and then, when the black-out was up, a candle, by whose orange flame she allowed him to undress her, piece by piece, as he knelt before her on the

24

threadbare hearth rug. As he dealt with her jacket and skirt, he was still talking about the landlady, Mrs Carman, with her bilious temper and bags full of odd-smelling possessions; when he pulled down her satin slip, he became more serious. How solemn his face then became, Mary could not say, as, acting on some childish impulse, she had closed her eyes in the hope of becoming invisible.

It was not all that she had hoped, when finally he lay on top of her, but it was enough for her to feel changed by it, in some way emancipated, bolder and brighter when she looked back on it the following day. David told her it was an adventure for him as well, something he had never tried before, though she thought he said that only to reassure her: how else could he so knowingly have touched her when she lay there naked as his model?

After Mary joined the WAAF, she was trained at first in London and continued to meet David when she was allowed. She had never had a boyfriend before and baulked at the word when her father used it, but when her embarrassment had subsided she was forced to concede to herself that this was what he was. The trouble was she had never felt the things that girls, according to friends and books she read, were meant to feel. She thought that perhaps her mother and father had so enveloped her in love that she had none to spare, or that any man would somehow have to become a part of her family, like a brother, before she could love him in return. This seemed undesirable, and for the first time in her life she fretted at her parents' tight embrace.

David's second application to join the army was successful, and he was despatched for preliminary training before taking a commission in a Shropshire regiment; Mary was posted by the WAAF to Norfolk, and their affair became one of leave-time assignations and weekly letters. One winter night, after a separation of six weeks, she arrived at Trinity Church Square only a few minutes after David himself. He looked unsoldierly in uniform, plump and vulnerable. He poured her a drink and sat on the bed in the corner, loosening his khaki tie, searching in the pocket of his tunic for cigarettes.

Sitting cross-legged on the arm of his sofa, Mary, half-swallowed by her air-force blue serge, her anxious dark eyes peering across at him, was struck by a strange sensation. The light by which he was lit, only a shaded bulb suspended on a flex from the ceiling, seemed to cast a glow about his head and shoulders, like an aura. His movements seemed to have slowed, as though he had moved into a separate world; when he raised his face from the flare of the match, it was radiant. For the first time, the contradictions of his comic face and serious manner were resolved: his expression, when he met her eye, was taut with tenderness.

She walked to him in a daze. She sat on his knee and put her arms about his neck. She buried her face against his shirt. She heard his voice at a distance going through a list of endearments and she wished that he could find more, that his voice would carry on speaking. A transcendence was happening in her, so light that she could not think what name to call it by; all she could tell when at last she pulled back her head from his chest and looked him in the eyes was that something was changed: she had tasted a power of emotion, and all her experiences from that moment would be seen in its light.

For seven months they saw each other as often as they could; then David's battalion was sent to North Africa, from where he wrote her airmail letters, the brittle paper crushed beneath his desperate endearments. Mary lived in a converted school and bicycled to the airfield where she was instructed in how to track the movements of enemy aircraft; but her nights before the radar screen and her mornings in the dormitory were filled with lightness, a sense that they were in some respect provisional, because what mattered to her was elsewhere: not in Norfolk, not in the German bomber stations of Norway, nor even in the deserts of Tunisia, but in a separate, more fully realized existence.

She watched a point of light on the circumference of the screen and saw the straight beam sweep and catch on it: bright representations, radiant particles, and meaning altogether elsewhere.

A telephone call from her mother in London informed her that David had been killed in action. His company had been on the wing of a British advance that was counter-attacked by the Germans; David had been buried on the battlefield, but in the wake of the successful

British action would be transferred to a Commonwealth war cemetery. Mary worried how he might have managed if he had lost his glasses at some stage in the fighting; she visualized him on a sand dune, swivelling round in blind desperation with sweat running down his cheeks, as she had seen him on the squash court, then blundering into a German gun.

She was able to think with clarity. When years had passed she would meet other men; the natural affability of her temperament would not change: but David was her one, her self, and therefore that aspect of her life was over. As a girl she had viewed her future as infinite and her expectations as limitless; but over them now she felt something slide and close.

2

In the morning Charlie van der Linden emerged from Number 1064, his hair still damp from the shower and with blood on the collar of his shirt from his peremptory shave. He felt too sick to have breakfast, but a taxi that Mary had called while he dressed was waiting for him; his own office was still in a hotel on Connecticut Avenue where his department was based until the new Embassy building was complete. Morning Prayers, however, the formal meeting that began each day, took place in the almost-finished premises on Massachusetts Avenue because it had a secure meeting room. The Ambassador was out of town, but the Minister, who would chair it, liked to draw on what counsellors had read to save him from the trouble of studying all the papers himself. As Charlie slumped back against the taxi's leather seat, he desperately scanned the papers to see what questions might be directed his way.

He pulled the remains of a crushed pack of cigarettes from his jacket and searched for a match. The trouble with Washington was that it was drastically short of drugstores, delis, bars or anywhere that he could get what he needed to start his day. One street of the inner suburb gave way to the next without so much as a general store or a laundromat to service the residential miles. He told the driver to divert to one of the

29

big hotels, where, while the cab waited, he ran into the over-heated coffee shop. He hated American coffee; it was always dusty, boiling hot and lacked the necessary caffeine. He drank as much as he could from a heated mug, managed half a Danish pastry, took two books of matches and left some coins on the bar.

By the time he reached the Embassy, he had flicked through the *Post* and the *New York Times*, but Morning Prayers were already under way. On hard chairs around the walls sat numerous grave-looking men, the economic and chancery first secretaries and the usual naval and military analysts. Charlie mumbled some apologies as he took his vacant place at the table.

'Good morning, Charlie. We were talking about Richard Nixon. Do you fancy a trip to California?'

'Not particularly, no.'

Charlie was feeling the exhilaration of a hangover that had not settled. A thin film had been shaved from his irises; the molecular movement of the surrounding world had increased in agitation by about half its normal speed; he could feel a slight flush in his neck and jaw, but the headache was still a distant threat. He felt bold, carefree, as he shakily rode the chemical balances of his system: he was essentially, he admitted to himself, still drunk.

Edward Renshaw glanced at Charlie, his eyes dilating for an instant as he took in the bloodstained collar. His own capacity for recovery was legendary, and he looked as pure and dedicated as the day he had first arrived in

Whitehall. He pushed back his hair. 'It's very difficult to tell at this stage, of course,' he said, clearly referring back to what was being discussed before Charlie arrived. 'But our analysis still points to Nixon — Kennedy in November and to a narrow win for Nixon. That's the assumption we're working on.'

'We'll see,' said the Minister, before beginning to analyse what a Republican government under Nixon might mean.

Charlie looked out of the window. He needed to prepare an excuse for not going to California. He dreaded the thought of having to ingratiate himself with Richard Nixon's staff, buying drinks and lunches for various small-town lawyers who had slapped Joe McCarthy on the back, inquiring about their plans for foreign policy, as though Nixon had any policy at all beyond getting himself elected. What was decisive for Charlie, however, was not his distaste for the work itself, but the fact that he found himself unable to fly without having swallowed three sedatives and half a bottle of scotch.

He also wanted to be in Washington to keep an eye on the stock market, to consult brokers in London and New York; it was difficult to stay in touch when you were in Santa Barbara, eight hours behind the start of dealing in the City. Charlie's portfolio of shares was now worth less than half its value three years earlier; he had borrowed more money to invest, but although he twice changed his broker, his inexplicable run, his own private bear, had continued.

Charlie held his face in his hands and rubbed

his eyes. Sometimes he wished he had not had children. It was not that he didn't love them; occasionally when he went into their room at night and saw them sleeping, he felt his stomach tighten as a feeling in him yearned protectively towards them. In the sober daylight, however, he found they were expensive, wearisome and always complicating the arrangements. Before, he had been true to some ideal he had developed of the way a man should live, without favour or obligation to anyone but himself; now he was preparing to persuade some adviser on the Nixon payroll that there was a coincidence of interest in the way they saw the Communist threat. Charlie had once been good at this kind of thing; his social ease and humour, coupled with degrees and honours he had acquired with the minimum of endeavour at ancient English and American universities, had fitted him in the eyes of his superiors for rapid advancement; they remained unaware of his difficulties, and his occasionally erratic behaviour was overlooked in the generally hedonistic atmosphere or accepted as the price of his talents.

After the meeting, he took a taxi to the hotel where his temporary office was on the first floor of the building. It was a converted bedroom suite, in the outer room of which, the former lounge, sat his secretary, a tidy American woman in a grey flannel skirt and black loafers.

'Coffee, Mr van der Linden?'

'Thank you, Benton.' He called her what everyone else did; no one seemed to think that

Patty, her first name, did justice to her severe efficiency.

'I read the Russians are going to put a dog in space,' she said as she placed the cup on his desk.

'Really? Make me some appointments, Benton, get me busy. By lunchtime I don't want to be free to travel.'

'Right away, Mr van der Linden. Any news about when we'll be moving into the new Embassy?'

'Can't tell you that, Benton. Classified.'

Benton's first job had been working with the British military in Washington in the last year of the War, which had given her security clearance at a level exceptional for a non-native in the Embassy. Charlie liked to pretend that this had been a serious mistake.

Benton paused with her hand on the telephone. 'By the way,' she said, 'did you hear they invented a new cocktail? It's called the Sputnik.'

'OK, what is it?'

'One part vodka and three parts sour grapes.'

'I like it. I'm surprised at a good American like you, though, telling such unpatriotic jokes. You might find yourself the subject of a Hearing.'

'Uh-huh.'

'I heard one, too,' said Charlie. 'You know Eisenhower likes to read science fiction. What does Khrushchev read?'

'I already heard that one,' said Benton, as she settled at the desk and began to dial. 'Science fact.'

Charlie gazed out at the frosted sycamore trees on the avenue. The people of the United States appeared to be in a condition of what his psychoanalyst in Bethesda called 'free-floating anxiety', expecting, for all their material comforts, to be overwhelmed at any moment by the superior technical weaponry of the Russian enemy or undermined from within by the machinations of its agents. They appeared to be losing the Cold War, and were always aware of that awkward fact. He knew one American family who had relocated to Montana to be beyond the range of Soviet missiles, but most seemed to have reached a compromise with their anxieties: to still the beating heart, they went hiking in the Blue Ridge Mountains, they experimented with European wines, they planned holidays with friends and affairs with the same friends' spouses; they listened to show tunes and jazz; they bought larger cars with bigger tail-fins. They opened charge accounts, bought new seasonal wardrobes and indulged their children in hula-hoops and Lincoln logs.

Charlie sighed and picked up the unopened mail on his desk. His stomach lining felt as though it had been scoured with wire wool.

★ ★ ★

Frank Renzo did not come downstairs until eleven o'clock. He found Mary on the telephone in the kitchen, explaining to Kelly Eberstadt that she might be late for their lunch appointment because of her sleeping visitor.

She hung up quickly. 'Did you sleep all right? How's your hand?'

Frank shifted round the room uneasily. 'I'd no idea what the time was. Did I keep you from doing anything?'

'No. No, I was just doing a little work and then . . . I'm going out in about half an hour. Can I get you some breakfast?'

Frank sat at the table while she made coffee. He leaned back in the chair and looked through the paper. He opened it only a few inches and held it at arm's length, as though worried that he might be blinded by the glare of its contents.

'What are these? he said, picking up a pile of woven name-tapes.

'They're for the children's clothes. We're sending them to boarding school in England.'

Mary turned back to the electric percolator. She was wearing a shirt-waisted catalogue dress just back from the cleaner; it was part of the family's agreed economy measures that she should cut back that year on new clothes, though she felt a little self-conscious about it as Frank scrutinised her from behind.

'You don't sound too happy about that,' he said. 'The school thing.'

'I'm not really.' Mary put the cups on the table and sat down. 'It's another economy measure. It's one of the perks of the job that when you go abroad your children get subsidised schooling in England. They've been too young until now, and anyway I wanted to keep them here. But Charlie says we can't afford the private schools here so they have to go back home.'

35

'You'll miss them.'

'I think I will.'

'You could send them to the public schools here.'

'We could . . . ' Mary felt uneasy, as though she were implying some criticism of American education. In fact, it was Charlie who had been against it: beyond the diplomatic vacuum, he pointed out, Washington was not an easy place.

'But I wouldn't recommend it.'

'What?'

'High school I went to in Chicago you just hoped to get out alive at the end of the day. My father made the mistake of settling his family in an all-colored neighbourhood. Jesus.' Frank lit a cigarette and folded up the newspaper. 'It's not as if there weren't enough Italian families in town. There were whole streets you'd think you were in Naples. You been to Chicago?'

'Not yet. But Charlie travels a lot, and when the children have gone off to school I'm hoping to go with him.'

'Nice guy, your husband.'

Mary smiled. 'Well, I think so.'

'So do I.' Frank stood up. 'I'd better get back to the hotel, get a change of clothes. No taste in music, though. Don't tell him I said so.'

When Frank had gone, Mary went back to sewing name-tapes on to Richard's socks (six pairs, grey, woollen, knee-length, the printed clothes list specified). She loved looking at his name in print: Richard van der Linden — so solid, so real. It was ridiculous: he was a creation of her and Charlie's imagination, an idea they had fancifully invested with a character, not a proper person with a grown-up printed name. Someone was bound to find them out sooner or later.

★ ★ ★

Charlie was due to have lunch with two congressional aides and had booked a table in the upstairs room at a recently fashionable Italian restaurant on 17th near the junction with L Street. The venue was convenient for one of his favourite bars, the tall sitting room of the Hay-Adams hotel, where the price of drinks was offset by the discretion of the assiduous staff. At twelve-thirty, he set himself down in a wing chair by the vast fireplace and lit a cigarette while the waiter brought his dry martini, straight up, with no risk of alcohol displacement by ice, and no olive or twist. With both hands, he raised the trembling meniscus to his lips and sucked; he closed his eyes as he rested his head against the back of the chair.

The bar with its exalted ceilings reminded him of childhood Gothic, the illustrations to fairy tales or the castle home of a sinister uncle. Logs crackled in the fireplace as the waiter answered Charlie's brief wave and replaced the empty glass with a new one; he lacked only a basking Irish wolfhound at his feet. It amused him to linger in this play world while a brief walk away the earnest young men in button-down collars pounded the corridors of the White House, gabbling, minuting, telephoning;

and five minutes' taxi ride the other way, the real city, the southern settlement hacked from the surrounding swamp, carried on in its impoverished way, unmoved by the proximity of world decisions and the jabbing fingers of a thousand intent stenographers.

The second martini filled Charlie with a sense of peace, though he could feel a tightness in the skin of his forehead and the approaching thrum of pain behind the temples. He unwrapped two Tylenol in his jacket pocket and sluiced them down; when he had finished his drink, he played briefly with the idea of having another. The moment of balance he was looking for, the instant of perfect pitch, was becoming harder to find each day. Once there had been a time when two martinis at noon had made him feel like a king; not only that, but the feeling had lasted, with a glass of wine here or there, for two or three hours, even sometimes until the evening scotch. In that mood, he could see all his troubles for what they were — insolent, negligible — and he could live off the feeling of reassurance. Now it was almost impossible to prescribe the mixture, or the volume, that would liberate that powerful sensation; and on the rare occasions that he found it, it seemed to last only a few minutes.

He was late for his two lunch companions, who were at the restaurant's downstairs bar, where, after the handshakes, he was offered a drink.

'What are you chaps having?' he said, peering at their glasses.

'Martini.'

'Well, I suppose I might as well join you.'

He took a second one up with him to lunch. The sight of the others drinking white coffee with their food made him queasy, and he pushed his buttered macaroni and *fegato alla veneziana* more or less untouched to one side. He drank some iced water and for a moment reached a stage of hot balance, as one of the aides talked of foreign policy realignments. Charlie was so bored that he thought he might weep, there at the table, in long hysterical sobs: he detested every word they said and the tawdry, life-denying world they represented. Perhaps all they really wanted was an invitation to the ambassador's residence, something they could tell their wives about or to which they even hoped to bring them.

Charlie's neighbour ploughed his last piece of chicken through the red sauce on his plate, then raised his cup, on which the milk had separated from the coffee, and sluiced it down.

'Excuse me.' Charlie rose from the table and went to the head of the stairs: he felt drops of sweat on his chill forehead and upper lip. The stairs looked vertiginous; the floor at the foot of them heaved beneath his gaze. Clasping the handrail, he limped down step by step. With all the mental power that had once been bent to solving academic problems, he forced himself to concentrate on negotiating the width of the slippery room to the door marked 'Signori'. The sweat felt like a full, cold moustache as he twisted the handle and went inside. He made it no further than the doorway before he vomited an arc of colourless liquid across the tiles. He pulled open the door of a cubicle and slumped down on the floor. His cheek was cold against the porcelain, but his head was too heavy to move.

★ ★ ★

After her lunch with Kelly Eberstadt, Mary had time to do some food shopping before she went to collect the children. Christmas was approaching. The lights were glimmering on early trees in the living-room windows of the residential streets; the gas station on Woodley Road had a giant spruce with flashing crimson bulbs; the supermarket had frosted greetings sprayed across the windows. Perhaps at this moment, a few minutes down the road, Mrs Eisenhower was putting some final touches to her own tree, which were sure to be stylish in a store-bought, Mamie kind of way.

Mary liked being in America at this time of year: people had not yet grown tired of the festival; its rigmarole still seemed to strike them as sincere and new, not exhausted by repetition. As she waited by the school gates, she saw Richard and Louisa emerge inside the wire-fenced compound and sounded her horn. Louisa looked up and waved unhurriedly; Richard was too absorbed by some cards he was showing a friend. Once they had climbed into the back of the car, Mary tried to find out how the day had gone. 'What lessons did you do?' 'History.' 'How was that?' 'Okay.' 'What else?' 'We had a spelling bee.' 'How was that?' 'Okay.' Louisa had developed a slight Maryland inflection which she could exaggerate at will; Richard's voice was unchanged by America.

'And we had A-bomb drill.'

'Yeah, our class went down to the basement, all in line, two by two. It was horrid and smelly. We had to stand by the furnace.'

'You're lucky. We had the emergency drill. You know, in the classroom? You have to cover your head so your brains don't blow out and dive down like this!'

'Ow, stop it, Richard. You hurt my leg!'

They were always hungry, having eaten their packed lunches at noon, and, as it was a Friday, Mary gave way to their clamouring insistence to stop off for a milkshake at the soda fountain. The traffic was so slow, she thought, it would make no difference to their journey.

The children ran ahead of her from the car across the lot, jostling and shouting. Louisa had Mary's small bones and dark hair; her younger brother was already an inch taller, strong, and pulsing with an unguided *joie de vivre*. At home, they often fought or played on their own, but when they were happy together they sank into a self-contained contentment that had a peculiar tranquillity, signalled by Louisa's gurgling laugh and Richard's uncharacteristic quietness. These moments were so few and so valuable to Mary that she could have named and numbered them; yet on the memory of these finite instants would be based an agreed history of their childhood.

41

Mary watched as Richard and Louisa reached up to the counter with their coins. Did strangers see them as just high-spirited kids, or did they know how provisional they were, and how gently they must therefore be treated?

It was later than usual by the time they arrived home, and the telephone was ringing in the hall. As the children dropped their bags and coats on the floor and ran upstairs, Mary answered it.

'Mary? It's Edward Renshaw. Charlie was taken ill at lunch-time. It's nothing to worry about, but some imbecile at the restaurant rang an ambulance and they've taken him off to hospital. Now he wants you to go and pick him up.'

'You sure he's all right?'

'Yes, he's fine. They wanted to keep him in overnight, but you know what Charlie's like.'

'I do.'

Calling instructions to Dolores and the children, Mary ran out to the Kaiser Manhattan, which, for once, started first time. When she arrived at the address in Bethesda she found Charlie sitting on a hospital gurney in a treatment room, looking pale and impatient: he was irritated that the staff would not let him smoke.

Mary kissed him and took his arm as she led him out to the parking lot; through the sleeve of her overcoat she noticed the tremor in his hand.

'What did they say was the matter?'

'The doctor said I should have my blood pressure checked again next week. He said I should get Weissman to do some tests — diabetes, that kind of thing.' That was not all the doctor had said.

'But he wasn't worried?'

'Not in the slightest. How's your day been?'

'My day? Fine. Very ordinary.'

'What time did that fellow leave?'

'Frank? Quite late. I thought I might not be in time for lunch, but it was all right. Now let's get you home and into bed.'

Back at Number 1064, while Mary was downstairs, telephoning Dr Weissman, Charlie put on some pyjamas and took a sedative from the bottle in the bathroom cabinet. A long night's sleep would help him to see things in the old perspective: he didn't need much, just a lucky break or a change of scene. He switched on the bedside light and reached over to Mary's night table for a book; he found a volume of stories by Irwin Shaw, which he began to read as Mary's anxious voice came up from the hall.

' . . . ask you for some tests. The doctor at the hospital thought he might have diabetes.'

Charlie pictured Weissman's snort. 'Sure, and maybe W.C. Fields died of too much Seven Up.'

One of the most touching things about Mary, in Charlie's view, was that she still viewed him as irreproachable. Of course she knew he drank a good deal, but so did all their friends in Washington, and none of them in Mary's opinion benefited from it as much as Charlie: no one became as magnanimous, as death-defying as Charlie late at night. She did not wonder why his previously frictionless movement through the diplomatic labyrinth now seemed fraught: there were political considerations in a large embassy like Washington; other men's lives and paths had to be accommodated; and he was only there to do a specific political job for a limited period. She repeated to him what the ambassadors in two former postings had told her: that Charlie was unique, one of the very best.

Louisa arrived with a cup of tea and kissed her father on the cheek. He held her to him for a moment, losing his face in her dark hair, which smelled of soap and cookies. He felt detached from her, he felt old and tarnished: how far apart had been their contemporaneous experiences of the day.

The other thing about Mary, Charlie thought when he was alone again, was that she lacked the capacity to envisage disaster. He knew that she had lost a fiancé in the war, but she seemed somehow to have eliminated the experience. It was not that she did not remember David, but that she did not allow the tragedy to alter her trust that all was well, that while she believed in those she loved, no harm could come to them.

Later, Mary brought him scrambled egg on a tray, and sat on the edge of the bed to eat hers with him. Charlie forced down a little and drank some black coffee, but was reasonably able to plead sickness as a reason for not eating. When Mary had gone back downstairs, Charlie reached for another pill and turned off the light. He fell into a profound and sweaty sleep, too drugged to dream or hear the telephone ringing by the bed.

* ★ ★

Mary picked it up in the kitchen. She heard her father's voice at the other end, and this was in itself a cause for anxiety. Her parents were unsure of the time difference between London and Washington and did not really believe, despite the evidence of their ears, that the telephone was capable of connecting them over such a distance; and even if it could be made to work, the cost of a call was certain to be punitive.

Mary stretched the long lead across the kitchen to the sink, where she was drying the last of the dishes. She stared through the window, fixing her eyes on the dark outline of a tree. In London, it must be nearly one o'clock in the morning, she thought.

'Can you hear me all right?' said her father suspiciously.

'Very well, thank you.' There was a slight delay on the line, but Mary had grown used to dealing with it: when you had finished speaking you had to stop and wait. She thought of RAF coastal stations; she was tempted to say 'Over'.

James Kirwan came to the point quite soon, as though fearful that the connection would not hold. 'Your mother's been feeling a little unwell and she's had some tests . . . there does appear to be some sort of growth.'

Although James spoke loudly, to give the sub-Atlantic cable every chance, what he said came to Mary in fragments, as though some self-defensive censor were breaking it up into morsels she could manage. She stared hard at the branches of the black tree. This was the moment against which she had prepared herself in her imagination for almost forty years. Until she had had children of her own she had not been able to contemplate the death of either of her parents; when the subject had arisen, in conversation or in her own imagining, she had said only: I just don't know what I'd do.

Now that it was here, or might be here, the first thing that she and her father did was to agree that everything was still all right. Each reassured the other: wait and see . . . nothing we can do anyway . . . know more next week . . . exactly.

They agreed that there was no reason for Mary to go back to London; then Elizabeth herself came on the line to lend weight to James's optimism. As a doctor, she brought some authority to the cheerful prognosis; she seemed in any case more interested in Louisa and Richard and whether the Christmas presents she had sent had yet arrived.

When she had rung off, Mary stood, staring out of the window at the leafless tree for a long time. Everything was all right. Her mother was alive, that was the important thing: nothing had changed.

She went up to the top floor and kissed the children goodnight. There was a photograph of her mother holding Louisa as a baby in the garden of the Regent's Park house on a summer afternoon. Perhaps even when she had taken it, Mary had been aware of how few such occasions there were: you talked them up into a life, a history, but in fact you could count the days on the fingers of two or three hands.

3

Dr Weissman ran liver function and other tests on Charlie van der Linden, but, to Weissman's irritation, the readings all fell within the prescribed range. He told Charlie that unless he cut down on the amount he drank he could not accept responsibility for what happened: there would be black-outs, accidents, organ damage. He recommended that Charlie go more often to see the psychoanalyst with whom he had begun treatment the previous autumn; he also prescribed barbiturates to help him sleep.

Charlie's absence from work excused him from the trip to California, but when he went back in January he found his diary uncomfortably full of the diversionary appointments Benton had made. His will to survive was still strong enough for him to recognize that a period of quiet efficiency was required of him. He did the meetings and he did the lunches; he went to the offices on the Hill and talked to congressional aides; in the afternoons he drafted convincing telegrams. He reassured London that Richard Nixon, for all his spotted past domestically, was unlikely to be a Taft-like isolationist in foreign affairs. He gave reasons. He wrote a memo on the significance of the Iowa caucuses and the New Hampshire primary. He kept to two martinis before lunch and nothing in the afternoon; when the vodka bottle in his desk

48

drawer was empty he did not, immediately, replace it.

At Number 1064 the first twelve weeks of the new decade were quiet with the stillness of life suspended. The children went, with other diplomatic exiles, to England, where Mary's mother met them at London airport. Mary was alone in the house. There were no school bags and coats dropped anyhow in the tiled hall; she did not trip on sections of Richard's wooden railway when she crossed the kitchen to the fridge; Louisa's painful practice at the piano no longer provided the lounge music at the cocktail hour. She went up to their rooms, but they were tidy now and she had no excuse to linger: for the first time in ten years the toys were in their proper boxes; the expensive christening mugs were not lying beneath the bed; a silver watch left to Richard by Charlie's father was no longer the damp treasure in a muddy pirate ship beneath the maple.

Mary picked out some of their books from the shelf, the ones from which they had learned to read, and, before that, the ones at which their consciousness had first flared up. Here was the story of a fire engine, the book itself broken and stained. At eighteen months old Louisa's eyes had widened when Mary read it to her: behind their gaze her mind was in the act of being made, lifted and stirred by news of the world. Every day Mary witnessed the intimate act of creation as Louisa began precociously to talk, speaking with exploratory gentleness, as though her tentative framing of a word was the first time it had found human utterance. Each syllable gave Mary a pathway into the mind she was anxious to reach, so that the eruption of love in her could find a channel and a home in the heart of this astonishing child.

She replaced the book on the shelf. The children who had sat on her knee were gone; each week they were replaced by new versions of themselves, epigones of the purer being. The love that welled in her was always readjusting to their changes, racing after them. Once when she knelt beside her bath, Louisa had looked her in the eye and, for no reason Mary could tell, said, 'Mummy, why do you love me so much?'

So much . . . Why indeed? thought Mary as she sat down on Richard's bed. The truthful answer was simple: because I believed you were the most wonderful and beautiful creature ever to have opened its eyes on the world, and I felt stupefied, blessed and transfigured that I should have been chosen to be your mother. She could not admit this; she only said, 'You funny monkey,' and kissed Louisa's forehead. What puzzled her was why this should be the nature of things: what plan, divine or biological, had been so arranged or had so evolved that a reasonable adult human should, in the course of her most natural function, be subject to this transcendent passion?

Mary went to the top of the stairs, reluctantly. It was not just the children's former selves that had vanished; it was the physical beings they had become who were absent. She longed for their skin, their hair, their necks, the touch of the muscle beneath their clothes; no one had told her how tactile was this love, how intimate the knowledge of a forehead's swell, a knee's flex, the edible cartilage and soft tissue of the ear, which she had sniffed and nibbled like a rabbit.

She went downstairs and sat alone in the living room. She must find something to distract her, to help her through: perhaps this was the time for her to write the book with which, Charlie was always boasting to their friends, she would one day surprise them.

★ ★ ★

That evening, after dinner, the telephone rang and Charlie reached across to answer it.

'Hi. This is Frank Renzo.'

'Well, hello.' Charlie fought for a moment to remember who he was. 'How's the hand?'

'What? Oh, it's OK. I find I'm back in Washington.'

'Again?'

'The paper sent me back. I have to do another piece.'

'What's it about?'

'It's a feature. Diplomatic life, how people view the election, that kind of thing.'

'I see. Where are you?'

'I'm in a hotel in Georgetown, but I'll be here for a few days.'

'Well, anything we can do to help?'

'Can I call in the morning?'

'I have to go to work, but I daresay Mary — '

'I appreciate it.'

Charlie put down the receiver. 'Are you doing anything tomorrow?'

'Was that Frank?' said Mary.

'He needs someone to show him round, I suppose. Make some introductions. I did promise. When he came to the party.' Charlie thought for a moment. 'Anyway, he might be useful. We could always use more contact with the papers in New York.'

★ ★ ★

The next morning Mary put on a dress she had bought from Lord and Taylor in New York the previous summer. It was in grass-green tweed, round-necked with a slightly gathered skirt; the magazine advertisement described it as 'deceptively casual' (perhaps it really meant 'deceptively formal') and as something the 'woman of today can wear at *any* time'. Mary liked it because it looked the kind of thing that Audrey Hepburn might have worn.

She arranged to meet Frank at the new British Embassy building on Massachusetts Avenue. Within a week of the van der Lindens' arrival in Washington, Mary had been identified as a wife who should be used as much as possible. Despite a little shyness, her buoyant character and essential good manners were viewed as assets; there was a tradition at the embassy that if someone was unmarried or his wife was indisposed he could call on the wife of a junior to be his hostess at a function, and Mary had, rather against her will, been used in this way.

Most of the British diplomats subscribed to what was known, after the Washington columnist who had invented it, as the Joe Alsop Amendment, which stated that with eight people at dinner there could be no bores present; with ten there could be half a bore; with twelve a whole bore could be absorbed; with fourteen, a bore and half, and so on. Half-bores, in Alsop's definition, were dull but very powerful men or vacuous but very beautiful women.

The new building was a functional rectangle of concrete, steel and glass in which the need for Civil Service gradings, competitive views and relative office sizes had prevailed over aesthetic design. It was being slowly inhabited, corridor by right-angled corridor, as diplomats temporarily housed about the city in borrowed buildings, hotels and office blocks moved in their maps, papers and Rolodex address finders. Mary waited downstairs in the glass-fronted lobby, chatting to the receptionist. Showing Frank around was a chore she felt she could have done without, and if Charlie was anxious to help him for some reason, she did not see why he could not have spared the time himself. She felt less than diplomatic — reserved, unwilling — when Frank crossed the floor, taking off a wide-brimmed felt hat and holding out his hand.

'I can give you a tour here to begin with,' she said. 'Then you'd better explain to me more exactly what you want.'

'Sure,' he said. 'You understand that this is entirely off the record.'

'Yes. The Head of Information's been in

touch. He's joining us upstairs.'

As they went across to the elevator, Mary said, 'By the way, how's your hand?'

'Oh, it's fine. It healed well.' He showed her a closed scar that ran down and disappeared beneath the cuff of his shirt. He flipped open a notebook he took from the pocket of his raincoat. 'All right if I take notes?'

'As long as — '

'Sure. Background only.'

They started at the top of the building, where the canteen would open in due course. The Head of Information, enthusiastic about meeting a new journalist, was waiting for them.

'You lead on, Mary,' he smiled. 'I'll just open a few doors, literal and metaphorical.'

There were one or two people already in their new offices to whom she was able to introduce Frank as they slowly descended through the building. Once they had been assured that they would not be quoted, most of them seemed happy to be distracted from their work and to answer his questions. He asked them what they thought of Eisenhower's presidency and who they thought the next president would be; he wanted to know what they made of Washington, how it compared with other postings and how they spent their evenings.

When they reached the ground floor, Frank said, 'Do I get to see inside the Ambassador's residence?'

'Yes,' said the Head of Information, 'I'm going to hand you over to the Ambassador's secretary.'

The ambassador was in New York, but they

were allowed to look round the residence, a mock-Queen Anne building next door to the Embassy with towering brick chimneys, mansard windows and creeper-clad walls at the rear.

'Charlie calls it Greyfriars,' said Mary as they walked over in the surprising warmth of early spring. 'He thinks it looks like a boys' boarding school.'

'It's sure big enough for one man.'

'It used to be the Embassy itself. It had all the offices until they ran out of space.'

They rang the doorbell and waited for the Ambassador's secretary. As they went inside and looked up at the white-stone staircase, Frank said, 'Jesus, it's like a kind of upscale restaurant.'

Mary smiled. 'Yes. Indian, I think. The man who designed it, Lutyens, did a lot of government buildings in New Delhi.'

Frank nodded. Mary presumed he knew nothing of India and the British Raj. She looked at him properly for the first time that morning: he was clean-shaven and neat, but with the same stray, fatigued look she remembered from before. He had mentioned that he was from Chicago and she wondered what difficulties he had found in extracting himself from the deprived neighbourhood he had described and heading East.

The Ambassador's desk was set with its back to Massachusetts Avenue. The polished expanse of wood was impressively clear; at the edge were three trays, marked In, Out and Destroy. Each was empty, and the only other items on the desk were two paper flags, American and British, and a well-consulted New York restaurant guide.

There was a leather-covered fender in front of the fireplace, wing-back armchairs and shiny bookcases with matching sets of leather volumes; there was a feeling of borrowed grandeur, dignity by the yard: the atmosphere was of a Manhattan gentlemen's club for graduates of not-quite Ivy League universities.

'What kind of guy is the Ambassador?'

Mary glanced up to see that his secretary was out of hearing. 'I think you'd describe him as an empire loyalist. He's anxious about Britain's declining role in the world.'

'Sounds okay for an ambassador. Does he like Washington?'

'I don't think so. He got off to a bad start. It was just after Suez, and Dulles called him in to his office. Dulles asked him why the British hadn't won and the Ambassador became so angry he had to leave the room.'

They went downstairs, where they were shown the gardens at the back of the building, with their soft, deep lawns, rose beds and herbaceous borders. Mary thought how out of place Frank looked in his New York newspaperman's clothes, a man of the streets with grass beneath his feet.

They walked back to the Embassy and out on to the service road that ran off Massachusetts Avenue. A delivery truck was unloading cases of champagne to the side entrance of the residence.

'Would you be free for lunch tomorrow?' said Frank.

'I'm not sure, I . . . '

'I have to go see someone else right now, but I'd appreciate the chance to talk a little more.

Could I call you in the morning and see if you'd have the time?'

'All right. Can I give you a lift somewhere? I've got the car here.'

'No, it's fine, I'll take a cab.'

Frank was still waiting by the side of the road, scanning the impatient traffic, when Mary drove past, but since he had been quite emphatic, dismissive almost, she did not stop or repeat her offer. Although it was nearly lunchtime, she did not want to go home to the silent kitchen, so she swung the car left and drove up towards the Naval Observatory from where she could drop down to Fiorello's, an Italian café she had discovered that overlooked the canal.

She took a table in the corner, and looked out of the window, towards the river and the Theodore Roosevelt Memorial. Few cities in the world could have had so many memorials in proportion to such a relatively short lifetime, she thought. Without thinking too hard, she could list the lapidary reminders of Lincoln, Jefferson, Roosevelt; the George Washington Memorial Parkway, the George Mason Memorial Bridge, the Arlington Memorial Bridge leading to the Iwo Jima Marine Corps Memorial . . . What were they so scared of forgetting?

★   ★   ★

For lunch the next day, Frank urged Mary to choose somewhere she particularly liked, as his newspaper would pay. Fiorello's was her own retreat, unknown even to Charlie, and she did not want to compromise her privacy; she chose instead the Old Firehouse, a large, traditional-looking place in Georgetown which the reliable Lauren Williams had recommended, and booked a table for one o'clock.

It was a day of early spring sunshine; there was some high, broken cloud, a light breeze and an almost-forgotten sensation of warmth in the air as Mary walked down 33rd Street from where she had parked the car, past the period houses with their shiny paintwork and the village shops where nothing of vulgar, corporate America had been allowed to penetrate. In the front gardens there were the shoots of croci and a swelling in the twig that presaged buds on the magnolia and cherry trees. There was something false about the houses, part colonial, part neo-Georgian, their period style enforced by statute after some adventurer had bought a plot and built a home from cinder blocks; but you would have to be a grudging person, Mary thought, not to feel uplifted by this island of civility, particularly when you turned on to the lively sidewalks of M Street.

She arrived a little early at the restaurant and handed her coat to the hat-check girl. She was wearing a beige cashmere sweater and a navy woollen skirt; her dark hair was pushed back from her face by two tortoiseshell combs. A waiter showed her to the back of the room: the table was in a booth with bench seats, one of half a dozen such on a raised platform; the napkins were white and starched, but the mahogany surface itself was bare. She lit a cigarette and sipped a glass of water as she waited; she began to read a copy of the *Post*, trying to interest herself in an article about the economic outlook, which told her that with falling GNP and the highest unemployment since the Depression, some urgent rejuvenating action was required.

'I hope I didn't keep you.'

Mary looked up from the paper in surprise, having neither seen nor heard his approach.

'Not at all,' she said, untruthfully, as Frank slid in opposite.

When his drink came, he stirred it quickly with the plastic swizzle stick, which he then knocked twice on the rim of the glass and flicked into the ashtray; it was a swift, practised movement with a defined sequence of sound.

He smiled as he took a long pull from the drink. 'Did you look at the menu?'

'Yes, I thought I'd have the chicken sandwich.'

The waiter was standing by the table. Frank looked up. 'We have one chicken sandwich here. And can I get the French onion soup, then the steak and salad? I'll have a beer with that. Do you have Schaeffer on tap?'

'Sure. And for the lady?'

'I'll just have a glass of water.'

'Glass of water,' Frank repeated.

Mary suddenly laughed. 'God, I sound like Franny.'

'What?'

'Franny. She's a character in a story I read in a magazine. I think it was the *New Yorker*. It doesn't matter.'

'The Salinger story?'

'Yes.' Mary was unable to keep the surprise out of her voice. 'You've read it?'

'Sure. It was a big thing a couple of years back. You like it?'

'Yes, I did. I thought it was very touching.'

'You think the kid's pregnant?'

'Franny?' Mary thought Franny was a dim but likeable college girl on the edge of a nervous breakdown caused by her insensitive boyfriend. 'I hadn't thought of that.'

'Maybe not. Anyway, she has the chicken sandwich, right?'

'Yes, and he has snails and frogs' legs.'

'Son of a bitch.'

Frank questioned her about Washington and how they lived; he opened his notebook and laid it beside his plate. He scribbled a couple of lines in it, left-handed, then laid down the pencil.

'We were in London before we came here and before that in Tokyo.'

'Tokyo?'

'Yes, in Japan. It's — '

'I know where it is. What was it like?'

'I enjoyed it, in a way. Before that we were in London and before that Moscow.'

'And that's in Russia, right?'

Mary found herself blushing slightly. 'Yes. Anyway, I hardly went there, because Louisa was ill and she was being treated in hospital in London.'

'Is she okay now?'

'Yes, but it was frightening at the time. She was very ill for a year. Eventually they discovered she had an allergy to wheat. As long as she watches what she eats she's fine. And then I was pregnant with Richard and it looked as though I might lose him. So what with one thing and another, Charlie was pretty much on his own in Moscow, which he didn't like.'

Frank pushed his soup bowl to one side; in the saucer were some crackers in an unopened cellophane pack.

'And what about you? You seem to me like a very happy person.'

'I suppose so. I have every reason to be.'

'Charlie?'

'Yes, of course. And our children.'

'Tell me about Charlie.'

Mary looked at the open notebook.

'Pardon me,' said Frank, swiftly putting it away in his pocket.

Mary thought of Charlie, and the thought made her smile. 'He's a remarkable man. He's . . . I don't know. I don't know where to start. Why do you want to know?'

Frank spread his hands. 'You don't have to tell me.' He cut a piece off the end of his steak with the knife in his left hand, speared it with the fork in his right, dipped it in sauce, laid down the knife and rapidly transferred the fork to his left hand, ready to eat the piece of meat.

Mary watched the shuttling manoeuvre.

'But maybe you'd like to tell me,' said Frank. 'Maybe you have things on your mind.'

'Well,' Mary hesitated: the thought of her family made her feel precariously fortunate. 'I suppose the first thing you'd say about Charlie is that there's not much middle ground. No moderation in anything. He's very kind, very clever, very funny. His moods, though. If you had to put them in order, they'd probably be elation first, then despondency. Then exhilaration, then despair. Things like pensive, hopeful or patient wouldn't come in until about number twenty on the list. I don't think content would come in at all.'

'What does he despair about?'

'I don't know. I don't think anyone quite knows, least of all Charlie. I think it's partly a fear of boredom.'

It was a long time since Mary had discussed Charlie with anyone, and Frank, in his abrupt way, was an effective questioner. He seemed always slightly to misunderstand, which made her eager to correct him, to clarify, and go on. She did not pause to wonder if this was professional technique. Frank seemed so disconnected from the world that she could not tell what he was thinking, or if he felt anything at all; yet talking to him did make her feel better. She had not been able to share with Charlie her feelings about the children's absence: she could not put into words her physical loss without sounding self-pitying. As for her mother, Charlie could understand and sympathize well enough, having lost both his own parents, but there was really nothing to say beyond the platitudes on which she and her father had fixed.

'You finished with that, ma'am?' The waiter held the plate with her half-finished chicken sandwich. She nodded, and he took it away.

'This thing with your mother,' said Frank. 'Do

you know how sick she is?'

'We're still waiting to find out for sure, but you know how it is with cancer. You have to be prepared for the worst. You expect it.'

'How old is she?'

'A fair age. Seventy-two. It's not that it's unfair. Most of my friends have lost parents, one or two have lost brothers and sisters, or children, which must be unbearable. But I suppose I never thought it would happen to either of mine.'

Mary took a cigarette from the pack Frank proffered. She said, 'You never get over the way you view them as a child, they seem indomitable, eternal, and their death is the worst disaster that could happen — the end of the world. Even when you've grown up, it seems to belong to an unforeseeable future. I find it hard to believe that that hypothetical future event has taken a form, now. It seems somehow too . . . specific.'

Frank said nothing. She felt him looking at her, his head on one side.

Mary gathered herself. 'Now,' she said, 'you must tell me about this article. Is this the kind of thing you specialize in?'

'Lately, yes.'

'What do you mean?'

'I'm a news reporter by nature. I like to be there. I don't want to be coming along a few days later to sweep up the crumbs.'

'But surely you're in advance here?'

'It's the same thing. It's not news. They'll run something like, 'City in a turmoil. Washington's foreign residents prepare for the post-Eisenhower era. Frank Renzo reports', or 'goes behind the scenes'. They like that. It's all bullshit really. No one's in a turmoil. Half the foreign nationals'll get posted somewhere else in a couple of years anyway. They have no stake in the city.'

'So why are you doing this job?'

'So I can get back to reporting. It's my punishment. I'm serving a sentence.'

'A sentence?' said Mary. 'What did you do wrong?'

'It wasn't funny.' Frank ran his hand along his jaw and shook his head. 'This country went through a bad time.'

'What do you mean?'

He looked at her for a while, then shook his head again. For an embarrassing moment, Mary thought she saw a tear in his eye, but when she looked more closely it seemed to be dry. He said, 'You ever hear of a guy called Joe McCarthy?'

'Of course.'

'Maybe I'll tell you one day. Other things. After him.'

Mary looked down.

'For me, the important thing is to try to get back on board in time to do the election.'

'I see. How long have you been doing your penance?'

'Four and a half years. So.' Frank pulled a roll of bills from his jacket pocket and tucked some inside the check. 'And what do you foreign nationals in turmoil do on the weekend? How do you confront the post-Eisenhower era?'

'I think we're confronting it from the deck of a sailing boat.'

'Sounds good.'

Relieved that the mood had lifted, Mary said, 'You could come along if you liked.'

'I figure I've taken enough of your time. Also, I'm not much good with water.'

'But I thought you grew up in Chicago.'

'Poor boys didn't get to go on the lake.'

They were at the coat check, where Mary fumbled in her pocket for some coins.

'I'll get it,' said Frank.

As they went out on to the street, Mary said, 'Call us if you change your mind.'

'Sure.'

Frank put on his hat and buttoned his raincoat.

'Do you want a lift anywhere?' said Mary.

'No, I'm in the hotel just down the street.'

She walked with him to the corner. Through an open car window they could hear a radio playing a song. 'What did Della wear, boy, what did Della wear . . . She wore a brand new jersey, she wore a band new jer-er-sey . . . '

'Drives you nuts, doesn't it?' said Frank, and set off across the street.

★ ★ ★

There were letters from the children on airmail paper. Mary read them standing in the kitchen, a foolish smile on her face. Both complained of rules, strange lessons, uncomfortable beds and disgusting food; but Mary was able to infer, if only from the vigour of their complaints, that they were in good spirits. When Charlie came

65

back from work, they sat in the kitchen and pored over the crinkled paper with its uneven pencil lines; Charlie laughed at the spelling and read out passages in which he imitated Louisa's baffled stoicism and Richard's lisping irritation.

It was a rare evening, with no social activity. To please Mary, Charlie put on the record of *South Pacific* in the living room and left the door open so that it could be heard in the kitchen, where he returned and sat with his legs up on the table, drinking scotch, while Mary cooked the dinner.

She was wearing white slacks and a loose pink cardigan; she looked girlish for a woman of forty, and the tidiness of her figure, which had not swelled or slackened after the birth of the children, emphasised this youthfulness. He went over and put his arms round her as she stood by the cooker, enfolding her in his tight embrace.

'You're as corny as Kansas in August, aren't you?' he quoted from the song. He kissed her neck beneath the waves of dark hair and ran his hands up to her breasts. She wriggled in his arms, pretending to be impatient.

'Pity I haven't found me a wonderful guy.'

'I can see a grey hair,' he said. 'Is that your first?'

'Don't be ridiculous. Pour me a drink.'

Back in his seat at the table, Charlie said, 'I had a talk with Duncan Trench today.'

'Lucky you. What did he say?'

Charlie looked up again at his wife's back. His affairs had reached a state of such emergency that he was no longer able to confide wholly in Mary. Yet the urge to tell was great, and he thought he might relieve it by revealing a controlled amount, a sample.

'I've had some difficulties and he thought he might be able to help.'

'But he's not in your department, is he?'

'Well, yes and no. He's in Chancery. It was all a bit vague.'

Charlie had, over the years, become adept at being not quite truthful with Mary. In the beginning it had mostly had to do with other women. The strategy of strongly denying any feeling for any woman to whom he was attracted was a failure; Mary could tell in an instant that he was lying. They had developed instead a process of bluff and double-bluff by which he was able to confess to degrees of mild personal interest, superficial carnal excitement and occasionally to a grand passion, though the people for whom these feelings were professed were never the ones for whom they were felt.

It had worked well, and Charlie superstitiously provoked Mary into reciprocal confessions, though her fascination with the TV repairman and proclaimed passion for the delivery boy were never convincing. Charlie felt it was enough to keep canvassing the idea and that this would act as a lightning conductor in the event of her actually meeting someone: there would be a way of talking about it, exaggerating and making fun of it. The truth was, in his view, that Mary was constitutionally faithful and that her emotional life was too heavily identified with his and their children's welfare for anything else to be conceivable; even to kiss another man would be like an act of cruelty to Richard and Louisa.

Mary put down a casserole of chicken à la king on the table. 'It's nothing sinister, is it?' she said. 'I mean, you're not doing anything . . . unusual.'

'No, no. People like me aren't allowed to,' said Charlie, pouring another scotch. 'Anyway. What about you?'

'I had lunch with Frank in this restaurant Lauren recommended.'

'Oh yes. What was it like?'

'Very Lauren. Regular. Neat. Quite nice.'

She said 'quite nice' in a way that Louisa had first used at the age of two; it had a world-weary, tolerant sing-song that had greatly amused Charlie. He had a keen memory for the linguistic oddities and failures of the children, some of which he had sardonically adopted as his own standard usage.

'What did you talk about?'

'You, mostly,' said Mary.

'You must have been desperate. Did you drink wine?'

'No, I just had water.'

'And I suppose he had chili con carne with milky coffee, did he?' Charlie shuddered.

'No. He had a drink. I forget what. Beer, I think.'

Charlie began to talk about American drinking habits, which still intrigued him. The telephone rang twice before the end of dinner: the first time was Frank Renzo to say he was free after all if the invitation to go sailing was still good; the second was Katy Renshaw, who said they planned to spend Saturday night in their country

68

cabin after sailing, so would the van der Lindens please bring warm clothes, overnight things and records.

'And a New York journalist, if you don't mind,' said Charlie.

'That's fine,' said Katy. 'Is he the one I met at your party? My sister's coming down from Boston.'

★　★　★

They left early on Saturday morning in the Renshaws' station wagon, Edward driving, with Katy and her sister, whose name was Sal, on the bench seat beside him, and the others in the back. The rear was piled with boxes of provisions, candles, gas lamps in case of electrical failure and extra blankets. There was only light traffic in town as they drove east and picked up route 301. Washington seemed unmanned by the weekend; the closure of its government buildings, institutions and attorneys' offices robbed the city of its *raison d'être*; the empty streets seemed sheepish and unreal.

Their early start meant that it was still not yet nine when they arrived at the toll booth of the Bay Bridge. From the shallow water in front of them the bridge rose up on its graduated stilts, like a gentle ramp at first, until it reached its main span across the bay to Kent Island. High above, the blue sky was broken up with white vapour trails from light aircraft going to the small landing fields on the island or the larger one at Easton on the shores of Maryland.

'Anyone got forty cents?' said Edward.

For once Mary was able to produce the right money from her purse; she found American coins hard to handle, those dimes, nickels and pennies: Charlie's solution was to throw anything less than a quarter into the children's money boxes.

Edward ground the column shift into first and they moved off across the bridge. The home-made appearance of its engineering reminded Mary of Richard's short and emotional encounter with Meccano; she tried not to look down at the surface of the roadway, the trembling rivets or the drop into the water as the car was swept along at a speed determined by the hastening vehicles around them. Edward turned on the radio, Charlie wound down the window and Mary lay back against the seat, gazing up through the windshield at the huge open skies above the bay, ripped and flagged with puffs of white vapour.

Half an hour later, they were afloat. The sailing boat at once caught the spring breeze, its mainsail bagging out greedily on the wind, as the bow carved a bubbling gash through the dark waters of the bay. The women, in headscarves and sunglasses, sat along one side of the boat, the men, according to Edward's barked instructions from the tiller, switched sides beneath the swinging boom to keep them on an even keel. Charlie, who had sailed before, pulled on ropes, or sheets as he knowingly called them, stiffening or slacking the spinnaker as the plaited cord ran through its screeching metal pulleys. No one on the boat could have said how seriously he took himself at his work, except Mary, who knew that his view of all human activity was satirical. His hair was whipped back and forth across his face, revealing patches of bare scalp from where it had forever retreated. Mary looked at him fondly; she laughed, with Katy and Sal, at his inappropriate flannel pants and nautical oaths. Frank passed round cigarettes as he ducked beneath the boom; once back in his seat, he held firmly to the rail with an expression of mild suffering.

'Better than Lake Michigan, Frank?' said Mary.

'Sure,' he said, and nodded at the view. 'Beats looking at Evanston.'

The shores of the bay were wooded on all sides; around the water, from vegetation protected and unchecked, there were wild birds calling; it was hard to believe that the world's future was decided just the other side of the dense woods, in a clearing in the jungle.

'Do you know those lines, Eddie?' called out Charlie from the bow. ' "The world diminished to a surge of wind,/ Flung clouds break up within my heart/ The fitful joy of breathing." '

'Sure,' said Edward. 'It goes on . . . wait a minute. Yup. 'Land listening for the hull's return/ Expands beneath the hammered blue/ And something, something . . . ascends into the dancing air.' '

'Something like that. Who's it by?'

'Search me.'

At lunchtime, they landed at a mooring Edward knew, where the man who ran it, whose

71

name was Kenny, had a floating bar. They clambered on to the end of the landing stage, the boat rocking with their transferred weight. They walked down between the rows of gently rocking boats, the sloops, schooners and skiffs, the motor launches with their covered cabins and the skipper's chrome wheel glistening beneath its self-important awning. There was something about boats and boat people that always made Mary want to laugh, though this was a tendency she had to check in front of those kind enough to take them out — not that Edward Renshaw seemed to take the matter very seriously, but Katy, his pretty Bostonian wife, was a person of some dignity.

On the door of Kenny's floating bar was a notice that said 'Berth Here', but when Charlie, who was first up, went shakily across the suspended wooden walkway and tried the door he found it locked. On the other side of the boat yard was a man in overalls, whom Charlie followed into a small tackle store.

'Is the bar open for lunch?' he said.

'Sure. But Kenny's not here right now.'

'Do you know when he'll be back?'

'About four, I guess.'

'I see.'

Charlie walked back across the yard, past a gasoline pump and an area of loose stones covered with rusting marine detritus, to join the others.

'Lunch is at four.'

'I have some sodas,' said Katy. 'It doesn't matter.'

'But what the hell are we going to drink?' said Edward.

Charlie said, 'I took a certain precaution.' From Mary's wicker basket he extracted a two-pint Thermos he had filled with dry martini.

'I guess I did, too,' said Frank, and pulled out a hip flask.

They sat at the end of the landing stage, with their feet dangling over the water. Charlie lodged a ham sandwich between his teeth as he used both hands to unwrap the glasses; when he had poured four measures of Martini, he broke the sandwich into small bits and threw them to the gulls.

'Sal's brought some chocolate cake,' said Katy, who, with Sal, had preferred Coca-Cola. 'She's just the best cook.'

'I thought Katy was the dessert queen,' said Charlie.

'Oh, no. Just you wait,' said Katy.

'Hey, quit fooling around,' said Sal. She was taller and thinner than her elder sister; where Katy's sleek prettiness was in her shiny chestnut hair and upturned nose, Sal was thin, with hunched shoulders and pale eyes. Mary thought Sal was beautiful, but Charlie always laughed at Mary's idea of what was attractive in women; usually it was nothing more than the opposite of herself. Mary anticipated a whispered discussion in the cabin that night in which Charlie would explode with derisive laughter.

Katy handed round some cold chicken, then some apples; when they had finished and congratulated Sal on her cake, it was warm

73

enough for them to spread out on the boards and close their eyes. Mary leaned against Charlie, who was having another drink, and angled herself into the sun. She withdrew, behind her sunglasses and her closed eyes, into a cocoon from which she could hear Frank's voice, low in conversation with Sal. She could pick out occasional phrases: Boston . . . Kennedy . . . Michigan primary. Frank seemed to be interviewing Sal as he had previously interviewed her in the restaurant, and Sal seemed to be responding happily: Mary could hear her occasionally shrill laugh and caught the scent of one of Frank's cigarettes.

'Wind's getting up,' said Edward.

'Oh dear,' said Sal, 'does that mean we can't sail any more?'

'On the contrary,' said Edward. 'The conditions are ideal.'

'Oh God,' said Charlie, as they piled their rugs and baskets back into the stern.

When they made their way out into the bay, a red-painted boat began tacking towards them: on the bow was a woman with binoculars held up to her face, waving her arm. As the boat came closer to them, Charlie said, 'Isn't it that bore from the French Embassy?'

A man with a blue yachting cap and shining new oilskins called out to them in French-accented English. Edward shouted back some sailing pleasantries and began to tack the other way, but the Frenchman was challenging them to a race.

'Around the island and back to the point!' he

yelled, indicating a small, tree-covered hillock in the bay, about half a mile north.

'Do we have to, Eddie?' said Katy anxiously.

'It really doesn't make any difference,' said Edward. 'It's not like a car. I can't make the thing go any faster, it's entirely up to the wind.'

'Won't we end up in the wrong place, though?' said Mary.

'It's all right. It's only an hour or so from here back to the car.'

'Think of the honour of England,' said Frank.

'Quite right,' said Charlie, who had been nodding off in the stern.

'Hey, I need you, Charlie. Get up there,' said Edward. He looked at Frank. 'And you. Give that rope a yank, or do I mean the other way round? You're the crew.'

The two boats carved their separate courses, crossing and recrossing like folded parallelograms, scrawling their joined lines as straight as the contrary wind would let them. Mary huddled down inside her jacket and rubbed her hands. From time to time she and the other women were required to lean out over the edge of the boat; then, as the boom swung across, they would scurry back beneath it, sometimes encountering Frank or Charlie coming back the other way on their urgent crewing business.

Edward kept a strong arm on the tiller, his eyes good-naturedly moving across the horizon, making sure the boats did not come too close. As they neared the island, it was clear that the French boat was ahead.

'Listen, skipper,' said Charlie, 'I don't want to

start a mutiny, but shouldn't you be splicing the mainbrace or something?'

'Put the bastard ashore,' said Frank.

'Hear, hear,' said Katy.

'Poor Eddie, he's doing his best,' said Sal.

The wind was picking up further as they rounded the island and headed back towards the point, and it was beginning to rain in small, stinging drops that whipped into their faces.

'I knew this was a mistake,' Katy whispered into Mary's ear.

Mary turned up the collar of her jacket and retied her scarf beneath her chin. The boat rose and smacked its wooden hull down on a rising wave. Sal screamed as the boards of the deck buckled under the impact.

'Ah, a life before the mast,' said Charlie, taking a swill from Frank's flask.

'Did you see the floor bend?' said Sal. 'I'm scared.'

'I think it's called a deck, isn't it?' said Charlie.

'If it didn't bend, that would be a problem,' said Edward. 'How are you feeling, Frank?'

'Pretty good,' said Frank, whose face was pale even on dry land. He was holding hard to the rail and seemed to have left the crewing work to Charlie.

As they neared the point, Edward made a sudden tack and caught the wind at its strongest; by the time he turned again, there was no distance between the two boats. For a hundred yards or so they ran along parallel, but as they were on different tacks, it was hard to tell who was ahead when they crossed the finishing line.

They waved to the French and turned for home.

'We won,' said Katy.

'More like a dead heat,' said Charlie.

'You can be sure of one thing,' said Edward. 'In their history books that'll go down as a crushing French victory.'

'Get me home, sweetie,' said Katy. 'I'm drenched.'

It took more than the hour Edward had promised for them to reach the mooring where the car was parked, but it was only a short drive to the cabin, which was at the end of a lane in an area of woodland.

'God, it's Walden Pond,' said Charlie, as Edward drew up on the track alongside.

'But it has hot water,' said Edward. 'Provided the yard man remembered to switch it on.'

The cabin consisted of a living area dominated by a cavernous fireplace, above which was a moose's head; the room was divided by a wooden counter, the other side of which was a primitive kitchen. A short passage, snared with nets and fishing tackle, joined the main room to two bedrooms at the back; a narrow stairway rose from an alcove behind the fireplace to a bathroom and a further bedroom in the roof. The cabin was surrounded by a wooden balcony that gave views into the forests; the windows had wire coverings of tight mesh against the ravening insects.

It was starting to grow dark as they unloaded the station wagon, and Katy showed Mary and Sal up to the bathroom, which, she had decided, the women should use first.

Mary and Charlie were given the upstairs room, where Mary undressed in preparation for following Sal into the bath. Charlie went through their bag, looking for spare socks.

'Bloody cold, isn't it?' he said quietly.

'It'll be fine once Eddie's lit the fire.'

Charlie put on two pairs of socks and climbed in beneath the eiderdown. He pulled it back on Mary's side and patted the bed invitingly. Mary pulled a dressing-gown over her underclothes and slipped in beside him; she felt Charlie's hand run up her thigh and curled in closer to him. They could hear Edward's voice from downstairs.

'Frank, can you give me a hand with some logs? They're in the crawlspace beneath the cabin.'

Charlie whispered into Mary's hair. 'Do you think Frank's ever seen a log before?'

Mary laughed. 'Do you like Sal?'

'She's all right. Kinda cute.'

'Not really your type, though, is she? Not like Katy.' She nudged him in the ribs.

'I don't know about that.'

'I'd better hurry up so I can help with dinner.'

Charlie squeezed her thigh beneath the dressing-gown. 'Go on, then. Did you see any wine down there?'

'Yes, there was a whole case in the corridor. But, darling, please don't drink too much. Promise me. Remember what Dr Weissman said.'

In her bath, Mary caught the scent of woodsmoke from below. She slid back beneath the steaming water and let it run through her hair; the taste of steam in cold bathrooms reduced her always to the condition of childhood, of the world outside banished by the familiar warmth. By the time she went down to help Katy, the fireplace was stacked with flaming logs and Edward was pouring drinks from the wooden counter. Katy had brought a clam chowder, which only needed to be reheated, and had put some potatoes in the oven to go with a honey-glazed ham; on the gas ring she was doing something New England-looking with corn.

'So you see there's nothing for you to do, Mary,' she said. 'Just relax.'

Mary did as she was told. Sal came and sat on the sofa with her, next to the fire, while Frank sat opposite them with one foot up on the low table next to a dish of potato chips and tomato dip. Mary noticed that Sal's behaviour towards him was coquettish, and that Frank seemed not to mind.

'So how are you liking the rustic life?' said Sal.

'It's different,' said Frank. 'You see a flame like that where I live, you call the Fire Department.'

'Do you like New York?'

'Sure, I like it. But if there was somewhere bigger or with more things happening I'd go there. Why would you want to be second best?'

'What's your apartment like?'

'It's in the Village. My office is downtown, so it's kind of convenient.'

'I'd love to come and see it. I had a boyfriend in the Village once. We used to have such a good time. All those galleries and everything.'

'You can stop by some day. Just give me a call.'

Mary found herself irritated by Sal's disingenuous manner. 'Have you finished your article, Frank?' she said.

'Yeah. Pretty much.' He smiled and stood up. 'I think I'd better go wash up before dinner.'

When Charlie came down he put a record on, lit a cigarette and poured himself a tumbler full of red wine, catching Mary's warning glance as he did so.

'It's wine,' he said, 'not even a proper drink.'

Edward Renshaw, fresh from the bath and wearing a red plaid shirt, insisted on dancing with Mary while the soup was heated. He pushed back the low table to make room, and whirled her round the floor to the hissing beat of Duke Ellington.

'Jimmy Blanton on bass,' he explained to Mary, 'so anyone can dance to it.'

Edward was a good mover, though Charlie always maintained his interest in Mary was more than just that of a man who liked dancing. His right hand was tight on her waist, and he pulled her pelvis close to his. Charlie responded by flirting with Katy Renshaw, ostensibly as a revenge, though conveniently it happened that he found Katy's primness oddly arousing. Katy was too busy directing them to their seats for dinner to take much notice.

Mary was flushed by the bay wind, the chowder and the log fire; her clean, almost-black hair shone in the light of the single bulb whose dim wattage had been augmented by two hurricane lamps on the mantelpiece and by a group of flickering candles on the dining table.

Charlie looked at her affectionately as he filled another glass of wine before turning with the bottle to Katy, on whose thigh, beneath its woollen skirt, his hand hospitably lingered. Over the competitive din of conversation, the sailing race inaccurately recalled, and the pleading wail of tenor saxophones, Mary could barely make herself heard. Having eaten her plate of honeyed ham, she settled back into her chair, hoping she had room for another of Sal's extolled desserts, accepted the wine that Edward poured for her, and lit a cigarette. She felt afloat on warmth and appreciation; she caught herself at an instant somehow exhilarated and admired, though no one at that moment was talking to her. Frank was listening to Sal's self-exploratory monologue in the next chair, his tired face intent with concentration yet simultaneously aloof. His eye met Mary's for a moment as he turned his head to locate an ashtray on the table between them; she noticed he had located some clothes of at least semi-rustic variety in his bag, a pair of beige cotton drill trousers and a holly-green crewneck sweater, which looked suspiciously new, as though purchased from a Georgetown outfitters for the purposes of the trip.

Mary had drunk more wine than usual, though no more than anyone else, she thought, as she swayed about the floor in the arms first of Edward, then of Frank. Charlie was roaring, on the edge, and kept turning up the volume of the music, replacing Edward's or Frank's choice of record with his own and abusing their ridiculous taste, their passion for the second-rate.

Katy remonstrated with him, but was herself too unsteady to be able to control him. She clung tightly to his arm as he filled another glass, and it was only when she showed signs of becoming lachrymose that Charlie saved himself from embarrassment by changing dance partners, pushing Edward towards his wife and pressing Sal's hand against his own heart in a nightclub clinch. Mary laughed, as Frank's light touch in the small of her back steered her between these harmlessly irresponsible friends, whom she loved, even Sal, she told herself, as they slid and shouted and held on to one another, filled by an effervescence that had welled up in them from the inexplicable pleasure of their lives.

Mary detached Charlie from a bottle of scotch that Frank and Edward, now seated at the table, had begun to pour into beer glasses. She guided him upstairs to the bathroom and administered to him as she had done so often to their children. His eyes were glazed, but they were still in touch with the world; they were not, as she had sometimes seen them, looking backwards into some blank plain inside his head.

When they were in bed, Mary said, 'What do you think they're doing now?'

'Who? Frank and Sal?'

'No! The children.'

'I sincerely hope they're asleep.'

Their conversation degenerated into imitations of Richard and Louisa, random phrases that evoked them, that conjured in this remote cabin their terrible sweetness, their idiotic grandeur in their apprehension of the great puzzle that the world represented to them. Mary curled closer to Charlie, her eyes brimming with the love that the words had set flowing in her; she smelled the mixture of wine and toothpaste on her husband's breath as he nuzzled her dark, wavy hair, felt his caressing hand come to rest at its favourite place, between her legs, as he began to fall asleep.

It was all right, she thought, everything would be for the best after all, because no illness, no death or treacherous cruelty could be strong enough to break up a world so fortified with love or a life so diverse and rich in the sources of its contentment.

4

Mary awoke from a dream of her dying mother to the sound of New York. They had been booked into a hotel on Lexington Avenue; it was twenty-four storeys tall, faced in red brick, and the howl of the avenue was conducted up its sheer sides. It had been chosen for its proximity to the Consulate, a short walk away on Park Avenue between 39th and 40th Streets, where, to Charlie's delight, it was housed in the National Distillers Building.

By the time Mary returned from the bathroom, the bellboy had called with breakfast and the newspapers. Charlie read rapidly through them, occasionally grunting or exclaiming, and passing them over to Mary as he finished. The bedside telephone rang and Charlie, saying 'I'm not here', handed the heavy, bleating instrument across the bed, its flex tangling in the remains of scrambled egg and brittle strips of bacon.

'May I speak with Mary van der Linden?' She half-recognized the voice. 'This is Frank Renzo.'

'Hello, Frank. How are you?'

'I'm sorry to call so early. A colleague of mine was at your consulate yesterday and heard you were in town. I wondered if I could repay your hospitality, show you something of the city.'

'The guided tour?' Mary tried to think of a way of stalling him; she had been planning to

84

spend the day alone, shopping in the morning, lunch downtown, then a gallery. 'That's very nice of you. I'd better check with Charlie what his plans — '

Charlie waved his hand dismissively, in an accommodating, don't-mind-me gesture that was the opposite of helpful.

'Well, I . . . I suppose . . . That would be very nice.' She handed the telephone back to Charlie. 'Thanks a lot.'

Charlie laughed. 'You getting the tour? It might be fun. I've got meetings at the Distillery all day anyway.'

After Charlie had gone, Mary dressed with some care. She wore a suit with a tailored jacket and a skirt which, though a little tight at the knee, would not prevent her walking with ease if it turned into a long day of sightseeing. Most of the women on Fifth Avenue, she had noticed the day before, were wearing hats, but she had never felt comfortable with anything on her head and resented having to wear proper hats to weddings or to the parties on the Embassy lawns. She put a scarf into her purse, next to the small leather photograph wallet with a picture of the children, checked her make-up in the bathroom mirror and set off.

Frank was waiting for her in the lobby. He looked distracted, as though the enterprise had been someone else's idea. He was wearing the suit with the nailhead pattern he had worn on the first evening he had arrived at the van der Lindens' party, Mary noticed, and his tie was already beginning to sink down from the top button of his pale blue shirt.

'Hi.'

He held out his hand.

'This is very kind of you,' she said.

'Do you have an idea what you'd like to do?'

'No. I rather hoped you'd have a plan. Perhaps we could go and see some pictures — whatever's on at the Met, for instance.'

Frank, who was carrying a felt hat and had a raincoat over his arm, looked worried for a moment as he inspected Mary; but he swallowed whatever misgiving he might have had and took her by the elbow through the revolving doors on to Lexington Avenue, where he hailed a cab.

'Aren't you working?' said Mary, straightening her skirt over her knees as she settled on to the slippery seat.

'No, I have a few days' vacation.'

'And you're not going away anywhere?'

'Oh no. You never know what might turn up.'

Frank barked an instruction to the driver and sat back. 'Guy just arrived from Puerto Rico. Doesn't know where the hell he's going.'

The morning followed no logical itinerary. Frank's version of the city was less influenced by architecture or appearance than by stories he had written and people he had met. It began with an hour among the rows of second-hand bookstores on Fourth Avenue, round Tenth Street, then went over to Tompkins Square — an interesting district, he explained, because the New York City Housing Authority had built its first project on Avenue A at Third Street. Mary could not see what was noteworthy in the depressed and menacing blocks, with resentful-looking youths playing softball behind wire mesh.

They walked up to Tompkins Square Park, where he showed her a small monument of two children, carved in relief on a stone background, looking at a flowering tree. The girl was seated, the boy carried a hoop; an engraved caption read: 'They were earth's purest children, young and fair.'

'It commemorates the loss of a steamboat,' said Frank. 'Thousands of people from this neighbourhood died on it, mostly Germans. Their families couldn't bear to stay in these streets afterwards, so they moved out and it was taken over by Russians. Around here you can still feel that sense of loss. Don't you think?'

The children reminded Mary of her own, and for a moment she lost track of what Frank was saying, as her mind turned over thoughts of family and bereavement.

'You can hear them talk Russian in the stores and cafés.'

'Is that so?' She rallied. 'And what do they think of Sputnik?'

'I guess they'd be pretty divided. Most of them came before the Revolution and they're not so crazy about Communism.'

Frank took her back to the Bowery and on to the end of Bleecker Street, where he pointed to a handsome, ornamented building.

'Know who designed that? It's Louis H. Sullivan, his only building in New York. You ever go to Chicago, you'll see his best stuff there.

We're pretty proud of him back where I come from.' He smiled. 'Is any of this interesting to you?'

Taken aback by his directness, Mary stammered slightly. 'Yes, of course. Yes, it's very interesting.'

'So, do I just keep on talking?'

'Yes. Yes. You do that.'

'We'll walk down to Chatham Square, where two El tracks used to meet. You got to imagine what it was like, the people in the dark beneath all that ironwork.'

Frank walked quickly, and Mary found herself struggling a little to keep up; she wished she had accepted an earlier invitation to take a break in some Russian, or possibly Greek, café. The lower reaches of the Bowery were lined with discount liquor stores, flophouses, pawnshops and hotels whose imposing names — the Grand Windsor, the Palace, the Crystal — were set in context by their modest claim to offer 'Clean Rooms'. Frank strode on, apparently unaware of the fallen men stretched across the doorways, talking of the movements of people and how he felt that, although the city was a thousand neighbourhoods, it had a single character as well.

'And what's that single character?' Mary asked.

'Search me. Jewish, I guess. You find Jewish stores and theaters, you're pretty close to the real thing.'

He took her suddenly by the elbow and steered her to the right, down Grand Street. 'You gotta see this.'

After a few blocks, he stopped in front of an Italian general store, so un-American it might have been transported whole from Verona.

'Louis Sullivan, Little Italy. Another home for you,' said Mary.

They went into the store, which sold straw ponies from Positano, devices for making lasagne, plastic gondolas, plaster saints and arlecchinos, coloured drinking glasses and 78 rpm shellac recordings of Caruso in brown paper covers. By the cash desk, there was a *Grammatica Accelerata: Italiana — Inglese*. A woman in widow's black smiled at them from behind a wooden counter; the homesickness was almost palpable.

'Breaks your heart, doesn't it?' Frank said.

'Yours, I think,' said Mary.

They went back on to the Bowery and continued walking south, where the street widened for the approach to Manhattan Bridge, a square triumphal arch that might have been commissioned by Trajan or Tiberius. A traffic cop stood in the middle of the road, his blue serge jacket double-buttoned beneath his chin, waving his white-gloved hands at the streams of arriving and departing traffic. He was yelling at the cars and trucks, his body a frenzy of agitation as though he was about to dance. Mary thought his wild gestures were those of anger, until he pointed at a truck driver and mimed a festive pulling of the klaxon; she saw the smile of gratification spread across his face as the driver noisily obliged.

Eventually, they reached Chatham Square, a

confluence of nine streets, whose buildings still looked unused to the sunlight admitted by the slum clearance of the neighbouring Green and the removal of its elevated train tracks. One street led west to the financial district, another north into the belly of Chinatown.

'Imagine the view you'd get on the train,' said Frank. 'You could look into people's front rooms in Harlem or Brooklyn. You could see them working, women in sweatshops, men in factories, the guy alone in the office at night, fiddling the books. Then you'd see the East River or maybe the sun setting on the Chrysler building. And right here underneath, almost in the dark, there'd be movie theaters and newspaper sellers, florists, bums. And up on the platforms there were little framehouses, you know a hundred years old with gables, kind of like England, I guess.'

Mary had begun to laugh. 'I'm sorry,' she said. 'Maybe you had to be here.'

'I think maybe I did.' She touched his arm lest he should take offence. 'But it does sound charming.'

Frank looked at his watch. 'Listen. I'll take you to lunch. Do you like fish? Ever had shad roes? Or a kippered herring?'

'Kippers? We used to have them every Friday breakfast when I was a child.'

'Come on, then.'

'But I didn't really like them.'

'Me neither. Too many bones.'

'Do we ever take a taxi in this tour?'

'No, it's just down on South Street, by the

market. Maybe after lunch.'

Frank took her beneath Brooklyn Bridge to a building near the waterfront. While he organized a table and went to make a telephone call, she walked through to the women's room at the back, which was down an unplastered brick corridor. The door handle was missing, though the tiled surfaces inside seemed clean enough, and she took some minutes to comb her hair and fix her make-up.

When she returned, she found that Frank had ordered her a glass of water and a dry martini. Across the street, they could see the huge open sheds of Fulton Market which disappeared off the edge of the island, their outer parts supported by piles deep in the East River. It was almost one o'clock, and activity was beginning to dwindle; the porters were pushing empty trolleys and men in rubber aprons were starting to hose down the floor.

'You like clams?' said Frank, looking at a board on the wall where the menu was chalked.

'What's good here?' said Mary, avoiding the clam question.

'Anything's fine, so long as it's fish. Why don't we get some crab?'

'Good idea.'

Mary was relieved to be sitting down at last, and surreptitiously eased off her shoes beneath the table: the giant square paving slabs of Manhattan had drained the life from her calves and heels. She lit a cigarette and offered the pack to Frank, who was stirring his drink with the end of his fork, since the restaurant had not run to swizzle sticks; he managed to make the same rapid sequence of sounds she had noticed in Georgetown.

There was a change in the atmosphere as the table required them, for the first time that day, to look one another in the eye. Mary was worried that, without the life of the streets to comment on, Frank might become bored by her company.

'So,' she said, 'tell me about your work. Why aren't you travelling somewhere if you're on holiday?'

'I don't care much for vacations. I travel a good deal for work, so if I get the chance I like to stay in New York.' He drained the glass and put it back on the table. 'Also, I don't want to miss anything. I think I told you I'm trying to get on to the election. Time's running out and I don't want to miss a break if it comes along.'

'I see. And were you reporting on politics before you did whatever it was you did wrong?'

'Yeah, pretty much. I did the Eisenhower — Stevenson election in '52. I guess that was the beginning of the problem. Eisenhower did this terrible thing in Milwaukee right at the end of the campaign. He rewrote his speech to please McCarthy. The local governor, a guy named Kohler, was frightened that if Eisenhower said good things about General Marshall, who McCarthy was trying to make out as some sort of Red, then McCarthy would make trouble for him. So Kohler got Ike to cut all the Marshall stuff out and Ike embraced McCarthy on the platform. But Marshall was not only a fine man, he had virtually created Ike as a politician, and

92

here was Eisenhower crawling to this toad McCarthy who was trying to ruin Marshall. It was a terrible moment.'

'But why on earth would Eisenhower be so frightened of McCarthy?'

'He was trying to please Kohler, the local Republican. But everyone was frightened of McCarthy, all the politicians. He showed he could get them beaten at the polls if he backed the other candidate. In the end it was as simple as that. They were scared of losing their seats. No one really believed all those Communist accusations. Not even Nixon.'

'Did you meet McCarthy?'

'Sure, he was a very friendly guy. He loved journalists. The press made him, by reporting his fantasies, so he was always buying drinks. I mean, really a lot of drinks. You know he died of cirrhosis? But it wasn't just trying to buy our friendship, he liked being one of the guys. He liked getting drunk with other men. I remember he ran a tab at the Pfister Hotel in Milwaukee. Unbelievable.'

'So he was an alcoholic?'

'I guess so. He was kind of amusing to be with, to pass an hour with. I think he didn't like women. He preferred men, if you see what I mean.'

'Yes, I think so.'

'That's where we parted company. That and the question of these Communists.'

'So what happened? You said that was where the problem began.'

While Frank was explaining, the waiter

brought the crabs with a bowl of mayonnaise and some ketchup in small paper cups. Frank told her that the FBI had helped to create the fog of distrust in which McCarthy had worked; knowing people were ready to sneak on their neighbours, the Bureau had been able to accumulate files on individuals who had only the most circumstantial connection with any left-wing activity — a foreign name, the purchase of a magazine, a wrong friend. Hardly any were believing Communists, but all were afraid of being reported, denounced and barred from work, knowing that they would not be offered a chance to defend themselves.

'They mounted a big attack on the press,' said Frank. 'Agents would just turn up at an office and tell the editor who to fire. I wrote a story about Eisenhower's speech. I'd been told by one of his aides how he'd cut out the pro-Marshall stuff. Even his own staff were appalled. My editor got a call a week or so later from the FBI. I was one of half a dozen reporters he was told to keep an eye on. He just told them to get lost, so I was okay for the time being.'

'The FBI came to your paper just because you'd been rude about McCarthy?'

'Pretty much. They could turn up at a women's magazine and tell the editor to fire someone and that was it. McCarthy and the FBI worked hand in glove. Hoover fed McCarthy a lot of material. McCarthy had this famous sidekick Roy Cohn, a revolting man, and Hoover was right up his ass. Pardon me.'

Frank looked momentarily embarrassed, and

Mary found herself smiling at his attack of decorum.

'I remember Cohn,' she said. 'But if your editor stood up for you, what finally went wrong?'

'I'll tell you about it another time.'

'But you weren't a sympathizer in any way?'

'Christ, no, Mary. I'm a reporter, I'm not a political guy. I mean, sometimes I don't vote, or maybe I'll have met one of the candidates and vote for him. The first time I ever went to the polls I voted Republican. I was sixteen years old and they came to my part of Chicago and handed out voting cards. All the kids on my block voted for Landon not Roosevelt. They'd enfranchised us. So why not?'

As Frank continued to talk, waving a crab leg, then cracking it at the joint, Mary watched his face in an absent sort of way. She had never, she thought, met anyone with eyes of quite his colour: they were pale blue, but round the edge of the iris were splinters of brown, like shards of cracked cob nut. Beneath the eyes, where the skin was discoloured with fatigue, she could just make out a handful of faded freckles of the same pale brown. She wondered what he had looked like as a boy, whether the freckles had bloomed then in soft skin, like Richard's.

The other thing she kept noticing was that, however much he disavowed any political belief, there seemed to be a sinewy sense in his conversation of right and wrong; he appeared indignant about certain things, committed to others. She wondered if he had inherited a

95

Catholic morality from his family, but it didn't seem to be a spiritual quality; she had the feeling that, however droll and dismissive his way of concealing it, there were a number of things he wanted to see done, by himself or others.

After lunch they took a taxi uptown to the Met, and at about four o'clock Mary was overcome by a desire to sleep. Frank took her back to the hotel.

'Well, thank you,' said Mary, as he went round the cab and opened her door. 'I enjoyed the tour.'

There was a moment of unease.

'Good,' said Frank.

'Thanks.'

'You know, we could do the second part of the tour tomorrow.'

'It has two parts?'

'It has a number of parts.'

'I'd better see what Charlie's doing.'

'Sure.'

'Are you certain it wouldn't be a nuisance for you?'

Frank's answer was lost beneath the driver's shouted question. 'You coming, pal?'

'I'll call you,' said Frank, walking round the back of the car.

Mary went through the swing doors. It was pleasant to have some company when sightseeing, she thought; you could go into bars and cafés without being stared at as a lone woman; it was good to have this fall-back for the next day if nothing else was required of her.

Up in the room, she took off her shoes and

96

skirt and curled up on the bed. She began to read her book, then found herself drifting off: the traffic noise from the street became part of an almost-dream, a pleasing soundtrack to the static images of no particular significance that were for her always the gateway to sleep: a tree, a gate, the corner of a house. The half-slip she was wearing could not prevent a draught reaching her legs and she pulled a cover over her, as, with her dark hair loose over the hotel pillow, she fell asleep.

★   ★   ★

She awoke when Charlie came back into the room. He leaned over to kiss her and lost his footing, so that he collapsed beside her on the bed, leaking fumes of alcohol. Mary sat up and stroked the hair back from his forehead.

'Are you all right, darling?'

'Boring bloody day. Christ, it's so bloody boring.'

It was an art, knowing whether Charlie should be indulged, rebuked or put to bed, but it was one in which Mary was practised. It was a failure to her if he could not be made to have dinner, but would only curl up with a bottle, rebuffing her attempts at friendliness. She decided to leave him where he was while she took a bath; sometimes a short sleep could pull him back on to the main line of the day, especially if followed by a shower and a large scotch on the rocks.

Mary sat in the deep tub, moving the hot water up between her legs and round her sides. She felt reinvigorated by her rest and wanted to go out to Chinatown, or Little Italy, or the Village: she didn't mind what they ate provided she could experience some more of the city. After twenty minutes she climbed out and wrapped herself in a towel. Charlie was where she had left him, snoring softly; Mary put on a robe she found in the bathroom and took him by the shoulder.

'Get off, leave me alone.'

'No, darling, you're coming out. Come on.'

She gauged that if she could withstand some abuse, Charlie was not so drunk that he could not be persuaded to co-operate.

'You have a shower and I'll ring for some ice. When you've finished I'll have clean clothes and a nice drink ready for you.'

Half an hour later, they were ready to go out, Charlie with hair still damp, but his mood somewhat restored by two large drinks and a cigarette. On Lexington Avenue he hailed a taxi.

'Where to, bud?' The driver craned round in his seat.

'Ask the lady.'

'I don't know. Greenwich Village. Anywhere down there.'

They pulled out into the middle lane, where they hit a run of green lights as the cab went loudly downtown, bouncing on the potholes, sounding its horn as it swung from lane to lane to avoid the dithering schmucks, jerks and assholes identified by the driver.

'This good enough for you?' he said, as they pulled up in Washington Square.

'Just let me out,' said Charlie.

'Thank you,' said Mary. 'This is fine.'

As they walked through the square, they noticed a group of young men lined up with their arms entwined through the double-barred iron railing, smoking, watching the people pass by. Although the night had turned cool, they wore only T-shirts, some of them rolled up over the bicep; they hung forward from the rail as though captive, yet with a hungry impatience.

'What are those men doing?' said Mary.

'Not something that concerns a woman. Where are we going?'

Mary led him down Sullivan Street for a couple of blocks, then turned left, where the sidewalks glowed under the light of neon signs. There were bakeries and greengrocers still open, bookstores and a low brick building with a circular sign announcing it as the Circle in the Square theatre. Coloured awnings led into various restaurants and bars, and they eventually settled on a corner building with scrubbed wooden floorboards and tables set in candle-lit booths.

As Mary ate her appetizer and looked across the table at his glazed but no longer hostile expression, she found her eyes sting with sorrow. She seldom allowed herself to remember Charlie as he had been when they first met: ebullient, clear-eyed, certain that he could reinvent the world or at least convert it to the invigorating plan he had for it. Nothing in her sorrow affected the love she felt for him or her devotion to their joint cause, the children, their domestic life together in their Washington street — the things he referred to as '1064 and All That'. She felt only an anguished sympathy for what he seemed to suffer and, periodically, a fear that it might have some awful outcome. When she had once confided her anxiety to Katy Renshaw, however, Katy had told her that there was nothing to worry about. Charlie drank only a little more than most men they knew. So what if he went to see a psychoanalyst? Everyone did, particularly in New York. Katy made it sound as though the sky over midtown was a jam of uninterpreted dreams, the drains below the fuming manhole covers a network of suppressed desires. Anyway, Katy said, men like Charlie and Edward were creative, unusually clever guys who needed to be allowed their foibles and their games, like when they tried to catch each other out with lines of poetry they pretended to have read but might instead have made up. Had Mary seen the pleasure in Charlie's eyes when he had passed off a line of his to Edward as one of Wallace Stevens's? It was a game; it was all just a game.

Such was Mary's temperament that she was inclined to believe her. All would be well, because all usually was well, more or less; and anyway, they were locked together in a common endeavour: dealing with Charlie was part of her life and she would have it no other way.

'I have to go to Chicago,' said Charlie, pushing a piece of chicken round his plate. 'Tomorrow. I have to take a plane from La Guardia at ten o'clock.'

'Why?'

'Don't ask. It's this bloody election. Trouble is, I don't think I can manage it. The flying.'

'You'll be all right, darling. You'll be fine. Have you got some of your pills with you?'

'Yes, I have. But I have to take so many that then I can't perform at the other end.'

Mary put her hand on his. 'Would you like me to come with you?'

'No, I'd hate that. You stay here.'

'All right. How long will you be gone?'

'Two nights. I'll be back on Thursday. Will you be all right? You can go back to Washington if you like.'

'I'll be fine. It's you I'm worried about.'

Charlie lit a cigarette and pushed his plate away. He held his head in his hands. For a moment Mary thought he was crying. Then he wrenched his hands away and pushed back the chair noisily, losing his balance for a moment as he stood up.

★   ★   ★

The next morning, in the taxi on the way to La Guardia, Charlie looked pale, and there was a tremor in his hand; but he was also quiet and resigned. Mary suspected that he owed his mood to one of the pills Weissman had prescribed, but knew he would be irritated if she asked. She stood with him on the ramp outside the departure building, checking that he had everything he needed. As she kissed him, she did up the middle button of his jacket, and patted his ribs, as though he were a child. She felt the little death of departure.

He licked his dry lips, turned, bag in hand, and made off through the revolving door.

Mary climbed back into the waiting taxi and told the driver to return to the hotel. She wondered how Charlie would manage the flight; she hoped he would not be so doped by the time they landed that he would be incapable of getting off the plane.

Back inside the hotel, she went to the front desk to collect the key.

'Mrs van der Linden?'

'Yes.'

'Message for you. A Mr Renzo called.'

'Oh. I see. Did he leave a number?'

'Sure did, ma'am.' The desk clerk held out a piece of paper along with the key.

Up in the room Mary paused before telephoning. She could perfectly easily spend the day alone, doing what she wanted to do. This would entail some of the things for which New York was more obviously well known: going to the Frick Collection and looking in some of the shops on Madison Avenue behind it; a light lunch overlooking the Park and then, one of her particular pleasures, a film in the afternoon, emerging while it was still light for a cocktail at the top of a midtown skyscraper, and the self-indulgence of a room-service dinner alone with her book.

Did she really want to be taken on another random and exhausting trek through low-rent neighbourhoods, plague areas, second-hand bookstores, streets with 'interesting' ethnic history, fish and garment markets, pausing infrequently to be presented with a glassful of stupefying iced liquor and a lecture on recent American politics?

It would be company, at least. She lifted the receiver and dialled. It was arranged that he would stop by the hotel at midday; Mary calculated that this would give them only an hour before lunch, and this time she would have some say over the venue. As a precaution, she invented a call from Charlie which she would expect at five o'clock; in fact, he seldom rang when he was away, but she wanted to have an escape route.

Frank called up from the front desk at ten to twelve.

'I'm a little early. I took the subway. I can wait if you like.'

'No, no. I'm ready.'

The elevator sank eighteen floors and the uniformed attendant hauled open the rolling accordion doors. Frank was standing by the desk, turning his hat slowly round in his hands. Mary moved swiftly across the lobby.

'Hi.' Frank took her by the arm and moved her toward the door.

Mary paused at the kerb, expecting him to hail a cab, but he set off on foot, down 45th Street, then right on to Third Avenue.

'How's Charlie?' Frank said loudly above the traffic noise, as they waited to cross the street.

'He's fine. He's had to go to Chicago. Where's the tour taking us today?'

'I haven't decided. I like it down here, though.

103

Toward Murray Hill. It's kind of blank.'

'You like that?'

'I like the fact that it's impersonal. No one troubles you. That's what cities are for. Frankfurters, cabs, you know. Loud noises. Come on.'

Frank walked more slowly than the previous day so that they could continue their conversation. He guided her over to Madison, past the J. P. Morgan home, back on to clamorous Lexington with its long blocks of furniture stores, then over again on to Third, where they walked down past the old gin mills. Despite the proximity of many skyscrapers, the city was less overpowering than in the seething boxes further west; there was a sense of the island sloping downhill to the East River and of the tight grid beginning to shake loose.

'When I first came to New York I had a room in a railroad flat way uptown on 95th, and I used to take the train down Third every morning.'

'Is that when you got the habit of looking into people's windows?'

'I guess so. They took it down a few years ago. I never imagined how pretty Third Avenue would be beneath the tracks.'

'Pretty?' It seemed to Mary a strange word for the blur of commerce, the undistinguished tenements, where a police siren had begun to shriek in front of a clothing store.

At lunchtime they took a cab back uptown to a chop-house on Lexington of which Frank spoke warmly. Most of the clients seemed to be businessmen in suits, sitting at a long mahogany

104

bar or gathered at tables with blue checked cloths, speaking with low urgency over their powerful drinks.

'So what's Charlie doing in Chicago?'

'I don't know. I've learned not to ask over the years.'

'Why? Is it confidential?'

'No, not really. Charlie's job really is to follow the election. We'd been in London for a bit and we were expecting to go to Paris. Charlie was Assistant Private Secretary to the Foreign Secretary at a very young age. They made him a counsellor when he was only thirty-six.'

'So he's what they call a high flyer?'

'It's an awful expression, but I suppose that's it. With the election coming up the Embassy political staff in Washington needed someone extra, and Charlie'd done a doctorate on American politics, so he was asked to come for a couple of years. He'd met Senator Kennedy when his father was Ambassador in London and it was thought he had some kind of special line to him.'

'And does he?' said Frank.

'I think so. He claims he remembers nothing about their meeting at all. He says he was drunk at the time. In fact he does have some kind of access. I don't quite know how it works, but I've seen the results. It's all a bit of a gamble, because at the moment it doesn't look as though Kennedy'll even get the nomination. But Charlie does other things as well. When someone's on leave or off sick, he'll cover for them, then you have to take over their speciality, which might be the Soviet Union or Indo-China or something. And he's supposed to liaise with the American press as well. They all are, to some extent.'

'So why don't you ask what he's doing?'

'Because he gets so cross with me.' Mary pulled a pack of cigarettes from her bag and offered one to Frank. 'Charlie's not a very happy man. He doesn't like the work. Or maybe he doesn't mind the work, he just doesn't like being alive. It's a kind of illness.' She paused. 'I shouldn't tell you these things.'

'We're still off the record, aren't we? Does he see a doctor?'

'Yes, two, but it doesn't do any good. One of them gives him pills and the other one, the analyst, just makes him talk. He's fuming when he comes back. The man never says anything, apparently, just sits there with his arms folded and hands him the bill at the end.'

'And what do you think the problem is?'

Mary sighed. 'I don't know. I doubt whether there's a single thing you could just identify and cure. I think the world has disappointed him, that's one thing. He can't bear to be bored. He's impatient. He drinks so much to try to drown out his need for stimulation, to stifle the clamouring in his brain. I think. I also think he feels the futility of everything more than most people. I mean, I know it's all pointless, that I'll just go on for a few years, then die — but I like it. I'm happy. This drink, this bar, my conversation with you. The thought of my children. I can't help it, I just feel uplifted by them. But I know that that's dishonest in some way, that I ought to take more account of the tragedy of existence, or whatever you might call it. Occasionally I feel frightened that in some way I'll get found out. That something will come along and I won't be ready for it. Or that when I die, God will say, 'Well, you had a good time, didn't you? Too busy to stop and think, were you?' Charlie's got it right, probably, but it makes him so unhappy.'

She was looking into Frank's eyes, which met hers without blinking. 'He's a nice guy, Charlie.'

'Oh yes. He's certainly that. He's a wonderful man.' Mary smiled. She hesitated for a moment, then said, 'Would you like to see a photograph of my children?'

'Sure.'

The waiter arrived to tell them about the specials, and Frank questioned him about their provenance and whether he personally would recommend them; Mary had noticed that he thought it a point of politeness always to engage the waiter in this way. She rummaged in her purse and came up with a folding leather wallet which she handed across the table.

Frank made admiring noises. 'Tell me about them,' he said.

Mary had the broiled snapper and a green salad, Frank had the chops with gravy and mashed potatoes. At her request he ordered her some white wine to go with her fish, after which she had a slice of key lime pie and a cup of black coffee. All the time, she spoke of the passion she felt for the children, and it warmed her even to mention their names.

As she replaced her cup in the saucer, she said, 'I'm sorry. I seem to have gone on rather. It's your fault. You shouldn't have asked me.'

Frank handed back the photographs. 'It's my fault. But they sound like fine kids.'

'They are. But don't get me started again. Tell me something about you.'

Frank pulled out a cigarette. 'You ever been to Indo-China?'

'No. But Charlie has. When we were in Japan.'

'I know. That's where I met him. He didn't seem to remember.'

Mary laughed. 'He was probably drunk. He certainly was at the party.'

Frank smiled. 'Me too. Should've switched to highballs earlier on.'

'Anyway. Tell me something about yourself. I'm embarrassed to have gone on so much about Richard and Louisa. It's a thing you should never do — bore people about how sweet your children are. Charlie goes mad when people do it to us.'

'OK. I'll tell you something.' Frank sat back and lit his cigarette from a book of matches on the table. His face was for a moment shadowed and illuminated against the dark wood panelling behind him. 'I have this plan. One day I'm going to build a house. Maybe in the Adirondacks, or the Catskills. It would have to be somewhere mountainous, with woods and a river nearby. But it would also have to be near a town with bars, bookstores, that kind of thing. I'd find an architect and we'd make the plans together. It would be large, but it wouldn't be pretentious,

108

not like a Hollywood mansion. It would be in a simple kind of style — pitched roof, clapboard, pretty traditional, I guess. But inside, there'd be three staircases, a lot of different passageways and corridors so that strangers could easily get lost.'

'It's important that your visitors get confused?'

'That's pretty central to the plan. It would have a lot of big store-rooms for fuel and liquor and household things so they could be kept right out of the picture. And there'd be a hall in the middle with a gallery running around above it.'

'And bedrooms?'

'Sure, we'd have bedrooms, with long views down the Hudson valley. And the bathrooms would have stone floors and plain walls. No tiles like you have in New York with 'roaches in the grout.'

'And who would live there?'

'Me. A few other people maybe.'

'And what would you do there?'

'Fish in the river. Shoot deer. Play pool in the pool room.'

'But you'd be bored. You like the city and newspapers. You haven't even got any country clothes.'

'Don't you think you could live somewhere like that without driving a pick-up and wearing a fur-trimmed hat?'

'You'd think so, wouldn't you? But it seems to be impossible.'

Frank laughed.

She said, 'Do you know, that's the first time I've seen you laugh.'

109

'Is it?' Frank ground out his cigarette. 'That's curious, because since we met at noon I don't think you've stopped.'

'Haven't I?' Mary found her cheeks burning. 'You haven't said anything funny, have you?'

'Not intentionally.'

Mary regathered her composure. She said, 'I think maybe you've just got a ridiculous face.'

When they went outside, a cab sounded its horn loudly next to the kerb; Mary looked up and down the avenue and saw that although the light had begun to fade, the frenzy of the street had not diminished. She had the feeling of how inessential she was to the life of the city; and, with her mother dying, her children and husband absent, how insubstantial was her existence.

★　★　★

Back at the hotel there was a message from Charlie to say that he would have to spend another night in Chicago and would not now be back until midday on Friday. He left a telephone number, which Mary called as soon as she reached the room: the invented excuse for her early return to the hotel had in fact materialized.

He was not drunk, but he was unhappy. Over the years, Mary had grown used to the sound of his voice, lonely and uncertain, trembling, sometimes breaking on the long-distance wires. She found it compellingly strange that someone so confident was capable of so completely unravelling.

110

She wondered what he did when he was away. He liked to disappear, to leave no trace, yet she knew that his need for human company was such that he would not be alone in whatever city he was staying. He would find a bar and inveigle himself into some sort of friendly exchange; even a conversation that bored him would be better than the terrible emptiness of his own company. The problem seemed to be that without other people there he was unable to shut out the clamour of the world's atomic pointlessness; it overwhelmed him.

She reassured him on the telephone as best she could, spoke to him of their children, told him about her day and said it would not be long before he saw her again. He was pacified when he eventually rang off. Mary loved him more for his bewildering weakness than for any of his explicable strengths and felt invigorated when she could be helpful to him.

Frank had said he would call the next day and, with the evening free, she had a cocktail in the hotel bar. As she sipped the drink, she read a magazine article about the Democratic primary in Wisconsin, where Muriel Humphrey's black-bean soup had not been enough to sway the voters behind her man. There was a photograph of Hubert Humphrey standing by a chrome-covered Greyhound bus and one of the improbably young Mrs Kennedy looking startled and lovely in a sleeveless dress with a heavy bead necklace. Senator Kennedy had pitched camp on the third floor of the Pfister hotel in Milwaukee, the article said, and she remembered Frank telling her about McCarthy's bar bill at the same hotel. The next contest, in West Virginia, would decide the nomination: if an overwhelmingly Protestant state could elect Kennedy as its candidate, the problem of his being a Catholic was buried and he could win.

Mary began to feel excited by the idea, not so much of a Catholic or a Democrat being president, but by the process itself; she could understand how passionately Frank must long to be part of it, to see at first hand what was happening.

Reluctantly she retired from the bar and went back to the room. At about nine she asked for a Caesar salad and a bottle of beer to be sent up, watched the *Arthur Murray Show* and *What's My Line* on television, then read her book until she was tired. She opened the window for a moment on to the howl and thud of Lexington, then decided to forgo fresh air and switch the air-conditioner to a cooler setting instead. In the clean sheets, she fell almost at once into a bottomless, but not dreamless, sleep.

Meanwhile, down in the Village, on the top floor of his apartment building, Frank lay back on the bed and lit a cigarette. The door through to the sitting room was open to allow him to hear the Lester Young record that was playing there.

He was finding sleep elusive, as he often did.

5

One of the things that kept Frank awake at night was thinking about the men he had killed. The speeches and the broadcasts that encouraged volunteers at the start of 1942 appealed to ideas of freedom and tyranny, to homeland and to the right to live in peace. They did talk of courage and the idea of 'sacrifice', so that those who enlisted were aware that they might not return; what they did not mention was that the purpose of being a soldier was to kill other soldiers, and that, for most men, each killing would have an individual flavour.

You were encouraged to forget because to mention it, even to think about it, was in bad taste. But it was there, and that was what it meant to be born an American male in his generation; these were the big facts, the capes and straits of the world in which you navigated.

And in the last ten years, the other given, the other unavoidable in his life, had been the manoeuvrings of the men in brown raincoats, agents of 'security' who had made his profession almost impossible to work in with freedom of thought, or at least with lightness of heart. Frank had no more wish to deal with them, to find an accommodation with them, than he had had with the Emperor of Japan. Some of what they did was necessary; much of it was not; but it really mattered very little what he thought,

113

because like the Depression or the war, they were bigger than individuals, and all he could do was play straight. He had himself belonged to no party and incurred no debts to the agents of the law; he had never played their game. The closest he had come to political action was to go with his brother Louis one night in Chicago, at the age of sixteen, to a meeting of the Young People's Socialist League in a basement on California Avenue, because Louis had promised him they would meet hot girls in low heels and leather jackets.

Frank climbed off the bed and walked through to the sitting room to turn the record over; it was the drowsy 'Peg o' My Heart', so he rotated the volume knob a few degrees. On his way back, he went to the window and lifted the lid on the noisy air-conditioner; he switched the dial to zero and hauled up the window. Night was so quiet in the Village, especially on a top floor, that he could hear a distant fight between two people shouting in Spanish and a crash of garbage cans, presumably from the restaurant on the corner of Grove Street.

He liked the sounds of the city at night, though he preferred a more solid rumble of traffic; nothing helped his wakefulness better than the sleepy kiss of car tyres on an uptown avenue after rain. He could gaze around the walls, the limits of a life he had made, let in the night or close it out, entirely as he chose, by listening to the street or to the music in the apartment.

When he went out from his newspaper office

at lunchtime to get coffee and a sandwich, he looked at men of his own age and wondered whether they too had killed others. The counterman at Schrafft's had a deft way with a knife when he made up the egg salad sandwich, but it didn't worry Frank. The fellow had probably been in the catering corps, or perhaps still living in Poland, or Latvia, in which case he might even have fought for the Nazis. What made Frank pause were the men in the suits and striped ties who rode the express elevators with their eyes locked on to the front pages of the *Times* and the *Wall Street Journal*. When he stood in the car with them he believed he could sense where they had been: Guadalcanal, Naples, Iwo Jima, Normandy. Their Yardley aftershave and Brooks Brothers clothing meant nothing to him; he looked at their hands, their haughty eyes, their fingernails: part the fronts of their drip-dry shirts and you could expect to see a patch of chest hair worn away by the dangling twin dog tags. Most of them had never knowingly killed a soul; some had been officers in a staff headquarters miles from the front; even the GI's just loosed off a few rounds, threw a grenade or two, but no one stood around to watch out for the results. But occasionally Frank thought he could sense a fellow killer who was now going calmly about his business, on the subway, strolling over Rockefeller Plaza, trotting down the steps to the bars of Grand Central for a drink before the evening train to Westchester or Yonkers, back to the embrace of his wife and child, a cook-out with the neighbours, ruffling their children's hair with the hands responsible for the unconfessed slaying.

It was not guilt that troubled Frank. The person responsible for taking those six lives was not himself but a numbered infantryman whose actions had won the gratitude of the society to which he returned. He himself was exonerated; he was not much given to introspection and hardly at all to guilt, but it surprised him, when he saw this city at a fine moment in its history, to think how many vice-presidents, short-order cooks, lawyers or construction workers, how perhaps even some of the jazzmen in Birdland or the Half Note, doped on heroin, giddy with improvised elations, had, like him, performed the drab act. What did women think? Did they mind? Was it merely an idea of 'good taste' that had ruled the subject unmentionable?

Roxanne, his ex-wife, had known. She had asked him once what it had been like. He thought for a long time before telling her, 'It felt like everything that happens to you. It felt like nothing at all.'

This was true; at least, it expressed the part of the truth that interested him: how something could be separated and shut off; how rapid was the mind's ability to digest and dismiss because its appetite for calm and gladness was over-powering.

The greater the distance of time from the killings, however, the more Frank thought about them. He did not scratch himself with the memory; he refused to admit any tremor of remorse; but he found them there, bulking solid and unchanged: they were something that would not move over and with which he had to share his life.

In a way that he could not understand, the memory was connected to something he felt about women. Occasionally he thought it was nothing more than the fact that women had not killed, and he valued them for that separate innocence, as though they were the guardians of the past or the intact connection to the previous and better world. But there was an element of female ignorance and complicity that was also, in a perverse way, exciting, because if women could be accomplices in this great deception they must be adept at other moments of disingenuousness and ignored shame.

Frank lay on the bed, thinking of Lester Young. A delicate man, exhausted by disappointment, he had taken a room in a hotel on 52nd Street and Broadway; looking down from his balcony on to Birdland, his own talent no longer in demand, he had steadily drunk himself to death on glasses of gin and sherry. When the news of Young's death came into the office, Frank volunteered to go and speak to the jazzmen who had been his friends; by the time he tracked down Charles Mingus, sitting among a group of red-eyed men in a small bar, Mingus had already composed his elegy, a tune he later called 'Goodbye, Pork Pie Hat'.

Lester Young had had an exquisite talent, Frank thought; Charlie van der Linden, on the other hand, had none. All Charlie's education came to nothing in the end because he could find no expression for the rage inside him. In that way, it seemed to Frank, these two most disparate men were similar, and he felt certain that Charlie would rush towards death in the same way. It was not enough to die, there had to be self-destruction; the debonair indifference to extinction, the flirting with and courting of it, was supposed to be a criticism of the inadequacy of the existence that preceded it. Of course, it was also a sign of unrequited love, since only those who had adored the possibilities of living could be so recklessly critical.

Frank lit another cigarette and watched the smoke rise. Then, involuntarily, he began to think about Mary, and once more, as he had done so often since the day of the van der Lindens' party in Washington, he tried to understand the feeling she had fired in him.

He closed his eyes and lay back with his head on the pillow. There was something in the pallor of her skin that was like an essence of femininity. It incensed him because it would not let him rest: he had to understand her, to experience exactly what she was; and although this undertaking had a sweetness in its urgency, it also seemed to him oddly perilous, as though if he failed he might tumble into some void that lay beyond her.

★ ★ ★

For the space of two or three days, the period coinciding with Charlie's absence from New York, Mary had had the curious yet exhilarating sense that time was distorted: it was both running headlong and, simultaneously, suspended. Charlie's return, now settled for Friday at midday, had seemed laughably remote, more like a hypothesis than a scheduled moment.

On Thursday morning she agreed to meet Frank for the concluding part of the tour; he arrived at the hotel at twenty-past eight, but she was ready to go. He looked preoccupied but well dressed, in a flannel suit she had not seen before and a knitted silk tie. She noticed his hands, the broad span with long, unexpectedly delicate fingers, clutching a roll of morning newspapers, already well worn. Mary felt strangely reassured, as though something worrying had been set right by his arrival; she felt galvanized by the possibilities of the day.

She did not know where they went. She talked without stopping, it seemed to her, though the object of her talk was to make him speak, to hear his voice. At some stage they visited his office, where Frank introduced her to the receptionists, then left her in the lobby area, watching the tape spool out the Dow Jones prices from a glass-covered machine, like manic shoots beneath a bell jar. She moved from foot to foot, a little embarrassed under the scrutiny of the two women and the young man behind the high-topped desk, hopefully eyeing the frosted glass doors through which Frank had disappeared. She felt as though she were living someone else's life. She felt very young.

They walked in Central Park, then sat on a bench where fierce spring shoots had broken through the city crust. Frank talked about his life as a child in Chicago, how his father had lived in a wooden rowhouse in the Back of the Yards, fighting for work in a market swamped with cheap labour as thousands of families moved up from the southern states, turning the South Side suddenly into a black neighbourhood. He spoke affectionately, with the indulgent humour of one who knew he need never return.

They roared downtown on the express subway from Columbus Circle to the other end of the island. Yet when they climbed the steps from the underworld, the people were still pressing through the grid, past the florists, the delis, the awnings, the hydrants; Mary wondered if someone called ahead to these robotic actors to tell them she was arriving, so they must put out their cigarettes, drink up their coffee fast and resume their heads-down bustle through the rectilinear set.

Then, at the bottom of Seventh Avenue South, near Carmine Street, it all broke up; the place became industrial, though on the sides of buildings the names of merchants and importers were vanishing, sinking into the cement, their endeavour not yet forgotten, the surnames with their European roots still legibly uptorn. They went to a bar, a small brick frontage in a row of warehouses overlooking the Hudson that Frank liked because it had a telephone box in the middle of the room, from which he once more called the office.

It was a narrow, dingy saloon with a dark dining room at the back; above the rows of bottles were earthenware jars holding bunches of dried twigs. Mary sat at the bar, as instructed, and sipped a martini that made her eyes water. Time was running faster than at any moment she had known; yet all her previous life was trapped and distilled into the instant. The small girl in blue taffeta opening the door to her party guests, the young woman in WAAF serge uniform, the mother returning home in triumph with her firstborn were reconciled and alive in her.

'They call this place the Ear,' said Frank, taking a stool beside her. 'The neon sign outside used to say 'Bar', but the curved parts of the 'B' broke off.'

She did not know if he was serious. It was not somewhere she would have dared to come alone, but with Frank she felt at home there; the crumbling warehouses seemed vital beneath his gaze; even a gloomy bar seemed radiant. Things fell into place for him: when he stepped into a void, a foothold invariably materialized.

She told him so, and he laughed, not unkindly. 'People don't normally speak that way at the Ear Inn.'

'It was a florid way of putting it.'

She looked down at the wood grain of the mahogany bar and at the small paper mat that was growing damp beneath her chilled glass.

In the afternoon they sat at a cement table in Washington Square Park, next to two Italians playing chess on the inset board.

'You haven't called the office for at least ten minutes,' said Mary.

121

'Yeah, I'm sorry about that. Thing is, I'm told Cordell's about to blow out. I'm getting this from Bob Levine, who's my buddy there. But it's not official.'

'Who's Cordell?'

'Webster Cordell's the Washington correspondent. He's been with the Kennedy campaign. The problem is that he seems to have fallen in love with the candidate. It's happened to a few of them. He's incapable of being critical. In fact I think he's playing politics rather than reporting it. The trouble is, he's a senior guy, he's senior to most of the editors. There's only the managing editor Bill Stevens who can take him off the story.'

'And if he got taken off?'

'I'd be the next in line. But I've been there before. It depends if the proprietor thinks I've done my time.'

'And have you?'

He shrugged. 'Levine says they were asking if I was in town.'

Mary felt unaccountably perturbed by this information. She ran her finger over a rough indentation in the table top.

'Do you mind if I ask you something?'

'Go right ahead.'

'Why aren't you married? I mean you're not . . . ' She waved a hand inexpressively.

'Repulsive?'

'Not completely. You're solvent. You're not a drunk. Though, come to think of it, drunks . . . '

'I was married for a short time. A girl called Roxanne I met in college. You didn't know I went to college, did you?'

'How could I know? You didn't tell me.'

'I went on the GI Bill after the war. If you'd been in the armed services the Federal Government paid your fees. My first week there I saw this beautiful girl walking through the campus one day and I followed her and asked her for a date. She turned me down. She said she had a boyfriend.'

'But you got your date?'

'I guess I wore her down. We were married two years later.'

'What went wrong?'

'There was nothing wrong. It was a passion that ran its course.'

Mary felt his gaze on her, as though he expected her to counter with an equivalent confession of her own, or at least to comment on the idea that such feelings were finite. She saw no need to indulge him; she felt protective of her intimate life and of the welfare of the children, which depended on it.

'How long did it last?' she said.

'Five years. She didn't want to come to New York. That was the breaking point for a lot of people. We were coming from the Midwest, that was the biggest wave of immigration to the city at that time, and for a lot of those people New York was like a foreign country. It was like going to Europe or Africa.'

'Were you sad?'

'I was sad because I had loved her.'

Mary looked down at the table and licked her lips. She swallowed.

'Couldn't you have stayed?'

'In Michigan? No.'

In the early evening, they were walking on another street and Mary recognized the Circle in the Square theatre.

She pointed in surprise. 'I was here with Charlie the other night. We had dinner just down there.' It seemed a year or so ago.

'Oh yeah?' said Frank. 'My apartment's not far from here. A few blocks up the street.'

Mary laughed. 'You weren't going to mention it? We were just going to walk past the front door and you weren't going to say a thing?'

'It's not a site of historic interest.'

'My dear Frank, the bookshops on Fourth Avenue are not a national monument. Nor is the spaghetti utensil shop or the public housing project.'

'You didn't like the tour?'

'I liked it a lot. Though I was never sure about its guiding principles.'

'Me neither. It's almost eight. Do you want to get some dinner? I guess you won't want to be too late.'

'No. No. Let's go and have a drink somewhere first. There's no hurry.'

While they drank cocktails, there was no sense in Mary's mind that the evening would come to an end: there was still dinner, the hours afterwards, maybe more drinks. Friday was a very long way ahead. They were in another restaurant and she could not stop talking, perhaps now inflamed by the wine she insisted he order, and the words were pouring out of her,

124

about her mother, her children, her life, and she was watching his face, no longer unreadable, but a screen of animated reaction, engaged, disbelieving.

But the fish had been and gone, the dessert, the coffee, more wine, more coffee, innumerable cigarettes, and she did not dare to look down at her wristwatch but was aware of two waiters standing in friendly but impatient proximity and of Frank rising in slow motion from his chair, taking her arm through the empty restaurant and of his face registering intense relief when she suggested a further bar, a café, some quiet Village nightspot and of their walking together for the first time quickly, with an identity of purpose.

On Cornelia Street there was a bar with tables on the sidewalk, and the night was warm enough for them to sit outside and order cognac. Mary tried to make hers last, but eventually the moment came and the waitress leaned over the table with the check.

'Maybe . . . ' Mary gestured interrogatively.

'You want another?'

'I shouldn't, but if . . . '

'Sure. Two more, please.'

With the euphoria of reprieve, Mary began to talk again, then stopped. She froze where she sat and drew her breath in tightly. So utterly had she misled herself that she had no idea what words were about to come from her mouth.

'Frank, there's something I want to tell you, something I want you to know. In the last few days I've formed a kind of . . . admiration for you. No, listen, please. I think . . . ' She found both arms rising of their own accord from the table; she felt like a puppet, being animated by someone unrelated to herself: even the words were not hers. She was speaking to him as though delivering a eulogy. 'I want you to know that I think you are the most remarkable man and that I've enjoyed your company more than I can say, more than . . . I don't know.'

She could still sense him trying to interrupt, but raised her hand again. It occurred to her that the reason she was sounding like someone awarding a school prize was that she was choosing unemotive words for fear of breaking down. She was finding it difficult to breathe.

She said, 'I want you to know for today, tomorrow, for the rest of your life how much you have meant to me, how much you have touched me with your . . . ' she smiled, feeling tears pricking at her eyes ' . . . your tour of the city. I want you to remember always what a fine man you are, or so you seem to me. I so much admire your dedication, how much you've done, how hard you've fought for yourself. And your kindness, your manners, your . . . Well, everything about you. I think you're wonderful. Wonderful.'

Frank sat staring at her for a few moments. He looked now exactly as he had on the first night she had met him, after the party, black marks beneath his eyes, his tie at half-mast, his cropped hair slightly rumpled.

He said, 'Have you finished?'

She bit her lip and nodded.

126

He said, 'I'm in love with you too.'

The words hit her hard. 'Is this . . . is that what . . . '

'From the day I saw you. Every second that's gone past I've become more convinced that you are the most extraordinary and perfect person in creation.'

'No, you are. The best.'

'I don't want to have a competition with you, Mary. Just believe that I'm right.'

Mary looked down at the table. She felt alarmed at the passion of his response, but not as much as she felt relieved. Above all, she felt an absurd sense of propriety: that something that needed to be said had been fully and properly expressed.

'And now?' she said. 'What do we do now?'

'You walk back with me to my apartment, then we say goodbye and I put you in a cab.'

'All right.'

'It's just a few blocks that way.'

Time, any more time, was enough. As they began to walk, he put his arm around her, and her tremor of guilt as she slipped her own arm round his waist was as nothing to her sense of rightness and decorum.

They were outside a tall 1930s apartment building on Bleecker Street. He looked down at her.

She said, 'Could I . . . come up? Just for a few minutes? A cup of tea or something?'

'Hmm . . . Maybe.'

Frank nodded a greeting to the doorman as they crossed the hall. Inside the elevator, he and

Mary stood side by side, staring straight ahead back towards the front door of the building, but as soon as the doors closed, they fell on each other.

At the top floor they pulled apart and walked down the corridor with exaggerated propriety. Mary stood well back as Frank fumbled with the key to his apartment; once inside, however, she began to kiss him again before he had kicked the door shut with his heel. She felt his hands running up inside her clothes and tore the shirt from the grip of his belt so she could feel the skin of his back beneath her hands. For several minutes they made no progress past the small entrance lobby of the apartment, but stood entwined in one another. Her face was turned up towards his, seeking his mouth from different angles, her eyes closed; his hands ran through her dark hair as though he would uproot it, while his tongue seemed to be searching for a withheld core of her. She noticed that while one of Frank's hands stroked her face, her ears, the outline of her jaw, the other had slipped beneath her blouse and swiftly sprung the stretched clip between her shoulder blades, so that before she knew it, his face was buried in her breasts, which he had worked free, so that they were both exposed while her back was still pressed against the wall of his entrance lobby, where the frame of a picture was pressing into her shoulder. He was talking to her, but she could barely make out the words because his face was buried in her flesh, from which he would not take his lips, until at last she pulled up his head long enough to kiss his mouth.

They moved into the sitting room, where Mary straightened her clothes to some extent and Frank eventually stood back.

She said, 'Frank, I must . . . '

He said, 'Of course.' But under the guise of helping her regain her dignity, he began to caress her again. She felt his hands run over her hips, down her thighs; she felt his fingers lifting the hem of her skirt and heard a callus on his skin snag for a moment on nylon before it touched flesh.

Mary pulled away again, kissed him and said, 'I must stop.'

'So must I. That's enough.'

But she kissed him again.

Frank said, 'I can't do this.' His hand was on the outside of her skirt, at the back, but feeling down between her legs, crunching the loose material up between his fingers.

'No,' she said. 'You must stop. I'm a married woman.'

'I know. And I'm a decent man.'

'Of course you are,' she said, leaning in to kiss him once more. After several more false stops and new beginnings, Frank turned violently away and walked into the galley kitchen at the end of the living room. Mary breathed in deeply, straightened her skirt and refastened her blouse; she pushed the hair back from her face and, seeing a tiled wall visible through a half-open door at the other end of the room, went into the bathroom.

She slid the light switch up and looked in

amazement at her guiltless face, bright in the mirror. Her brown eyes stared back candidly. This is not me, she thought. Yet she felt no guilt at all: her composed features bore no mark of shame; even her lipstick was barely smudged. She lifted her skirt and straightened the ivory slip with its embroidered hem. What was the point, she thought, when she might soon be hoisting it to her waist? She clipped the bra together with a momentary tremor at the thought of how easily he had sprung it open. How often, how many . . . But when she looked down at the basin and saw the impatiently squeezed tube of shaving cream, the tin of sticking plasters, the still-damp brush and dime-store soap, she was filled with tenderness.

She did not linger over her reflection; the face she wanted to be looking at was his.

Frank was leaning over the record-player. He looked up when she came back into the room. 'You found the bathroom.'

'Yes, thank you.'

'I thought you'd like to hear some Miles Davis,' he said. He paused for a moment. 'He's pretty darn good at a time like this. Here. Have a beer.' He passed her a cold glass. The sound of a breathy, muted trumpet came up softly.

'It's called 'Stella by Starlight',' he said.

She nodded, like a child under instruction.

'Now you sit down there,' said Frank, pointing to an old couch on one side of the room. 'And I'm gonna sit on this bar stool right here.'

Mary did as she was told and sipped at the beer, which was very cold.

Frank looked at her, with his head on one side. 'You just stay there,' he said. 'Where I can look at you. Don't move. You want a cigarette?'

'About ten.'

The music coiled about the space between them; the trumpet was mournful, caressing, but with some suggestion of menace. Mary looked down at her lap.

'That's it?' she said.

'That's all. That's all there is. The rest is . . . night-time. Forgetting.'

'But I'm crazy about you. I'm demented. Do you know what it's like for me to say that?'

Frank laughed. 'Yup.' He held up his right hand. 'Remember this?'

'What?'

'This scar. No, don't get up or we're dead. Here, I'll hold it under the light. See?'

'Of course. That first night when you came to our party. The car door or something. There was blood everywhere. What was it?'

Frank leaned over to the kitchen counter and picked up his key ring, which had a small penknife attached. He held it up. 'This.'

'What do you mean?'

'I cut my hand with this knife.'

'While you were fixing the car?'

Frank laughed. 'What car? Why would I have a goddam car? I came by cab. I just flew in from New York that day.'

'So how did you cut your hand?'

'I told you. With the knife. I cut it on purpose so I would have an excuse to come back to your house.'

Mary's eyes widened. 'Because?'

He nodded. 'Because of you.'

Eventually Mary began to laugh. 'It was rather a clean cut, wasn't it, for a greasy car tool.'

'I thought I could count on Charlie. He'd want someone to sit up and have another drink with.'

'Don't mention Charlie.'

'No, I think we have to keep mentioning him.'

Mary swallowed a little more beer. She was finding the separation from Frank difficult to maintain.

She said, 'This is going to change my life. You do understand that, don't you? I've been married for however many years it is. And I love my husband. I haven't the slightest intention of . . . leaving him, or anything like that. And my children. I love them with a passion you couldn't possibly understand.'

Frank smiled. 'And now this.'

'Yes. I mean, I just don't want you to think that is the kind of thing that happens to me. Or something I wanted to happen. It's the last thing I wanted. It's probably different for you. Being a man. Single.'

'Sure.'

'No. You've got to tell me seriously, Frank. You have to.'

Frank coughed. 'All right, I'll tell you. I've never felt anything like this. From this moment on, everything is changed. Is that good enough?'

'I . . . think so,' said Mary. 'I think so. Do you know what time it is?'

'It's twenty to three. I think you need to go

home now. I'll come down with you and get a cab. And you might want this.' He handed her a book of matches with a phone number written inside the cover.

Fifteen minutes later they were still in the lobby inside the front door of the apartment.

'The only way I'm going to manage this is if you walk, like, twenty feet ahead of me,' said Frank, kissing her ear. 'And keep that distance.'

Alone on the back seat of the cab, Mary closed her eyes against the confusion of feeling that was overpowering her; there was a certain, remote dread that this unexpected joy was going to be paid for at a very high price. Ecstasies did not come free. Then she opened her eyes again and looked soberly at the passing store fronts of lower Sixth Avenue, the garbage cans and stacked crates of empty bottles, the street corners that reeled by as the lights yielded their sequential greens. There was no confusion, really, when she came to think of it, just this desperate elation.

6

Charlie looked in a deplorable state when Mary glimpsed him through the glass screen at La Guardia, waiting for his bag to come off the carousel. He was red-eyed, unshaven and apparently unsure which suitcase might be his; he picked off two quite different-looking ones before settling on his own. When he finally came through the door, he smiled, a defeated grimace, and she saw the tension dissolve from the lines of his face in his relief at seeing her; she threw her arms round him, finding the rush of faithful love rise up in her unchanged.

Back at the hotel, after a long bath and a gin and tonic from room service, he rallied a little. Mary cleared up and repacked the cases, while he dressed in the bathroom. She found the book of matches with Frank's telephone number and tried to memorize it so she could throw away the evidence.

'Whose number is this?' Charlie would say.

'It's . . . Katy Renshaw's brother's. She said I should give him a call if I had time, but I didn't.'

'What does he do?'

'He's . . . a journalist. No. He works on Wall Street.'

'I'd like to meet him. I'll ask Katy about him.'

'No. No. Don't do that. He moved. Katy doesn't talk about him. She denies his existence.'

'It's not Katy's brother's number, is it, Mary?

134

It's Frank's. You're having an affair with him, aren't you? I'm divorcing you now and I'll get custody. You'll never see the children again. My lawyers will see to that. Take your case and go now.'

She would have to keep it simple. 'It's Frank's number actually. He showed me round while you were away. It was fun.'

Before Charlie emerged from the bathroom, she had refined her guileless explanation and practised saying the word 'Frank' in a normal voice. Then she thought this sounded suspiciously ordinary and that she should perhaps plead a theatrically exaggerated *tendresse* for Frank, as though she were trying to divert Charlie's attention, as she suspected he had sometimes done with her (that Japanese girl, Hiroko, for instance), from the true object of a problematic affection. It could be like one of those crime novels in which a suspect is discovered with the knife in hand in chapter two, after which the detective goes through a maze of bluff and counter-bluff only to reveal in the end that the killer was, though for reasons and in a manner entirely unforeseen, the suspect with the dripping knife in chapter two.

On the other hand, Charlie might have read such books, and . . . Mary shut the suitcase. This was unbearable. She loved Charlie. Nothing had changed between them. She had done nothing with which to reproach herself; on the contrary, she and Frank had behaved — it seemed to her — with a painful self-restraint. Now she would return to the business of her family and her life, her reputation intact, and devote herself to Charlie's happiness.

She put the matches in an inside pocket of her purse and zipped it up.

'There's a train at six o'clock,' she said.

They sat side by side in the Pullman car and she tried to discover what had happened in Chicago.

'I was talking to some people there,' said Charlie. 'The Democratic organization, you know. Daley's people. There's a feeling Kennedy could win this, if he gets the nomination. They truly believe he might pull it off. Seems unlikely to me, but you never know. Also, I was meant to check on a few things while I was there.'

A waiter leaned over the table with their drinks and a bowl of pretzels.

'What sort of thing?'

Charlie ran his hand through his hair. 'Everyone in this country is anxious at the moment. They think they're about to be annihilated by a hydrogen bomb.'

'Are you talking about Communists?'

Mary's plastic swizzle stick clinked swiftly on the ice, the glass and the ashtray.

'Yes,' said Charlie, leaning back. 'The day when the shoe-shine boy or the lady in the laundromat was thought to be in the pay of the Kremlin are behind us, I think. But they don't like foreign visitors. They have to be looked at closely. And they really do believe the Russians have more powerful missiles. They believe they're losing this war, the Cold War, the only one that matters.'

'But why you, Charlie? What's it got to do with you? Why do you get into such a state?'

Charlie turned to her, his eyes filled with tears. 'People ask me questions. But I'm all right, sweetheart.' He raised his glass to her and drank, then put his hand on her arm. 'We'll be all right,' he said. 'Won't we?'

★ ★ ★

Number 1064 came into view through the taxi window, and as they unloaded their bags from the trunk and walked up the path to the house between the blossoming trees, Mary felt the familiar centripetal forces drawing her into her own home and the home of her children; at the same time she felt the falling anguish of separation from what she most wanted. The circuitry seemed confused, the polar forces variable.

Inside the house she had the comforting sensations of return and belonging; she noted with approval that Dolores had polished the tiled hall and sorted the mail; she saw that some bulbs she had planted in a pot on the kitchen window sill had begun to sprout. She went about preparing supper, scrambled eggs and bacon, while Charlie read through his letters with occasional derisive oaths.

As she stared at the aluminium of the pan, on which the slimy yellow mixture began slowly to coagulate, she saw through the metal atoms of its surface to another room, in which the air was filled with the sound of a soft, insinuating trumpet, and she was charged with an exhilaration so powerful that even the memory of it was hard to keep in check. She noticed her lower lip begin to tremble.

She was out of control. She shook her head, and salt drops fell into the hardening egg. Without daring to raise her eyes from the stove, she reached out a hand to the work top where her cigarettes habitually lay and fumblingly withdrew one.

'Christ!' said Charlie, throwing down a letter.

She took the book of matches and struck one. She pushed the eggs, which were done too soon, on to a cold ring and turned the flame up on the bacon.

'Who are these people? Fund managers. They couldn't manage a bloody piggy bank.'

She sucked on the cigarette and held the smoke in her lungs till she felt giddy. Still looking down, she reached out for her glass and raised it to her lips. Her nose was running, but she did not want to blow it for fear of attracting Charlie's attention. Her eyes were burning red.

She tried to imagine what sort of figure she made, standing there, and she had a picture of herself as her mother used to describe her when she was five or six years old: like a real person, only smaller. This sentimental memory did not help; it reinforced the sensation that she was being run over by some force greater than she could withstand. She raked her fingernails into the palm of her hand.

For Christ's sake, she thought, I've seen death

and birth, I'm forty years old. I can bear this, I can bear this.

She felt Charlie's arm suddenly on her shoulder. She swung round and buried her face in his chest, feeling her nose and eyes dampen his clean shirt. She sobbed within his innocent embrace.

'There, there,' he said. 'You've been so brave and I've been so useless.'

He clearly thought she was upset about her mother, and even in her distress Mary recoiled from the idea of such an alibi.

'It's not that,' she said. 'It's . . . I don't know what it is.'

In the moral no man's land into which she had apparently been swept, the second evasion felt less reprehensible than the first.

★　★　★

The next day, she telephoned her mother, and they spoke for almost an hour. Mary offered to go to London and help look after her, but Elizabeth dismissed the idea impatiently.

'I'm perfectly all right. I'm still running the house. The last thing I want is another mouth to feed.'

When she spoke to her father, Mary asked to what extent this bravery was a front. He told her Elizabeth had had a tantrum of vintage proportions a day or so before and they agreed that this was a good sign. He promised to call if there was a change.

As for the other developments in her life,

Mary decided that all she could do was say nothing, remain speechless and perhaps misunderstood, because that was the only way she could be sure of doing no damage. She planned her day in such a way that she was primed for jollity when Charlie returned from work, and he, meanwhile, was so absorbed in his own difficulties that he appeared to see no falsity in her manner. It was a pity, she thought, that she had such a reputation for happiness; a melancholic could have passed off the behaviour she wanted to indulge in as no more than a periodic fit. But in her any sign of despondency, even a weary sigh, would be considered grounds for concern by those who loved her.

In the afternoons she lay on the bed and tried to catch up on the sleep that was eluding her at night. She discovered that it was better if she lay on her front; it was as though her physical weight helped compress the anguish.

As for a larger strategy, she had none. There were two imperatives of which she was aware, the well-being of her children, her husband and her parents, her primal care for them, which had not altered; and then her love for Frank, and his for her, which had a power that seemed to her not just primal but almost moral in its urgency. She could not establish an order of preference between the two; as well ask her to distinguish between a tree and a cloud: no crude ranking could reflect the reality of either.

She became sure that her decisions were right, or at least not wrong, but they had one weakness: they left her without a plan of action, groaning on the bed, forcing her belly harder against the mattress. When she telephoned Frank's number in New York, she felt no guilt towards Charlie; in fact, there was a certain self-righteousness in her manner towards him. How many women in her situation would have shown such restraint? If the price of that was a couple of forlorn phone calls, then Charlie was a luckier man than any other husband they knew. As for the calls themselves, made surreptitiously when Charlie was at work and Dolores out of earshot, the furtive comedy they provided was all the lightness in her day.

Her success in reaching him, on the other hand, was nil. By the time Charlie left for work in the morning, Frank had evidently departed for his newspaper office; by the time he was back in his apartment at night, Charlie was also back at Number 1064. One evening, when Charlie went to a reception without Mary, Frank, it appeared, also had a dinner date. Charlie did not return till one in the morning; but by a quarter to one Frank was also still out, presumably at the Vanguard or some other smoky room where the tenor saxophone was hopping over the piano rhythm. Mary did not let herself dwell on the thought of whether he was there alone; there was not enough room in her heart for that kind of self-torture, and in any case, she believed what he had said. For him too, everything was changed, set in the altered light of his feeling for her.

She spoke instead to her parents in London, surprising them frequently by the miraculous submarine connection. She gathered herself to reassure them; by scouring her store of imaginative sympathy, by the effort of will involved in comforting her mother in her last months and her father in his impending loss, she brought some solace to herself.

In her afternoon rests she sometimes thought of herself as a traveller in a dark wood. She was confronted by paths into the forest, by the need to make pitiless choices. This was the lot of a woman of her age, to take on the lives of those older and younger than herself, to carry the weight they could not bear; while her own private grief, a disabling, more vital version of something she had known when young, was fated to be seen by her in the uncompromising perspective of her imagined self when old, where all passions came to the same inevitable end.

★   ★   ★

'Frank?'

She heard his voice answer at last. She sat down heavily on the kitchen chair.

'Is this Mary?'

'Yes. How are you?'

'I'm okay. I didn't hear from you, but I didn't like to call. Are you at home?'

'Yes. Charlie's at a party. Dolores is at the pictures.' The mention of Charlie in this deceitful context almost took away the pleasure of hearing Frank's voice.

'What are you wearing?' he said.

'I beg your pardon?'

'I want to be able to picture you.'

'Well . . . Just my day clothes.'

'Don't be shy, Mary. Remember the night you left?'

'I do, Frank. Oddly enough, I do.'

'Well then.'

'A cream blouse with a broderie anglaise collar and a black woollen skirt and loafers and a pink cardigan. It doesn't really go. I just threw it on. I was chilly.'

'Not in your summer dresses yet?'

'No, it's quite cold here. What about you?'

'Just an undershirt, suit pants, bare feet. I was writing a piece. The building's always warm.'

'I've missed you, Frank.'

'I haven't breathed since you left.'

Mary found her face muscles aching from a strange reflex grin in which they had set themselves. She began to talk softly to him about how she pictured his apartment and him in it; this led her to his mouth and how soft it was to kiss. She heard him laugh.

She said, 'And is there a record playing in your apartment?'

'Yeah, it's still Miles Davis. It's 'On Green Dolphin Street'.'

'That's what was playing when we kissed.'

'Or wasn't that — '

'No. That was it.' Uttering the word 'kissed' had produced such a fierce, illicit thrill in Mary that she could not be bothered about song titles.

'So nothing's changed,' said Frank.

'Are you sure?'

143

'I'm sure. Unfortunately, I'm sure. Do you remember after dinner?' He, too, started to go over what had happened between them that night, as though anxious to establish that it had not been a dream of his own alone. She laughed when his narrative slowed down at the moment he kissed her breasts; he seemed to hope he might relive it by the close retelling, and, though it was shocking to be spoken to in such a way, she did not deter him.

It was Frank who eventually said, 'Maybe we shouldn't be speaking like this. When am I going to see you?'

'I don't know.'

'I don't think I can find a pretext for coming to Washington. I have to be here.'

'Oh God,' said Mary, feeling the fixed smile disappear.

'I think I could bear not having you if I could see you. Does that seem so very much to ask? Just to look at you?'

Mary had the sensation of falling. 'I'll fix it,' she said.

'What do you mean?'

She felt blood scalding her face. 'I'll come.'

★   ★   ★

The following morning, while Mary was reading the newspaper in the living room, the telephone rang. It was Duncan Trench, asking if he could come round and see her. He told her it was something that needed to be treated with the utmost discretion, and he would therefore be

144

grateful if she could make sure the maid was not in the house.

Bewildered, Mary put down the receiver. In as far as Duncan Trench had registered on her mind at all, it was as an irascible, bluff colleague of Charlie's whose disagreeable manner could be partly forgiven by the fact that he was clearly naive and often drunk. Could it be that chub-faced Duncan had all this time been nursing a passion for her? She shook her head. Not everything confidential had to do with amorous feelings; it was more likely that Duncan wanted to talk about Charlie's work or, more probably still, his health.

She heard no car draw up outside, so Duncan's ring at the doorbell took her by surprise. She opened her arm towards the sunny living room, but Duncan had already bolted ahead of her.

'Can I get you some coffee, Duncan? Or a drink?'

'No. No, thanks.'

He walked over to the phonograph. 'How does this thing work?'

'I'm sorry?'

'This thing. I want to put a record on.' He began wrenching at the arm and twisting the knobs.

'Let me show you. Anything in particular?'

'Something noisy. A brass band or something.'

'I'm not sure how much brass band music we have. Would Duke Ellington be all right? Or Count Basie, perhaps?'

The needle dropped on to the record with an

145

amplified thud, then skated over the surface for a moment before it settled in the groove.

Duncan turned the volume up to the maximum. He put his face close to Mary's. Despite the rhythm of the music, she did not feel like dancing.

'You probably know what I do at the Embassy,' he shouted.

Mary recoiled from the blast of American cigarettes and hotel coffee on his breath. She knew quite well what he did at the Embassy, but thought it unwise to tell him so.

She put her hand on his shoulder and reached up to his ear. 'Not really.'

'I'm not a career diplomat, like Charlie or Eddie Renshaw. I work for a different organization. Have done since I left Oxford.'

'I'm sorry?'

Duncan grimaced. He leant down to Mary's level and put his lips to her ear.

Fighting with the sound of Duke Ellington's rhythm section in one ear (Jimmy Blanton on bass, as someone had pointed out the other day — Frank, perhaps; no, on second thoughts, it might have been Eddie, in the log cabin) was Duncan bellowing in her other ear the word: 'Intelligence'.

Mary stood back a pace and looked at his flushed cheeks and low forehead with its wiry hair surround. 'Intelligence' was not the first word that came to mind.

'I see,' she said. How long ago that weekend on the Bay now seemed; her mother had been still healthy and Frank just a visitor that

146

someone — who? — had asked along.

Duncan was still shouting. ' . . . even with our closest allies. Of course, our work here is quite different from what we do in, say, the Soviet Union, or even one of the Arab countries. There's a lot of sharing. We co-operate closely with American security.'

Mary said nothing.

Duncan looked exasperated. 'The FBI,' he shouted.

'Yes, yes, I understand.'

'Just a little favour I wanted to ask you.'

Mary found it difficult to make out exactly what Duncan was saying, but she caught enough of it to understand. 'You're very well regarded,' he was saying. 'A new Yugoslav couple's just arrived. We're particularly interested in her. We wondered if you could make an effort to be her friend, keep your eyes open, then have the occasional chat with me.'

'Tell me what Charlie's doing,' said Mary. 'Is he working for you?'

'No. Not allowed to, though we share information occasionally. We're all on the same side after all.' He coughed. 'I can't pay you, I'm afraid. It's just something for your country.'

Mary looked at Duncan's anxious face; there was a line of sweat on his upper lip.

'I'd like to help, Duncan,' she said.

'But?'

'What?'

'I said, 'But'. I hear a 'but' coming.'

'But I'm going to live in New York for a bit.'

Duncan looked dumbfounded. 'Charlie never

mentioned anything.'

Mary herself could barely believe what she had said. 'I haven't told him yet.'

Duncan looked at her in disbelief. Mary went over to the record-player and turned it off.

'There must be other people you could ask,' she said. 'Other wives. What about Katy? She's very social.'

'She's American. You're the one we want. And it would do Charlie no harm.'

It was quiet in the room. Mary looked down at the floor, then up again. 'I wish you hadn't said that last bit. About Charlie. That's really not fair.'

Duncan shrugged.

'Anyway, I can't help you, Duncan. I'm just not going to be here.'

'How long will you be away?'

'A couple of weeks or so.'

Mary went over to the mantelpiece, where she found a packet of Charlie's cigarettes. 'I've had a difficult time recently,' she said. 'My mother's dying, my children have vanished. I think I need a change of air.'

Duncan nodded, with an appearance of concern. 'Yes, I know what it's like. Ladies. You need . . . Anyway. But two weeks is all right. I'll ring again.'

7

The Red Caps wheeling baggage down the platform at Baltimore wore their peaked hats pushed back on their heads and walked with a slow, distracted motion, as though they were no more willing or engaged in their work than their fathers had been in the tobacco fields. There were three rivers to cross on the way to New York, and Mary was counting them off impatiently as the train rolled out of the station, gathered gratifying speed towards the Susquehanna and swept her on through the drab marshalling yards of Philadelphia to the Delaware.

She remembered a painting of George Washington crossing the river; the state had been the first in the union, and in the making of the new country the river had had some symbolic force, a Rubicon after which . . . From the train, she saw neat clapboard houses with short wooden jetties and small boats jostling on their ropes; she heard in her mind the irritating song, 'What did Della wear, boy . . . ' It had been playing through a car window when she first had lunch with Frank in Georgetown in that innocent age.

Mary saw the skyline of New York approaching, but the train was still in fields; there were raised highways flying to the left, signs of construction to the right, but no suburban crescendo, no spread or graduated entrance to the city. Then they came to a steep-sided cutting and vanished suddenly into the dark; the locomotive slowed as it rattled through an underworld of rusted sidings and wrecked trucks, a place where trains came home to die in the glow of lanterns that hung from the bricked vault, so that the final crossing, beneath the Hudson, seemed less like the Rubicon than the Styx.

Mary found a cab up on the ramp and emerged once more into the unyielding grid, where there were no more curves or meadows or boats at mooring, but an equation to be solved using numbers and right angles only. Her hotel was near the station; she had found it in a guidebook that recommended its handy situation, clean rooms and reasonable prices. She made her way to the desk, checking that she had a supply of dollars and quarters to distribute to the willing hands.

The lobby of the hotel was dark and smelled of cleaning fluids; the crimson carpet looked damp, as though it had just been shampooed. The desk clerk found her name, handed her a key and asked if there was anything she wanted; Mary felt that in his voice she detected a note of scepticism.

'No, no, I'm fine,' she said, following the bellboy to the elevator.

The room turned out to be two rooms: a small lounge gave on to a large bedroom. There were walk-in closets and a bathroom with mysterious old-fashioned plumbing that included a fourteen-inch tubular chrome upstand next to the tub.

'It's okay?' said the bellboy.

'Yes, yes, of course,' said Mary, fumbling in her purse.

There was also, on the nightstand by the bed, a telephone. First, she went to the bathroom, splashed water on her face and combed her hair. It was half-past six and there was a chance he would be home. She picked up the receiver, then replaced it. How desperate was she? She could at least unpack. Eventually she came to it. Seated on the edge of the bed, she heard the single calling ring go out, and imagined the instrument bleating on his desk; to arm herself against the worst, she pictured absence, an empty room. She swallowed hard to clear her ears; she thought she might not hear his voice over the roar of expectation with which her body was already clamouring.

This is not good, she had time to think as the ringing sound went on: this desire is excessive and is demeaning me.

The sound of Frank's abrupt answering voice filled her with an exultation that swept away misgivings. He was amazed to find her in New York, and his surprise for a moment overcame his delight, so that Mary asked him to reassure her that he was honestly pleased. This he was able to do, with passion, and soon Mary felt herself settle into the arms of his conversation, the short sentences, the fuzzy baritone, the sardonic edge of it at war with the warmth of what he said. She surrendered herself to it.

151

In the bath, her hair wrapped up in a cap, she lay back and tried to calm herself. She thought of Richard and Louisa, five hours ahead of her, asleep in their draughty dormitories; of her mother watching the lights of extinction grow large; and of Charlie mounting the steps of the plane, awash with sedatives and scotch. She thought also how her mother would still have enough strength to admonish her for her selfish immorality.

She put on a short-sleeved navy woollen dress she had bought from Bonwit Teller on a previous visit to New York; it was billed as evening wear, but she thought it casual enough for whatever Village dive they might find themselves in later. She made up carefully in the steamy bathroom, rolling mascara along the lashes, her face elongated by the effort of opening her eyes. When she had finished, she looked at her reflection one last time. 'What are you doing?' she mouthed at the glass. She turned away with no sensation of having made a choice.

It was a warm dusk on 35th Street as she walked briskly across to Broadway. When she felt the chrome handle of the taxi spring the catch inside the yellow door, she wondered if she had ever felt more invigorated, more charged with the voltage of the moment. A few minutes later, she was there: she climbed out and watched the cab pull slowly off down Christopher Street, then took out a book of matches on which she had written the address. She crossed the street to

Frank's building, the tallest in view among the low Village houses. She breathed in deeply as she pushed at the art deco outer door and walked across the polished hall, past the doorman.

'Mr Renzo? Sure, ma'am. Fourteenth floor.'

The elevator rose slowly. On the previous occasion she had not had time to examine the inside; now she saw a seat, a concealed telephone, a safety inspection certificate. The numbered lights flicked through their inevitable sequence till she was delivered at her destined floor; when the doors ground open, he was waiting.

'I came back,' she said.

★   ★   ★

The scene of the almost-crime was thrillingly intact.

Writhing in his arms, Mary found herself in danger of repeating the same sequence of events with the same unsatisfactory conclusion.

Frank seemed to sense something similar and guided her to a couch while he went to the kitchen bar to make a drink. She watched him rattle the cocktail shaker and pour the liquid into two glasses. On the bookshelf near his shoulder was a photograph of a slightly younger Frank, shirt-sleeved, in an office; across the desk was a young fair-haired man, his face a compacted smile of youthful energy.

'Who's that with you in the picture?'

'That's Billy Foy. He was my best friend. We first met in the army.'

He handed Mary her drink and smiled as he backed off. 'You stay right there. Then we'll both be all right.'

There were some awkward pleasantries and reassurances, then silence.

Mary sipped her drink and looked up at him.

Frank smiled back at her and raised his glass.

She said, 'I know what you're thinking.'

'Yeah, and I know what you're thinking. And it ain't gonna happen.'

'No. It certainly isn't. So now let's think about something else.'

'Where's Charlie?'

'He's in Boston for a couple of days.'

'Right. Did you see the paper? The Soviets shot down one of our spy planes over Russia. A U-2. It means the Summit in Paris won't take place.'

'That's worrying.'

'It is. Things are coming a little unglued. The pilot can expect to get fried. And it's bad news for the President. It's a worry for the whole world.'

Mary swallowed. 'It's so strange, isn't it? We carry on as though nothing was happening. And yet . . . '

'We go sailing on the lake, we drink cocktails and we dance till dawn. But . . . ' He shrugged.

'I know,' said Mary. 'It might all go up.'

'Any day. Have another drink.'

When he refilled her glass, he stole a kiss from her mouth.

'I had some good news today,' he said, as he

retreated to safety. 'The managing editor called me into his office and asked what my plans were.'

'You mean . . . '

'They've taken Cordell off the Kennedy campaign. There's one hell of a row about it. Kennedy's press people are furious for one thing. And Cordell's threatening to resign.'

'And don't tell me,' said Mary. 'They're sending you.'

'It looks as though I finally served my time.'

Mary licked her lips. 'And when do you begin?'

'Next week.'

'So you won't be in New York next week?'

'Some of the time. The heat's off a little since West Virginia. Now that Humphrey's pulled out. Kennedy'll go back to Washington or Boston in between trips.'

'Why . . . Why does this mean so much to you?'

'It's all to do with a Chicago boy called Emmett Till. I'll tell you over dinner. Let's go uptown someplace, get away from the goddam Beatniks. Where's your hotel?'

When she told him, Frank said, 'Christ, how d'you end up there? Though I guess you're well placed if you like shopping at Macy's.'

In the taxi going to dinner, Mary was aware of the same facial ache she had noticed when talking to Frank on the telephone. Could it be that even the news that he was not going to be in New York after all had failed to remove the smile from her face?

155

After dinner, Frank deposited Mary at her hotel and took the cab on home. He thought of stopping off at a jazz club, but decided to keep it for an evening when Mary could come along too.

Her presence was torturing him. After years of feeling that his life had stalled, that he was somehow disconnected from his own destiny, he now felt everything coming together at the same time. He was so blinded by Mary that he preferred to act on easier impulses. First, he would settle the question of his professional life, by making sure that he did a better job on the Kennedy campaign than anyone else. He had waited so long to be rehabilitated by his newspaper that when the moment came he felt no triumph or righteous vindication; he felt merely determined.

Almost five years earlier he had arrived in Sumner, Mississippi, sent from New York as a reporter on the trial of two local white men accused of murdering a fourteen-year-old Negro boy called Emmett Till, who, on a vacation from Chicago to see family in the South, had apparently made the mistake of being disrespectful to a white woman, wife of one of the accused, when he went in to buy bubblegum from the store where she worked.

It was the first time the northern press had sent reporters en masse into the South. After the Supreme Court had ruled against segregation in the case of Brown v Board of Education the previous summer, the papers sensed a show trial of southern values, a test case of 'separate but equal' development that would demonstrate what Negro lives were really worth in the Delta. The reporter who normally covered the South was temporarily on leave. Frank volunteered for the job, assuring the managing editor he would keep cool in the atmosphere of southern hatreds and, when there was still some doubt about his suitability, pointing out that he had known dozens of children from the same school as the murdered boy, McCosh Elementary on the South Side.

The Greyhound bus dropped him two miles outside Sumner on Highway 49, leaving him to walk into town through a wall of September heat. The land was so flat that the horizon was visible all round, edging down into the cotton and soybean fields; the two-dimensional landscape made it hard to say how far it was to the scant farm buildings and bare rectangular dwellings that stood like cut-outs in the middle ground beneath the low, pressing sky.

Frank pulled his notebook from his pocket to note the roadside sign, 'A GOOD PLACE TO RAISE A BOY', that welcomed the visitor to Sumner. He checked the words carefully, one by one (all capitals, above a Coca-Cola sign), as he had taught himself, to forestall the sub-editors' surly inquiries. The journalists were assigned rooms in a boarding house, whose female owner sat outside, fanning herself in the thick air, watching with distaste the northern city men, their superior manners, their jostling for the house telephone.

Frank noticed that almost all the local men seemed to be armed. Old boys in straw hats sitting out on the veranda had shotguns across their knees; twin barrels poked from farm débris in the back of a pick-up truck; even in the grey brick courthouse, he saw more than one pearl handle sticking out from a straining waistband. When the film-crew cars went off to a nearby airfield in the late afternoon to get the footage on the plane to New York, there was no more noise in Sumner. The dense air blotted out sound: the crack of a door slamming was enough to make you start, and the people watched the incomers with silent, hostile eyes. At night, when he lay in the suffocating darkness of his narrow room and heard the distant baying of hounds, Frank wondered how many other black men and boys had been beaten, then thrown, like Emmett Till, into the Tallahatchie River.

Some of the reporters, who had been warned not to go out after dark, were afraid for their lives; some affected southern accents to try to blend in; but, as Frank explained to a nervous young man from Boston, they were both white, and because of that were protected by law: that was what the case was about, after all, and whether a young Negro enjoyed the same legal safeguard. Yet despite what he said, Frank felt uneasy; he felt the hatred, which pressed into his skin like the airless heat.

It was different for the black reporters. 'Hello, niggers,' said the sheriff, as he showed them to a segregated table in the courtroom. Though two-thirds of the people in Tallahatchie County

158

were black, the jury consisted of twelve white men, ten of them from the poorest, most backward hill section of the county. Frank grew to know their faces, their blank farmers' features, impermeable to weather or to words. Only one wore spectacles, an older man with a pinched, beaten face; Frank wondered if the others had not tired their eyes. Perhaps the fact that they read nothing but only gazed over the interminable flatlands for indications of rain or darkness had kept their vision healthy. There was one younger man who wore a checked shirt and diamond-pattern socks; the others all wore white shirts, mostly short-sleeved, and loose cotton pants. Their black-banded straw hats hung on a line of hooks attached to the green plaster wall beside them.

The evidence presented to them was easy enough. Emmett Till had either wolf-whistled at, been verbally suggestive to, or touched the waist of, a young and desirable white woman called Carolyn Bryant in her husband's store, Bryant's Grocery and Meat Market in the small town of Money. The prosecution suggested he had done no such thing, but that he always made involuntary whistling noises when he spoke because of his stammer. It made little difference: Till was a lippy young man; and, as a city boy from Chicago, he had failed to understand the rules of the South, where male Negroes averted their eyes not just from white women but from representations of them in posters or photographs. Therefore he was murdered by Carolyn Bryant's young husband Roy and his older

159

half-brother, a heavily built man called J.W. Milam.

Bryant and Milam had called at the house of Emmett Till's great-uncle in the night and asked if this was where the boy who had made advances to the white woman was hiding. The great-uncle, an elderly sharecropper called Mose Wright, apologized for any misunderstanding, but the two men took Till and drove him to the river, beat him till his facial bones were crushed and one of his eyes was hanging out, shot him once, tied a seventy-pound fan from a cotton gin round his neck with barbed wire and threw him in the water.

Mose Wright went to the stand and was asked by the prosecution to identify the two men who had taken his great-nephew in the night. Milam leaned forward in his chair, took a cigarette in his fist and gazed with intense fury into Wright's face, as though challenging him to risk his own life. Under the fire of hundreds of white people's eyes, Wright slowly raised his hand and pointed. He said, 'Thar he.' Trembling, he moved his hand and pointed at the other defendant: 'And there's Mr Bryant.' After a half-hour cross-examination by the defence, who called him 'Mose', Wright was allowed to leave the stand. He returned to his seat and collapsed into his chair with a lurch as the nerve went out of him.

The defence had no trick, no absence of a smoking gun or last-minute alibi. They began by suggesting that Emmett Till's mother had wrongly identified the body of her own son. Till's mother, a city woman in a print dress, black bolero and a small black hat with a piece of veil, replied that if it had not been Emmett she would not now be in the courtroom but would be out looking for him. Defence counsel, a man called Breland, remained seated as he cross-examined Till's mother, occasionally slicing the air with rigid motions of his hands. He referred to her as 'Mamie' and maintained that a body had been planted in the river by a mischievous civil rights group looking to make trouble; the sheriff of the county speculated in the witness box that the 'real' Emmett Till was living somewhere in Detroit.

At the lunchtime recess Frank would go outside and watch the crowds press up to the sandwich and soft-drink concession. Milam and Bryant sat on the steps of the courthouse, handing out ice-cream cones to their children and laughing; old white men sat along a bench, while black people gathered at the foot of a Confederate statue inscribed 'THE CAUSE THAT NEVER FAILED' (all capitals). Mose Wright walked across the lawn to them, his blue pants hoisted high by brown suspenders over his clean white shirt. He looked pleased to see his friends, but crushed by the gravity of what he had done. In an effort to escape the heat, Frank went into a drugstore where a large fan was churning the air; on the counter was a jar for donations to the defence fund of Milam and Bryant.

Afterwards, back inside the courtroom, the mother of Bryant and Milam massaged their shoulders and bathed their temples with a damp white cloth: this truly was a case, Frank thought, about mothers and sons. The members of the jury smoked and crossed their legs; the man with the tie ran his finger round inside his damp collar. Bailiffs came and went with pitchers of iced water.

Frank wondered what was going on in these men's minds. Their loyalty to local tradition was greater than their respect for federal law; they would not have phrased it in such a way, but the truth was that, to them, disrespect was a crime worse than murder. Therefore they were not listening; they were not open to argument. A young man called Willie Reed, eighteen years old and barely articulate, testified that he had seen Emmett Till in the back of a pick-up belonging to Milam and that he had heard the sound of someone being beaten up. It made no difference.

That night Frank paid ten dollars to borrow a car and drove to the little town of Money, where Emmett Till had made the mistake of being too forward with Carolyn Bryant. The town had one paved road, along which were ranged a school, a post office, a place for ginning cotton and three stores. The headlights of the car picked out one with a large Coca-Cola sign at the front; this was Bryant's Grocery and Meat Market, which, they had been told in court, specialized in selling snuff and fatback to the black field-hands who lived in the tar-paper shacks along the unmade roads nearby.

Frank did not know what he had come to find, except that he wanted to have a clearer picture of where the thing had happened. People in the courtroom talked with drawling familiarity of

Bryant's store; the strategy of the defence was to stress the normality of the two men, how regular they were, how easy to understand and how representative of the place from which they came.

Most journalists, in Frank's experience, were frightened of being caught out, exposed as naive or ignorant. They were afraid of being telephoned by an editor the following day and asked why their story did not match that of their competitors. They therefore accepted with earnest nods and without question what they were told; they wanted to get the labyrinthine story and all its bizarre details into one of the simply labelled boxes that their editors would understand. There were numerous familiar categories on offer: Jim Crow lives; southern test case; miscarriage of justice; the world watches. Bryant and Milam were 'World War Two vets', Bryant a 'much-decorated' one, while his wife was a 'former beauty queen'; the difficulty was only in knowing which angle was the most comfortable. Beneath the hard male banter, each reporter was frightened of being found out; most of them therefore compared notes and stories, particularly where two papers came from the same city. The most obvious rivals were therefore, for reasons of common self-interest, the most ardent collaborators. The aim of each of them, in the end, was to report on events in such a way as to render them comprehensible, to remove the strangeness by using recognized and reassuring phrases. In New York Frank had frequently discussed this tendency with Billy

Foy, who, in the course of a long evening in Herlihy's Saloon, had once defined the ultimate aim of such reporters: to write about extraordinary new events in such a way as to render them *already familiar*. Frank could remember the emphatic movement of the hands with which Foy had gleefully italicized the last two words.

Yet even the peripheral details of the Till case were outlandish. As a Chicago man, Frank did not know what a tar-paper shack was until his headlights picked one out; having worked in the stockyards he knew which part of the hog provided fatback, but some of the city men did not know if it was something you ate or smoked or used to wash the automobile. He felt as though he was in a foreign country, and in his reports he tried to make the Emmett Till story sound almost incomprehensibly strange.

He wondered how many men the gross and unrepentant Milam had killed in Europe during the war, and whether his service had made it easier for him to murder Till. The unit in which he fought would certainly have been segregated and if he had shot Germans who looked like he did without compunction, the idea of firing a gun into Till's dark head might have been untroubling to him.

Frank drove back to Sumner in the darkness, the windows of the car wound down, letting in the swampy night air. He thought of a sentry he had himself killed on a bridge in the Rhineland during the advance into Germany of 1945. As the lieutenant in charge of his platoon, Frank thought it unreasonable to give the task to anyone else. It was a moonlit night and he had a clear shot on the young German's back; despite the fact that the safety of all his men was at risk, some scruple made him wait until the sentry was facing him. The bullet went through the neck, and when Frank and his sergeant reached the body the tongue had been uprooted and was lolling out of his mouth like an ox's tongue ready to be rolled and pressed. He was heavy to shift, and Frank pulled a sacro-iliac muscle as they heaved him to the edge of the bridge; it was a familiar, domestic pain, a version of a football injury, quite out of place at this moment of killing and emergency. They dropped the German in the river; unlike Bryant and Milam, they had no concern about whether the body floated.

The next day the jury took one hour and seven minutes to acquit Milam and Bryant; one juror later said they could have done in it ten minutes, but an officer of the court sent in cold sodas and told them it would look better if they could spin it out for a while. There was an intake of breath in court when the foreman gave the verdict; for a moment there was a silence of shame. Then Milam stood up, lit a cigar and grabbed his wife. The defendants each had two small boys, who ran into their fathers' arms to celebrate; photographers climbed on desks and tables. Within a few minutes the courtroom was empty except for the paper cups, piles of cigarette ends and a few abandoned spectator chairs that the American Legion had hired out at two dollars a time.

165

★ ★ ★

After he had returned to New York, Frank continued to write about the case. In Mississippi the verdict was well received, but almost every newspaper outside the South was shocked: their reactions varied from disappointment to outrage. Some writers praised the impartiality of the judge; they saw some hope in the fact that the jury had reportedly not been unanimous at the first count. Then they turned away, because there was only so much wringing of hands that could be done over a state that was still part of a union.

Frank was so troubled by what he saw in Sumner that he turned to the foreign press. With the aid of a dictionary, he translated *Le Figaro* ('scandalous . . . worldwide indignation') and *France Observateur*, which thought the trial more outrageous than that of the Rosenbergs, who had been electrocuted for unsubstantiated treason the previous year. The paper's German correspondent put into English for him a piece that claimed the trial showed that 'the life of a Negro in the Delta is not worth a whistle'. Combining the European response with his own reactions to the trial, Frank wrote an article for his newspaper that began: 'When something happens to unite various observers into moral outrage, a reporter's first instinct is to suspect that they are all wrong. A few days on the case will reveal what has been neglected or overlooked — the shades and details that make a more interesting truth. But the case of Emmett Till looks like an exception . . . '

He quoted from the comments of the foreign press to show how the case had caused America's stock to fall in the eyes of the free world, and, more shamingly, the un-free world. The war against the Russians was apparently being lost in space and in the development of arms; the United States was now in danger of squandering its only unassailable advantage: the moral superiority conferred by constitutional rights.

Ten days later his editor received a visit from two agents of the FBI, who were compiling reports which would, unofficially, be handed over to the Senate Internal Security Subcommittee's investigation of the press. It was known that they were actively investigating six employees of the *New York Times* alleged to be Communists; even the music and the dance reviewers of the *Times* were on an FBI Security Index that permitted them to be deported to detention camps if an 'internal security emergency' occurred.

Knowing this, Frank's editor had expected a call. There were three journalists on his paper they were interested in, one of whom was Frank Renzo, about whom he had previously received a complaint after his coverage of the Eisenhower — McCarthy speech in Milwaukee three years earlier. The editor thought he did well to protect his man's job. The agents suggested 'for his own peace of mind' that Frank be switched to some non-contentious area of the paper. This the editor refused; though he offered a guarantee that Frank would do no reporting of a directly political nature. 'It's a good deal, Frank,' he said. 'It's the only way I could get the bastards out of the office. At least this way you don't have to testify to the goddam Senate committee.' He assured Frank it would be only for a short time.

Meanwhile in Sumner, Mississippi, Bryant and Milam, immune under the Fifth Amendment from being prosecuted twice on the same charge, told a magazine journalist who paid well for their story how they had murdered Emmett Till.

★ ★ ★

'That's why it matters so much to me,' said Frank as he ended his story. 'Being back in business. It's not just my own work, it's kind of a philosophical thing.'

'I understand,' said Mary. 'And you're forgiven now? It's all OK again?'

Frank nodded. 'The atmosphere's improved a good deal, but you can never be truly sure. There's a guy at the *Times* has never gotten off obituaries.'

'But the political atmosphere's easier now, isn't it?'

'Yes. We don't have McCarthy any more. Or Eastland, who chaired the Senate committee on the press. He was a segregationist from Mississippi who believed in white supremacy. He said the Supreme Court had been brainwashed by Communists. He had a lot of journalists sent to jail for pleading the First Amendment. That's why my editor wanted to keep me and Billy Foy

168

out of it all. He knew how dangerous it was.'

'You look upset.' Mary reached out a hand to him.

'Billy was my best friend. He came from a dirt poor family in Columbus, Ohio. We met in the army, in the same platoon. It was his idea to become a journalist. We both went to college on the GI Bill after the war. He came to New York six months after me. He was clever as hell, but he was the sweetest guy. He loved the work, it was all he'd ever wanted to do. And he was a natural at it. But he'd written a lot of stuff about the South that got right up Eastland's nose and he'd been looking for a chance to get Billy. The FBI, as luck would have it, had already done a security investigation on him.'

'I thought that was only for criminals or undesirable aliens.'

'Not then. More than fifty people at the *Times* had been investigated. The FBI gave a lot of stuff to the committee. Just like they did with McCarthy.'

'And what happened to your friend?'

'Billy was subpoenaed to attend. He took the Fifth and that kept him out of prison, but everyone who took the Fifth got fired. It made it look as though you were a Communist. Even after he'd left the paper, the FBI wouldn't leave him alone. They harassed him, they chased him. They were blackmailing him to inform them about other people. One day he threw himself from the eighteenth floor of his apartment building. Goddammit, Mary, he was thirty-five years old.'

169

8

Frank took the train to Baltimore with Mary. She kissed him furtively as he climbed down on to the platform, where the sun was shining with the taut early promise of summer. He stood by the exit with a portable typewriter in its brown case and a carryall he would not need to check at the airport; his first assignment with Senator Kennedy was at Hagerstown, Maryland, and Mary could sense the strain in his waiting body as he glanced back, caught between two poles.

Mary continued the journey to Washington and was back at Number 1064 in time to welcome Charlie from Boston. She asked the Renshaws to come to dinner that night. She knew that they were almost the only couple in Washington who did not in some way exasperate Charlie and she wanted to re-establish the normal rhythm of their lives, as though nothing had changed. She telephoned her mother in London and spoke to her for half an hour; she would have taken longer but her father warned her that, despite the gaiety of her manner, Elizabeth often seemed weak. He said he would call on Mary if he needed her, but for the time being they did not expect a visit until they came to collect the children at the end of term.

It was a warm spring evening, sunny without the heaviness that came in full summer, and they cooked steaks and chicken on the barbecue in the backyard. Charlie stood at the grill with a white apron wrapped around him, pouring sidecars from a jug into some new glasses he had brought back from a shop on Boylston Street.

'The importance of the glass, Eddie,' he said, handing him a refill. 'If I am remembered for only one thing in my life, I would be happy for it to be that. Forget my contribution to international relations, my learned papers on the Communist threat and the economy of Europe.'

'I think I already have,' said Edward Renshaw, as he turned the squat glass appreciatively round between his fingers. 'But this . . . this is a real discovery.'

'Yes,' said Charlie. ' 'Significance that each has lived/ The other to detect/ Discovery not God himself/ Could now annihilate.' '

'Emily Dickinson.'

Charlie went inside to search for the book, so he could complete the stanzas of the poem they had forgotten, but returned empty-handed, cursing his haphazard shelves. The Washington night sank warmly on to the paved yard and Mary brought out storm lanterns into which the moths blundered noisily.

'These bugs are killing me,' said Katy.

'You need more smoke,' said Charlie, handing her a pack of cigarettes.

'Thank you,' said Katy. 'You glad to be back in DC, Charlie?'

'Yes, but I'm off again any minute.'

'Boston again?'

'God, no. Oregon. I'm required to spend some time with the Catholic Senator. He's supposed

171

to be my special subject. I'd almost forgotten.'

'The one you said could never win the nomination?' said Edward.

'That's the chap,' said Charlie. 'Anyway, he hasn't yet. There's still Stevenson, Symington and Johnson to come.'

'Looks like it, though, doesn't it?' said Katy, wrapping a cardigan across her shoulders.

'I think so,' said Charlie. 'But he won't beat Nixon.'

He reached, smiling broadly, for a wine bottle through the mess of plates with their charred remains, melted ice-cream and cigarette ends stubbed into the rejected parts of chicken that had been still pink at the joints. Mary watched him pour and could sense the largesse, the moment of equilibrium rushing through him with the wine.

'What about you, Mary?' said Edward. 'Did you enjoy New York?'

'What did you go for?' said Katy. 'Just a vacation?'

'Yes, pretty much. I like the city. I've always enjoyed it. And if Charlie's going to be away on his travels, who knows, I might go back.'

'You sound as though you have a little project going on,' said Katy.

Mary peered into the darkness to see what degree of playfulness was registering in Katy's eyes; but through the smoke and the blur of the lamp she could see only the pretty outline of her jaw and the soft swell of the cardigan on her shoulders.

'Well,' she said, 'it's funny you should say that.

You know how Lauren's always saying how cultured I'm supposed to be, coming from Europe, and Charlie's always telling people I'm writing a book.'

'Am I?' said Charlie.

'That's what you told Lauren,' said Katy. 'You said she'd won prizes in college for her writing.'

'Anyway,' said Mary, 'I thought perhaps I would. With the children away and so on. I mean, why not?'

'Would what?' said Charlie.

'Write a book. I know it sounds ridiculous, it sounds so presumptuous, but, well — '

'What about?' said Charlie.

'I'm not quite sure what it's about. I think it's about New York. And children.'

'It's like a guidebook?' said Katy.

'Not exactly.'

'I can't wait to read it.'

Charlie laughed. 'I think you'll have to. The poor girl's got to write it first.'

'Do you like the idea of your wife's being an author?' said Edward.

'Sure,' said Charlie. 'The new Emily Dickinson. Or more like Edith Wharton, perhaps.' He filled his glass. 'Or Grace Metalious. In fact, that's what we really need. A *Peyton Place* would do fine. Then I could retire from the service.'

'Does she know enough about suburban adultery?' said Edward.

'I'm sure I could find out, Eddie.'

★ ★ ★

173

From Maryland, Senator Kennedy flew to Oregon to address a Young People for Kennedy rally at Portland. With him on the press plane went Frank Renzo; behind them went an aircraft with the sound and camera people, dismissively referred to as the 'animal plane'; and on a commercial flight the following day, in an aisle seat ('something as far from the bloody window as possible') booked by Benton at the embassy, went Charlie van der Linden.

A cherry-and-white cab pulled up outside Number 1064 to take Mary to Union Station; ten minutes later the announcer called out 'All Aboard' and that evening she was back in New York. She had kept her room in the drab hotel in the Garment District, where she went to the manager's office to negotiate a long-term rate. She agreed a price, calculating as she did so by how much it would further overdraw the family account.

In a drugstore on Seventh Avenue she bought some ballpoint pens and a large blue exercise book with a high school daily schedule printed inside the front cover. She pictured Charlie beaming over a mugful of Wild Turkey: 'My wife can't join us tonight, Ambassador. She has to be in New York, where she's doing 'research' for the book she's writing.' It was impossible to count the number of inverted commas with which he would surround the word 'research'. How preposterous, how absurd it sounded: she, herself, an author. *The Ailanthus Tree: A Memoir* by Mary Kirwan; and on the back flap: About the Author: 'Mary Kirwan was born in

London, England in 1920 and is married to a British diplomat. They have two children and are presently living in Washington, DC. Her hobbies are reading and listening to music . . . Her husband's hobbies are drinking liquor, taking barbiturates and benzedrine tablets, smoking cigarettes and misquoting poetry. She wrote this book so she could pursue a platonic but passionate adulterous love affair in New York City with a newspaperman she barely knows, who is mostly out of town. Miss Kirwan, a British university honours graduate who enjoys the musicals of Rodgers and Hammerstein, is already hard at work on a sequel: *From the Outside Inwards: Cutlery Conundrums and Other Scenes from Diplomatic Life . . .* ' Hmm . . . Better a novel, really, she thought: something with a title that suggested an elegant melancholy — *A Shaded Street*, or perhaps *The Reluctant Dancer.*

It was ridiculous, but she started anyway, and watched the coarse paper of the book, that should have filled with some schoolchild's homework, clog up with lines of spilling reminiscence. The coming death of her mother had provided the frame in which all else was now contained and intensified: matters that had seemed provisional or capable of endless procrastination had acquired the dull imminence of fact: death happened, death was coming and she herself was going to die, inexplicably, unsatisfactorily, like her mother, like everyone else, with burial, extinction, no questions answered and no ends tied off. And in the

175

middle of all this weight, of all this duty that accompanied her previously denied middle age, there had come this rapture. At this moment, for the first time in her life, she had experienced the transcendent combination of the fierce tenderness, such as she felt for Richard and Louisa, with the physical desire that had once before raged, many years ago, with David Oliver, and which she had resigned herself never again to know. The simultaneous experience of the two feelings was not a simple addition of their respective effects; it felt to Mary as though the force was squared. She could not imagine how she was supposed to deal with it; but it felt like death — imperative, unavoidable, the only issue.

She had found a deli called Nathan's, where she had breakfast every morning. The elderly waitresses with blue hair soon lost their initial gruffness as they refilled her coffee mug (too hot and too weak — Charlie was right), brought fresh orange juice ('oring juice', they called it, as though unable to manage two 'j' sounds in succession) and plied her with eggs over easy, sunny side up, home fries, wheat toast, omelettes, brittle strips of bacon, paper tubs of pale butter and miniature containers of jelly ('Raspberry? Grape? Whaddaya like today?') that they pulled from the pockets of their aprons.

She read the paper, lighting a cigarette, trying to prolong the pleasure of being there, as she looked for Frank's byline. She liked it, she would have been happy never to have any other breakfast than that provided in the wooden booths divided by their low partitions with patterned panes of brown and crimson glass at head height, with Sadie hovering at her elbow with a coffee refill, Mike the bearded cook in his crumpled hat beneath a sign that read: 'Special. Don't Cook Tonite. Whole Roast Chicken. Plus One Pound Kasha Varnishkes. Plus 1lb Potato Salad or Coleslaw.' She liked it all as though her life depended on it.

After breakfast she returned to her hotel room and settled down to write in the exercise book till about noon, when she would take the subway downtown to Sheridan Square. Frank had passed on a piece of advice he had received from a woman friend: she should smooth the back of her skirt down carefully before she sat down, as the seats in some subway cars had rough rattan surfaces that tore your nylons, 'And you know what it's like when you get a run in one of a new pair.'

Trees, trees, she thought each time she emerged in the Village: trees, and streets with curves and names; yet in this temporary escape from right angles there seemed a decadence, a flexed temptation. She followed a regular course: from Seventh Avenue South down West 11th Street, a peaceful, tree-lined thoroughfare of Italianate rowhouses with half-basements and pink geraniums in the window boxes. There were one or two plaques on the walls that suggested the street had long been too grand for the bakeries, Mexican craft shops and blue jeans that Frank despised. Then she looped on to Bleecker Street and paused to look at Frank's apartment building. She gazed up to the top floors, unable to make out which window was his, with its view of the Hudson and the Jersey shore. She went back a block to West 10th and looked again. There, behind that square of impersonal upper window, that was where her life had changed.

Afterwards she took a different route each day, looking for a bar or café where she would feel at home. On this morning she walked for a few blocks down Bleecker, then turned south. Houston was not a street, but a highway of cross-town traffic, and a division, too, a Delaware, below which was Hell's Hundred Acres, an industrial district of cast-iron buildings, sweatshops, strikes and factory fires. A block or so down she saw a neon Café sign and decided to brave Houston to reach it.

Installed at the bar, she took out a magazine and leafed through it as the barman presented the requested Bloody Mary with a casual flourish. She was only the second customer in the place, which had a clean, morning smell and an atmosphere of expectation. Behind the bar an enormous selection of bottles was ranged on a wooden counter, beneath which was a row of brass-handled drawers. An indolent, two-bladed fan rotated in the ceiling, and behind the stool where Mary sat, on the other side of the long, rectangular room, was a row of tables set with red gingham cloths. On the wall above were photographs of prize-fighters, many signed to the bar: watchful faces, some African in reluctant origin, some Slav, like Fritzie Zivic, staring with violent monochrome trepidation, fists raised, at their new unconquered homeland. You could

178

almost hear the roar of their endeavour.

Mary was too happy in her surroundings to read the magazine, but flicked through the advertisements, with Frank's voice in her ear. The men's clothes all promised something more impressive than pants and coats. 'Glen Guard: the trademark of the confident man!' 'The Bowler Homburg — the new Hat of Influence', at Saks. 'Strook — for the self-assured look. Some men are born relaxed, some achieve relaxation through Yoga or Zen and some find relaxation thrust upon them via suits of Folkweave Tweed.' The gentleman in the picture had certainly achieved a self-assured air; so much so, Mary noticed, that next to his folkweave tweed suit he was clutching a nine-inch upright model of a US Navy Polaris missile.

Every page seemed to have some relevance to her own unusual circumstances. She could send a Western Union candygram, a two-pound box of chocolates with a telegram attached — five dollars plus the cost of the words — to Eugene, Oregon. But to whom would she address it?

Her small anguish at the thought of Charlie staggering once more across the tarmac to the waiting plane was replaced by a shameful idea: she could volunteer to accompany him. And if he was going to be close to Senator Kennedy for a time, then inevitably she would come across others who . . .

The bar was slowly filling with workers from the factories, regular customers known by name to the barman, also with one or two office clerks in suits and neckties who had ventured down from the Village into the cast-iron neighbourhood. Mary felt she should vacate her stool for these people whose claim was superior to her own, but she was enjoying being there and ordered a sandwich to justify her presence.

The barman brought another drink, which she sipped, feeling not so much a weakening effect of alcohol as a slight intensifying of the moment. She flicked the page and read the words 'Hold that Tiger with an Easybaby Car Belt' over a picture of a cross little boy standing on the back seat of a car. His face reminded her of Richard's when he was two or three, and from her purse she surreptitiously slipped the wallet with two photographs and gorged her hungry gaze on them beneath the cover of the mahogany bar rail.

'Club sandwich, ma'am.'

Mary looked up with stinging eyes. 'Thank you.'

After lunch she went back to the hotel and wrote a long letter to each of the children, describing the wonderful city of New York. Then she wrote to Duncan Trench, explaining that she planned to be out of town so much in the near future that she would regrettably be unable to help him with his request.

★　★　★

There was no flight number for the press plane, no check-in; you walked across the airfield apron, left your bag beneath the open hold if you wanted it stowed, then climbed aboard, found a seat and, when the attendant had shut the cabin door, you took off. There were seat belts, but no one wore them because they prevented you from turning round and sharing drinks and notes with the reporters in the row behind.

There was a murmur of anticipation as the small aircraft reached the steepest angle of its climb. The curtain at the front parted, Senator Kennedy emerged and sat down on a wooden tray; he joined his hands round his feet and tobogganed down the aisle into the restraining arms of his junior press secretary at the rear of the plane.

The senator passed within a foot of Frank Renzo as he rushed by; Frank saw the straight hairline, the close-shaved skin of his young face, the narrow eyes opened to their widest extent in alarm and triumph as he defied the advice of his back doctor to deliver what the boys on the plane had been asking for. Forgive me my sins, his wild gaze seemed to say, forget my reckless love of women, overlook my wealth and East Coast homes, because at heart I am like you.

Frank noticed the stitching in his clothes, his manicured hands and the easy manner that came from years of parties in Hyannisport and Martha's Vineyard, of dating debutantes and making furtive love also to their mothers; of yacht clubs and dinner parties, cigars and tennis; of law school and oak-panelled rooms and charge accounts on which you bought shirts by the dozen. Frank found they raised in him an instinctive distrust — a reaction he could no more control than the reflex of a struck knee.

'Frank,' said the *Sun*'s reporter, a man called Potter whom Frank had met on previous assignments and admired for his hardheadedness, 'you're going to love Jack. The guy's got class.'

'*Jack*? When did you start calling the enemy by his first name?'

Potter laughed. 'You'll see.'

Frank looked at Potter sceptically. Was this the man whose angry rectitude had chilled Senator McCarthy, who had in public told Chiang Kai-shek's adjutant that he was a liar?

Everyone around the candidate seemed dizzy with uncritical affection. 'If you're new on the senator's campaign,' the press secretary told Frank, 'you need to look out for the jumpers.' As Kennedy's car drove slowly down a prepared route, a number of women in the crowd would jump up and down on the spot: schoolgirls in bobbysocks, mothers with babies in their arms, ladies in suits and high heels — age seemed not to be a factor in their excitability. Those who held hands as they jumped were known as double-leapers, those who hugged themselves in glee if Kennedy caught their eye were 'clutchers'. Most dramatic were the 'runners', women who attempted to break the police line, reach the motorcade and steal a kiss from the candidate.

The senator, Frank noticed, seemed at best indifferent to the response he prompted and often perturbed by it. His speech, which varied little from day to day, was a sober account of Republican failings in office and a reasonable list of improved policy expectations at home and abroad under his presidency. There was nothing demagogic in his style, yet something in his presence seemed to excite, so that the steady paragraphs beat the air as though uttered with full oratorical intent. The logical conclusion of his argument was often lost before the end, to the speaker's evident exasperation, in the clamour of hysterical applause.

Frank was exhausted by his induction to the job. Pierre Salinger and the other press secretaries had viewed him with distaste after the removal of Webster Cordell, believing Frank would naturally over-correct his predecessor's uncritical fondness for Kennedy. He was not invited to informal briefings in hotel rooms; he was the last to be told of any changes in a prepared speech. He therefore relied on the kindness of colleagues, rapid shorthand and what he hoped would be the superior powers of his own observation. None of this endeared the candidate to him, but he allowed neither his treatment by the press aides nor his instinctive recoil from Kennedy's gracious manner to influence what he wrote. He watched and listened ravenously, put down what he saw and heard, checked it three times over and took it to Western Union.

* * *

Coming and going in the hotel lobby, Mary lingered as she passed the desk, looked the clerk in the eye and gave him an extended greeting, so he would be reminded of the telephone call for her that he had taken earlier and would produce from the pigeonhole behind him a message of transfixing love.

Late one afternoon, he did stop her on her way in and handed over the piece of folded paper she had so fiercely imagined. She read it as she crossed the lobby. 'Will be returning evening 20th. Two days, then Augusta.' She paused at the elevator, turned and walked back to the desk.

'This message. Can you tell me who it's from?'

The clerk took it from her hand and looked at it. 'Let me check.' He went into the glass-fronted office behind the desk where Mary could see him questioning the obese female telephonist.

He returned and handed her back the piece of paper. 'I guess it's from your husband, ma'am.'

'Yes . . . Yes, I guess it is. Thank you.'

Up in her room, Mary sat on the bed and clutched herself. This was the pain of death and nothing she tried could make it stop.

I am a woman of some standing, she told herself through the hands she had raised to her face: a mother, a person others are entitled to look to with some confidence for rational behaviour and good example. I cannot therefore allow this to happen to me.

She went to the bathroom, steadied herself against the basin and splashed water in her face. She looked into her eyes, the dark brown irises, and tried to see shame or sense.

When she had calmed herself, she called room service for some tea and searched her purse for change with which to tip the bellboy. After he had been and gone, leaving behind the wheeled

184

wagon with the tea things, she turned on the television, kicked off her shoes and lay down on the bed.

A New York early evening programme was interviewing a number of famous people who were in town that night; through the fuzzy monochrome of the screen, presumably receiving insufficient signal from a cloud-piercing roof antenna, a man in a bow tie was speaking to the camera: 'Later in the programme we'll be talking with Lucille Ball, who's staying at the Plaza, but right here in the studio we have a whiff of *Gunsmoke*, yes it's Marshal Matt Dillon himself, Mister James Arness . . . '

The telephone rang.

★　★　★

An hour later, Mary was sitting on the subway — her flannel skirt carefully smoothed before she risked the snagging seat — heading down to the Village. The street numbers in the bare, tiled stations counted her rapidly down to zero. She tried not to hurry as she went through the turnstile but to keep some dignity; the fact that Frank had called to say he was back in New York did not mean to say she had to lose all sense of her own freedom of action.

As the elevator rose in Frank's building, she tried to organize her thoughts. He was waiting at the open door of his apartment down the corridor, and she had just enough presence of mind to keep herself from running.

When she had extracted herself from his arms,

Mary felt disappointed. Nothing had been solved by his absence or return and they took the same wary positions on either side of the room.

'You look exhausted,' she said.

'I haven't been to bed for three days. I had a lot of catching up to do out there. I haven't even had time to shower since I got back. You were too quick for me.'

'You can go and have a shower now if you like. Shall I make some tea or something?'

'Sure. There's some in that cupboard there.'

Embarrassed by the thought of having been 'too quick' for him, Mary found a small pleasure in marshalling cups and a pot, moving among Frank's possessions, using them as her own. She saw him emerge, damp-haired, from the bathroom in a dark-green robe and go into the bedroom next door, but ten minutes later there was no sign of him and the tea was growing cold.

Mary went cautiously to the door of the bedroom and knocked, the cup of tea in her hand. There was no answer, so she pushed the door open a little and peered round. Frank was lying on the bed asleep, still in his robe. Mary smiled as she crossed the room and set down the cup on a table by the bed, next to a crumpled pack of cigarettes. She touched Frank's arm and shook it lightly, but he did not stir.

She sat on the edge of the bed and looked at him. He lay on his back with his arms loosely folded across his chest, like the figure on a crusader tomb. The breath was hauled up slow and deep from his lungs and blown out almost soundlessly through his nose. Where the robe

186

was open she could see the light covering of hair on his chest; there was a place where it did not grow, as though it had been worn away by the friction of some heavy object.

She reached out a hand and touched the pale freckles beneath his eyes, then ran the back of her hand down his cheek, which was shadowed and rough from the time-change and the late night. She touched the soft membrane of the lips with the tip of her finger.

While he was unconscious, he lay within her power. She looked at each indentation of his features, thinking she might reduce them to so many pores and lines, might banish the power which, when animate, they held over her. It did not work: the more she looked, the more forlornly she loved him. If she could not profit from his sleep to break the spell, she thought, perhaps she could use it in a different way.

She went back into the lounge to fetch her purse, from which she took a powder compact. She climbed on to Frank's bed, pulled the skirt up her thighs and straddled him; he stirred but did not wake as she settled lightly on his hips. With gentle strokes she covered the dark rings of fatigue beneath his eyes, and made pale the growing shadows on his jaw. She could not bear the thought of all the years she had not known him, how much of what was rightly hers had been withheld. By covering the marks of the years, she might recapture them: she might make time run differently.

She felt herself aching with the furtive control she had taken over him. If she were to take some pleasure of him while he slept, he need never know; and somehow, then, it would not count. After all, could they be lovers if one of them did not know it? She pulled the tight skirt higher, so it bunched above her hips, rose up on her knees, gently untied the cord of Frank's robe and parted it. She closed her eyes and let her left hand slide down over the fabric of the skirt, then inside, where it felt her own flesh.

She heard her breath coming harder when his voice interrupted her, 'Keep your eyes closed.' She felt her face flare and burn as his hand pushed aside her clothes. He had one hand on himself and one hand on her hip as he carefully guided her downwards. She sighed as she sank and fell.

9

Charlie woke up, but did not know where he was. He looked into his memory, pressed the usual buttons of recall, but nothing came. He dragged his eyes around the room and saw it as a savage might see his first interior. It appeared to be a hotel: his unopened case was on the folding baggage holder; on the glass top of the chest of drawers were keys and coins. His jacket, the sleeves bunched inside out, was lying on the carpet and next to it was a lassoed necktie. He lifted the bed covers and looked down: he was dressed in his shirt and underwear.

Carefully, distrusting the impact on his eyes of light and air, he made his way to the net curtain and pulled it back. In front of him was a city park: a big open area of green with sparse trees crossed by paths on which a few figures walked. He went to the desk and found some writing paper in a leather-bound blotter. The hotel was in Boston. He looked again out of the window. The Common. Boston . . . Beacon Hill . . . Tea Party . . . Back Bay . . . Irish Catholics. Kennedy. Patches of the previous day began to take shape in his memory like disconnected areas of a photographic print emerging in solution. Charlie remembered the senator making a speech to a lumber company in Eugene, Oregon. But from where had he then flown to Boston? Portland? Seattle? And who had told him where to go?

Presumably he had undressed himself, as a kindly helper would have hung up his jacket. From the back pocket of the suitcase, he pulled out a fifth of Wild Turkey, his emergency supply, went to the bathroom for a glass and drank it half-and-half with lukewarm water from the faucet. Then he pulled off his clothes and stood beneath the shower, from whose retractable head two dozen needles pierced his hunched shoulders.

A few minutes later, he picked up the telephone and asked for breakfast to be sent to the room.

'We could send up some coffee right away, sir,' said a male Bostonian voice. 'And maybe a sandwich. But we can't do breakfast. It's two forty in the afternoon.'

Charlie sat on the edge of the bed. He wanted Mary to be with him. From her sprang strength and clarity of purpose. She had made all the decisions about the children, the house, how they lived, whom they invited over. Even the Kaiser Manhattan had been her idea, and that was what he loved about her best: you could leave it all to her, but she would make interesting choices. All Charlie had been supposed to do was keep his own career on course, to choose between jobs, perform them diligently and not offend his superiors.

He lowered his head into his hands. He felt tired with the exhaustion of all the failed centuries. He was not exactly hungover; he barely had hangovers any more, just days of gastric terror and mental absence. He sometimes pictured the workings of his mind as the jewelled movement of a Swiss watch, trembling with expensive fibrillation, into which he had poured sand. Yet what had he or the world lost by this wantonness? There was no sign that a careful husbanding of the machinery would have produced anything that would have helped to give value or meaning to his or any other existence. There was nothing he could do that could not be done by other over-educated people in the State Department, the World Bank or the Diplomatic Service. As for power . . . Those who sought and won it had a talent for self-abasement and sycophancy, an indifference to shame, an ability to believe the fatuous and the untrue. And all of this was in the service of . . . Of what? Of seeing their hand on a lever, their name on a box.

It was not possible by art or politics to transcend the self-renewing strictures of the daily world: of that Charlie felt sure. He noticed — bore witness to the fact — that people could nevertheless perform with antic gaiety within those confines, could plan and act and laugh as though nothing were wrong, as though the design were not irremediably flawed. The more he lived, the more certain he became that the key to being able to act in such a way (for what that way was worth) lay not in analysis of the problem, not in intellectual effort, not even in experience or good fortune, but merely in the chemical inheritance that people called temperament. He saw it a little in Katy Renshaw and sometimes in Benton, his stern secretary; it was

191

in women more often, it seemed, than in men (though in himself it could be chemically induced); but mostly he saw it in his wife.

It had taken him several years of marriage to appreciate that this was what had drawn him to Mary; that this was his chance of survival, the blind genetic cunning that found him his mate and simultaneously tricked him into thinking it was something else — her dark eyes, her forthright emotions or the modesty of her touch.

In the bathroom he went through his washbag, looking for aspirin, then returned to the telephone and dialled the number of his house in Washington. His head was filled with the logic of despair.

Give me something against reason, he thought. Give me hope. Give me a voice that, however unreasonably, likes living.

★　★　★

Mary lay beside Frank in his bed, kept awake by the thunder of the air-conditioning. She had one thought only through the small hours: I am not the kind of person who does this.

There were people who 'had affairs', as the phrase went; there were people who were what they called 'unfaithful'; but all their deceptions seemed banal to her. They were all failures of the imagination because the constant reinvention of her married love was more romantic than any furtive double-cross could be. She was not the kind of person who did that. She was the kind of person who had a sense of value, who loved her husband fully, organically, in a way that easily encompassed his shortcomings. She was the kind of person who did not see the constraints of marriage as a sacrifice of freedom but as a necessary discipline that intensified the rewards of love, both in her husband and her children: marriage was moral and it was indefatigably interesting.

She was wearing a cotton shirt of Frank's and it was uncomfortable when she turned on the mattress; even though it was an old one, there was a stiffness in the seams, and periodically she had to heave it out from beneath her hip.

Mary could not bring herself to think about what they had done. Once the taboo had been broken, there had seemed no reason to hold back; if they were convinced that the purity of their feelings justified their actions, then the candour of the actions might as well do justice to the fierceness of the emotion. Not that she had thought it through so clearly, on the floor of the lounge, standing against the kitchen counter, in the shower, or kneeling on the bathroom floor. She felt herself blushing in the darkness.

She wanted to return to safety, but home no longer represented a refuge. She had infected Number 1064, and she acutely regretted it; she doubted that she could ever recapture that glad innocence and a squeeze of panic went through her. The hotel room was the best place she could think of: hers, yet neutral; and there she could sleep, reorganize her thoughts and decide what she was to do. In the course of the long night there were no thoughts too radical: leaving

Charlie, moving to New York, arranging visits to the children, forsaking both men to be alone. In the morning she was certain of two things: that she remained devoted to her life at home and would not change any aspect of it; and that more than anything at that moment she needed Frank's reassurance that what had passed between them meant as much to him as it did to her.

She looked at his sleeping face for a long while, then got up and crossed to the window, where she looked east, over Little Italy, hoping for the sun to rise.

★　★　★

Frank was dreaming he was back in the Solomon Islands, where he had spent three days in a foxhole with a man from Jamestown, North Dakota called Aaron Godley. The platoon had been cut off by a Japanese counter-offensive and, with stragglers from various other units, was stranded in the jaws of an unpleasantly intense two-pronged attack, waiting for the reinforcements promised on the surviving field telephone.

Godley had always been the runt of the platoon, the one who would first be picked off by predators, and even within his own pack was the object of bullying derision. He was forgiven for the fact that he could not read a compass and that his kit was always deficient in some crucial respect; his colleagues were grateful that Godley's obvious failings distracted the drill sergeant's attention from their own. His problem was that he was inauthentic; his jokes were not funny, his attempts at comradeship were transparently self-interested. He fastened too quickly on to the slang, the nicknames and the running gags that others had in twos or threes, promiscuously switching from one sub-group to another, looking for any sign of welcome; his desire to be accepted was too palpable, and nothing he did seemed natural. He could not even march properly, sometimes making his right arm swing with the right leg, the left with the left, so that he jerked along like a man with tin legs.

Frank felt sorry for Godley because he knew what it was like to be lonely, poor, not there, where the warmth of life was. Yet he felt that he had figured something out for himself: like the other men in the platoon, like Billy Foy, for instance, he had discovered there was a road to friendship and acceptance and that it lay in not caring what others thought, but in finding your own dignity. While he did pity Godley, it was impossible not to dislike him; like the others, he recoiled from him because he embarrassed them: he vulgarly displayed the cravings and the weaknesses that they had learned to hide.

In their foxhole, Frank saw Godley unravel as the intensity of the Japanese fire increased; he learned the smell of his body, of its skin and its excretions. He saw that there was a void in him where the affections and the self-respect belonged; it was not just that he had been driven frantic by the bullying: it seemed to Frank that he could never have been valued by anyone. He jabbered at the sound of gunfire, clasped hold of Frank's arm, and it was clear that the emptiness in him was total, that any arm about the shoulder, any reassurance would be the first occupant of that vacant space of unlove.

They received orders to advance to a new position. It was a day of awful heat and Frank welcomed the idea of any movement that might help them refill their water bottles and escape from their inadequately buried waste. They climbed over a ridge of sand and ran for cover in some dense tropical vegetation at the top of the hill. There was rifle and machine-gun fire from the left, where the temporary Japanese positions had been alerted by American ground support aircraft that movement was imminent.

As Frank pulled Godley down beside him, they had a clear view of a Japanese machine-gun post, dug in about fifty yards below, towards the beach. Frank shot the gunner through the cheek; Godley hit the man feeding the gun, also in the face, causing a spill of brain and blood over his shoulder, and turned to Frank with a delighted expression that implored him to concede that now, surely, he was acceptable.

The platoon dug in where it was, waiting, since the enemy had retreated, for the order to advance. It rained hard in the night, and Frank slept with Billy Foy, who had joined them with a battered ridge tent. They awoke in the morning sun to an unfamiliar splashing sound. Godley's dead Jap was wedged against the gun, still upright, though with the top part of his skull missing. Into the water-filled cavity, from ten paces away, Godley was tossing pieces of coral.

Three weeks later, on leave in a steamy North Australian town, Frank and Godley were in a group of six who went to a brothel. It was with relief that the five of them watched Godley being escorted down a dim corridor by the madam of the house. At last Godley did not need one of them to hold his hand; the girls, mostly refugees from the Philippines, were used to all kinds and conditions of men, and he would not feel threatened; perhaps he would even emerge with some self-esteem. Frank's girl took him to a small bedroom where a large three-bladed fan in the ceiling stirred the clammy air and a window overlooked a market where chickens squealed in wooden cages. Frank, who had never previously visited a whore, was not sure to what extent the normal rules applied. Was he meant to kiss her, for instance, to imitate affection? Should he put her pleasure before his own? Or would that provide an unwelcome distraction in her work? Was she in fact capable of pleasure in her professional circumstances? She could have been no more than eighteen years old, but she smiled and undressed with a swift confidence that was not arousing.

To each encounter he carried the sum of all such previous experiences. Others in the platoon talked of girlfriends at home, girls they'd picked up on the road, of what they had done to them, and how; the anatomical details were garish, if not always convincing. Frank found himself touching his Filipina in a certain way that a previous lover had liked. Each act was a

197

summary or palimpsest of what had gone before, the lives of vanished lovers and their bodies visible for a moment through the years, reincarnated: the kiss on Mimi Lever's sensitive ear, the circular caress enjoyed by Anne-Marie Warshanky, and by her sister Donna, the rotary movement that Sassie LaSalle had most liked and which always made him envisage, to his private shame, a ship's turbine.

When he made love to Mary, he was anxious not to appear indelicate, as though he had some bestial expectation; yet at the same time, with no way of telling what her experiences of the act might be, he wanted not to disappoint. At the beginning the figure of Charlie hung comparatively over his every action; later he felt the need to transgress fully, to make the crime fit the punishment.

In life Godley had returned from his room down the corridor of the brothel with a look of smug bravado; in Frank's dream, Godley's girl turned out to be Mary.

He awoke with sweat on his upper lip and his heart plodding in lumpy protest against his sternum. He remembered what had taken place the night before and looked across the bed; but where Mary should have lain asleep, the sheets were corrugated and empty. Frank pulled on his robe and went through to the living room, at the far end of which, at the kitchen counter, he saw her making tea.

'Good morning,' he said.

★　★　★

Mary had made love to only two men before, and had not discussed with female friends the details of the act. For her it had been a physical expression of an abstract emotion: an emblem, almost a metaphor, even if it was a confusingly blunt one that produced auxiliary emotions of its own. It had also carried with it a sense of surrender, or at least a statement of trust; there was after all nothing more of herself that she could offer.

With Frank, she was anxious that she was not doing things the right way, but rather was drafting him into a ritual that had developed long ago between her and Charlie. She worried at first that the limits of her marriage and her life were transparent to him and could be deduced from her staid or unsatisfactory movements. Then, later, she stopped sensing the ghost of David Oliver or Charlie because she became too intent on Frank, on the illicit excitement of this new sensation at a time in her life when almost everything was familiar.

'Good morning,' she replied.

Where on earth, she was thinking, can I go from here?

10

'Mrs van der Linden called. She's still in New York. She said she told you. She's coming back tonight.'

'Thank you, Benton. I expect she did tell me. I'd forgotten.'

Benton put some telegrams from London on to Charlie's desk. 'We have a date for opening the new building,' she said. 'September twenty-fourth.'

'Who's cutting the ribbon? The queen?'

Benton consulted a memorandum on her desk. 'No, it's Mr Selwyn Lloyd.'

'The Chancellor of the bloody Exchequer! God, you'd have thought they could have done better than that.'

'What's Mrs van der Linden doing in New York?'

'She's writing a book, I believe.'

'A book? Like a mystery story?'

'Complete mystery to me, Benton. I think she misses the children. I think that's the problem.'

'How do you manage at home on your own?'

'It's only been a day or so here and there. She just takes off when I do. When I'm in town she comes back. And I have Dolores. If you like chili con carne.'

'How did you get on in Oregon?'

'Very well, thank you.'

'And Boston?'

'Not so well. I think I may have missed a lunch appointment.'

'With Senator Kennedy?'

'Among others. You sound appalled, Benton. I think you have a soft spot for him.'

Benton crossed her legs with a fierce nylon crackle. 'I guess he is kinda cute.'

'He's a politician, Benton. That means he spends his time calculating how much he lies to whom and trying to prevent different factions from discovering that he has made them incompatible promises. Imagine the nervous stress.'

'Mrs Kennedy's attractive, though.'

'Undeniably.'

Charlie looked down to his desk, where a telegram from the Foreign Office was asking the Ambassador to respond to a story in the London *Times* about Senator Nixon's projected defence policy and how it would affect NATO. The *Times* article was itself a development of a piece in the previous day's *Post* to which no one, least of all Charlie, had paid much attention.

A note from the Head of Chancery was attached to the telegram. 'In view of your brilliant fire-fighting operation last week (complete silence from London) I wondered if you could let me have a draft reply to this? By 3.30 p.m.?' Charlie groaned quietly and reached for the telephone.

★　★　★

Mary waited for Frank in a bar, a typical Frank rendezvous between Park and Broadway, a few blocks up from Union Square. It was a long room whose ceiling was the colour of New York brownstone with cracked fleur-de-lys motifs in the plaster and a four-lamp glass-shaded chandelier. Three men in hats sat staring upwards at the blank television screen mounted on a bracket at the end of the bar, their faces averted equally from their own reflections in the long mirror behind the stepped rows of bottles and the steady photographic gaze of Theodore Roosevelt. A door at the far end of the room was marked MEN.

Mary ordered a Seven-Up and opened her paper. It was twelve-thirty and her train was due to leave in two hours; she had been back to the hotel to find a message from Dolores that Charlie had been trying to reach her in Washington. She viewed 1064 and All That with a mixture of feelings: fear, that she had tainted something sacrosanct, and hope, that the house would still provide a refuge from the turmoil of her feelings.

'How ya doin'?' She felt a hand on her shoulder.

Frank was suddenly at her side. 'Let me have a beer, will you, Ray?'

'Fine, fine,' said Mary.

'You like a real drink?' said Frank.

'No, this is okay, thanks.' Mary saw the rings on her left hand and slid it down beneath the rail; she felt that everyone in this man's bar was looking at her. She had changed her clothes back at the hotel and washed with scrupulous care, but a physical reminder of the night before had made itself felt as she leaned forward to take a cigarette from her purse.

'Still shouting for that bunch of losers?' said the barman as he pushed the beer over to Frank.

'Listen, we have the most valuable player in the National League.'

'Ernie Banks? He's just a big black slugger.'

'Oh yeah? And the Yankees? You're nothing without Yogi. Think you're still so great?'

'We are great, mister, that's the truth. Mickey Mantle, he's the best you ever seen.'

'More speedy than a slugger, more sluggy than a speedster and less of both than either. Was that what the boss said?'

'Hey, don't give me that Stengel crap. Pardon me, ma'am. He don't talk good, but he can sure coach a team.'

'Do yourself a favor. Get over to Chicago and see a real game.'

'Hey,' the barman chuckled as he turned away. 'Chicago. That's a good one.'

Mary waited for someone to speak English again.

'So,' said Frank, turning to her. 'You sure you have to leave?'

'I do. Charlie's back home and I ought to go and look after him.'

Frank nodded, saying nothing.

'But I could come back if you like,' Mary wanted to say; but she judged it wiser not to.

Frank put his hand on her arm. 'Are you all right?'

'Yes, I'm fine. And you?'

He nodded. 'I'm all right. I'm glad you could come along. I'm sorry I had to leave in a rush this morning. I slept too late. I was tired. You know, after all — '

'Yes, yes.'

'All that campaigning, I was going to say. I have a break now. For a coupla days.'

Mary felt a twist of anguish. 'Just when I'm not free,' she said. 'And then what?'

'California, New Mexico, Minneapolis. I have one day back in New York — on the seventeenth, I think. Then two or three days at the end of the month. Then there's the Convention in Los Angeles. And after that, at some stage, I'll switch to Nixon for a while.'

'I don't think I can live without seeing you,' she managed also not to say. She looked away, but remained calm. She had been in love with David Oliver, a great passion that had grown slowly; she had also been in love with Charlie van der Linden, and the easy nature of their superficial exchanges deceived no one as to the force of their mutual reliance.

But Frank. Good God, she thought as she looked down to her hands twisting in her lap beneath the mahogany rail. Everything had come at once, the tenderness, desire, the sublime simplicity of happiness that depended only on his presence and his face, the fierce knowledge that told her it was him or nothing but the void. And that it should have come at this time in her life, when she had thought such things were past. Let the more loving one be me . . . Wasn't that a line that Charlie used to quote? In God's name, she thought, let the more loving one be someone else: for me it is beyond endurance.

'So what happens now?' said Frank.

Mary puffed at her cigarette and ground out the stub in the ashtray. The thing about being forty, she thought, was that while you had the feelings of a twenty-five year old, at least you had some dignity.

'I don't know, Frank.'

Dignity? She had no dignity at all. She thought of what she had done and it was not dignified. So maybe she had . . . Self-control. Not even that: as soon as she had heard his voice on the telephone, she had leapt on the train to New York; as soon as he was unconscious she had more or less assaulted him. Self-control in public places. Yes, she would allow herself that: she was not going to cry or faint, like poor Franny in the story, but it didn't seem much of an achievement for twenty years of adulthood, childbirth, raising children and all the wisdom and serenity that that was meant to bring.

She felt his gaze, looking down because he stood while she sat, and she thought of him on the first night they had met, slouched in their armchair, with his insanely distracted enthusiasm for some jazz trumpeter, dripping blood on to her maple parquet.

Through her mind were going all the possibilities, rapidly flipping over, like cards on a Rolodex. Stop this now and leave; never see him again: she could picture the scene quite easily. Explain to Charlie what had happened; make arrangements for a compromise. She could visualize responses and consequences; she could see arms raised, heads lowered; she could see these and many other sequences in stark dramatic outline, lit and ready to be shot. They flickered through her mind, but she could not light on one of them, because none had integrity. The only real possibility was to be passive, to endure, and see what happened; the feeling itself was the master of them both and they would have to yield to it.

Still she needed something from Frank.

'I have to go soon,' she said. 'I have to settle up with the hotel.'

'I thought you were keeping the room.'

'There doesn't seem much point. You're not going to be here and I can write the book at home while I look after Charlie.'

'I thought he was supposed to be following Kennedy as well.'

'Not all the time. He'll go to the Convention, I suppose, and — '

She felt her wrist being squeezed violently. 'Keep the goddam room, Mary. I'll come back. Every chance I get.'

'That hurts, Frank.'

'So did this.' He pulled back the cuff on his shirt and pointed to the long scar that he had cut with his knife, leaving his crimson trail through the kerbside snow.

Mary looked into his eyes, which were shining with some white intensity, like the eyes of a teenage boy in a desperate neighbourhood. She felt the immense loosening warmth of relief.

206

He let go of her hand. 'Sure you don't want a drink?'

She looked at her watch and worked rapidly back, calculating what time was left to her. She could squeeze the minutes; with seconds of such intensity, she could knead them into days.

'All right,' she said.

★   ★   ★

From the hotel she took her bag and walked to Pennsylvania Station. She could not rid herself of the feeling that everything she did was being done by a stranger who temporarily inhabited her skin. She presumed that her mind was deluding her; that to protect her from the roar of experience it was offering her this illusion that someone else was in control, as people in shock or grief are separated from their too-harsh reality.

She went into Penn Station through the main entrance, on Seventh Avenue, between the repetitive line of Doric columns, out of the sun, and down a long arcade of steel-framed shops, separated by honey-coloured marble. Each store had its own cast or pierced decoration, and with its orderly profusion of high-quality goods, the arcade reminded her of Naples or Milan, a kind of national boast beneath the domes of electric light suspended at intervals in spherical clusters, like ripe glass fruit. In Italy she would have lingered to buy a straw donkey or plaster Colosseum for the children, but there was nothing about her transit through Penn Station that she wished to remember.

At the end of the arcade she descended the stone staircase into an enormous space that had been modelled on the Roman baths at Caracalla but which reminded her, in its superfluous, ballroom grandeur, of St Peter's in Rome. From half-moon clerestory lights at each end, broad rivers of light poured down into the monumental space, illuminating the towering Corinthian columns around the buff-marbled walls and the iron lamp standards on their plinths. Mary thought for a moment of the thousands who had passed beneath the coffered ceiling of the seatless waiting room throughout the war: people of the West returning to ancestral Europe through this stone gateway. The six-storey columns and marble walls, ecclesiastical and permanent, made the passing appointments with the trains below seem insignificant; in this cathedral no anxiously desired connection made any real difference to the travellers as they panted on towards their little destinies.

Mary looked about her for the ticket counter. Some committee of Pennsylvania Rail Road officials had installed a modern booth that mimicked those of the new international airport at Idlewild. Perhaps they had been embarrassed, in the age of Sputnik, that the railroad connection of Manhattan to the West was begun in a model of a 2000-year-old European bath house; in any event they had suspended a glass oval on thin steel wires, like a clam shell in a church.

Having bought her ticket, Mary found herself

with ten minutes before her train left. With an overnight bag only, she strolled past the chrome-trimmed interior concessions, a bar, a florist with deco lettering, Savarin's restaurant and a tobacco shop where she asked for a pack of cigarettes. Her mouth felt dry from the martini she had drunk with Frank, and, overcoming her unease with American coins, she bought a paraffined-paper cup from a vending machine for a penny and filled it from a drinking fountain as she went down the steps from the classical waiting area to the gothic steel of the concourse below, where elegance gave way to power. In repeating loops and intersections above her head, the lattice of functional metal bent and bubbled under its glass ceiling, like the Gare St Lazare in Paris imagined for a world more filled with possibilities. Huge steel pillars rose in bolted verticals, supporting splayed arches in a show of colossal, calculated strength.

Mary boarded her train and found a seat by the window. There was a tightness in her chest as the locomotive took the strain and jerked the carriages as it picked the current from the rail and the train crept slowly out beneath the Hudson. Mary gazed at the subterranean tracks and sidings that converged and crossed like veins and arteries in the lamp-lit darkness; she saw the abandoned trucks and rusting engines she had noticed in the Stygian fog in her entrance to the gridlocked city. Fifth and 58th; Sixth and 21st; Seventh and 34th: she thought of all the factors, all the sums and all the calculation in the right-angled world that she was leaving, where everyone was searching for a new prime number.

Suddenly the daylight burst into the carriage, the train gathered speed; they were out in fields, in countryside, with a high blue sky above them, cool and free, shaken loose from the tyranny of the grid, and she felt the blocked air rush out of her with a gasp.

11

Frank was on the afternoon press flight from New Mexico to Minneapolis, where Senator Kennedy was due to speak at a Jefferson-Jackson day dinner. It was a day with no slack in the schedule, but the reporters had just had four days' rest in California and many of them had found it difficult to fill the time.

Frank went down to the waterfront in San Francisco because he wanted to hear something his brother Louis had once described to him: the wild and unexpected honk of seals. In August 1945 Louis had been on a troopship in the Bay, waiting to depart for the invasion of Japan. Many of those on board had already fought the Japanese in the Pacific and were finding it difficult to envisage the scale of what it might be like to fight for two years or more in Japan itself against an entrenched army on its home soil. One morning as they were laying out their kit for inspection, news reached them that the United States Air Force had dropped atomic bombs. The ship lay at anchor in the sunshine for a week before the men were allowed to disembark; from the shallows they could hear the applauding seals. They had been ready to invade.

In New Mexico the newsmen raised their eyebrows and muttered as they climbed aboard the aircraft, shepherded along by the campaign staff anxious to deliver the candidate to

Minneapolis in time, but they could not conceal their delight that the game was on again. Although he nodded and exchanged brief greetings with his colleagues in the morning, Frank did not like travelling in a pack; it went against what, to him, was the point of journalism. When he left Michigan in 1951 to take up his job in New York, he covered the mayor, the Yankees, the Mob; he was on call for fires, homicides and accidents. It was thought to be a shrewd move to put an out-of-towner on the local job; he was encouraged to find his own stories, away from the other reporters, and he liked the days he spent alone in the less-regarded areas of town. Yet everyone in the news room wanted to travel; the ambition of most was to be a foreign correspondent, which implied that you were either a man of education and taste, speaking a different language and charging your expensive life to the newspaper, or that you were a Green Beret to be parachuted in to salvage truth and colour from a tangled foreign conflict.

The following year Frank was taken out of the city to follow Eisenhower's first campaign for the presidency, and one morning in the autumn of 1953 he received a call from the foreign editor, a studious man called Maxwell Johnson, asking him to step into his office.

'I'm told you speak French,' Johnson said.

'I picked up a little towards the end of the war.'

'Girls and menus? That kind of thing?'

Frank thought for a moment. 'A little better than that.'

'Know where Saigon is? I hear things are going to warm up there. We're pouring money in to help the French. They've got some crazy plan to lure the Vietminh out of the bush and blow them away once and for all. They're setting a big trap. Question is: who's going to fall into it. Normally we'd send Wes Cornish, but after three years in Korea he's beat.'

In the news room Frank looked at French Indo-China on the map of the Far East; he followed the course of the Mekong back into the hills and looked at the names of the cities: Phnom Penh, Da Nang, Hanoi . . . It was not far from places he knew; he could almost have been on leave there with men of his platoon, Billy Foy, Wexler, Douglas, Kilkline and the wretched Godley. But for its proximity to China, the country looked a secondary, marginal kind of place.

He found a room in a side street off the rue Leclerc in a large wooden house that reeked of opium. A family lived below, but all the upper rooms were let and there was a communal air about the building, with women sitting, gossiping on the stairs and landing. He had to share a bathroom with two other tenants, one of whom stole the blade from his razor if he left it on the basin. His room was spacious and cool, with wooden blinds and an immense, steady fan in the ceiling. It was easy to meet people in Saigon; the officers of the Press Liaison Service called him daily to let him know how well the French forces were progressing and to invite him up north to see for himself; two American special advisers called Barrett and Walther took him to the Croix du Sud, a restaurant with a Military Police post just inside the door and wire mesh over the windows against grenades. They explained the John Foster Dulles strategy of 'massive retaliation' over *escargots* with Brouilly and *navarin* of lamb and *pommes dauphinoises* with Côtes-du-Rhone.

'There's every kind of loser in this place,' Frank wrote in a letter to Billy Foy in New York. 'At least with 'advisers', you know what their game is. But I met a guy called Moone the other day, a thin streak of East Coast piss, looks like a ghost with bad skin, about twenty-five. He took me to this place the Charrette Rouge and asked me a lot of questions over the frogs' legs. I never did discover what he wanted, but he had a bad gleam in his eye.'

It was a lacklustre war. Occasionally there would be the sound of mortar and rifle fire from the outskirts, but it only happened after dark, and the French and Americans knew which side of the river to stay and where not to go when night had fallen. 'You never see the Vietminh,' Frank's letter went on. 'You can hear their weapons, and if you go north in a press plane you can see the French bombing the jungle where they think they're hiding. Of men, women or children there's no sign. They're ghosts in the wood, shoeless men in the forest. They rearm their front line by carrying stores on reinforced bicycles. This war could go on for a hundred years and the people in Saigon would hardly know. They play checkers and mah-jong and some crazy dice game. It's kind of picturesque, the women sitting in their loose silk pants and mollusc hats. The Americans and the Europeans drink pastis and vermouth, though you can get scotch if you ask around. The locals smoke opium and I have a friend who wants me to try it. She says you should be careful because the French run a monopoly on the low-grade stuff.'

The friend was a lover, a twenty-year-old girl with large eyes whose Annamite name was unpronounceable to Western tongues and who had been nicknamed Tilly by her previous boyfriend, also an American. She was slim and modest, with a light touch in her fingers but a stubborn and persuasive character that revealed itself to Frank slowly over the months. She required movie magazines and chewing gum and that he should have no other lover; in return she slept in his room if he wanted it, or went back to her grandmother's house if he did not. She liked to sit cross-legged on the edge of his bed, beneath the bundled haze of the mosquito net, and gaze at him as he typed on the Smith-Corona portable; something about the make and size of him seemed to amuse and fascinate her. She talked of how it would be when they were married.

Frank took coffee at ten at the American Legation and looked through the rival newspapers; the situation was covered mostly from Washington, where it was a matter of furious debate. The French government had long since stopped paying for its army, which was now funded by the United States; American planes and material followed the dollars, and naturally they needed mechanics to service them. The point at which engineers became troops was a matter of intense concern, since it would then become an American war, something not even Dulles wanted. His strategy was to present the conflict as one in which other nations must take an interest: supporters of the nationalist Vietminh were Marxist in their belief, the State Department argument ran; therefore they must be allied in some unspecified way to the Soviet Union; therefore the French must not be defeated. Dulles turned the full force of his persuasion on to Winston Churchill, a man with some record in conflict, but received in return only a lecture on colonialism and the loss of India.

The papers gave him the politics; for the local developments Frank would go before lunch for a drink with an officer in the French Sûreté. It might be Chevannes, a heavily perspiring man of about fifty, who, after handing over a list of the previous night's arrests and charges, would turn the conversation to the question of whether Asian girls made better lovers than European, a subject in which he was indefatigably interested. Frank suggested he should try a particular half-caste girl he had been told was available for 300 piastres; coming from both cultures, she would offer scientific evidence better than anything in the Kinsey Report. On other days he would have his drink with Bretenoux, a thin man with a high colour who felt homesick for his village in the Lot and would require Frank to join him in a game of boules in the courtyard.

Nowhere could a war zone have been more torpid, Frank thought, as he walked down the dusty streets with their Second Empire façades and backyard chicken runs. America was there and not there in this humid and beautiful backwater; the wishes of the Dulles brothers, the tense edicts of Langley and Foggy Bottom, the phrases such as 'line of dominoes' were discounted and absorbed by the air in which they were uttered, with the smoke of opium and the steam of noodle soup from the open-backed kitchens. It was a lazy town, unwilling to confront the world; it reminded Frank a little of New Orleans, and it seemed to him a natural home for people on the run from their responsibilities.

He had not pictured himself as such a person, yet he felt liberated by the life he led. Chicago and its icy winters, the offices and streets of the Loop, seemed to have been experienced by someone from another generation, unrelated to himself. He believed he had shed the memory of the streets where he had grown up, that the War, then college had cleared his mind. Yet perhaps these things were still in him; perhaps even his attitude to Tilly, frictionless as it seemed, was influenced by the circumstances of his youth. Did she represent the rejection of a Catholic upbringing whereby he was meant to marry an Italian, or did she show that he still had a need to grab something wherever he went, something to show he was not just another self-invented man with no belongings in the world? He believed neither of these things, yet Saigon was certainly solving something; and how could you feel relieved unless you had been in pain?

The city made him feel he could be many people, that in his middle thirties he was nowhere near the finished version of himself, and that even if he ever got there, that too might turn out to be provisional — not a stable compound of temperament and experience, but a bundle of momentary inclinations.

★   ★   ★

Frank crumbled his bread roll and sipped the iced water on the table. Kennedy's speech in Minneapolis had a little more Democratic self-congratulation than usual for the sake of his Jefferson — Jackson day audience, but otherwise varied little from the set routine. Alcohol was not served, and when Frank returned to his hotel he went to the bar.

After two whisky sours he felt better, and was thinking of going up to his room; he was returning to New York the following morning and had arranged to see Mary in the evening. From the reception area he heard an English voice.

'Can you tell me where the downtown is?'

'What exactly are you looking for, sir?' said the desk clerk.

'Anything. Some sign of life.'

The voice, though neither raised nor slurred, was recognizably Charlie van der Linden's.

'What do you mean there's no downtown?

There must be.' Charlie's manner was playful rather than abusive. Frank found a smile twitching at his lips, but made no move from his seat.

It was inevitable, he thought, that Charlie, thwarted in his search for action, would resort to the hotel bar, and a few moments later he was aware of a tall presence and an English voice muttering amiably beneath its breath a few feet away.

Frank turned to him in the cocktail gloom. 'Welcome to Minneapolis, pal.'

Charlie peered for a minute, partly because it was so dark, partly Frank thought, because he was trying to remember his name. 'Frank!' he said triumphantly. 'Christ, it's nice to see you.'

Frank had never before come face to face with a man with whose wife he was sleeping, but the tone of Charlie's voice was familiar enough: it was that of a lonely traveller whose problems have suddenly been solved.

'Have a drink,' Charlie said. 'God, what a place.'

Frank thought any sign of reserve might seem suspicious, so accepted the drink and the prospect of a long evening. It was the last Kennedy event Charlie was required to attend before the Convention, and he was clearly relieved that the end was in sight.

'You heading back to Washington?'

'You bet. Even the tedium of the embassy's preferable to . . . this.' Charlie made a gesture that included hotels, travel, politics, teetotal dinners and all of Minnesota.

219

But your wife won't be there, thought Frank. She'll be naked in my bed.

Charlie looked at him and smiled. Frank looked back into Charlie's face. Its handsome lines were starting to break up; the cheeks were badly shaved, there were gathering pouches on the jaw and fleshy rings developing beneath the eyes. Frank smiled back candidly.

He drank quickly, to quell his misgivings and to catch up with Charlie. He started to grow used to the strange nature of his situation; the guilt began to ebb. It reminded him of what he had told Roxanne about killing a man. After a while it feels like everything you do: it feels like nothing at all.

By the time the barman said he would like to close up, all that Frank felt towards Charlie was a sentimental warmth, a desire to put his arm around him in a sincere embrace. When Charlie mentioned the supply of scotch in his room, Frank accepted with vehement gratitude. By two in the morning, he was even drunker than Charlie; he was sitting on the edge of the bed, haranguing him about the FBI.

'This beautiful country . . . Such a time in its life. But those bastards, you know, they killed my best friend . . . They almost finished my career. They're in everything. A mist you can't see.'

'I know,' said Charlie, blinking at Frank's passion. 'There was someone I met in Vietnam — '

'Yeah, what the hell were you doing in Vietnam? I meant to ask you.'

'We were in Tokyo at the time. The

Ambassador was getting leant on by the Foreign Office in the usual way. Eden was getting an earful from Dulles about why didn't Britain join in. And we'd just finished in Malaya, given up India, we didn't want to get involved in a French problem, particularly when they'd been so useless in the War.'

'Sure. But how d'you get up to Dien Bien Phu?'

★ ★ ★

Charlie was leaning against a warehouse off the Boulevard de la Somme, overlooking the Saigon River, where American planes were being unloaded from transport ships by the light of flares. He had been taken to dinner at a restaurant on the Boulevard Charner and afterwards felt the need to see something for himself, without Barrett and Walther interpreting everything for him through the lens of American interest. He had asked if they could organize for him to go up to Dien Bien Phu, where the French were preparing for a decisive head-on conflict with the Vietminh, but they seemed unwilling. He thought that perhaps they had scented a gestating disaster, which made him more curious, but without the help of an authorized agency he could not make the trip. His British colleagues had been correct but unco-operative, and he had just arrived at the stage in his life when he was becoming reckless.

He was mildly drunk on French wine and had his fortune told with cards on top of an upturned crate in front of a warehouse. 'You will be a rich man,' the fortune teller told him in his almost incomprehensible French-Vietnamese. 'You will be rich in love. You will not live to old age. Many dangers lie ahead.' Seldom could a greasy Jack of Clubs have been so eloquent, Charlie thought, as he produced some coins from his pocket and moved off.

There was still activity on the Boulevard de la Somme, with barbers shaving customers by torchlight beneath the trees and stalls selling noodle soup or rice with fermented fish sauce. On the waterfront, Charlie kept a distance from the ships, whose unloading was performed under armed guard. He lit a cigarette and leaned back in the doorway. His thoughts turned to home and to Mary, whom he pictured reading alone in the bare sitting room of their Tokyo apartment, her ear tuned to any sound that might come from the children's room, where two-year-old Richard lightly slept. Mary had her self-balancing temperament, her inner gyroscope; Louisa had her quietly intense interests; he himself still had the capacity for exhilaration; but Richard had something none of the others did: a riotous passion for each day and a delight in its details. His demands were irresistible; his candour disarmed rebuke. He had become seigneurial in his attitude to their discreet Japanese lodging; when he returned from his walk in the park, he would go into the living room, throw open the door on to the terrace and, standing on the threshold with his rosy genitals resting on the ledge of his half-mast pants, micturate resoundingly on to the gravel.

At the thought of his small son, Charlie was smiling a little in the gloom when a voice made him start. 'Pardon me. You got a light?'

In the glow of the match, Charlie saw a young man with an unmistakably American crew-cut. 'My name's Moone. Buy you a beer?'

Charlie's instinctive recoil was lost to his reflex affirmative. In a brightly lit café over cheap half-litres of beer, Charlie told Moone he was a salesman for electrical goods.

'Sure,' said Moone.

They talked about the war. 'The French are doing a pretty good job up there,' said Moone.

'I hear they're surrounded.'

'You want to go take a look? I could fix it for you.'

'Why would I want to do that?'

Moone shrugged. 'Just thought you might be interested. There's been a flow of visitors for weeks. Reporters go up all the time. I know people who could fix it. Soon the rains'll come and it'll be too late. Know how much rain they'll be getting in the next three months? Five feet. You hear that? Five feet. So now's the time to go. But not if you're not interested.'

'No, I'm not.'

After two more beers, Moone made another suggestion. 'You ever smoke opium?'

Charlie smiled at the tidy young man with his sky-blue seersucker jacket and cleanly shaved face with its coins of topical acne. 'I suppose you can fix that too,' he said.

'It's not difficult,' said Moone. 'There's a

223

dozen places in this block. I know the best. You know how it feels when you drink a big dry martini before lunch? Feel like you're king of the heap? It's a lot better.'

He led Charlie to another café, then up two flights of stairs to a dark landing, where he told him to wait. Eventually, a young Annamite woman came out and led Charlie into a dark sitting room with low couches round the walls. Moone, who was already sitting down, grinned at him encouragingly as the woman set to work, heating a bubbling lump of brown opium over a flame.

'When she gives it you, suck it all down in one go,' he said.

The woman looked bored by the procedure, though her hands moved dexterously. The pipe was made of bamboo, unadorned, with a bowl cut into it where the woman kneaded the gum on a pin. When it was ready, she plunged it into the bowl and reversed the pipe over the flame, so the opium drew smoothly as she held the pipe out to Charlie. She helped keep it steady as he sucked in the smoke and held it in his lungs. As soon as he had exhaled and released the pipe, she began the process again with a weary efficiency; it made Charlie think of a waggish landlord in a village pub with his regular tankards and china beer handles.

After his third pipe, he felt no alteration in himself or his body, but what he could only describe as a philosophical shift of gravity. The world had shed a skin and revealed its magnificence. Charlie could see that he had previously been deceived into thinking that there was something bitter, tense and self-defeating about the brief human passage through an existence devoid of meaning. Now he could see that the world was not like that at all, but an intricate mechanism of boundless yet quite lucid beauty which was entirely comprehensible to the regal power of his intellect. There was no fear, no doubt, no death; the idea of calamity or grief was absurd. He could perhaps imagine unhappiness, but only as an hypothesis that had no real existence. The truth of bliss, meanwhile, was everlasting and was underwritten by the calm and powerful reality of the revealed world.

Some hours later, Moone drove him back to the Hotel Continental and saw him up to his room. When Charlie awoke, it was almost eleven and he found a note with Moone's telephone number, saying, 'Call me if you change your mind about the trip north.'

The thought that transcendence could be achieved for so little trouble was a poignant one to Charlie, who was finding that moments of contentment had begun to grow elusive. From his hotel he cabled Tokyo about the possibility of a trip to Dien Bien Phu. It was ill advised to go without knowing who his sponsor was, but he felt confident, in the residual elation of the opium, that all would be well; it would, at the very least, be interesting. The head of his section replied that a major action was thought to be imminent, but told him to trust his own judgement after he had consulted his colleagues in Saigon. Charlie followed the first part of the advice but not the second because he was too impatient with the prudence of bureaucracy. He took the risk. He telephoned Moone and was instructed to report to the military airbase in forty-eight hours' time. Moone left some press accreditation for him at the reception of the Continental, stating that he worked for the BBC; Charlie winced at the deception but thought that he had reached a point from which he could not turn back. His fellow passengers were mostly journalists, though there were a couple of overalled mechanics and one or two others Charlie did not care to ask about. They flew for almost four hours in an American Dakota to Hanoi, then refuelled for the flight west to Dien Bien Phu.

As they began their approach, Charlie noticed that the French camp was in the bottom of the valley; it was a cul-de-sac, from which the only exit was the airstrip itself. It looked like a vast prehistoric village whose inhabitants, not having discovered how to build, were sheltering in various holes in the ground. They saw regular red flashes of Vietminh artillery fire from the intense jungle on the hills; the sound followed a few moments later, then the upward trickling smoke. To have allowed the enemy to take the high ground above a position from which you had no guaranteed means of escape struck Charlie as, to say the least, unorthodox. The second thing he noticed as they came in was that they were under fire; and the third, as they touched down, was that the temporary runway, made of pierced steel plates, was holed by

226

artillery shells. Beside the strip, abandoned, were the still-smouldering remains of an American Flying Boxcar transport and a Cricket reconnaissance aircraft. Red dust was blown through the steel plates of the runway by the propellers as the plane taxied down into a bunker at the end of the strip. They climbed out and went inside a depot where they were given tea by a Senegalese corporal. Charlie spoke as little as possible to the others for fear of giving away his ignorance of journalism. Eventually a French major came in and introduced himself.

'You are the last group of journalists we shall be entertaining. Consider yourselves fortunate, gentlemen.' He spoke in English, with a light Franco-American accent.

He described for them how French para-troopers had taken the area the previous fall and how the engineers had demolished the housing that existed in Dien Bien Phu, previously some sort of administrative outpost, then built a system of strongpoints protecting the centre, which consisted of the depot where they were sitting, the airstrip, the hospital and the headquarters of the camp commander, Colonel de Castries. Each strongpoint had a woman's name — Béatrice, Eliane, Gabrielle, Huguette and so on.

'The locations have been carefully chosen and each has been designed and reinforced by the engineers.' The major paused and gave a small cough. 'There is no truth in the rumour that they are named after Colonel de Castries's mistresses.'

Some of the American newspapermen laughed obligingly.

'The strategy of General Navarre remains the same: to entice the Vietminh out of the jungle into a place where the superior weaponry, training and manpower of the French army can be decisive. Dien Bien Phu is the ideal battleground for us since they must place their artillery on the reverse side of the hills where our planes can destroy it. We will run offensive actions from inside the camp to drive their infantry into the open.'

One of the American reporters, a paunchy grey-haired veteran with a cigar, had a question. 'Couldn't help noticing the fire from the high ground as we came in. Looks like they have some pieces on this side of the hill.'

'We are mounting regular air strikes,' said the major. 'If you look out of the window you can see another flight about to take off.'

'Yeah, but suppose they put the airstrip out of action. How are you going to get out?'

The major smiled. 'They will not, my friend.'

'But suppose they did.' The newsman removed the cigar from his mouth and examined its sodden end.

'The only way out of the camp is to march out victorious. Now then, you will be divided into smaller groups and each will be taken to see one of the strongpoints. You will be billeted there tonight and a flight will take you back to Hanoi tomorrow. Enjoy yourselves, gentlemen.'

Charlie was driven in a Jeep with four other reporters over a trembling Bailey bridge that spanned the narrow Nam Yum River, already beginning to swell with early showers, up a rough road that, at least until the downpours came, was still passable to a sturdy military vehicle.

'C'est la Route Quarante-et-Un. On va à Béatrice,' said the Algerian corporal who was driving. 'La plus belle des maîtresses du colonel.' He showed a gold tooth as he laughed.

Charlie found himself smiling a little as they jolted up the road; there was something profoundly strange about this clearing in the jungle where the flower of St Cyr officers, their heads full of European gunnery tactics, had brought a collection of troops to provoke a people they hardly knew in a colony that had been returned to them after the disgrace of Vichy only because the Americans and British had no use for it. This giant folly of pride, greed and quixotic ambition was about to receive, as far as Charlie could see, a cataclysmic judgement.

Béatrice turned out to be on top of a hill, where it could control Road 41. If any Vietminh artillery was placed on the hills opposite, the corporal explained, the French fighter-bombers and heavy howitzers would silence them at once. Once the Jeep had deposited them, however, it was clear that well-placed enemy artillery was already hitting a strongpoint on a hill to the west.

The corporal laughed. 'Ça, ce n'est rien. Ce n'est que Gabrielle qu'ils essaient de réveiller.' There was another flash of gold.

In a temporary building in the main complex of Béatrice they were left for half an hour until a press liaison officer could be found. Two other

American reporters who had been at Dien Bien Phu for almost a week came in to join them. One was a loud, florid man, complaining about military censorship; the other was lean and quiet with a distracted look in his eye.

Their new guide was a man with considerably less *joie de vivre* than the major or the corporal before him. A pale, bespectacled Parisian captain called Rigaud, he took them to inspect the trench system that his men had dug forward to repel any infantry attacks; it had communication trenches leading to the rear area and a system of reinforced dugouts where radio, first-aid posts and some of the officers were housed.

Charlie turned to the quieter of the two new reporters. 'Christ,' he said. 'It's Verdun.'

The man smiled faintly and looked at the press tag Charlie was wearing round his neck. He held out his hand. 'Frank Renzo,' he said.

'Charlie van der Linden.'

'You Dutch?'

'No, English. I had a Dutch grandfather who came to London on business and married a local girl. Otherwise I'm all English. Have you been here for a while?'

'A few days.'

'Were you in the army during the War?'

'Sure was.'

'So was I. Tell me, am I missing something or are the French about to be buried?'

Frank said, 'See that jungle there? For five months tens of thousands of men and women have been bringing supplies up here. Coolies paid in opium, trucks, mules, reinforced bicycles

230

— they've brought thousands of tons through hundreds of miles of jungle and the French can't see a goddam thing. They've bombed some of the routes, but they haven't found most of them. The Vietminh tie the branches of the trees together overhead to make a tunnel. They have guns all over the hillside — this side, not the other side, where the book says they're meant to be. The Americans have shot infra-red film to try and find them and it's come back blank.'

Charlie looked at Frank and smiled. 'Is your paper interested in this?'

'Not really. They're more interested in Senator McCarthy. I can't get that sonofabitch off the front page. But the *Washington Post* said that if the French are defeated then Paris'll feel the same as London did after your English general surrendered to Washington at Yorktown.'

Captain Rigaud's answers to the reporters' questions were brief and ill-tempered until they returned to the main building at dinnertime. As the mess corporal brought in more bottles of Gevrey-Chambertin with which to quell the taste of the chicken curry, Charlie and Frank managed to manoeuvre Rigaud to one side, where he became mournfully confidential. He told them in English that hardly any of the buildings in the camp were properly reinforced. There was a drastic shortage of timber, and when engineers were sent out to cut trees they were attacked by Vietminh patrols. When they destroyed the local houses to find more materials they succeeded in making all their inhabitants into Communists. The enemy outnumbered them by five to one, Rigaud had been dependably informed. Although his men had started a number of brush fires, there had not been enough time or manpower to burn back the surrounding jungle, with the result that the enemy had laid a trench system that finished, in some places, only fifty metres from the French lines. Sapping out from the front, the Vietminh had then dug mines and filled them with explosives, which they were waiting only for the word from General Giap to detonate.

Rigaud held his scholarly head in his hands. 'I just keep thinking of Paris. The shame of this. I think of how the radio stations will play solemn music and the traffic will stop along the Seine. The rue de Rivoli, the Quai des Grands Augustins.'

The other journalists had left to play cards at the far end of the tin-roofed mess, and the hurricane lamps shed a harsh glow along the empty table. Frank poured more wine into Rigaud's glass.

'You married?' said Charlie.

'Yes,' said Rigaud. 'Since two years. I have one son, who is with my wife actually in Paris. She's expecting another baby. If it's a girl she will not be called Béatrice.'

'What's going to happen?' said Frank.

Rigaud sighed. 'The rain, that's what will happen. In three months there will fall one and a half metres of it. And we'll fight. The Foreign Legion is here after all. The Algerians are good if their officers are good. We have also T'ai tribesmen, but you have to place them between paratroopers and Moroccans, otherwise they run away.'

Charlie said, 'How did you get into this position?'

'A complete failure of Intelligence,' said Rigaud, lighting a French cigarette. 'We were misinformed about their numbers, their weapons and their supplies. Also, their general is better than ours.'

'Where do you suggest we go tomorrow?' said Frank.

'Hanoi. The Hotel Métropole. Have a pastis for me.'

At midnight the other journalists were taken back to the depot at the camp centre for the morning flight, but Charlie decided he would like to see some more. He said goodnight to Rigaud, who made off for his quarters, unsteadily, taking a candle and a copy of Montaigne's *Essais*. Frank had disappeared.

Charlie slept well on an army cot in a storeroom. He was not frightened of the crunching mortars or the occasional thump and screech of artillery. He had been an infantryman himself for two years from 1942; he had commanded a company in Tunisia and Italy before being transferred to Intelligence. The situation in Dien Bien Phu was bizarre, but it was not boring, and it appealed to his sardonic sense of history; at this stage of his life his nerves were still well sheathed.

There was nothing to eat for breakfast, though there was the sound of mortar fire directed at Road 41. Béatrice was surrounded, and it took a battalion guarded by two tank platoons to get drinking water up from the river.

Charlie saw Rigaud at the end of a corridor, running to a communication room. 'You'd better get out,' said Rigaud, who looked pale and hung-over. 'We're clearing the road now. The corporal will take you back to the airfield.'

Charlie walked to the edge of the position, where thick barbed wire was mined with anti-personnel charges. In the valley below he could see French fighter-bombers coming in from the south-west, over strongpoint Dominique, and setting fire to the road, the adjacent trees and any enemy soldiers in the way with napalm bombs. Towards eleven it was considered quiet enough for vehicles to move off, and the Jeep went back along the blackened road, where a platoon of T'ai tribesmen were bayoneting the burned Vietminh survivors. Charlie had never seen the effects of napalm before, nor smelled its fierce odour.

In the main depot area, he made contact with the urbane major of the previous day, who seemed pleased with the way things were going and happy to accommodate Charlie's desire to stay a little longer.

'Nation shall speak unto nation,' he said.

'I beg your pardon?'

'The BBC. Is that not your corporation's motto?'

'Yes, of course.'

In mid-afternoon, two French reporters landed in a Dakota, and that evening Charlie dined with them and the major in the officers' mess. The cheese course was interrupted by the sound of shells landing on the airfield outside the window and the Frenchmen, who knew the situation well, went to investigate this unsuspected enemy firepower. Twenty minutes later they were brought back into the mess by stretcher-bearers. One was dead and one was missing his right foot. Charlie asked the major if he had seen Frank, but apparently he had made off somewhere in Huguette with an Algerian driver he had befriended.

The next day Dien Bien Phu came under attack on all sides, and in the evening came the news that Béatrice was already on the point of falling. The reinforced bunkers, the trenches, the dugouts and the little tin-roofed buildings had collapsed one after another beneath a bombardment that exceeded the direst intelligence estimates. The Vietminh infantry had poured through the rudimentary trench defence system, up the hill and on to the heights. The French commander was dead; almost all the senior officers were dead; it was believed that the handful of men left were commanded by master-sergeants.

Charlie was denied his request to be shown another defensive strongpoint; the major, whose *joie de vivre* was evaporating, told him to stay in the depot, where he sat up during the night, thinking of Rigaud and wondering how the news would be broken to his young wife in her modest apartment. He pictured her as a thin, severe, woman with dark hair dragged back into a bun; he imagined her living in a modest flat in

Neuilly, bare apart from a few coloured toys for the two-year-old boy.

The duty Charlie had least enjoyed during his own war was writing to the families of men who had been killed. It was necessary to be straight and simple, to talk of country and duty, then briefly to conjure some individual detail, if he could, about the dead man. It was the replies that he dreaded. They varied in their degree of literacy and their length, but almost all had the same modesty: a submissive stoicism that placed the will of a formless providence above the most fiercely valued, deeply loved possession that they had ever had. 'We would have kept him,' one had said, 'but God knew best.'

The letters made it impossible for him to waver; as his battalion worked its way up Italy, he thought of the addresses from which the letters had come — the houses, lanes, the terraced streets of industrial towns — and pushed himself through the swirling blood of the River Rapido and on through the early rains of winter up into the hills, where his company was supplied by sodden mules. After four months of shellfire, some close at hand yet making little noise, some distant but making him leap in fear, he had eventually come to think himself immune. He did not hear the one that hit him, though he was aware some time later of gentle hands removing his helmet and of shocked voices commenting on what they saw within.

He was nursed in a hospital in Florence. The shell fragment had pierced his helmet and his skull, but as far as the doctors could see it had caused no damage to the brain itself. The condition of his twenty-four-year-old body, fatless, undamaged by alcohol, conditioned by continuous physical endeavour, had enabled him to survive. When he was able to know what was going on, he was told that his company had been cut off in heavy fighting: some had been killed, some taken prisoner, and the survivors were being reassigned to other units. His own company had ceased to exist.

As he gradually regained his strength, Charlie went for walks about Florence, to the churches and to such of the museums as were open. He was susceptible to headaches and amnesia, but what he could never forget were the letters of condolence that he should have written. He presumed that his second-in-command would have taken on the task, but later he learned that he had been killed. He could not bear to think of the modest houses where they would pull the curtains early and feel the bitterness of loss because the parents or the wife had not received the words of comfort that were his to write.

Florence in winter was dark with the chill of the Middle Ages, and Charlie felt himself flood with its coldness as he walked by the river or dined alone in an under-stocked restaurant lit by candles. While his company had existed, it had been possible to believe in something beyond the foul-mouthed humans who comprised it; he had been able, if not quite to share, at least to be inspired by the sentiments of the dead men's families. Now everything seemed reduced to its essential parts; the frescoes and statuary of the

237

city that had once seemed to transcend their origins to reach a universal eloquence had come to look like nothing more than assertions of existence, limited by the prevailing ignorance of their time.

On the third morning in Dien Bien Phu, he was ordered to leave the camp. A place had been found for him on a press plane. It belonged to an American journalist who had gone missing, and they were anxious to evacuate all civilians — 'while it's still possible' were the words the major did not utter, but which clearly lay behind his urgency.

In the afternoon the French artillery laid its largest barrage so far towards the western hills, while such planes as had been able to take off attacked the eastern Vietminh positions. Under this defensive cover, the French engineers with their American technicians went out on to the runway to remove the damaged steel plates and cobble together a usable surface with replacements.

Charlie watched from inside the depot with the major, whose demeanour was that of a man who has been appallingly deceived. To take his mind off what was going on, Charlie talked to him about France, the places he had visited and the writers he had enjoyed.

'Rigaud is dead,' said the Major. 'I've just heard.'

Towards dusk Charlie was told to go to the bunker at the end of the runway, where two Dakotas full of wounded men were turning their engines over. Torchlight messages were shot from the darkness of the runway ahead, as the French barrage momentarily stopped and the Vietminh guns began to find the range of the airstrip again.

Inside the bunker the pilot revved the engines until the noise sounded as though it would not only burst the airframe but bring down the concrete shelter itself. Eventually the lightless plane shot forward on to the holed steel of the runway, bouncing and roaring as the shells lit up the jungle on both sides. The nose lifted and Charlie saw the pilot's hands shaking as he tried to hold the plane steady. As they rose above the camp, they saw the boiling orange of tracer fire coming up towards them from the anti-aircraft batteries concealed in the trees, but the propellers kept on churning up the humid air as the aircraft steeply rose, then banked, and headed east, towards the haven of Hanoi.

★ ★ ★

In the hotel room in Minneapolis, Charlie rotated the empty glass in his fingers for a moment before leaning across where Frank was sitting on the edge of the bed to reach for the bottle.

'What did you do in Hanoi?' said Frank.

'Had a pastis at the Métropole. Then caught a flight back to Saigon. There was a message for me at the hotel from this character Moone asking me to call to fix a rendezvous. I never went. I reported back to the Embassy in Tokyo. I didn't tell them I'd been up north, I just said that on no account should we get mixed up in this fiasco. I think they'd already worked that one out. When did you get out of the camp?'

'A few days later. In a helicopter ambulance. I'd missed my place on the plane.'

'Maybe that was the one I took. Maybe you saved my life.'

'I don't think so,' Frank said quickly. He did not want some entanglement of gratitude. 'When the French surrendered I finally managed to get a piece in the paper. Not the front page, though. Page three. The front page was still McCarthy. We never could get American readers interested in that place.'

'Just too far away to seem real, I suppose.'

'Sure. Where did you go next?'

'London. That's what you do as a rule, you alternate a stint abroad with a spell at home.' Charlie had some difficulty with the sibilants. 'I'd done Moscow and Tokyo so I was due some paperwork. I was meant to go to Paris next, but then they decided they'd send me over here. Soon after we'd arrived in Washington I got a call from someone who said he wanted to meet. He seemed to know a lot about me. I met him for a drink in a hotel and he dragged up a lot of stuff out of my past.'

'Like what?'

Charlie sighed. 'Well, Moscow for a start. That had been my first posting. I was on my own there most of the time because Mary was looking after Louisa in London. This man seemed interested in who I'd known there. Also about Tokyo. There . . . there was a girl in Tokyo. Her name was

Hiroko. It was just an innocent thing, a flirtation really.'

'Did Mary know?' The name was awkward in Frank's mouth.

'God, no. We hadn't been married long. I mean the children were, whatever, two and four or something. And Mary was a different matter anyway. She was the woman I was going to spend my life with. She's an extraordinary person. There's no one else like her.'

Charlie stopped and looked at Frank, as though the rhythm of the exchange required him to say something, and he nodded politely. 'Sure.'

'Anyway,' said Charlie, 'there was this girl, Hiroko. It was happening to diplomats all the time. They were being set up with girls, compromised, then blackmailed. But I wasn't set up, it was my initiative. And it was usually by the Russians. I mean, this creep in Washington was American. And there was other stuff. They mentioned opium. It was as though he was trying to make out I was some kind of drug dealer.'

'What did you say?' said Frank.

'I told him to fuck off. But I kept getting calls. They seemed to be searching for something they could latch on to.'

'Did you tell your boss?'

'I couldn't. I'd lost a lot of money in Tokyo, dealing in shares. And . . . It was difficult. It was complicated. I hadn't quite played by the rules, financially, but I desperately needed the cash.'

'But these problems started in Saigon?' said Frank.

'I think so.'

'Sounds like this guy Moone was on the case, doesn't it? I remember him, the little piece of shit. A kind of informers' informer. No real affiliation, he'd take it up the ass from anyone.'

'The odd thing was', said Charlie, 'that at the end of the war, I'd been posted to army Intelligence in Berlin. It was fascinating work, and when I was demobilized in '46 they sent me for an interview with someone from an anonymous department of the Foreign Office. He said I was the kind of man they were looking for . . . linguist, patriotic, whatever. He wanted me to go and train at some place in Portsmouth. I knew what he was suggesting, but I wasn't interested. I looked under the desk and I noticed he was wearing sandals.'

'In London?'

'Yes.'

'And that's what decided you?'

'Pretty much. He had maroon socks underneath.' Charlie smiled briefly. 'I could see the way Europe was shaping up, I could see what scope there was going to be for this kind of thing. But I was idealistic. I thought the war had been worth fighting and I didn't want to go off and start recruiting Nazis to work for us against the Russians. So I applied to the Diplomatic Service and took the exam.'

'You went in the front door.'

'Yes. And that's the way it's been. But about every six weeks I had to go and see this man called O'Brien in a hotel in Arlington. There's some other monkey in a mac with him. I got so worn down by it. In the end I called on Duncan Trench. He's supposed to have a job in Chancery, but everyone knows what he does.'

'I think I met him at your party,' said Frank. 'Guy with a face like a blowfish?'

'That's him. He says he can get them off my back. In return I just have to 'keep in touch' as he calls it.'

'Doesn't sound too good.'

'The trouble is, I'm in a bad state. I can't even get on a plane without taking a truckload of sedatives. And, you know, I go to see this analyst, and that's all complicated because they bring that up, too, O'Brien and the other gorilla, as though they've read the file and discovered some big secret I've confided to the shrink. Christ, if only. We're both in the complete bloody dark.'

Frank pulled the last cigarette from his pack on the table. He could already feel his hangover beginning, the liver cringing, the brain expanding hard against the skull.

Charlie stood up, slowly, and went over to the window, where he pulled back the curtain. He breathed in very deeply, though Frank heard the constricted emotion in his chest as he did so.

'Isn't that a pretty sight?' Charlie said. 'Sunrise over Minnesota.'

He turned round and stood with his back to the window, where the grey light filtered through. 'I tell you what,' he said. 'If it wasn't for Mary, I'd just finish it. I had a life and it interested me, but I lost it and I don't know when. Florence, maybe, or Saigon. Somewhere. Somewhere I lost it.'

Frank said nothing.

Charlie said, 'I have to help Mary. I think she's having some kind of breakdown because of the children. My analyst told me it happens to women at that time. The children disappear and they wonder what their life's supposed to be. I'd have the children back, but I can't afford it. So she has this book she thinks she's writing in New York. I have to let her go and do it. I suppose she'll come through it. But if it wasn't for her, I'd just . . . finish. Give up.'

Frank looked down. 'What about the kids? Surely they're worth — '

'No,' said Charlie. 'Just Mary. She is my child. It's through her I feel anything that's left on earth for me to feel.'

12

It was a bright July morning and Mary was reading the newspaper; she sat beneath the basketball hoop in the backyard at Number 1064 with the remains of breakfast still on the table before her. The headline on the main story had the two-sentence structure she liked: 'Kennedy Heads for Los Angeles, Has Chance to Win on First Ballot'.

'The upcoming Democratic Convention is generating an unusual excitement,' wrote the editorial-page columnist, a violent drunk and philanderer, according to Frank, 'even among those not politically minded. It was one thing for John Kennedy to have overcome Hubert Humphrey in the Badger State, where his father could ensure that every sheriff race was well funded in his favor. It was a greater achievement to have persuaded the Protestant voters of West Virginia that his religion was of no consequence. But Los Angeles will be quite a different task for the likeable young senator from Massachusetts. Here, without Pop's help, he must sway the union bosses and the power-brokers of Chicago and the South — in the convention hall, with the big contenders still waiting their moment to enter the race. It is no exaggeration to say that America holds its breath to see if the young man can pull it off.'

Mary put the paper down beside the coffee

percolator. Excitement was intense in Number 1064 as well, even among those not politically minded. Charlie had suggested she accompany him to the Convention and she had agreed to go, ostensibly both to keep him company and to visit Patricia Rosewell, a friend from London, who had been fruitlessly inviting the van der Lindens out West since marrying a Californian lawyer and settling in some remote canyon five years earlier. Patricia had sounded pleased at the prospect of seeing them and talked of putting on a dinner party for them. Was there anyone they would like her to ask?

Charlie was dreading the visit to Los Angeles, but knew that he could not decline or sidestep it. He had kept the extent of his problems largely hidden from his superiors; the loyalty of colleagues such as Edward Renshaw and his own adroit handling of two potentially awkward demands from London had diverted critical scrutiny. His closeness to the Kennedy campaign, however, had been much talked of in his department and the Convention was the place where he had to demonstrate it.

After sleeping through most of the flight, he emerged from the airport building on Mary's arm and went unsteadily towards the taxi rank.

Patricia's house was approached by a winding road flanked by hissing green grass where the sprinklers played in front of Mexican adobe façades, Gothic turrets and timbered Tudor bungalows rendered oddly homogeneous by the bland wash of sunshine in which they glowed. Patricia's own dwelling was in the ranch style with a wooden veranda and views down to the Pacific, or at least to the turbulent haze that lay across it.

She took Mary and Charlie into the backyard and sat them beneath an orange tree, among white oleanders and strident purple bougain-villea, while she fetched iced tea.

★ ★ ★

Meanwhile, in his functional hotel room in Santa Monica, with whitewood table lamps and Formica surfaces, Frank laid out the Smith-Corona, pens and a notebook. He called room service for some beer and potato chips, then settled on to the bed to do some telephoning.

It was extraordinary how much journalism in the end came down to the same thing. In Saigon or Washington, Dallas or Seoul, it was a list of telephone numbers culled from friends and colleagues, a spiral ring-bound notebook, three pillows behind the back, and the telephone receiver lodged between shoulder and ear while the minutes to deadline ticked away on the bedside clock. Sometimes he never even had time to look out of the window.

He disliked the first moment of the call, when he had to introduce himself. He had heard one or two others in the newsroom — Headley Adams, for instance, with his Harvard manner — and noticed how they seemed at once to be taken into the confidence of the person they had called; within a few minutes Adams was laughing with his bench-made shoes up on the desk and

247

inviting the stranger to lunch at his club. Billy Foy maintained there was a form of words with which they did it: a Masonic trick or incantation that was universally recognized. 'Listen Frank, it's like when you pick up the phone. Someone asks for you by name, do you say, 'Yep' or do you say 'This is he'? These guys say something, I can't figure out what, and it means, 'Can I kiss your ass for twenty minutes but I promise not to drop your name, or to screw your daughter, and I'll vote Republican if that's what you'd like.' It's a bond, it's a brotherhood of classy guys. You with me?'

Frank worked his way down the names on his list, marking off those who would call back or could not help. He wanted to know who Kennedy's choice of running mate would be if he won, and his problem was that the press secretaries still viewed him with suspicion, particularly when his reports had been less adoring of the candidate than his predecessor's; they also knew that he would switch to the Nixon campaign after the Convention, so that he was not a good investment of their time.

Frank took a cab downtown to Pershing Square and found a place reserved for him in the Press Room at the Biltmore; there was a telephone, an ashtray and some paper cups, one of which he went to fill at the water dispenser. Other reporters lounged about the room, reading the newspapers, gossiping about the first ballot.

A young man in a blue bow tie, someone new to Frank, said, 'Stu Symington's still the best bet.'

The others in the group looked sceptical, but a little worried.

'Kennedy'll make it all right,' said one of the older men. 'It won't be a stampede, but he'll get it.'

'If he gets Illinois and Pennsylvania,' said the assured youth with the bow tie. 'But it's a big if. Otherwise Symington has to have a chance. Or Stevenson. It's not too late for Adlai.'

The men dispersed to their typewriters and telephones, muttering dismissively, but manifestly upset by the young man's conviction that the outcome was not yet decided. They wanted no surprises; they wanted to be right; they wanted the same story.

'You Mr Renzo?' It was a young woman with a Kennedy button on her bosom.

'Yep.'

'Message for you.' She handed him a piece of paper, and a small device attached to her belt let out an electronic squeal. She unhooked it and lifted it to her mouth. 'Sure. I'll be right over.'

Frank looked at her in surprise: it was the first time he had seen people communicate in this way. It would, he thought, have been helpful in Guadalcanal.

The message was from Mary: a telephone number. Frank put it in his pocket. He did not want thoughts of Mary to distract him; he would not think of her sitting up there in the canyon in her summer dress, slim legs tucked in beneath her as she read her book, waiting for his call, her dark hair pushed back by sunglasses, smiling with those full lips that always looked to him as though they could have been sculpted from clay then decisively finished at the edge with a sharp knife. Her lips were very . . . how would you put this . . . three-dimensional.

He called the number anyway and spoke to Patricia Rosewell, who put Mary on the line.

'Hello, Frank. Where are you?'

Her English voice sounded cool, yet heavy with possibility; it sent a shudder through him, as when someone is said to walk over your grave.

'I'm at the Biltmore. You coming down?'

'We'll come on Monday, for the count.'

Her daring amazed Frank. She must be lying to Charlie, at least by omission, but she never seemed tense; and if she wanted to see him in New York, she just took the train.

'I'll be working through the count,' he said. 'I won't see you. I have an early deadline because of the time difference. Where's Charlie?'

'I don't know.' There was a pause, then Mary said, 'Why don't you come up here for dinner? Patricia's inviting a few people.'

Frank rapidly calculated what he needed to do and whether he could make it in time.

★   ★   ★

The sun was sinking as the taxi went up Sepulveda Boulevard and right on to the ridge of Mulholland; the driver went slowly, as though uncertain that he was allowed on such an elevated road, anxious not to trigger some neurotic security system. Beneath and to the right, Frank could still just make out the tall buildings of downtown, dim giants in a grey steam bath.

Night had fallen by the time they arrived; it was hot and heavy with the sound of hummingbirds and cicadas. Frank had showered in his hotel, but the humid interior of the car had made his clean shirt stick to his back beneath his suit. He ran a finger round his collar as he walked up some crazy paving between the sodden lawns and rang the bell; the maid, in a pink apron and frilled hat, showed him outside to a table with a linen cloth and a bar set up on it. A Spanish-looking man trowelled out chunks of ice into a glass, poured bourbon over it and wrapped it in a paper napkin. Frank took the drink on to the veranda, where he caught Mary's eye in the lamplight; she came through the dozen people that separated them and laid her hand lightly on his wrist.

'Come and meet Patricia.'

Frank could sense how much Mary was enjoying his presence and the formal way in which she introduced him to his hostess, a tall woman with an equine face and uncorrected teeth.

'Hi, Charlie,' he said, turning to his right.

'Hello, Frank. Enjoying yourself? Got a drink, have you?' Charlie seemed reasonably in control.

'Come on.' Frank felt Mary's hand on his elbow. 'There are some more people you should meet.'

Away from Charlie, Mary's manner relaxed again as she introduced him to a group of three women on the edge of the veranda. All the guests were in suits or cocktail dresses, but while the others were talking Democratic politics, these three were discussing their vacation plans.

'Is that a Chesterfield?' said one of them, watching Frank take a cigarette from his pack. 'May I?'

'Sure.'

Mary was leaning with her back to the wooden railing, so that her hair was for a moment outlined by the light of the torches planted in the lawn behind, and it reminded Frank of the first time he had seen her, standing in front of the lamp in the living room at Number 1064. She stood watching him with a half-smile on her face, as though she was expecting him to perform for her pleasure.

The other women drew him into their conversation about the merits of Maine, Mexico or even Europe for their next trip, and they seemed to defer to him, to seek his opinion with particular urgency. All the time, he sensed the dangerous languor of Mary's body; she was wearing a dress with a full-bodied skirt, a cotton print of enormous roses on long green stems, and he saw the way her thighs were arched forward as the small of her back was supported by the rail of the veranda. She had one shoe off and was carelessly rotating it on its heel with her toe. While he heard the words of idle conversation — beach, hotel, weather — he suddenly pictured Mary naked beneath her knee-length dress; he saw it rise up her thighs and felt his hand run up beneath it till it touched the fine black hair on its shy promontory and the

252

parted flesh beneath; he caught her eye and he knew with certainty as he did so that she had registered what he was thinking, and that she approved.

'I guess Europe seems a long way to go,' he said thickly, ashamed of the picture in his mind as he tried to grapple with the conversation.

'So have you been to Europe?' one of the women asked him.

'Yeah,' he said, gathering himself a little. 'But only to take life.'

'Come and get some dinner, you guys,' said Patricia Rosewell's husband. 'Juan's set up a barbecue. We have shrimp and corn and steaks with his special chili sauce.'

In the dark press of people moving off the veranda and down towards the garden, Frank stood behind Mary and allowed the back of his hand to brush over her dress.

★ ★ ★

He slept badly that night. The rattle of the hotel room's air-conditioner did not disturb him, in fact it reminded him of home, but thoughts of Mary would not leave him. It could not really be that she had lost that English innocence, that motherly sweetness that made her sing 'Some Enchanted Evening' in his shower; yet on the dusky veranda she had seemed like a force of nature that had somehow sought out the landscape of his longing and moulded itself to each contour. He went to the bathroom, splashed water on his face and took some

253

aspirin; but he was weary and red-eyed when he woke the next day.

He made it to an unscheduled press conference where Lyndon Johnson's aide, John Connally, pointed out that Kennedy was suffering from Addison's disease, a degenerative malfunction of the adrenal gland that, in the absence of regular cortisone treatment, would eventually kill him. Pierre Salinger, Kennedy's press secretary, put out a statement saying that the claim was 'despicable'. It seemed to Frank that it certainly showed a degree of desperation on Johnson's part, and he decided to go and see if the other purported front-runner for the nomination, Stuart Symington, was also being forced to consider extreme disclosures. He was particularly interested to see whether he would mention the activity that Kennedy himself referred to as his 'girling'.

It was easy enough to find out where Symington's headquarters were, and Frank walked slowly down the hotel corridor, bracing himself for the encounter. He would need to talk his way past the security and the administration, but he calculated that Symington would want to be interviewed.

The door to the suite was open, but the rooms were empty. There were mimeograph machines, several desks set up with extra telephone lines, noticeboards and charts of the states and their delegate strengths; there were typewriters and soda machines set to dispense free drinks, but there were no people. If Symington's own team had evidently concluded that Kennedy was going to win on the first ballot, there seemed little left to do but report the voting.

He was late arriving and the hall was already full. The delegates with their placards and balloons and their striped hats did not look like political movers; they looked like vaudeville players or workers in a candy factory with an open day for children. Seated on the press platform, Frank felt a mild revulsion from them, something he sensed, from their resigned looks, that was shared by the other reporters. Only the young man in the bow tie still looked as though he expected a surprise; Frank saw him point to the galleries, which were filled with excited, chattering people.

All sense of world-weariness evaporated when Eugene McCarthy spoke to nominate Adlai Stevenson. The mounting passion of the speech went through the hall like wind through a cornfield; the people in the gallery revealed themselves to be Stevenson's as they raised their arms and cheered in response to McCarthy's unexpected eloquence. Frank thought for a moment of his part-namesake, Joe McCarthy, dead of cirrhosis at forty-eight three years earlier: what he might have given for such oratory. Typewriters began to smack and clatter in Frank's ears, as East Coast reporters set to work, frightened by the thought of missing a sensation to their early deadline, while the Biltmore echoed to the sound of Stevenson's name and stamping feet.

Frank checked his watch. There was no way of knowing if the galleries' enthusiasm would actually affect the voting of the delegates, but if he waited till the count was done it would be too late to write the story of Kennedy's dramatic setback. He would have to write it for real, as though it had happened, then, if it didn't, he could change a few words and drop the whole description down the story. When the Philadelphia caucus resulted in sixty-four of its eighty-one delegates going to Kennedy, he began to tone down his account of the great upset, but it was not until the end of the roll-call, when Wyoming pushed Kennedy over the limit, that he was finally free to reorder the pages, change 'developed unstoppable momentum' to 'momentarily threatened' and 'major upset' to 'predicted outcome', briefly describe Kennedy's surprisingly limp acceptance speech and hurry up to the Press Room with his copy.

The next day he heard that Kennedy had asked Symington to run for vice-president. The consensus in the Press Room was that Kennedy had made a mistake; that Symington, as one of the grander columnists put it, was far too shallow a puddle to jump into, and that Kennedy could not beat Nixon without Lyndon Johnson's help in delivering the South. Frank sent over news of this development, telephoned the office to make sure they had no queries, then took a taxi to a restaurant opposite the end of Santa Monica pier, where he had arranged to meet Mary. He drank a dry martini and looked out at the ocean, lying limp against the shore, sparkling beneath the indefatigable light.

He relaxed. They were a long way from

Hagerstown, Maryland, and further still from New Hampshire, with its icy covered bridges, where the campaign had begun. He looked at two Hispanic boys playing ball, heading off along the pier; a girl was following down the boardwalk with a pink hula-hoop. He wondered if politics meant anything at all to them. He himself had been invigorated by the process he had witnessed, but he doubted whether it was of much consequence to anyone beyond the obese women in paper hats on the convention floor and the swarthy union gangsters. He knew that Kennedy's father had said that if his son was not nominated in Los Angeles, he would himself vote for Nixon in November. In his reporting, was he much more than a valet to these rich men?

A waiter was leaning over his table. 'Sir? Mrs van der Linden's sorry, but she can't come. She'll call you later.'

★ ★ ★

Mary had received a call from Dolores in Washington to say that her father was trying to reach her, and so unusual was it for him to resort to the telephone that Mary feared that it could only be bad news. She calculated that it would be a little late for comfort in London, but if her father had thought it important enough to call, then she should risk disturbing them.

Her mother answered. The sound of her voice was other-worldly. Mary stood by a picture window, framed by potted palms, looking down towards the Pacific. High in the almost cloudless sky she could see the vapour trail of a silently ascending airliner; at her feet was the polished wood of the floor, reflecting the even Californian sunshine. In her ears was Elizabeth's voice, a little tired, sometimes echoing or delayed, but bearing its essential load: her brisk and habitual indifference to her own comfort; the minor friction of historic rules and remembered battles from Mary's childhood; but above all a comforting partisanship, the fussing, unconditional flow of a mother's love.

It was eventually Mary's father who, after various inquiries about the children and inconsequential pieces of news about London, revealed that Elizabeth had been back to see her specialist. He reported that the cancer had spread and was now inoperable; they could do much to limit the pain, but she would die within a few months.

Mary replaced the receiver and breathed in deeply. She had no desire to weep or rail against what was happening. Her mother, after all, was still alive. Nothing had yet changed.

★   ★   ★

Frank received no call from Mary the following day, so telephoned her the morning after. She explained what had happened and he tried to offer his condolences. He found it difficult, recognizing that in some ways, for all that he felt for her, he scarcely knew Mary. He was relieved that she did not take advantage of his vulnerability on this point; it would have been easy for her to vent a little constricted emotion at his expense, to indulge a petulant self-righteousness about how Frank had never even met her mother. But she took his sympathy graciously, as though Frank were the family's oldest friend, and he admired her for it.

'By the way,' she said, 'Charlie wants to speak to you.'

'Frank? Did you hear about Johnson?' Charlie sounded sober. 'Apparently Kennedy's offered him the vice-presidency.'

'But he's already offered it to Symington.'

'I know. Perhaps he wants to have two.'

'That's crazy.'

'Unprecedented, I think. He's sent Bobby to persuade Johnson to turn it down after all.'

'Jesus, I should go,' said Frank. 'But I can't get past security at the top of the elevator.'

'He has a private lift. Ask the blonde girl at the desk.'

'What's the suite number?'

'Hang on. It's . . . 8315. You going to go?'

'I might as well try.'

Security in the Biltmore Hotel had slackened in the chaos, and Frank found it easy enough to reach the bedroom of Number 8315, which acted as a waiting room to Kennedy's office, housed in the sitting room beyond. Periodically, a woman Frank heard referred to as Mrs Lincoln came in and out of the office; through the open door he briefly glimpsed both Kennedy brothers, Sargent Shriver and John Connally talking and waving their arms; one of them was invariably on the telephone.

There were six others waiting in the bedroom, including a perspiring man with a cigar who called Mrs Lincoln 'Evelyn, honey', but was referred to by her only as 'Senator Bailey' in return. Frank made his request to speak to the candidate. He was sure he would be rejected, but it was helpful to him to be this close to what was going on; Mrs Lincoln said he would have a long wait and told him to help himself to a glass of water. Pierre Salinger appeared from the corridor and went through into the office without knocking; a few minutes later he stuck his head round the door and said, 'Four o'clock in the Bowl downstairs. The announcement. Tell the press.'

Mrs Lincoln reached for the telephone.

'Bobby can't get Lyndon to un-accept,' said the senator with the cigar, smiling widely.

'What do they tell Symington?' said Frank, presuming on the emergency of the moment to join the conversation uninvited.

'Nothing,' said a third man, standing with his ear to the office door. 'Symington knew all along that Jack'd have to ask LBJ. He told me so.'

The traffic of people through the suite continued for another hour. Voices were occasionally raised, but Frank sensed also a comic edge to the commotion; many of these men and women would have no finer moment than this, no time at which they would feel more wanted or more usefully alive.

At five to four Mrs Lincoln stood up portentously and coughed. She opened the door to the office again and for a moment there was silence as the occupants looked out. Kennedy sat behind a desk in his shirtsleeves, leaning back with his hands behind his head; he was smiling. Really, thought Frank, the panic over the identity of the potential vice-president was morbid when Kennedy himself was so young.

A few moments later, they filed out of the sitting room, and those in the bedroom stood back to let them pass. Kennedy smiled at them as he went through, followed by his brother, Shriver and Connally. They were all straightening their ties and jackets, pulling themselves up importantly as they strode out over the patterned carpet.

'We're going down to the Bowl,' said Salinger. 'It's Johnson.'

Frank followed the men down the corridor to the elevator, stepping aside to avoid a room-service wagon that had been left outside number 8309, with a half-eaten hamburger and a glass of untouched iced water with the Biltmore's corrugated paper cap on top of it.

13

The further the van der Lindens' hired Citroën DS travelled into the western parts of Brittany, the more the aroma of pâté, apples and baguette was exhaled by the soft crimson upholstery; each time the hydraulic suspension levelled out a rut, it released into the car the memory of the picnic purchased from the boucherie-charcuterie in the village outside Rennes. The fierce brake was nothing like the spongy pedal on the Kaiser Manhattan, and Louisa and Richard complained at the way it catapulted them into the back of the bench seat in front when Charlie touched the sensitive button with his foot. Mary periodically withdrew the red Michelin guide from the glove compartment as she guided Charlie through the more tangled town centres, hoping that a 'TOUTES DIRECTIONS' would come to her aid. Forwards to her was always north, and she had to twist the fat red book around so that they were travelling up the page at all times — a manoeuvre that she tried to conceal as far as possible from Charlie's sideways glances.

In their absence at school the children had both grown: Louisa's cotton dress was halfway up her thighs and Richard had to leave the waistband of his shorts open. They had developed new enthusiasms and a new argot in which to express them. Mary found that she could no longer follow everything they said — their references to school rituals, peculiar teachers and apocalyptically embarrassing events. They had withdrawn from her a little; they had developed the 'independence' of which the school prospectus boasted, though it looked to her more like a survival reflex. They had been through some sort of cold fire together and had the sardonic shorthand and stoic intimacy of old lags.

The holiday had had a tense and lowering start when they went to stay with Mary's parents in Regent's Park. Elizabeth made every show of normality that she could manage, and the children appeared not to notice that she spent most of the day in bed. Mary was both proud of their tact and resigned to their youthful self-absorption; they played familiar games in the London garden, climbing a half-fallen elder tree, dressing up in their grandparents' old clothes from the loft and leaving behind them a trail of plastic toys that crunched beneath adult feet. The atmosphere in the house was that which people call 'life suspended', Mary thought, though really it was death, not life, that had been temporarily held at bay. When it was time to say goodbye, Elizabeth's brisk fortitude gave no indication of the fact that it was likely to be the last time that she would ever see her grandchildren. Mary did not know whether to stress the gravity of the occasion to Richard and Louisa or whether they already knew quite well but had decided not to make a fuss. So the goodbyes passed off normally, with no more than an extra pressure of the hand, a slight prolonging of the hug, a lingering wave to vision's end from the back seat of the taxi to suggest that it was more than a routine *au revoir*. Only people in their wretched middle age had to face the truth, Mary thought; the slipped responsibilities of the old and young were hers alone to bear.

It was growing dark as they approached their French destination. Mary had found an advertisement in the London *Times* that promised a roomy traditional house with the seaside, tennis and fishing nearby. They had previously taken holidays in hotels, but the state of Charlie's finances made it impossible. He would not have gone on vacation at all, had not the illness of Mary's mother made a trip to Europe inevitable; even the price of an empty house, where they would shop and cook for themselves, was unsustainable until Mary had the idea of inviting another family to share it. The Renshaws were going to Nantucket, and the only European friends of which they liked both partners had already made plans; but Lauren Williams, who had never been to Europe, was enthusiastic, even when Mary stressed how primitive it would be. Her husband — whose name, Mary reminded Charlie, was Vernon — was amenable, and the deal was done. Through someone at the French Embassy, Lauren conjured up a teenage girl from Vannes, who would act as mother's help. The apparent size of the garden convinced Charlie he would have to spend no more than the duration of meals listening to Lauren's animated reminiscences of people he had never met and what they said to people he had never heard of.

Charlie was tired after his day at the wheel and the children's listless bickering had made his nerves shrink and tighten; their raised voices and sudden squeals cracked like rim-shots on the drum of his ear. He had swigged only once from the bottle at lunch for fear of falling asleep, and now he wanted to lay himself down in cool sheets with a pitcher of iced wine at his side, with a window overlooking the orchard through which a cool breeze would mingle with the exhaled smoke of a Pall Mall cigarette. Since most of the villages had similar names, Saint Brieuc, Saint Brion, he and Mary had taken to pronouncing them in an excessively anglophonetic way to avoid confusion. Once, on honeymoon in Italy, such games had seemed a comic way of sharpening the excitement; to Charlie, with his smashing headache, they were by this time an indispensable shortcut to deliverance.

The Citroën slid out of one more rocky town, and Charlie prayed it was the last limp hôtel de ville tricolore he would see recede in his wing mirror as, a mile or so later, they found themselves at an unmarked crossroads. It was almost dark, and Mary had to open the passenger door to shed some light on the map.

'Your guess is as good as mine,' she said.

'That's no good to me,' said Charlie. 'You're the navigator. You have to know. I can't do both.'

Mary glanced across at him in the dusk. 'Don't be cross with me, darling. It's just

265

impossible to say. We should have brought a bigger map.'

Charlie inhaled tightly and made an effort to be genial. 'From my time as an infantryman, in the course of which I have to say I was lost for almost two years, I would say it's definitely that way.'

He pushed the column shift into first and swung the car decisively to the right. Mary read from the owner's directions: 'After about half a mile, you will come to a farmyard with a small stone calvary by the roadside.'

''One ever hangs where shelled roads part,'' said Charlie.

'What?'

'Wilfred Owen.'

''Follow the cart track till you come to a grassy triangle.''

''In this war he too lost a limb.''

''If you come to the boulangerie, you have gone too far.''

'I never go further than the grassy triangle.'

'Daddy! There it is.'

Charlie slowed down and switched the headlights to full beam. In addition to its hydraulically pumped suspension, one of the peculiarities of the car was that its headlights were directional: by use of the steering wheel, Charlie was able to wash the Breton countryside with shafts of bright illumination. Beneath a chestnut tree, they picked out the figure of a hanging Christ.

'The girl's a genius. Let's go.'

'' . . . for two hundred yards, being careful to

266

avoid the ducklings which — ''

'To hell with the ducklings.'

'' . . . past the gate posts, then pull in at the second entrance.''

The rough stones of the the farmyard crunched beneath the Citroën's sedulously levelled entrance; Charlie switched off the engine, and the big car sank to its knees as the suspension hissed away. The children's good humour was restored at once as they clambered from the back and ran round the house to look for a way in. The key to the front door was eventually discovered beneath a pot; Mary occupied herself with the children's clothes, while Richard and Louisa sprinted over the wooden landings. Charlie went in search of liquor.

The house was certainly traditional. It dated from a time when Bretons regarded 'France' as an invented novelty that would not catch on; it had been unaltered since before the Revolution and had resisted all incomers from the threatening Republic, particularly cleaners. There was fresh linen on the beds and the bare floorboards had been perfunctorily swept, but there were cobwebs in the corners and the bedrooms gave off a dry, exhausted smell. There were two bathrooms whose giant cast-iron tubs had rusted water stains, while, through connections to its unknown burial place outside, the septic tank had left a reminder of its proximity. As Mary made her quick inspection, she thought of a farmer's daughter drawing up her knees for warmth and holding on as the telegram boy

267

brought news from Verdun, a French hell in which her brothers and lovers were so reluctantly engaged. She pictured earlier inhabitants, Bovary-type girls wandering through the orchards in their dreams of desire, aching to be free of the anonymous countryside where even Quimper and Vannes and Concarneau seemed unreachably distant. This desire to be loved, without which they would not be alive . . . Silly girls, she thought, folding Louisa's clothes into the drawer of a walnut chest.

Mary's unhappiness at being separated from Frank took the form of anger. She was impatient with the children and found that she disliked the dirty rustic house — miles from America, pointless. She had an aching wish to be back in the United States, to taste cheeseburgers made from grain-fed cattle that gave them that loose texture, to drink a cold martini with an olive; to sit at her corner table in Fiorello's and look down at Teddy Roosevelt on his island while she ate the chocolate dessert with a large espresso in which floated a twist of puckered lemon peel.

The owners of the Breton house had assured them that Madame Bobotte, a neighbour, would have called round in the afternoon to leave them milk, bread and some emergency supplies until they could get to the shops the next day, but a thorough search of the kitchen showed that Madame Bobotte had failed to oblige. There was no address or telephone number for her and it was now too late to find anywhere open, so Mary went through the various cupboards to see what she could find. Behind a floral curtain on a wire, she discovered a fridge with a levered handle like those on the door of a butcher's cold room. It was admirably cold inside, but empty except for a swollen ice-tray dusted with frost crystals of an age to grace a mammoth's tomb. In the dresser were many china dinner services, lidded soup tureens and piled plates of every size, but no food. A pine corner cupboard disclosed some packets of rat poison, a few bottles of dried herbs and a brush made of tied twigs.

Charlie rummaged at the back of his case for his emergency fifth of Wild Turkey. The water in the bathroom ran cloudy in the toothglass, which he cleaned and rinsed with a practised forefinger. Bourbon was the finest disinfectant known to him, and he had no scruple about draining a glass of half whisky and half warm *eau de robinet*, with which he swilled down three Tylenol from his washbag.

He went downstairs to find Mary struggling over the gas in the kitchen. After he had discovered the butane cylinder on the floor, concealed behind another floral curtain on a wire, and spent some time turning the tap this way, that way and halfway, the burner eventually ignited with an explosive thump, causing Mary to leap backwards with a squeal. Charlie resumed his search for liquor, while Mary lifted down a blackened skillet from its hook.

Eventually she was able to offer a dinner that consisted of last year's walnuts fried in nut oil with anchovies, accompanied by most of a week-old baguette sliced and fried, for variation, in olive oil with pepper. There was half a bar of chocolate in the car. Mary drank water, the children drank a diluted grenadine cordial, both chilled with the slightly defrosted and rinsed mammoth's ice, while Charlie drank something he had found at the bottom of a cupboard in the sitting room. It was a pure spirit, but with an oddly viscous surface and some sprigs of herb or plant in the bottle.

'It's rather good actually,' he said. 'Some sort of *eau de vie*, apple or prune or something. You want to try some?'

Mary shook her head. 'It looks disgusting,' she said.

She watched the children's faces as they ate. There was just enough food and it was just sufficiently edible to pass for dinner; together with the sugar of the grenadine and chocolate, it lifted their spirits.

Charlie lit a cigarette, drained his glass and smiled. 'Marvellous supper,' he said. Mary noticed that he had not actually eaten it, but then he hardly ate at all any more.

He began to speculate on the people who lived there, their observation of obscure saints' days, the pious names of their numerous children, their repudiation of alcohol and their fanatical dislike of food. 'We never eat in any month that has a vowel in its name. Which particularly rules out *août*.'

The light was on behind his eyes, Mary saw, and Louisa's extraordinary laugh was gurgling up like water from an unblocked drain. It was almost like the old days and she had to look away.

* * *

It was a beautiful morning, cool and fresh, with air that no one, since the Atlantic rocks were formed, had breathed before, and the promise of sunshine to come. Charlie rose early and drove into Saint Brioche, as he now called it, to buy supplies, which included a plastic paddling pool and water pistols. When he returned to the house, he saw Mary in her white nightdress boiling water in the kitchen. She gestured to him to be quiet, miming that the children were still asleep.

The Williamses arrived shortly before noon with their twins, Douglas and Elliot, and Marie-Laure, the girl from Vannes. Vernon Williams was a bespectacled, unathletic man in his late forties who worked at the State Department. He climbed out of the car and shot his hand out at Charlie to be shaken; Lauren offered her cheek, which, Charlie noticed, was fragrant and freshly powdered even after the tiresome journey.

Mary took the Williamses upstairs to show them where they were sleeping; the children greeted one another with muted hostility, then ran off wordlessly into the garden where there were two barns in states of dangerous disrepair. Charlie slunk down to the orchard with a book and did not return until summoned for lunch, which Mary and Lauren had laid out beneath some pear trees at the back of the house.

Vernon Williams folded away his copy of the *Herald Tribune* and helped himself to cold chicken. 'I can't believe they don't have a shower here,' he said.

His wife laughed. 'It's Europe, honey. Things are a little different.'

Marie-Laure, the mother's help, piled her plate with chicken legs, pâté and salad and lowered her head to the task with small grunts of appreciation. Charlie poured some wine.

Mary said, 'We thought we'd stay in tonight. I'll make dinner, so you can all just relax.' It was the kind of thing Charlie had heard her say a hundred times: helpful, accommodating, selfless. But was he imagining it, or was there an edge of sarcasm, almost of despair, in her voice?

He looked at her, in her navy cotton shirt, white slacks and loafers; she looked a little tired, he thought, but the good thing about Mary was that you never really had to worry about her.

In the course of lunch Charlie was able to disengage his mind and drift. He generally knew what people were going to say from the first few words of their sentences; after that it was a question of keeping an appearance of interest as they struggled on towards the end or, in Lauren's case, were sidetracked before they reached it.

'You look so remote, Charlie,' people used to tell him, which was true, but a quarter of an ear was enough to keep up with what was being said; the remaining part of his attention searched for something else to occupy it, and it was the opinion of his psychoanalyst in Bethesda that this was the root of his problem: that he could not find a constructive or creative outlet for the rest of his mental activity, because he had no talents. So he drank to kill it off. He drowned it.

'Shouldn't I be a repressed homosexual at least?' Charlie had said. 'Or the victim of some forgotten childhood cruelty?'

The analyst did not smile. 'Would you like to be?' he said.

Charlie drank enough wine at lunch to make it possible for him to sleep through the hours from three till five, a time of the day he particularly disliked.

It grew hot in the afternoon and Mary changed into her bathing costume. It was a bikini, the first she had ever owned, black, with trunks that stretched to a squared-off end a little way down the thigh; when she lit the gas to boil water for tea, she felt the warmth of the flame against the bare skin of her belly. Despite being called Sir Winston Churchill Five O'Clock, the tea was too weak to restart Charlie's day with the jolt it required, and he spent another hour on the bed doing a two-day-old *Times* crossword.

★　★　★

Mary laboured alone over dinner. Cooking on holiday, with no guests and worries about time, was normally something she enjoyed, but she felt angry with the recalcitrant stove and annoyed at the stupid Williamses with their gormless children. She could not explain her frustration to anyone, but the pressure of it mounted so much inside her that she had to find some way of venting it. She let out shuddering sighs and swore at the kitchen implements, at Brittany, at the girl from Vannes and at her mother for dying.

At seven o'clock she called Charlie to the kitchen to help her light the oven. Twenty matches later, Charlie summoned Vernon Williams.

Vernon lay on his back on the red tiles of the kitchen floor.

'There's a little hole, just there.'

'Maybe you should light the element on the top.'

'Or is that the grill?'

'Are you sure the gas is on, Charlie?'

'Do you have another match?'

'Is that a pilot light? That's working anyhow.'

'Well, that argues that at least the gas is connected.'

'Didn't they teach you anything at Harvard?'

'Have you tried that little hole up there?'

'This is the last match.'

'Are you all right?'

'Yes. I just banged my head on the door trying to get out of the way.'

'Made a hell of a bang.'

'Still, at least it's working.'

'Yes. What exactly did you do?'

'I'm not too sure.'

Normally this holiday ritual delighted Mary, but she could see no charm in it this time. She banged the cast-iron lid on the casserole and shoved it into the feeble oven. Lauren took the children off for a bath and Charlie poured drinks in the living room. He carried a glass of whisky, Lord McGregor Genuine Scottish from the *épicerie* in Saint Brioche, through to Mary in the kitchen and, to her irritation, put his arms around her as she stood at the sink. She turned to him and forced a smile, pushing a strand of dark hair back from her eyes. He helped himself to one of her cigarettes, which lay in their usual place, next to the cooker.

'Since when have you smoked Chesterfield?'

'I . . . I don't know. They didn't have any Winston. By the way, there's no washing machine here. I'll have to take the clothes to a laundry. Did you see one this morning?'

'I'll go tomorrow.'

Mary cooked a large dinner for them all to make up for the privation of the night before: eggs with home-made mayonnaise and the last of the anchovies, a beef bourguignon with mashed potatoes, and apple pie from the patisserie. Lauren told a long story about Kelly Eberstadt's first husband.

'And what do you think, Mary?' said Vernon Williams. 'You've been very quiet.'

'What do I think about what?'

'About Kelly's husband and her remarriage.'

'I don't have a view. I don't know any of the people. What does it matter anyway? You mate, you die.'

Charlie glanced at her and dismissed Richard and Louisa with a nod. Mary drew up her bare feet beneath her on the chair and lit a cigarette.

'Well,' said Vernon Williams patiently, 'I guess it matters to Kelly.'

'Jesus,' said Lauren, 'these bugs are regular man-eaters.'

275

★ ★ ★

The next day, after the early run to Saint Brioche, Charlie took a pile of books to a deckchair he had installed in a quiet part of the garden, beneath an apple tree, next to a low brick wall with a long view down towards the sea. He was not concerned about Mary; her sharpness was no less than Lauren Williams's conversation deserved, and privately he was pleased by it, wondering if it would allow him to say something similar when Lauren next dilated on her nanny's family's holiday arrangements. It was true that it was unprecedented for Mary to behave in such a way, but the cause of it was clear: her mother. It would pass, and, in any event, worry about Mary was a feeling that the years had removed from his emotional repertoire.

He began to read. These days he could seldom summon the concentration necessary to get through a book and he took it as a good sign that he had managed a hundred pages the day before. *Ars longa, vita brevis*, his father used to warn him, but over the years Charlie had discovered that *ars* was not as *longa* as people made out. Provided you had done the classics young and could clear a couple of youthful summers for Tolstoy, Proust and some of the longer-winded Americans, there was not that much bulk to be afraid of; most of the rest could be taken piecemeal over twenty years. His tolerance had very greatly diminished with age, however, and he reviewed the contents of his teenage shelf — Thomas Hardy, D. H. Lawrence, Fielding, André Gide, Zola, Dostoevsky and Dorothy L. Sayers — with incredulity. He had no desire to re-open a single volume. He disliked all Greek literature, all travel writing, most biography, all narrative poetry, all detective stories, Jane Austen, Trollope, Browning, in fact all Victorian writers except Dickens; also Shaw and anything written in England since the War. His positive canon, a small and shrinking one, included most things Latin, Rilke (though he had read only translations), some of Dickens, Melville, Tolstoy (not *Resurrection*), Conan Doyle, P. G. Wodehouse (but only Jeeves), Montaigne, Emily Dickinson and recent American poetry, particularly Wallace Stevens and the promising Robert Lowell.

The conviction that he had exhausted the world's literary output did nothing to raise Charlie's spirits. The book he was reading was a biography of Melville; normally, he avoided lives of writers, but his admiration for Melville was such that he overcame his scruples. From what he could gather from novelists' own diaries and letters, the urge that was common to them all was a need to improve on the thin texture of life as they saw it; by ordering themes and events into an artistically pleasing whole, they hoped to give to existence a pattern, a richness and a value that in actuality it lacked. If after reading such a novel you looked again at life — its unplotted emergencies, narrative non sequiturs and pitiful lack of significance — in the light of literature, it might seem to glow with a little of that borrowed lustre; it might seem after all to be charged with some transcendent value.

These poor writers depicted themselves engaged in this heavy task: from people they knew or met, they gathered characteristics for their imaginary humans; from conversations, they pulled out thoughts that could be developed into themes; houses they had visited were relocated and refurnished; other writers were absorbed, assimilated for what they could unwittingly donate; from some less recognizable source the power of pure invention was mobilized, while over it all the artistic intelligence shaped an entity that would thrillingly exceed the sum even of these rich parts.

To Charlie, it looked like very hard work. Then the writer's biographer took it slowly back to pieces: the magnificently complex heroine, he claimed, was after all a mixture of the writer's aunt and his mistress; the atmospheric shooting lodge was only the guest house where they took their holidays, moved to Lombardy from Felixstowe; the pained love affair was in fact a sublimation of the subject's interest in teenage boys. So there was no transcendence after all; there were mixtures, but there were no compounds, because everything could still be reduced by the biographer to its elemental pointlessness. What could conceivably be the purpose of such an exercise? Charlie thought. Did biographers of bridge builders believe that the river was better off unspanned? Did whoever wrote a Life of Newton maintain that the heavens should never have been charted?

At lunch, with wine, Charlie elaborated his theory.

'So after the glorious attempt to make the work float free, to make art, to cut the umbilical cord, along comes this plodder and tries to tie it up again.'

Vernon Williams said meekly that he enjoyed political biography and Marie-Laure looked up once from her piled plate of sausage, cheese and the night before's fried-up potato. Exhausted by his literary aria, Charlie took himself off for a rest, while the others prepared to drive to the beach.

When he awoke, the house was silent. The alarm clock told him it was five o'clock, which was a good time to ring Duncan Trench in Washington. Morning meetings would be over and he would be at his desk; Charlie reckoned the café in Saint Brioche with the telephone by the WC would also be open. With great reluctance, he hauled himself off the bed, made a cup of tea with two bags of Winston Churchill and some sterilised milk, then went out to the Citroën.

'Répression de l'ivresse publique'. How many draughty French cafés have I stood in, Charlie thought, reading through this ancient statute about drunkenness? It had taken him a quarter of an hour to reach the international operator and he wondered how a country with such a primitive telephone system could do business with the world.

Eventually he heard the sound of Duncan Trench's irascible voice. 'What? Yes, it is. I'll have

279

to call you back on a secure line. What's the number there?'

'Christ knows. I'll go and find out.'

The woman behind the bar suspiciously supplied the number, and after twenty minutes and two glasses of pastis, the telephone in the pungent vestibule finally rang again.

'Right,' said Trench. 'What is it?'

'It's your weekly call, Trench. I'm 'keeping in touch'.'

'Hmm. Not going through Paris, are you?'

'No.'

'Fancy a detour?'

'Don't bend the rules.'

'I could make it worth your while.'

Charlie looked down at his feet, where the rope soles of his espadrilles had started to fray at the toe. 'Goodbye, Trench,' he said, as he replaced the receiver.

★　★　★

On the beach Mary sat with her back to a stone wall looking down towards the sea, where Lauren and Vernon Williams were launching an inflatable boat for the children. With her forefinger, she inscribed Frank's name in the sand, then looked at it for a long time, stunned.

She wondered if subconsciously she wanted to be found out; had she deliberately left Frank's pack of Chesterfield cigarettes, which she had come across at the bottom of her purse, where Charlie would see them? She stood up and sighed. With her bare heel, she kicked over the

280

letters of his name and hated the fact that even this small, petulant action gave her pain.

As Richard and Louisa splashed in the shallows, waiting for their turn in the boat, Mary remembered childhood holidays of her own on the beach in Norfolk. She had been alone usually, content with her bucket and spade, her skin itching beneath the woollen costume as she searched for different-coloured shells.

What a strange child I must have been, she thought, skipping over the sand in a world where time did not move, believing that my taste of sea air and ice-cream and salt water was definitive, that my parents were as enduring as the sea-wall. Now I see my children and I know that they are figures in a lantern show, that their sense of permanence is an illusion, because all around us time is unstoppable.

When Louisa came back, shivering from the sea, Mary wrapped her in a towel and strapped in her arms so tight that she could not move. She had three small moles below her left ear in the shape of a half-moon and, while she kept her daughter prisoner, Mary kissed each one.

14

In New York Mary was woken by an explosive noise, as though the scaffolding on a skyscraper had collapsed and all its constituent parts had hit the sidewalk simultaneously. It had taken her many such awakenings to work out that it was the sound of a dumpster truck going over a pothole, so that its empty container, what in London they would have called a skip, rose and smashed down on the steel chassis. She drifted off to sleep again to be woken in due course by a sweeter sound, the pattering of rain on the air-conditioning condenser outside the window. She looked over from the bed and saw the usual pigeon, a piebald veteran of the gutters, cowering in the lee of the brick shaft, fourteen storeys high.

Mary smiled and stretched beneath the covers, delighted not to be in Brittany. She had come in from Washington the night before and had gone without dinner; she felt the call of Nathan's griddle and its homely waitresses. The rain had eased by the time she went out and made the short walk across town. She settled into her preferred nook, glassed off from the rest of the room, and ordered coffee, 'oring juice' and the breakfast special plate, number three. She looked at the paper while she waited, searching for Frank's byline. He was covering the Nixon campaign, and she had briefly glimpsed him on a television news bulletin during the Republican Convention in Chicago. When Governor Rockefeller introduced Nixon 'and his poor wife with half a flowerbed on her shoulder', Mary was still wincing in sympathy with Pat Nixon, the embarrassed wife who did indeed look as though she had been unearthed from a herbaceous border, when a rogue camera caught Frank among other monochrome pressmen. Mary felt obscurely gratified, as though this proved he was not cheating on her. Frank was supposed to be with Nixon as he fulfilled his ambitious pledge to visit every state in the union, but in Greensboro, North Carolina, Nixon had injured his knee so badly in a motorcade that he had had to go to hospital. After a few days Frank persuaded the office to let the local reporter keep an eye on the bed-bound candidate while he returned to New York; he said he would call Mary when he got in that evening.

'So how is he?' said Sadie, filling Mary's coffee cup.

'Who?' Mary had been so deeply lost in thoughts of Frank that she presumed she must have missed something. 'Nixon?'

'No.' Sadie had a harsh, drawling laugh. 'Your man. The one you're here for.'

Mary felt herself colouring. 'My God. Is it that obvious?'

'My age, I know the symptoms. You want ketchup with that?'

At least Sadie had not disapproved of her, Mary thought, as she set off after breakfast. She needed to do some shopping, and on Fifth

Avenue she turned to walk uptown. Charlie never appeared to notice what she wore and she was not certain if Frank did; in fact the only person she discussed clothes with was Katy Renshaw, who passed on various fashion magazines when she had finished with them. As far as she could make out, Frank liked quite conventional clothes, if only for the pleasure of removing them. His one stated view was a horror of Bermuda shorts, particularly when worn with Shetland sweaters; he had recently discovered that on Madison at 55th there was a Bermuda Shop, several floors dedicated to knee-length shorts.

'My God,' he said, 'it's like those well-bred girls who work at the White House, called things like Pooky or Fiddle or Squidge. They all wear those things. Pretty girls, but . . . '

'Oh yes,' said Mary. 'Though I don't suppose that stopped you dating them.'

'All of them,' he said, 'except Fiddle. I don't think anyone dated Fiddle.'

Mary found that the problem with shopping in New York was that there was an epidemic of Dacron. In *Harper's Bazaar* she saw a 'sleeveless blouse of tulip print cotton with a button-through skirt in gendarme blue' at Abercrombie and Fitch; but when you looked closely the dress version was admitted to be a blend of cotton and Dacron. A charming dress at Bonwit Teller was similarly blighted.

As much as anything, however, she enjoyed just going into the shops and putting herself in the hands of assiduous sales staff. An elderly male assistant in Bergdorf's found her looking with interest at a washbasin in the corner of the showroom.

'It's to demonstrate our waterproof fabrics, madam. Perhaps you'd care to see one of our raincoats tested?'

There was a gravity in these people, she thought, however opulent or garish the shop in which they worked. They said things like, 'It's a beautiful shoe,' or, 'You won't regret it, ma'am, it's one of our most luxurious fabrics.' She pictured their rides into work each day from some rundown apartment in Queens or Brooklyn and wondered if at night they took home tales of the rudeness and vulgarity of their customers as they counted off the slow months to retirement.

In B. Altman, Mary sat on a couch, waiting for an assistant to become available. She flipped through a copy of *Vogue* as she sat, wondering if she should buy a Triumph Foundation Garment ('if you dare to be hated by other women', the advertisement simpered), a Sarong girdle or Dupont nylons, 'because every fashion needs a stocking all its own', pink, blue, green, tan, and 'You say, 'What a feeling of chic,' and He says, 'Mmm,' and need We say more!'

'What can I help you with today, ma'am?'

The attendant was a woman of about her own age, well dressed and impermeably made up.

'I need a dress that I can wear to a restaurant uptown and to a jazz club basement.'

'In the same evening?'

'I'm afraid so. Probably.'

285

An hour later, Mary stood in the doorway with two packages. The assistant told her she was not tall enough to carry off the amount of petticoat in the black silk organdie dress she had wanted; so instead she bought a sheath of combed cotton with black coin-sized dots on a beige background and a sleeveless silk dress of a dark and shimmering colour of which the saleswoman's description 'crème de menthe' fell pitifully short.

The clouds had cleared and the sun was beating on Fifth Avenue as she emerged into the light; yet the first cooling suspicion of autumn in the air tempted her to walk back to the hotel. She found her step light and easy on the huge paving slabs as she approached the Public Library with its friendly stone lions. She would stay on Fifth until she reached her own cross-street because who would actually choose to walk down Sixth?

Mary smiled a little to herself, caught out in the sheer pleasure of the city. The avenues on top of the camber, from Lexington to Seventh, always seemed to her like sprinters in their lanes, muscling and gasping their way up the course — with one just ahead, until you glanced down a cross-street to the north side of the intersection, and saw a higher number — all the way up to a finishing line at Central Park South. Broadway swung, louche, from lane to lane, courting disqualification, until, just before the tape, it veered off track completely to be swallowed by the crowds of Amsterdam; Fifth continued suavely north as far as the Harlem River; but unlovely Sixth, the avenue where buildings were always going up or coming down, home of the jackhammer and the pneumatic drill, still blinking at light let in by its uprooted El, Sixth, the avenue of Radio City, of windows of electric gadgets, of Florsheim and Walgreen, was defeated by the race and expired at the finishing line, where it sank unmourned beneath the hooves of the snorting cab ponies.

Back at the hotel Mary walked slowly through the lobby, making sure the desk clerk noticed her, but he merely nodded as she walked past to the elevator. She hung up the new dresses in the walk-in closet and wished she had more clothes to fill the empty space. The hotel was a converted apartment building, and what it called a suite (there was no other kind of accommodation) had once been home to a couple, perhaps even a family. The cheap floral curtains at the window did not pull, but were decorative strips only; light was blocked by white plastic roller blinds at night and, during the day, by grimy sheers which Mary stood on a chair to roll up and tuck beneath the valence.

The telephone rang, and she threw herself across the bed to scoop it off its hook. It was Frank and he wanted to meet her at six-thirty in the bar at the top of the Rockefeller Centre.

'Another tall building?' she said. 'Couldn't we meet downtown somewhere?'

'I like tall buildings. And I'm meeting someone at five just nearby. Don't be late.'

She protracted the conversation for a little longer, but he was calling from the airport and needed to move on. As she replaced the receiver,

Mary was aware of the ache in her facial muscles that told her she'd been smiling fixedly again.

In the sunshine of Herald Square, she stood for a moment deciding where to go. Downtown to her left she could see the Flatiron, nosing skew-whiff through the grid; to her right were the dun brick cliffs of Broadway; behind was a palimpsest of New York endeavour, the black names of superseded garment enterprises fading into brick: Bo-Peep Mfg Co, STYLE UNDIES, Weber Blouses; while opposite was a winner of the battle to survive, R.H. MACY, whose giant cast-iron-framed department store dominated the block. She had pictured him as a puritanical Kansas draper with rimless spectacles, something in the Harry Truman line, and had been surprised when Frank told her he had had his first shop in Nantucket. Perhaps Captain Ahab had hunted Moby Dick in a Macy's oilskin.

She walked uptown a couple of blocks, then turned right on to 37th, a street she liked for its long view across the island; had it not been for the slight elevation of Fifth Avenue you could have seen straight through from coast to coast. She called in at a friendly-looking lunch place — deli, café, diner, she was never quite sure of the definition — and took a seat at the counter. There were sandwiches of the usual combinations, though what they were pushing was provolone or chopped egg with anchovy. She asked for a roast beef with mustard on wholewheat bread and a Rheingold Extra Dry beer, which the counterman produced at once in an iced tumbler.

Mary paused for a moment as she sipped and felt the cold intoxication trickle down inside.

'He called me in,' said the man on the next stool to his companion. 'He was in sportswear. He wanted to expand. I had an opportunity.' He chewed noisily on his corned beef sandwich. 'Can I get another pickle here?'

Mary felt dispensable to the life of the city, with its hustling for a break; there were few places on earth where her absence would be quite so unremarked, but this did not bother her in the least. There was no doubt that the intensity of her inner life had made her more than usually observant of the place, as though she sought to locate some correlative of her elation in glass and steam and stone; but the indifference, for example, of self-absorbed Park Avenue to her passing steps did not cast her down.

Then her mind turned to her mother. She had spoken to her father before she left Washington and he reported that Elizabeth, while weakening, was in good spirits; there was no reason for Mary to be in London yet, though there would shortly come a time. Her father strongly resisted her offer of going then and there; he said it would be more difficult for him; he suggested that her presence would intensify the bizarre uncertainty, his feeling of time suspended.

Since the day Frank had returned from Oregon and she had gone softly into his bedroom with the tea, Mary's sense of time had been similarly affected. Dying, loving, facing some wreck of truth and choice: so long as time did not move, nothing changed, everything was possible. She could have more than one life; she could be with Charlie, with her absent children, with Frank and with her mother, alive or dead. Would her mother, when dead, be any more absent than her children were now? She was not bound to choose, not this instant, perhaps ever — to bow to the literal pressure of a clock.

As she stood up to leave, she slid the picture of Richard and Louisa furtively from her purse. She kissed their small, ridiculous faces. 'It'll be all right,' she murmured. 'I promise you. Somehow . . . I'll make sure it's all right.'

★　★　★

She began her preparations at four-thirty, with an hour-long bath, but she was so excited at the prospect of seeing him again that she could not make the time pass. She had exhausted her repertoire of Rodgers and Hammerstein and spent twenty minutes making up, but still it was too early to be the ten minutes late she planned. Eventually she settled on the cotton sheath with the dots and set off once more into the streets.

She wanted to linger in front of shop windows, but it had clouded over again and was beginning to rain, so she arrived at the Rockefeller Center, breathless and five minutes early. The elevator rocketed her upwards through the circles of purgatory, and as she entered the bar on the sixty-fifth floor, she breathed in deeply, trying not to smile too much in her lofty paradise.

He was not there, and a waiter took her to a

table at the edge, by the window, to wait for him. Manhattan lay steaming under drizzle and cloud. She could vertiginously make out the symmetry of the Empire State Building, stepping inwards as it neared the top, the golden radiator caps that crowned the Chrysler and the uncompleted Pan-Am giant rearing up over Grand Central. She ordered a gin and tonic from the swift-footed waiter who had appeared at her elbow.

She imagined Frank at ground level, hurrying down his numbered street, lost somewhere in these insoluble equations. She scanned the horizon as though she might see this little figure, her microscopic destiny, like an atom flying in chaotic mass. On the East River was the huge blurred outline of the Manhattan Bridge; beyond the Hudson she could see the lights of Hoboken, refulgent, foggy yellow on the water. She gulped the drink. My darling, she thought. Come soon. Come before I die of wanting you.

When he came, she found it hard to speak and asked him questions so that he would have to do the talking. What was it in that face that was a self-renewing source of wonder to her? Each time she looked away, she found she had forgotten it; she could not memorize its features. She could enumerate them if he was not there: the blue-brown eyes, the bony forehead with a hint of vein running up into the cropped hair with its early dusting of grey, the lean cheeks, slightly tanned, the long, narrow-bridged nose and the incongruous handful of freckles beneath the eyes. But the composition would not stay in

291

her mind as a completed picture. Was this evanescence the key to its peculiar power over her, or was it the other way around: did the fierceness with which she gazed at him cause the loss of focus? It didn't matter, because the result was the same, a hunger for his presence that his presence could not sate.

They each had a second drink before Frank called over the waiter and settled the dizzying check. In the elevator, Mary clung hard to the deco handrail and swallowed aggressively to uncork her ears. Her legs wobbled slightly as they emerged and walked over the floor, to which, she noticed, some cruel engineer had given a slight and unnecessary slope. Frank hoisted his umbrella and put an arm around her shoulders as they went outside; she leaned into his sheltering embrace.

'I booked a table at a place nearby,' he said. 'We can walk if you like.'

The restaurant was a house number added to a street number divided by the number of an avenue, but inside it was a world. A huge cold room, with a door like a large version of the fridge door in Brittany, lay to their right as they went down a dark woodlined corridor. In its lit refrigerated space hung rows of beef carcasses. The dining room was low-ceilinged with a collection of delicate smokers' pipes suspended by hooks; on the walls were framed playbills, and the light, from innumerable candles, was orange and low.

Frank smiled at Mary as she settled on to a wooden bench with her back to the wall so that she could face out into the room. He offered her a cigarette and she remembered how Charlie had noticed that she was not smoking her usual brand in France. She did not mention the incident to Frank, however, because they did not talk about Charlie: he was from a different life, her other life, and there was no need to complicate things.

Frank ordered half a dozen oysters, but they brought seven, to show that this was a magnanimous place for American people. In other ways, it was a typical Frank selection, Mary thought: it had all the things he liked, snapper, scrod, bluefish, blackfish, broiled, charred, scarred, and steak, of course, with pots of creamed spinach and baked potatoes big as footballs. Intimidated by the sight of so much meat through the window of the cold room, Mary ordered fish.

Frank talked, and Mary heard herself talking, though by the end of the night she had no recollection of what they had said. Perhaps it was on this occasion that he explained to her the difference between cherrystone and little neck clams; perhaps he told her his thoughts on Richard Nixon, how as a congressman he had sponsored the McCarran Bill, which allowed US citizens to be picked up on suspicion of subversive sympathies and sent to FBI detention camps ('concentration camps' some people called them) without trial; or perhaps this was one of the evenings on which he told her of his life in Chicago, of the terrible jobs he had done before the war, as a porter in the slaughterhouses and, when he tried to improve himself, as a stock-boy in a candy factory for sixty cents an hour.

He may have smiled when he spoke, because when he recalled bad times he seemed not so much bitter that they had existed as grateful that there had been a means of escape. Sometimes Mary thought she saw him shudder with the sheer relief that he had become something, someone, a man who could go into a steak house, order what he wanted and tip the waiter handsomely. It always surprised her, this sense of striving in him. Because she loved him so much, admired him and in many ways deferred to him, it seemed extraordinary to her that he had had to strain so mightily to create the man he was. His grace, to her, was given.

He flung on his coat and took her out again into the rain, where he hailed a taxi with a stockyard whistle and ordered the driver downtown. Sliding on the slippery back seat, they moved into each other's arms, staying fixed together till the cab pulled up alongside some steps going down into a basement where a bulb hung over a rainy doorway.

Inside, they elbowed and slid their way through the press to a corner where Frank was greeted with familiarity by a tall waitress.

'Wanted to take you to the Five Spot,' he said in Mary's ear, 'but Ornette Coleman's pretty much taken up residence there. I think you'll like these people better.'

There was so much smoke beneath the low ceiling that at first Mary found it difficult to make out the stage, a tiny raised platform only a few feet away over broken glass and a sticky floor. She tried to concentrate on the music, focusing on one player at a time. The saxophonist, a burly man in a pork pie hat, closed his bulging eyes when he played his solo, but occasionally the lids would half open to reveal the whites only, the irises having slid up in rapture out of view. The pianist, a white man with college-boy spectacles and a striped blazer, seemed barely to touch the instrument, his long fingers resting flat and delicate on the keys, his right leg, never near the pedal, jerking up and down to the awkward beat. Though the horns played into microphones, the volume was low enough for conversation to be heard over the quiet passages, and aficionados next to the stage would look round accusingly if a noise disturbed their trance.

'Apparently', said Frank with his lips against Mary's ear, 'Coltrane's left Miles Davis. Some guy just told me.'

'Is that bad news?'

'You could say so. They had the best little band there's ever been. They're on tour in England. I blame you.'

A man with a beard and a pipe moved in front of their table, blocking Mary's view; his head nodded up and down incessantly and there was a self-congratulatory smile on his face. Mary studied him and his girlfriend, a young woman with a boy's haircut, a black roll-neck sweater, slacks and pumps, until Frank said something in the man's ear that caused him to move over.

On stage the bassist, whose forefinger was splayed flat from plucking, had his moment alone, before the trumpeter picked up some bleak and lonely notes that only he seemed to know where to find, floating out in the dark somewhere, spearing each one like a bubble he was bursting. It was an extraordinary sound, Mary thought, lyrical, yet desolate. She turned to see Frank's face tight with pleasure. The trumpeter's fingers lay flat across the keys, squeezing and releasing as he blew, so she could sense the resistance of the air beneath his hand; when he inhaled it was not his cheeks that filled, but some odd pouch beneath his ear. His eyes were fixed, open and disconsolate; once he lowered the horn from his mouth and a long tongue shot out across his lips. Behind him the drummer worked his brushes in a circle without taking them from the skin; he cocked his head towards the fragile movement, like a doctor performing some delicate investigation.

In his apartment, later, Frank played her Miles Davis and John Coltrane playing 'So What' and 'Freddie Freeloader'; he seemed mollified to think that, with all their drugs and furies, they had at least managed to record some songs together. They were in bed by now and Mary stroked his hair as the sound of the trumpet drifted through the open door. She looked back towards the living room, and saw his unfinished drink on a table by the window, and the dotted sheath that had gone the way of all dresses, lying on the floor beside it.

'What are you doing?' he said. 'With your fingers?'

'I was writing my name on your skin. Like this. My full name.' She traced out the letters, Mary Elizabeth Kirwan, over his shoulder.

'Egoist,' he said.

'Write something on me,' she said.

He rolled her on to her front, and traced something with his finger down her spine.

'What's that?'

'My army number. I think. Good God, you know, I think I may have forgotten it.'

'Good.' She kissed him.

At first when they had made love, Mary was surprised that a woman of her age should still have a hunger for these actions, ungainly, coarse — and pointless, too, because she took every precaution that they should not end in pregnancy; she would not have thought that she could still feel so desperate to perform an act which she had mentally relegated to her past.

But when Frank touched her, with the music still drifting through the door, she pictured for a moment the drummer's circular caress of the skin. As her thoughts became less coherent, she closed her eyes. She did not think she was 'good' at this, if there were standards or comparisons; and it was odd that the feelings she had were so little like love as she understood it — what she had felt for Charlie, or her mother or her children. The deeper into sensation she went, beneath his weight and his urging, the more it was like going into a room of utter darkness, which she felt was familiar from a time before her birth; it was something other, or beyond; it was like death, or very near it.

When she returned and found herself still lying there, with his adored face close to hers on the pillow, there was nothing for her to say.

In the morning she awoke to the high metal screech of the garbage trucks collecting on Grove Street. She was alone in bed.

Frank came back with bagels and muffins and a selection of newspapers, which he let fall on the table before he set about making breakfast. When she had returned from the bathroom, Mary sat on the couch and leafed through the papers while she waited for the coffee to be ready.

'Sorry I was out for so long,' said Frank, from the kitchen. 'I got talking to the Super. Giovanni. He always wants to talk about di Maggio and Crosetti and when the Yankees won the pennant in '41. You like your bagel with sesame seeds or plain? He thinks I'm Italian. He can't believe I don't speak a word of the language. Then it's how Rizzuto replaced Crosetti because shortstop was an honorary Italian position. And I made the mistake of mentioning a couple of guys who'd played for the Cubs, Cavarretta and Dallesandro, but Chicago doesn't count for Giovanni, it's only the Yankees.'

'Is this American football?' said Mary. 'Or basketball?'

Frank put a tray on the coffee table and sat down next to her. 'Best not to ask,' he said. 'What would you like to do today?'

'I have to go back and change,' said Mary.

298

'That's the first thing I have to do. Then, I don't know. Maybe I could come back, wander round the Village a little. Have lunch.'

'Or I could come up to join you. We could — '

'But, Frank, I like it down here.'

'Okay. I tell you what. If you really like it, there's a guy I met in San Remo's the other day who asked me to some party tonight. Poetry, mime, that kind of thing.'

She saw his suppressed grimace. 'You sure?'

So they did what Mary had always wanted to do, wander from shop to shop, from Pierre Deux antiques on Abingdon Square, via Li-Lac Candies to Zito's bakery and Chumley's defunct speak-easy. Frank, initially reluctant, told her that Minetta Street was on top of an old trout stream called manetta, the Canarsee Indian for 'devil water'. Mary did not know if he was serious, but she liked his commentary as they walked down streets which to her looked fashionable in a bohemian way, with goods displayed across the sidewalk, as in Europe. They had coffee in a pavement café near the Sullivan Street Playhouse, and Mary felt hungry from the morning's walk. She scraped the grains of brown sugar from the bottom of her cup.

'And what would you like to do now?' she said.

Frank looked at his watch. 'It's getting close to lunch. Me, I guess I'd like a dry martini and a steak as big as a butcher's apron, then maybe go back to the apartment and . . . ' He spread his hands delicately.

'I recognize that phrase,' she said. ' 'As big as a butcher's apron'.'

'It's famous. It's from that story by Irwin Shaw, 'The Girls in Their Summer Dresses'.'

'Yes, that's right.' Mary nodded. Something made her feel uneasy. 'You read that, did you?'

'Sure. Not quite your American primitive.'

'Of course.' Mary frowned, then gathered herself. 'Well I'm hungry too. Let's go down there, shall we?'

'You don't want to go there. Below Houston Street it's kind of a slum. Hell's Hundred Acres. I only go there to report industrial accidents.'

'I'm sure I went there once when you were away. A lovely bar.'

'Well, maybe there's some places. Perhaps the Beatniks are moving in. After all, when a slum's hit the bottom there's only one way it can go.'

'Up?'

'No. An artists' colony.'

Mary hung on to Frank's arm as they forded the torrential traffic of Houston. Eventually, they came to an averagely blackened industrial building that stood out from the others by virtue of a primitive awning and a string of white fairy lights. They went inside and found waiters fluttering laundered cloths over scrubbed wooden tables, welcoming them with even-teethed smiles as they set down the glasses.

Frank muttered, 'Give it a try?'

The food that came was Italian, but seemed to Mary better than the usual scaloppini at Monte's or the Gran Ticino with their headachey Chianti in straw-covered bottles.

She felt troubled as they ate. 'That story by Irwin Shaw. Did you like it?'

'Yeah. Sure. It said something, I guess.'

'Yes, it did. It said that men were incapable of being faithful to one woman because they would always be distracted by these girls on Broadway in their summer dresses.'

'Fifth Avenue, wasn't it?'

'It doesn't matter. But is that true? Are all men like that?'

' "What a pretty girl. What nice legs",' he quoted.

'That'll do, Frank.'

There were few other people in the restaurant and it was astonishing to Mary to think that such sleek and glorious wine, that food of a subtlety she had tasted only once before, on honeymoon in the Piazza Navona, could be produced and served with a speedy democratic glee from what was, in effect, the back end of a garage. New Yorkers never seemed to wonder at these discrepancies.

Frank ate with his usual efficiency, the cutlery shuttling back and forth between his hands, the left-handed stab of the fork preceding the vigorous but silent chewing.

'You watching me?'

'How come you never get fat? And how come you're always hungry?'

Frank drank some wine and put his glass down. 'First one, I don't know. Second one, I guess I'm making up for lost time. If you've ever been truly hungry, you never pass up a chance to load up. It's kind of an instinct.'

301

'Were you that poor?'

'Sure. But the army was the worst thing. Once we ate a dog.'

'In the Philippines?'

'No, it was in Germany. Near Cologne. We drew lots for which bit we'd have. It was a German Shepherd bitch. Billy Foy got the ribs, lucky bastard. I got the jaw.'

'What was it like?'

'Pretty good.' Frank pushed his plate away. 'Pity the teeth were still in. Have a cigarette. You've put me off my lunch now.'

In the early evening they went to the address given them by Frank's acquaintance in San Remo's; it was off Cooper Square near the jazz club, in a cold-water flat on the fifth floor of a brick building with padlocked toilets on the landings.

As Frank pushed at the open front door of the apartment, he turned to Mary. 'It's your world, sweetheart. You asked for it.'

Mary's first, rapidly replaced, impression was that they had surprised some construction workers on the job. Two women in overalls were in conference with a dozen men in blue jeans, pea jackets and navy surplus clothes; their paint-smeared fingers needed only a lunch pail to grasp for the illusion to be complete. They glanced towards Frank and Mary, but only one or two nodded in greeting. With a bottle of Dixie Belle gin he had bought on the way over, Frank mixed them both a drink.

'It's a long way from the Embassy,' Mary whispered in his ear.

The gathering was a party but also a performance; so long as you had contributed something, no one seemed to mind who came and no one seemed to be in charge. The barfly from San Remo's who had invited Frank was nowhere to be seen.

When about thirty people had gathered, a man with a corduroy jacket and heavy glasses asked them all to move to the side of the room, as a dance was about to begin.

A woman bound up in muslin, part bride, part mummy, came into the room on pointed toes. Her eyes were rimmed with kohl and her hair was scraped back from her shiny face. A pattering of tabla and maracas began from a corner where a bearded man was sitting cross-legged. The dancer looked about the room, her gaze challenging and bleak; a male performer with wild, curly hair in a soiled dhoti followed her into the centre of the room and prostrated himself before her as she pirouetted. Three other women entered in due course and proceeded to make patterns in which the single man seemed imprisoned. Mary found it difficult to take her eyes off his thin legs, which were coated in black hair through which she could see the almost fleshless sinews stretch.

The original female dismissed her hand-maidens and pressed herself against invisible objects while the abject male cowered. Her unbound breasts leapt within the muslin as she trailed and arced herself about the room, her bare feet occasionally screeching on the linoleum floor. For all its lack of inhibition and despite the loosening dhoti's tendency to gape, the dance was unerotic, its severity maintained by the challenging stare of the female principal.

A sequence of chants, in which all five performers joined, brought the first entertainment to an end. The dancers left, unsmiling, to prepare a second piece.

'Eva's a genius,' said the woman next to Mary, one of those in overalls.

'Sure she's a genius,' said a bear-like man on her other side. 'The other great thing about her is that she owns no underwear. Drives Emilio crazy. Thinks a gust of wind's gonna catch her out some day.'

'Even when she's dancing — '

'Sure when she's dancing. Know what they pay for this place? $85.90 a month including utilities. How d'you think they manage that? Hey, you wanna try some of this?'

He held out an oversized home-made cigarette. 'I got it from this cat at the Vanguard.'

'I don't use tea,' said the overalled woman. 'You carry on.'

'I'm all set. You wanna try some?' He was offering the lumpy tube to Mary, who could smell its bonfire-incense smoke.

She had the feeling that if she declined, she would somehow reveal herself to be an impostor, so held out her hand and placed the damp cardboard end between her lips, where she cautiously inhaled. She puffed twice before handing it back to the bear-like owner, who seemed pleased to be reunited with it. A circle had gathered round them and for the first time

Mary found herself included in the party.

'D'you know Jane Freilicher?' the man who had done the introducing asked her, indicating an elegant young woman of European beauty who seemed to have drawn four men to her side. 'She's a genius. They say her pictures lack passion, she can't make up her mind, but I don't think so.'

'Another genius,' said Mary. She looked around for Frank and saw him leaning over the phonograph in the corner of the room, a record poised between his palms. 'Are you a painter, too?' she said.

'No, I'm a dealer,' he said. 'This is Little Helge. You met her? She's at the Stella Adler School of Acting. She's very, very talented.'

Little Helge shrugged, but did not demur. 'What about you?' she said to Mary, who felt her clothes being rapidly scanned.

'I . . . I just came with Frank,' she said lightly, nodding towards the corner of the room.

'Sure,' said Little Helge. 'But for yourself, what are you doing in New York?'

The group around her was suddenly silent. Their different conversations about Larry Rivers and old Barney Newman, Bill de Kooning and Frank O'Hara had all ended at the same moment; now everyone seemed to want to know what Mary did.

'I . . . I'm writing a book,' she said.

'Well, that's swell,' said Eva the principal dancer, who had rejoined the company. 'What's it called?'

'It's called . . . ' The sound of the record Frank

had put on filled the room. Mary looked towards him in panic. 'It's called 'On Green Dolphin Street',' she said.

Frank had joined the circle standing round her. 'I thought it was 'Stella by Starlight',' he said.

'I changed it,' said Mary. 'Anyway, I never could tell the two apart.'

The man with the marijuana laughed, Little Helge turned to speak to someone else and the circle dissolved.

It was nearly ten by the time they left and it was dark as they walked down the Bowery to the corner of Bleecker Street. A doorway bum with boiling red sores on his face was drinking dinner from a brown paper bag. He called out something incoherent, desperate, to Frank, who paused and dropped a quarter into the grasping fingers scorched black with grime.

Up in the apartment Mary put on a record and went over to the couch, where Frank had picked up the newspaper. He opened books and papers no more than halfway, and held them at arm's length, as though scared of being dazzled by the banality of what he read.

This habit of his was a loved and integral part of her life, Mary thought, but how many books would she actually see him hold? There was a finite number and it was not a large one. She had once felt that what she loved and valued was made eternal or innumerable by her passion for it, but in the last few months — belatedly, perhaps — she had come to recognize that the instances of bliss were numbered as unforgivingly as the streets of the city, and that the edge of the island, once only a dream of explorers, was now in plain view.

In the morning she lay in bed, watching him dress. He did up his belt first, before tucking in the shirt, which seemed to her illogical; Charlie got the shirt tails comfortably arranged before buckling up. On the other hand, when Charlie came to fit his tie, he turned his shirt collar up, so that when he folded it down again there were invariably flecks of blood on the tips from where it had touched the shakily shaved underside of his jaw; Frank never lifted the collar, but slotted the tie around it.

He smiled as he felt her watching him. 'Gotta look good for the office.' He reached for his jacket. 'Can't you stay till tomorrow? I should be back by six.'

She shook her head. 'I can't leave Charlie on his own.'

The mention of his name deflated her. She loved him as much as ever, more perhaps since she had betrayed him; but he raised the morbid question of time.

Frank's face looked suddenly exhausted, shot with the fatigue of his life's exertion. He paused in his dressing.

'What do you want from me, Mary?'

'I want you to prove to me . . . ' she spoke slowly, taking his question literally, 'that time doesn't matter.'

'What do you mean?'

'If you say that only what lasts is worthwhile, then nothing is valuable, because everything passes. Isn't it enough that something should have existed, just once? Don't you think it continues to exist in some world where the pettiness of time is not so important?'

'I don't think I understand.'

'I love you so much that I can't believe that what we feel began only when I met you and will end when I stop seeing you.'

Frank nodded. 'That I understand.'

'Therefore the idea of a starting point or an end is in some way mistaken. Therefore, therefore . . . There is a world outside time, which . . . ' She trailed away.

'Where we can be together but you can still have your other life?'

'Something like that, but not just a convenient solution. An explanation, a way of properly ordering value. An eternity that is more than just time without ending. A place where time runs in a different way.'

Mary could not explain what she meant because her strong beliefs would not form themselves into words. She felt that she could not secure the bliss that should be hers because of some verbal shortcoming, the unwillingness of what she passionately felt to make itself available to words. It was hard to bear.

Later Frank kissed her and gave her the key to the apartment to leave with the Super when she went.

She watched him leave the room, heard his footsteps outside, the slide of the lock in the front door of the apartment and the reverberating slam.

15

The taxi crept through Hounslow on its way in from London Airport, past the smoky terraces, the wet school playing-fields and concrete parades of low modern shops, while overhead a plane dipped in above the power lines. Mary cleared a patch of glass with her hand on the misted window and saw the stationary traffic on the other side of the Bath Road, the commercial lorries and vans, the Rileys, Fords and Singers, fuming at the lights.

Her mother's imminent death made her see everything as though for the first time. When they reached her parents' street and Mary looked up to the top window of their house, she could feel the draught about her three-year-old ankles as her mother held her to the glass and pointed to her favourite star. The pressure of the emergency had the effect of stripping time away: the intervening years appeared to have been false or non-existent.

Her father opened the door and hugged her. For a moment all was well. On the oak floor of the hall the threadbare runner was still in place; the walnut sideboard held its usual load of unread newspapers, orphaned keys and post too dull or intimidating to be opened.

James Kirwan carried his daughter's case to the bottom of the stairs and motioned her into the kitchen, where he made a pot of tea. Mary felt light-headed, perhaps from the journey, but also, it seemed to her, with a kind of relief. Her father was there, unyieldingly kind, with his adored and reassuring face; on the terrace, through the french doors from the kitchen, the usual assembly of pots and tubs were throwing out their shoots and flowers beneath the metal frame that ran the width of the house with its load of dead vine and dried ivy that was her father's perennially unsuccessful attempt at a green bower.

Mary took her cup of tea and smiled at him; her pleasure at seeing him again was so great that she began out of habit to adopt the slightly skittish manner that, for a reason neither could remember, had long ago become the norm between them. He was unchanged and continuing; it was going to be all right, Mary thought. In any case, just how ruinous could this thing be? They would manage, they would survive. Death would be . . . it would not be the end of the world. She gathered herself, patted her father on the hand and stood up.

This was the moment at which she could repay all that they had given her: the indulgences of forty years, their unconditional love. It was good that this effort should be required of her now, when she was strong and clear in her mind, toughened by the demands of motherhood and by the strains of marriage. If her parents' love had been for any purpose, beyond the spontaneous joy of itself, it must have been to make her whole and balanced, capable of dealing with such natural events. By her resolution she would relieve her mother of any worry about what would happen when she was dead, and take from her father as much of his grief as she could.

Yet as she climbed the stairs to her parents' bedroom, her strength evaporated. Her legs would barely take her weight; instead of feeling calm and ready to accept the burden, she felt her heart's affections ripped apart. She thought of Frank, Charlie, Richard and Louisa and felt herself so fragmented that she barely knew what she was doing.

She knocked on the door. Her mother's voice called out thickly and Mary went in. Elizabeth raised her hand, as though embarrassed for any inconvenience her situation might be causing. Mary leaned over and embraced her, then sat down on the edge of the bed.

'How are you feeling?'

'Fine. These drugs are marvellous. Tell me about your flight. Was it on time?'

As Mary described her journey, she registered details of her mother's appearance. She had lost weight, but she was not unusually pale; her hair was recently washed; she looked no iller than she had on the occasion a few years earlier when she had contracted pleurisy.

Yet she was already dead, given over to the other side; and all the time that Mary talked to her she had the sense that her mother had detached herself. In the way that humans always push forward, because that is the only direction they are adapted to follow, she was reconciled to the crossing. She had left them, and Mary was shocked at her complicity.

311

Perhaps the exhaustion and sleepiness that the illness brought on had helped in some way to ease the separation. When you had flu, Mary thought, you did not care what was happening downstairs in the house, provided that, for the time being, you did not have to join in; perhaps, with the obvious adjustments in proportion, this was the same process.

Until she did die, however, there hung over the time that remained a portentous quality; her mother's words had a significance beyond their meaning because they might be her last. And while she was still alive death remained defeated, no matter how imminent it was; she was still Elizabeth as she had been for seventy-two years, with no change in her place in the world and in the living affections of those in the house.

They talked about Louisa and Richard, whom Mary would take out from school one day. Mary imitated the children as she spoke, and decorated the story of their holiday in France with details and some exaggerations she knew her mother would enjoy; she could feel her fond maternal gaze on her as she spoke.

When she had finished, Elizabeth squeezed her hand and said, 'Happy girl.'

It was, thought Mary, a good beginning, with everyone playing the appropriate and traditional part; it was therefore with a lurching sense of shock that she became aware, after a day or so, that her father was still hoping that her mother would survive. He had either not understood or had refused to accept the prognosis, and once Mary saw that this bewildering hope remained in him she believed she should try, as gently as possible, to disabuse him.

In their transatlantic letters and telephone calls, they had proceeded one step at a time: the next test, the next consultant, everything still open-ended for the time being and likely to end well. Presumably James had clung so tightly to this pattern that he could not believe it when they had reached the end. At dinner one evening Mary asked about his plans for the future, about whether he would stay in the large house alone, and all his answers were provisional. Eventually she saw that he was not going to accept anything until it happened, perhaps not even then, and that the burden of inevitability was for the time being hers alone.

Mary saw how her father's spirits lifted if Elizabeth ate even half a bowl of soup; it was as though he thought this was the beginning of a full recovery. 'There,' he would say, bringing down the tray, 'now if we can just get her to eat some toast with it and then perhaps a bit of dinner tonight, then we'll be on the right track.' His love was so instinctive that it could not adapt to reality; it overrode the facts.

Food became important in the house, and the success of the days was measured by Elizabeth's meagre consumption. Mary saw the dreadful effort it cost her to force down the invalid food from its bright bottle, the little fillets of sole, the painstakingly reduced clear soup or the triangles of lemon-sprinkled smoked salmon with which they tried to tempt her. But it all revolted her and each dry swallow was a testament only to her desire to please her family; for herself she would clearly have preferred to die then and there than prise her throat open one more time.

Downstairs, on the other hand, Mary found herself shamefully hungry: joints of beef and chicken came and went; her father ate pork pies, red cabbage and huge apple tarts from the bakery on the corner. They sat opposite one another at the family dining table, James in Mary's old place, Mary in the seat occupied by David Oliver on his first visit to their house, and guiltily ate prawns with home-made mayonnaise, then pork chops with mashed potato dotted black with pepper, rhubarb with cream, ending with English cheddar and French bread to go with the remains of the wine.

At night Mary retired to her childhood bedroom at the top of the house and took down from a shelf the books to which she had always returned at difficult times. She did not cry; she had not cried since her difficulties began and she felt it would be inauspicious to give way.

She lay in bed and thought of Richard and Louisa in a cold dormitory, wrapped in the self-protective acceptance of childhood. She thought of Frank, five hours behind, or maybe more, as he trudged wearily behind the would-be president, and she thought of Charlie, back in Number 1064, walking his daemonic tightrope, while downstairs her mother's life receded, the unthinkable emerging into the numbered minutes that remained. Mary felt ripples of panic run through her as she stared at the dark ceiling.

It was not just that, when her mother died,

everything would be changed; the problem was that the death threw doubt over all the years before: to think that this meaningless termination was what all the time was lying in wait seemed to undermine the value of the happiness they had accumulated. The photographs in their frames and albums looked ridiculous: her mother in the picture in their bedroom was not a confident young woman in the flower of early motherhood, but a victim, ignorant of the casual annihilation that awaited her. They had thought that the albums with their pictures of holidays and celebrations represented something durable or worthwhile: Richard's christening (that hat!), lasting happiness, Elizabeth's fiftieth at Le Touquet, enduring satisfactions, silver wedding party, landmarks and stability. She could see now that they were self-deceptions because death was the ever-present figure that, only now could they see, had made them all along a family of four.

* * *

On the third day the doctor came. It was not the usual one, Macdonald, who was on leave, but a locum called Charvis, a pale, plump man with sweaty hands, keen to impress with his air of gravity.

After a long consultation with his patient, he came down to the sitting room.

'How is she?' they asked.

'She's fine, she's doing well.'

'How long is it going to take?' said Mary. This

315

was a brutal question, but she wanted her father to hear the answer.

'Well, she is getting weaker,' said Charvis, 'but it's impossible to say.' His grave but sympathetic voice made the whole thing sound open-ended.

They discussed the various medicines in her room and their different properties; Charvis wrote a prescription for morphine and handed it to Mary.

'There's no shame, you know, in letting her go into hospital. They have some beds in the Twilight Room. The only thing that's making her unhappy is the thought that she's being a nuisance to you.'

For the first time since she had been in London Mary felt a convulsion of grief, but she bit the inside of her cheek, determined not to weaken in front of her father. When, later, she went out of the house to fulfil the prescription, she felt lightened and relieved to have escaped from the still air and the density of good intentions, from the feelings that were stifled partly out of consideration for others and partly because they were too large to apprehend.

Elliot's the chemist was an old-fashioned shop with coloured-glass dispensing jars in the window. Mary remembered scuffing her school shoes back and forth on the floorboards when she went shopping with her mother as a child. She recalled running errands here for her father, returning with bottles of shampoo and razor blades; then, when her mother had had a hysterectomy, handing over to the severe lady chemist with blue-grey hair a list of requirements it took her twenty minutes to collect from different shelves. For Mary, when a comedian began a story, 'A man goes into a chemist's' or when a character in a novel went into a pharmacy, no matter in what country or period, it was always into Elliot's fragrant premises that he came.

She handed the morphine prescription to the man at the dispensary counter, someone new to her. He studied it and quickly glanced back at her over the top of his glasses with a look of transparent sympathy. Mary sensed that the two other people waiting for their prescriptions had also somehow guessed; she was grateful for their silent compassion, but was bound too tightly to the chain of her own events to feel any comfort from it.

It was this visit for which they had all been waiting; the hundreds of toothpaste and soap calls had been, in the end, of no account: they had only postponed it. Mary could discern no significant difference between herself as a child and herself as she stood there now, and in that case the life between was lost: death had drained the years of purpose.

★   ★   ★

Yet every night, exhausted by emotion and the battle to retain the value of the past, she slept deep and dreamlessly. In the morning her discovery that her mother was still alive was joyful, but touched by disappointment: she

317

wanted Elizabeth's ordeal, and her own, to be over.

Her mother was in pain and Dr Charvis came to give her an injection; he again advised that she could be taken into hospital, but the three of them had agreed that she should die at home. Mary thought that Charvis wanted to save her father and herself from anguish, but by bearing up they could honour her mother's wish and spare her a small but final indignity.

As the days wore on, Mary found herself hoping that this would be the end, that today would be the day of release, even though she knew it would liberate them only into an unknown world of grief. Yet every day her mother roused herself again. Her spoken wishes were to depart, to stop bothering them; but her consideration for them was powerless in the face of her body's tenacious instinct to continue: she could not reach this animal stubbornness with her good manners and overrule it. She showed a spasm of her peculiar anger, as though the victim of her final loss of temper might be herself, for her inability to die.

Mary and her father also continued living; for long periods of the day they had no alternative but to carry on with shopping, cooking or reading the newspaper. In the evening they would do the crossword together in front of the fire and several hours would pass without their talking about illness or death. Mary told her father about life in Washington and her anxiety about Charlie's health, her worries about the children and her hopes for their future.

318

One afternoon Mary went up to the bedroom to see if Elizabeth would like some company; there was little to say, and her mother was too weak to talk, but she felt she might enjoy the closeness. She took off her shoes and sat on the bed next to her, propped up on a spare pillow. They managed a few words about the newspaper and the progress of a man called Beeching, who had been appointed to investigate the rural railways, then Elizabeth fell into a sleep which, though helped by the morphine Mary gave her, was troubled.

Above the shadows thrown by their hair, Mary's thick waves of almost-black, Elizabeth's grey and squashed by sleep, was a small oil painting of a cyclamen. When as a child Mary had brought her Christmas stocking to the bed and sat shrieking gleefully among the torn wrappings on the eiderdown, while her prematurely woken parents gazed on fondly, the cyclamen had been in the same place. So much else in the room seemed immutable to Mary because it was older than she was: her mother's silver hairbrushes, the glass-topped dressing-table with its frilled skirt beside which she had waited impatiently while her mother powdered and dabbed; the chest of drawers with pictures of Elizabeth's parents and of James as a young man in army uniform.

Elizabeth had been a nurse in wartime, going to France in 1915, and then to Serbia; it was her experiences there that had made her determine on her return to become a doctor. As a girl, Mary had often been told of the wounded soldiers in the hospitals; her mother spoke candidly of what they had suffered and had herself been transformed by what she saw. Mary could not bear to think that all her experience, the friendships she had made in those extreme moments, then valued and cultivated in the years that followed, that all the wisdom, anecdote and sense of value her mother had so tactfully acquired would now be lost. There was a delicacy and decorum in her, a sense of how things ought to be done, which, when she was dead, would be lost to an impoverished world.

Beside the bed were three pairs of glasses, two of them in their correct cases, the third neatly folded away, and it struck Mary that this might have been the first time that her mother had managed to have all her spectacles in the right place at the same time. Childhood astigmatism and short sight, discovered in her teens, had been complicated by middle-aged presbyopia that had meant reading at arm's length with various combinations of single-lens and bifocal glasses halfway down her nose, lodged on her head or, more frequently, mislaid. The hunt for mother's glasses had been one of the daily features of life in the Regent's Park house, and their loss was one of the things that regularly caused Elizabeth to become short-tempered. As Mary saw the wandering glasses safely gathered in, she thought of everything they had transmitted to her mother's toiling brain, the natural world, the severed limbs of soldiers, the rudiments of medicine, the faces of those she loved, works of art in France and Italy, the first sight of her only child, the billions of printed words by which she had taken her bearings in the world. The glasses were now folded shut.

Mary looked round the room again. In addition to the various bottles there were a wheelchair and a commode provided by the local hospital: for all their determination that her mother should die at home, something institutional, the aura of the Twilight Room, had insinuated itself into the house, had stolen in like smoke beneath the door. That morning Mary had begged her father to go out for half a day, to do as she had done and breathe some air that was not compressed by altruism and throttled grief, but he had refused in case he should be absent when the moment came.

She bent her head down to listen for her mother's breath, as she had with Louisa when she was in her cot. She would feel obscurely guilty if she alone were present when the breathing ceased. She had never thought that her mother could die; death was for other people: God would make an exception for a woman so loving, so wonderful in her life. She had cradled the heads of the dying; she had dressed their wounds; she had studied long into the night to realize her vocation, wearing out her poor eyes in uncongenial scientific work so that she could help the sick in peacetime. It was true that she had sometimes lost her patience with her family or colleagues, but she had harboured no spiteful thoughts, she had maintained her sly humour and her love of friends. There was something wrong with a world or a god that would let this

321

woman go, when outside in the streets were many people older than she was who should go first; or bitter, selfish people with no interest beyond themselves, who could far more easily be spared . . .

Mary managed, with an effort, to check her petulance. She went outside and walked down to her mother's rose garden, a semi-circular area with a small, weathered brick wall around it and a path made from broken paving over which she had ridden her first bicycle. She wanted to cry, but could not make the tears come; they were locked up in her, packed down tight. Eventually she forced one out and then one more, but they were not really tears, they were like drops of bile, hauled out painfully, threatening to choke her. She watched the wet mark each made on the lichen-covered paving as the stone absorbed it.

That afternoon there were signs that her mother was beginning to win the struggle to be free of life. Low murmurings came from her room and James hurried upstairs to be with her. Mary lingered in the sitting room, glancing through the window at the normal world outside. She had felt the thrilled glances of the neighbours, who had seen the taxi and the suitcase with its BOAC tag and knew that she was there until the end; she knew that they had watched the increasing frequency of the doctor's calls, seen him shuttling fatly up the path with his leather bag. Mary longed to be back in that outside world, but wondered if she could ever reconnect with it in the same way.

She heard her father call and she ran upstairs.

She looked interrogatively across at him, but he shook his head. Mary sat down on the bed and looked at her mother's face, now stiff with strain; it was as though she were thrashing against invisible restraints, the webs and roots of the clinging life instinct that bound her. She sighed and Mary went to the shelf to pour out morphine, which she tried to force through her mother's clenched mouth. It made a pink mess down her chin and on the front of her nightdress.

James, never a devotedly religious man, knelt on one side of the bed in prayer, asking God to take away his wife. Mary knelt on the other, thinking: she will never hold me in her arms once more; all I want now is to feel one last time her loving arm around me, but I will never, never feel it again.

The light of the afternoon drained away outside. Mary looked across at her father and she bled for him, seeing the strange calm that had come over him, because she knew it was still, even at this stage, based on hope. Each pretended to the other with silent eyes that they could manage and were unperturbed by what was coming. As the hours went on, Mary began to fear that they would have to give in and call for the hospital to take her mother away; neither she nor her father would be able to watch any longer. But when she faltered, he would hold out his hand to her across the counterpane, and clasp her fingers; when he weakened, Mary would be in a state of numbness in which she could encourage him in return.

The evening turned to night, and as Mary gazed out through the uncurtained window to the distant lights of Primrose Hill, wondering what further agonies they had yet to cross, she noticed that her mother was lying still.

She lowered her head and pressed her ear against her face. There was no sound of breathing. Feeling unqualified, she pressed her fingers into the veins of the wrist to feel for a pulse. There was nothing. She tried both wrists, but when she let the second arm go, it fell on to the bed, and she did not wish to abuse her mother's vulnerable dignity any further. She had never seen a dead person before. About the quiet body there was a sense of absence: she lay like a queen; she gave the impression that she had left them for some place unimaginably rarefied and serene.

Shocked, Mary looked at her father, rose and left the room. She walked downstairs and stood alone in the hall, then went through the french doors into the garden, breathing deeply. She knelt down on the grass and rocked with her hands behind her head. She had been prepared for the protracted anguish and the final shock, but the one thing she had not foreseen was the exact tenor of the end, the grandeur.

As she knelt in the darkness, with the dim sound of London beating on the wind, she felt chastened by what she had seen. She remembered how her heart had lifted when the midwife held up before her eyes the bloodied, squawling figure of her firstborn child, the sense of something elemental, of which she was an instrument. The moments of birth and death had been unimaginably similar, and to have been there until the end of her mother's life seemed at the final instant not so much an agony as a momentous privilege. She lowered her head to the ground, tore out small pieces of grass and let them fall on to the back of her neck.

When she thought that her father had had long enough alone, she stood up and returned to the house. She saw James gazing dry-eyed out of the sitting-room window, his hands in his trouser pockets. She went up the stairs and into the bedroom where her mother was lying. She touched her cheek with the back of her hand and kissed her forehead; she was frightened of how it might feel, but the skin was cool and reassuring. Then she laid her head on her mother's chest, lifted her limp arm and wrapped it round her own shoulders, embraced at last.

★   ★   ★

Mary went to her father in the sitting room. He seemed incredulous, as though something quite unforeseen had taken place. With his head on his daughter's shoulder, he stared ahead like a man in a trance. She made him sit down on the sofa while she went to make a pot of tea.

When she returned with a tray, she found him poking at the embers of the fire; a small flame curled up and he threw on a dry and splintered log, which at once began to burn, filling the room with a sweet smell of wood. It was not a cold night, but the flames were living and warm.

They suggested also funeral pyres, and Mary thought momentarily of Dido, Iphigeneia, rituals of mourning and dispatch. The points of reference were bleak but somehow just; she felt herself to be part of a primitive experience. There was even a tremor of comfort in feeling that she was at one with people who had lived with stones and fire.

She thought also of the log fire in the Renshaws' cabin, how she had smelled it from the bathroom above and allowed herself to be happy, refusing to admit what was about to happen. She drew the curtains and handed James his cup.

'I can't quite believe it,' he said.

Mary bit her lip. She thought her duty was still to be calm.

They began to talk about Elizabeth and about their lives together. James went to the shelf and brought over a photograph album, with the help of which they reconstructed the days of Mary's life and of her parents' marriage, as though they both needed to be reassured that they had really taken place.

Until they called the undertaker and set in motion the clumsy processes, the rituals and the forms, the headstone and the services, there was a period of intimate calm when Elizabeth was still theirs. It was the middle of the night; there was no longer any sound of traffic outside, just the occasional crackle of wood from the fire, which James had built into a blaze. It was a relief that there was no need any more to pretend that everything was somehow bound, however improbably, to return to normal; at least they could now admit that all was changed.

They talked with a candour induced by the knowledge that there was nothing left to conceal; they remembered what Elizabeth had been like, what they had loved about her and what they had never understood, the mysterious motivations, the corrugations of her individual temperament. For long periods they were quiet, exhausted, but with a sense that something had happened in its proper place; they were made silent by awe.

When dawn came, James went to the table in the corner of the room and poured two glasses of whisky, in which they drank to her life. Then he went upstairs again and sat by the bed; at nine o'clock he came down and told Mary to telephone the undertaker. He retired to the garden when the men came; he averted his eyes from their straining and heaving and their unintentionally comic manner.

The time difference meant that it was not until the afternoon that Mary was able to telephone Charlie in Washington. He was sitting in his office, catching up with what he had missed at the morning meeting from Edward Renshaw.

When Mary put into words the events of the previous twenty-four hours, her sequence of thought was suddenly interrupted by a memory of Louisa as a baby first walking in her parents' garden, and of her mother's face filled with rapture as she watched the small girl, with her blazing blue eyes behind thick lashes, solemnly explore. It was this image that prevented her from speaking, and in Washington, down the Atlantic cable, Charlie heard the silence as she tearlessly struggled to expel the weight of loss — of mother, of child, of all that patiently accumulated joy — from her throttled lungs.

16

In the television studio the carpenters were hammering at trestles, while a floor manager moved two lecterns on to a stage under the instructions of a man with a crew-cut called Don Hewitt. A vacuum cleaner started up as the set was inspected by various grave men in suits, Nixon's runners, who asked that two tiny spotlights be trained on their man's eyes to brighten the darkness of his campaign fatigue. Kennedy's advisers glanced at the set and reported no difficulties.

Frank checked his watch. The debate was due to begin at eight-thirty Chicago time, which meant that East Coast papers would be holding the front page and he would have to file his story paragraph by paragraph as the event proceeded. The reporters who would pose questions would remain in Studio B, but the bulk of the press would take the broadcast by monitor or by radio feed in smaller rooms within the Channel 2 building.

Don Hewitt, who was directing the programme, whistled loudly to attract the attention of one of the workmen; his tie was at half-mast and the stresses of the moment were legible in his face. If he was suffering so palpably, Frank thought, how bad must the candidates be feeling? He had seen Nixon arrive at the building earlier that afternoon, and as he stepped out of the car he struck his injured knee against the edge of the door. A spasm passed across his face, from which the blood was vanishing; but he mastered his pain and struggled into the building, where he made a show of being companionable with the CBS executives, slapping one on the back and even joking with a press photographer. The most recent opinion poll showed him leading Kennedy by one percentage point.

Nixon had addressed five different Chicago wards the night before, and Frank went with the entourage for the pleasure of seeing parts of his home town again. The names of Dearborn, Wabash and La Salle were as much a part of him as his fingernails, but some of Nixon's Californian aides were puzzled at the length of the great thoroughfares, unable to tell from a street number whether they were aiming for a teeming junction in the Loop, a residential backwater in the northern sprawl or a South Side project; late at night one staff car lost its way following local instructions to Go-Eathy Street, unaware that this was the historic pronunciation of Goethe. Then in the morning Nixon addressed the Carpenters Union; when reporters asked whether he should not be preparing for the evening debate, his campaign manager replied that the vice-president had knocked out Alger Hiss and outpointed Mr Khrushchev: debate, indeed, was his specialty.

Frank sat in the studio. Something of the nervous atmosphere had infected him; he was powerfully aware of being at home, that a fifteen-minute ride down Michigan Avenue would take him back to where he had begun and where he never wanted to return. A Nixon aide leaned over him. 'Frank, you're a local. Is there a pharmacy near here. We need some 'Lazy Shave'.'

'Why not get the guy a real shave?'

'His skin's so thin that even if he's just had one, his face still looks dark beneath the lights. Gotta cover up.'

'There's a drugstore two blocks down on Michigan.'

Nixon was standing on the stage, talking to Don Hewitt. He wore a pale suit and tie, and the collar of his shirt was at least an inch too big for him since he had lost weight in hospital. There was an awkwardness about him that had always reminded Frank of someone he had known, but it was not until that moment that he recognized who it was. Godley. Aaron Godley, the man in his platoon who could never fit in; the man who wanted passionately to be liked, but who was so inauthentic, so lacking in spontaneous life, that when marching he could not make his arms swing in time with the appropriate leg.

At that moment Kennedy sauntered on to the stage in a dark suit and tie; the photographers were drawn to him, leaving Nixon standing lonely and aghast. Eventually Hewitt was able to bring the candidates together formally.

'How're you doing?' said Kennedy.

'You had a big crowd in Cleveland,' said Nixon, flatteringly.

Hewitt asked the candidates if they wanted

331

make-up and Kennedy declined; Nixon gruffly followed suit, as though he did not want to play the girl. Frank wondered if they had found the 'Lazy Shave' yet.

The huge television cameras were wheeled up close, then, under instructions from the gallery, backed off again as each candidate took his place at his lectern.

'Can you hear me now speaking?' said Kennedy. 'Is that about the right tone of voice?'

When the technical checks were over, they retired to their separate rooms. Frank and other reporters were shown to their places by Channel 2 secretaries while the small invited audience took their places in the studio seats. Frank was on his own in a booth with a television monitor, a telephone line and his typewriter. He called his office in New York to make sure there had been no change in procedure, then settled down to wait. An audio speaker in the corner of the room was relaying the dialogue between the floor manager and the director.

'Ten minutes to air.'

On his monitor, Frank saw Nixon reappear on the stage, where he mopped his brow with a handkerchief. Don Hewitt, wearing a jacket by now and with his tie properly done up, came to join him, more out of compassion, it seemed, than necessity.

He went over the rules one more time and Nixon nodded, his gestures alternately dismissive and ingratiating, as though he wished to show that as Vice-President he was superior to a gimcrack medium such as this, but also desperate to be accepted by its leading players.

' 'Cut' means that's it?' he said.

'Get out gracefully,' said Hewitt.

'Five seconds.'

'Aah . . . '

'What I mean is, you want to quit quickly. How, how much?'

'What I figure is,' said Hewitt calmly, 'when you see thirty seconds . . . '

Nixon patted him on the shoulder, as if to show that he knew all this, really, but was above it. He was alone again, staring fixedly at the studio door, through which Kennedy was expected to emerge.

'Five minutes to air.'

Frank checked his typewriter ribbon and licked his lips. He felt an ache in his stomach such as he had not felt since the minutes before his platoon was ordered to attack.

'Three minutes.'

Nixon was staring at the closed door like a man hypnotised.

'Two minutes. Running up. Sound.'

The door swung open. Kennedy strolled across the platform to his place; he barely glanced at Nixon as he went by.

★　★　★

Mary eyed the television high up on the wall in the New York bar where she had met Frank the morning after they had first made love. Throughout the crowded room, the faces of the drinkers were turned up towards the fuzzy

333

screen, which was concluding a New Magic mascara commercial. It was noisy with the hum of male gossip and friendly derision; the barman, whom she remembered Frank referring to by name as Ray, made sure that his own shouted badinage gave no sign of preference for either candidate. Mary smiled uncertainly at him when he brought her drink, wishing she knew enough to engage him in talk of baseball or whatever game it was that he and Frank had discussed.

She looked back to the screen and imagined families all over America gathered round their new television sets, their TV dinners on their knees in the living rooms of their little box houses. What an extraordinary country this was, she thought, with its prodigious ability to invent itself and then persuade the world its innovations were inevitable. The commercial break ended and a resonant male voice regretted that viewers would not be able to see the programme that normally aired at that time, the *Andy Griffith Show*.

The bar went suddenly quiet as the screen showed two men standing uneasily behind their lecterns with a third, the 'moderator', Howard Smith, at a desk between them.

'Turn it up, Ray!'

'Switch the channel, whydontcha! We're missing the game.'

Through the snowstorm on the glass Mary could see a bleak grey set, into which Nixon in his pale suit seemed to blend; on being introduced, he twitched and gave a little half-sardonic bow; Kennedy, dark-suited, inclined his

334

head fractionally and stared past the camera like a mountaineer surveying a distant crevasse.

To Mary, her head full of death, the remarkable fact about either man was that he was alive. She felt an edge of jealousy towards each of them, as though it were she herself who had been deprived of life, or that they breathed at her mother's expense. How dare they carry on as though nothing had happened, as though domestic policy, the subject of the first debate, had any lasting importance? She wanted to communicate to them as they stood in their distant studio, feeling no doubt that some tide of history was running through their fingers, that no such thing in fact was happening; that for all the eyes upon them they were merely shadows on the grass.

'Mr Smith, Mr Nixon,' Kennedy was saying, 'in the election of 1860, Abraham Lincoln said the question is whether this nation could exist half slave or half free. In the election of 1960, and with the world around us, the question is whether the *world* will exist half slave or half free . . . '

He had a slight lisp, Mary noticed, and he pronounced the word 'harf', in what she presumed was a Boston accent; but she could not concentrate on what Kennedy said. She had returned two days earlier from London in order to be with Charlie for the opening of the new Embassy; she was exhausted by the time change, the conversation that had been dredged from her at the party following the ceremony, but above all from the weariness that was her way of feeling grief.

She had still shed no tear for her mother, but her limbs ached. For days after the body was gone, she walked about the house with her father, her arm through his. He would go from the sitting room to the kitchen, where he would stand and stare out on the damp garden, then walk down the hall to the dining room and gaze out at the street, where the people contrived to carry out their business as though nothing had happened.

The smell of polish and cut flowers remained unchanged. The latch on the kitchen door snapped and echoed as before; the landing window, still scarred from the tape of the black-out, trembled in its loose frame when the autumn wind blew; the cistern rattled and clanked as it had done on the day of Mary's birth. Everything was the same; nothing was the same.

James could see that the future was a place without comfort, but it was not the future that concerned him; it was the past, which, like Mary, he felt had deceived him and only just revealed what down all the long years it had been planning. He had thought himself content in that expanse of time, had believed it to be his friend, but saw it now for what it had been all along: a smiler with a knife.

Mary hated the people at the funeral, the old colleagues and friends with their good intentions and fond memories; the walking sticks of the elderly were not inconvenience enough for their continuing possession of life. She had been persuaded to believe that at someone's death their true worth would be made clear to the world, that a summing up of their life would officially value and appreciate all that they had been, leaving them secure in history's esteem.

Yet in the church off Primrose Hill, where people shuffled in from the rain over the tiled floor, shaking umbrellas, exchanging stoical pleasantries, there was no final reckoning, no true audit of the soul. Elizabeth's brother looked tired; her oldest friend could not be there. The eulogy, delivered by the senior partner at her medical practice, was inadequately prepared and dull. The mourners trudged out, many of them declining the invitation to return for lunch on the grounds that they had trains to catch, dogs to feed, work to do; Mary wanted to stop them and send them back inside, sit them down and lecture them, to ask if they could not see how terrible and unfair was this thing that had happened. Instead she played the hostess at her father's house, dispensing casserole and wine, lightly accepting offered consolations, but embarrassed by the terrible meekness of the old people, who were powerless to stop the disaster that was coming for them as well.

★　★　★

Frank kept his head down as the debate proceeded, scribbling notes, then hammering at the typewriter. He would leave the opening paragraph till last, in case something dramatic happened, but he already had a draft of it: 'The first televised presidential debate, which took place in Chicago at 8.30 p.m. CST last night, was a genteel affair with no clear winner. Vice-President Nixon had the edge in such policy debate as took place, but Senator Kennedy, by sharing a platform with the senior man and not being outgunned, showed himself a worthy candidate. He laid to rest any doubts on the 'experience' question.'

Frank barely had time to glance to the screen, but when he did so, he saw Nixon talking about what he called 'the Whydowse', implying that he had spent much time in its offices and corridors, while Kennedy looked on, head to one side, half smiling, as though slightly puzzled by his opponent, but hugely indulgent of him.

When Frank spoke to Rewrite in New York, they showed the surly lack of interest that was their house style, asking 'How're you spelling that, bud?' after any proper name, until Frank bluntly reminded them that deadline was approaching.

On the monitor in his room, unseen by Frank as he scribbled more notes on farms and taxes, Nixon wiped sweat from his chin. As the television reporters put their prepared questions, Kennedy addressed himself grandly to the watching nation, while Nixon talked at his opponent, accumulating small points at his expense.

Kennedy gazed into Frank's room, statesman-like and detached, from the unseen monitor, while Nixon's sweat glands poured out invalid excrescence through the streaked 'Lazy Shave' of his hospital-reduced jowls. But Frank did not see him; he saw only his own fingers as they smacked the chrome-ringed qwerty and hjkl through the paper and carbons on to the rattling inky platen of the Smith-Corona.

★ ★ ★

'Drink, lady?' said Ray. 'It's on the house.'
'Thank you,' said Mary.
As Ray took away her glass and brought a new one, she looked back at the screen, where the debate was coming to an end. Kennedy looked extraordinarily composed, she thought, for the pursuer, the junior partner. She could never understand why he was considered so handsome, with his pudgy face and narrow eyes weighed down by permanent bags, but he certainly looked elegant, whereas poor Nixon looked like a clerk who had been pulled out of his office late at night to stand in a police line.
The broadcast ended and she had caught no sight of Frank. He had promised to be back in New York the next day, so there was only the night to pass, she thought, as she went out on to Park Avenue.
Back in her hotel room, she telephoned Charlie at Number 1064.
'When you comin' home, Mrs van der Linden?' said Dolores. 'Mr van der Linden, I don't know where he is, but he's not lookin' good. He tell me not to worry, but I tell you his hands is shakin' when he goes to work in the mornin'.'

Mary picked at a loose thread on the bedcover. 'I'll be back on Wednesday. I'm taking the after-lunch train. Tell Charlie I've booked that restaurant he likes, near Dupont Circle, for dinner. I'm paying and — '

'Another thing, that lady telephoned from England. From the kids' school. She wants you to call when you have the time. She says it's not urgent, but she sounded — '

'All right. I'll call tomorrow when — '

'And your Pa called. He sends his love.'

'Thank you, Dolores.'

Mary replaced the receiver.

There is a battle going on for my soul, she thought, and I cannot just give it to the highest bidder. I have an interest in it too; I am player as well as arbiter. In Frank I have found something beyond me, beyond my understanding; this is where some irreducible core of me is destined to be, even if not in this life.

She took out the notebook in which she had begun to write her memoir, her novel, whatever she had most recently called it. There were about thirty pages of reflections and straight narration; there were also descriptions of the places she had been and — she had to concede — slightly incoherent accounts of her state of mind.

There were brief notes of dreams as well, though she dreamed the same thing night after night: that she was lifting her mother in her arms, carrying her weight and laying it down softly — on a bed, in a car or in a grave. Her mother was alive, but Mary's momentary delight at this discovery was dashed when it turned out that Elizabeth was also dying, always dying, never well again.

She wrote in her book, 'I have a duty to many people and somehow I will discharge it. I have a duty also to some continuing part of myself. I have discovered this essential identity through my feeling for Frank because that emotion has ripped open my self-protective layers. I see now what I am. It's not a question of 'happiness'. I don't value my own more — or much less — than anyone else's. It's something more urgent than that, and more lasting; it's a question of being faithful to an essence.'

She scratched a few words out: it was not right. She wanted to elevate the dilemma above the mundane distinction between selfishness and altruism, but the words on that higher plane were hard to find.

She tried from a different angle. 'I've heard people talk of the agony of moral choice,' she wrote, 'the anguish of life-shaping dilemmas. Well, I feel agony and anguish all right, often at the same time, so they make me tremble (though not weep). But I have never had much sense of choice. To have him, be with him, see him, be part of him is a natural imperative, because in some way he is me, my inner self. It's not just him that I yearn for when I call. It's myself, my previous life, my next life.

'So in fact there is surprisingly little choice. The possibility of not calling does not exist.'

★ ★ ★

341

When Frank had finished writing his article, he telephoned the desk in New York to see if they had any queries and, once given the all-clear, went back into the studio where many people he had not seen before were thronging excitedly about the platform. The reporters who had listened to the debate outside had gathered to compare notes, while most of Channel 2's employees seemed to be joining in the party.

Pierre Salinger, Kennedy's swarthy press secretary, was pushing through the crowds with a euphoric smile, trying to reach Don Hewitt on the other side of the studio.

'It's a triumph,' he said to anyone who would listen. 'We never dreamed it could go this well. The polls are giving it to us by two to one.'

'But, Pierre, on the tax issue — '

'Forget the tax issue. Jack came here tonight as the underdog and he leaves as the front runner. Nixon's got it all to do.'

'Didn't you think Nixon scored some points later on when — '

'Did you see the way the guy looked? Did you?'

'No, I got it through the audio feed.'

'He looked terrified, like a rabbit in the headlights. He was sweating. It was Jack who looked like the vice-president. Nixon looked like someone being interrogated. And then that reporter Vanocur got him with that question, you know when Ike was asked if Nixon had come up with any policy idea in eight years as Veep? And Ike said, 'Give me another year and I might think of one.' Vanocur sank his chances right there.'

Frank stayed close by. He discounted most of what Salinger was saying as wishful thinking; it was quite clear to him that Kennedy had scored no decisive points in the debate. On the other hand, something was worrying him.

Bob Finch, Nixon's campaign manager, was giving an interview on the other side of the room in which he also claimed victory for his man, pointing out that the vice-president had scored on the questions of farms — Jack Kennedy had clearly never visited a farm except to canvas support in Minnesota — on schools, on subversion and on the question of a candidate's age. All this was true, Frank thought, but there was no smile on Finch's face.

He went back to the Democratic side, where Salinger was in full flow, rebuking a reporter's scepticism, still with a smile. 'You think the guy in the bar in Madison, Wisconsin looking up at some fuzzy Admiral TV set is going to give a damn about the fine print of the budget? He wants to see a president on his screen. He wants to see a man look confident, like a naval hero in World War Two, not some poor guy writhing and sweating up like that, all desperate to please. I tell you, mister, you just saw the next president of the United States walk out that door and his name is John Fitzgerald Kennedy.'

Frank went over to a huddle of reporters at the side of the room. They had all shared his own view of proceedings, except those who had watched it on a screen, who believed that Kennedy had made by far the better impression.

Frank decided to go back to his room and

read through what he had written to see if he should add or subtract a paragraph. He found Pierre Salinger coming the other way.

'Hi, Frank. How're you doing? Enjoy the show?'

'Sure.'

'So. Whaddaya think? Show me your copy.'

'I beg your pardon?'

'What did you say about it? Let me have a look. The other guys let me see.' He began to tug at the carbon copies sticking out of Frank's jacket pocket.

Frank looked at him steadily. 'Fuck off,' he said.

★　★　★

Mary made dinner in Frank's apartment the next night, linguine with scaloppine, a dish she knew he liked at the Gran Ticino; afterwards she made zabaglione, protesting that without a copper pan it would not taste right. Frank had drunk bourbon all through the preparation of the meal and was in high spirits by the time it reached the table.

'I was worried,' he said. 'I thought I'd screwed up until I read the others. Russ Baker in the *Times*, even Joe Alsop in the *Post* who thinks he's the biggest noise on the Hill, they both called it a draw. You just couldn't see how badly Nixon came across unless you watched it on TV.'

Mary smiled at him as she carried the food over to the table. Frank was in full flow. 'Have you noticed, you can always tell a bullshitter by the way he introduces his own name into a story. Like Alsop, he says, 'So the President called me at home and he said, 'Joe,' he said, 'I'm sorry to call you at home, Joe, but you're the only man who can help.''''

He drained the straw-covered bottle of Chianti into their glasses and opened another one. 'Come and sit here,' he said, when he had finished. He put his arm round Mary, as she sat poised on his knee, then slid his other hand up her thigh.

'Zabaglione,' she said, standing up and straightening her clothes.

Frank laughed. 'I love the way you do that thing with your skirt.'

'What's that?'

'The kind of shaking down the hem in that schoolmarmy way.'

He liked to watch her in the morning; even when she appeared fully dressed and on the point of leaving the apartment, she would suddenly lift the skirt to refasten a stocking or straighten the hem of the petticoat, then tug down the skirt itself again with a reproachful, wriggling movement. She could never be ready enough for the day, he thought, for all its eventualities. Mary, Mary: what was she expecting out there?

She brought the dessert to the table and stirred the pan over a candle.

'Just to make you feel you're in one of those Village places you so dislike,' she said.

Frank stretched out his legs and watched her. It was a miracle that this woman had come for

345

him from the other side of the world, from that antique world of England, kings and fog, and that they had found each other. He had not known what was inside his head until she revealed it to him.

He took their wine glasses into the bedroom where the warm air was pumped from the furnace hundreds of feet below them; it was hot enough for him to undress her without her having to reach for cover, and she let him take his private pleasures of her. For once, Frank felt sufficiently euphoric that no shadow hung over him, no knowledge that the indulgence of his feeling for her would end. The drink made him feel powerful, as though he could make love to her indefinitely; he heard her sigh and call out to him. Perhaps at last, he thought, he had touched the core of her.

He took her face within his large hands, the hands with which he had dragged himself, almost literally he sometimes thought, from boyhood, the hands with which he had fashioned himself a life; he raked his fingers through her hair, down to the skull, as his body filled hers. All the way, he thought, I will go all the way, till I find her; and with her head between his hands he too let out a cry, because he felt pity on her soul.

17

Frank took some teasing in the office over his even-handed report of the televised debate. 'Hey, Frank, they fired Cordell for being up Kennedy's ass. Maybe they'll have to take you off Nixon for the same reason.' 'Call for you, Frank. It's Pat Nixon. You free for dinner Friday?'

He did not worry; he did not bother to quote the rival reporters coming to the same conclusions. If he had called it the same way as Joe Alsop, how could he be wrong? The editor asked him to write a follow-up piece on an inside page that explained the mechanics of how the press had worked and tried to estimate the future power of the new medium. Frank raised a casual finger to his tormentors, or smiled. It was not necessary to point out that he had almost lost his job and had spent six years in journalistic exile for writing articles that opposed all that the younger Nixon had promoted, as congressman, lawyer and counsel for various committees, because everyone in the office knew it.

When he returned to the Nixon campaign, his only misgiving concerned his absence from New York. He did not want to be separated from Mary, yet the residual elation of her company was enough to sustain him for a while. In his forty years or so of being alive, he had not actively sought happiness; he had experienced it most often as a side-product of striving after

347

something else. What he had felt since knowing Mary had redefined his view of the future, because he had not previously considered anything so abstract and unstable as emotion to be worth the effort of pursuing.

As he sat on the plane one late October morning, watching a brownish pattern of Midwestern prairie drift slowly by beneath them, hearing the chatter of reporters in the row behind, he admitted to himself that he could never see anything in the same way again. If Mary should die, or leave him, or in some less dramatic way deprive him of her presence, he could neither recover from the loss of her nor deal with the unfulfilled capacity for love that she had created in him.

He thought back to the morning he had recognized Charlie at the Spanish embassy party in Washington. He remembered him quite well from Dien Bien Phu; he recalled liking Charlie's rough indifference to the French army's dilemma in the elephant trap it had dug for itself. Perhaps Charlie had exaggerated his infantry officer's cynicism, but his attitude was appealing to Frank, who had been forced to cultivate a worldliness he did not feel in the Pacific. It didn't matter what your childhood was like; nothing in Chicago prepared you for Guadalcanal, where everyone, from the hoariest marine sergeant to the freshest army reinforcement, was making it up as he went along.

He had been glad to accept Charlie's invitation to Number 1064 that evening, even though he suspected Charlie had no clear recollection of who he was. When he first saw Mary standing in front of the table in her sitting room, his response was the exact opposite: although she was a stranger, he had the sense of already knowing her profoundly well. The way that he then behaved, forcing a re-entry to her presence, was unprecedented, but that was inevitable because she had opened up in him a depth of anxiety and desire that he had never previously known, and a new fever demanded a new remedy.

As the weeks went past, he did not scrutinize his feeling too closely; he felt a little ashamed of it. It seemed to show that in his marriage to Roxanne — sincerely enough undertaken, he believed — he had been ignorant. He seemed to have lived all his life until this point as though in some restrictive dream. The things that had driven him — a desire to escape, to have money, respect, education — appeared in retrospect to have been coarse and unambitious urges, hardly better than those of the man in the Levittown house who yearned for a larger tail-fin on his car each year.

He was worried, too, that his feeling for Mary was in some way decadent, unmanly, though he felt man enough not to flinch from it. While the passion that he felt strongly intensified the experience of being alive, it also felt inexplicably dangerous, as though if he pushed through the feeling — forced his hand through the web — or orchestrated it to its natural climax, what lay beyond was annihilation.

The stewardess brought him a glass of orange

juice, which he drank quickly as he looked out of the window over the torn wisps of cloud. What Charlie had told him in Minneapolis had worried him. The FBI was no longer as powerful or belligerent as at its high noon, when its uncorroborated suspicions, fed to and repeated by ambitious men in senate committees, could deprive a man of his livelihood, his passport, his friends, his bank account or, in Billy Foy's case, his life. Yet Frank knew how tenacious the agency still was in questioning people, how large and random were its powers. Charlie had manifestly passed the day when he could withstand such an inquisition; Frank worried for his state of mind and, more pressingly, that Mary might somehow become entangled. The thought that she might, to save her husband, be obliged to become some sort of informer was not something he could bring himself to imagine. Could he still love her? Would it be worse to lose her, or — with all it would mean for his integrity — to keep her?

Nor could he resolve what Charlie had told him, as the dawn was breaking, about how much he depended on his wife. Of course Charlie loved Mary; of course she was his light, his child — whatever the word was he had used: you would not be married to Mary and not feel that, Frank thought. The fact that Charlie valued her so much made Frank like him more, but there was nothing he could do to resolve their impasse. He was locked into it, like the other two, and the trivial questions of adultery — to tell or not to tell; to know or not to know — were of no interest to him. Perhaps, when Charlie spoke to him that night of his feelings for Mary, he had been warning him that he already suspected something; perhaps it was an appeal to Frank's finer feelings.

Frank swallowed and looked down at the cracked shiny leather of the empty seat next to his. He had 'finer feelings', all right, a 'nobler nature', all sorts of impulses toward fairness; but the intensity of his passion for Mary had banished them to some mental Alaska, far beyond reach.

★ ★ ★

Charlie was scanning the newspapers, about to leave for work from Number 1064, when there was a ring at the front door. A large man in a raincoat with a bovine face was leaning against the door jamb; on his chin, a piece of cotton wool was stuck to a shaving cut. He opened a wallet to reveal an FBI card.

'You Mr van der Linden? We'd like to talk to you.' He nodded his head towards a second, smaller man with a felt hat.

Charlie sighed. 'You sure you're meant to be here? Do you think there's been a crossed wire? I don't see O'Brien any more. That's all over.'

'I don't know any O'Brien. Is it through here?'

Charlie stood back from the door and followed them into the living room. He picked up his coffee cup and drank what remained in it.

'Your wife here?' The taller man had reddish hair, a Celtic look, Charlie thought, though well enough Americanized by now.

'No,' he said.

Neither agent sat down; the smaller one took off his hat and looked about the room, picking up photographs and papers. The one with the shaving cut leaned against a radiator.

'Where is she?'

'She's in New York.'

'What's she doing there?'

'She's writing a book.'

'What's it about?'

'I don't know. She hasn't told me.'

'Shouldn't she be here with you?'

'She is. She only goes for a couple of days at a time.'

The agent picked up the newspaper. 'You come across a guy called Frank Renzo? A reporter.'

'Yes.'

'Know him well?'

'No.'

'Where did you first meet?'

'In . . . I forget. At a party probably. Embassy reception, that kind of thing.'

'You sure? He's not a DC man. He's based in New York.'

'Maybe in New York then. I meet a lot of people in my work.'

'Maybe you met him someplace else. Maybe you met him in Vietnam.'

'I don't recall.'

'You seem a little nervous. You want a drink?'

Charlie shook his head.

'Sure about that? I got some Wild Turkey in

the trunk of the automobile if you're out of it.'

'I'm sure.'

'What were you doing in Vietnam?'

'My job.'

'And what was Renzo doing?'

'I've no idea. I don't recall meeting him.'

The smaller man pulled a book off the shelf. *The Man with the Golden Arm*,' he said. 'You like this writer? Nelson Algren.'

'Not particularly.'

'He's a Communist.'

'Is that so?'

'This guy Renzo,' said the man with the cut. 'Your wife know him well?'

'She's met him three or four times.'

There was a silence. The two agents walked round the room, their paths crossing by the doorway. Neither went near the window. Eventually the larger one said, 'She see him in New York? On these visits of hers?'

'It's possible. I doubt it. She works. She writes this book.'

'You're not worried about her all on her own there? She an attractive woman?'

'I am a little worried.' Charlie paused and looked at the man's blank eyes for a moment while he fought among his conflicting thoughts to assemble a response. 'She's had a difficult time,' he said. 'With the family. That's all.'

'Think she could tell us a little more about this guy?'

'I doubt it. Why are you interested in him?'

'He's being posted to Washington after the election.'

'Do you check out all the reporters who come here?'

'He has a history.'

'What kind of history?'

The agent shook his head.

'I suppose he's a 'Communist' too, is he?' said Charlie. 'I thought we'd left that game behind us.'

Neither agent spoke. Charlie watched as the larger man gently teased the piece of cotton wool away from his cut, then seemed to think better of it and stuck it back. He looked an oaf, Charlie thought, a comic figure really, but there was something about his bulk that was menacing; something unsettling also in the way that, while neither gave a name, both conveyed the impression they knew more about his own life than he did himself.

Charlie said, 'Does Frank know he's being moved to Washington?'

The larger man shrugged. 'Promotion, isn't it? Closer to the heart of things. He ever speak to you about being investigated?'

'No.'

'Ever mention Emmett Till, the Negro boy who — '

'I remember the case. But I haven't talked to him about it. I've told you, I hardly know him.'

The smaller man looked round from the bookcase. 'So when d'ya last see him?'

'A few weeks ago. In Minneapolis.'

'What d'ya talk about?'

'I don't recall.'

'Don't recall much, do you? Is that because of

354

the liquor or because you don't want to recall?'

Charlie said nothing. He could feel sweat bubbling out on to his upper lip; he wanted a drink, now that they both kept mentioning it: he badly wanted a drink. Years ago he had led his company in a beach-head break-out, into a tempest of machine-gun bullets, and had not hesitated; but these lumpen, unaccountable men filled with him a dread he could not manage.

'Listen,' said the smaller one, 'we're not trying to frighten you. We're just asking if you'd be willing to help us. And I'm sure you would be.'

'Did Renzo talk about his wife?' His partner resumed the questioning.

'I didn't know he was married.'

'Divorced. She runs some kind of store in Ann Arbor — books, magazines. D'you know the city? Kind of a hang-out for intellectuals.'

'It's a university campus, if that's what you mean.'

'This Renzo guy, is he an intellectual?'

'No. You wouldn't call him that. Clever enough, perhaps, but that's a different thing. He's a newspaperman.'

'But he went to college, right?'

'Search me.'

'What about you, Mr van der Linden?' It was the short man, who had apparently finished his inspection of the bookcase, lighting a cigarette as he did so. 'You go to college?'

'Yes. It's considered usual in my work.'

'What year you go there?'

'Before the war.'

'You know any of those English guys who

355

ended up defecting to the Soviet Union?'

'No. They were before my time.'

'And they were posted here, weren't they? Diplomats here in DC?'

'I believe so.'

'Were you at the same college?'

'Same university.'

'Still plenty of Communists in your day?'

'I suppose there were a few. But just undergraduates. Boys, really.'

The dark man dropped his cigarette on the maple parquet floor, stubbed it out with his shoe and moved towards the door.

'Your wife tell you any more about this guy, you let us know. You know how to reach us.'

Charlie nodded.

The larger man turned back to Charlie from the doorway. 'You want a lift to your office?'

'A lift? Christ, are you out of your mind?'

Charlie watched as the two men left and walked away to wherever they had deemed it safe enough to leave their car, before going on to trouble someone else's day. He stood in the doorway, staring after them as their feet went over the sidewalk down which Frank had first laid his trail of blood back to the van der Lindens' house.

★ ★ ★

When Mary returned late in the afternoon, Dolores passed on the various telephone messages that awaited her: Kelly Eberstadt and the dentist; Katy Renshaw, asking them to

356

dinner; her father; and Kelly Eberstadt again.

'You ring Mr van der Linden?' said Dolores reproachfully.

'I did. But I'm going to call again. I'm going upstairs.'

Mary carried her case up to the bedroom, hung up the dresses in the closet and threw the dirty laundry into the basket in the bathroom. She kicked off her shoes and climbed on to the bed, where, with her feet tucked beneath her, she took a picture of the children from the bedside table and stared at it. The last time she had seen them was when she had taken them out from school the day after her mother's funeral.

She had borrowed her father's Rover to drive up from London, a black car with shiny leather seats and an inner ring of chrome within the steering wheel that operated the horn. It was so heavy to steer that she felt the muscles of her arms straining beneath her sleeves as she slowed down for the corners.

St Anthony's lay at the end of a long drive flanked by dripping evergreens. Owners of some great houses sometimes planted lime-tree walks or avenues of oak, but the gentleman who had once owned the early Victorian mansion had had a weakness for spruce. The gables were intermittently visible through the prickly green foreground as she motored up the drive, the heavy Rover clunking almost axle-deep into the rain-filled potholes.

She parked in a gravelled area in front of the oak front door and went quickly up the steps beneath her umbrella. She rang the bell and waited for a minute until she heard the clacking of the school secretary's keys, which she wore for some reason on a chain against her bosom.

Inside, Mary was met with the smell of wholesale floor polish, old chrysanthemums and gravy. The secretary took her up a broad wooden staircase to the headmaster's study and invited her to sit down while she waited. Mary inspected the school photographs on the walls. The First XI football team, 1959, looked out at her from the steps that led up to the front door: eleven boys with cold knees in woollen shorts. They did not look much of a team, she thought; some of them looked unathletic and afraid. St Anthony's was a rarity in offering co-education and was favoured by parents who lived abroad, people who, like Mary, felt guilty and anxious at sending their children away but comforted themselves with the thought that at least brothers and sisters would look after one another.

Stunned by her mother's death, she nevertheless felt impatient to see the children; the anticipation made it impossible for her to sit. She found smiles of fondness twitching and passing across her face as she waited.

From downstairs there was the sound of a bell being rung, then a pregnant moment before a cacophony of voices and running feet. Mary strained to pick out the steps that were hers, the flesh she had made. Eventually there was a knock at the door. She composed herself: they might be accompanied by the secretary or the headmaster and she did not want to embarrass them. It was Richard, alone, in his grey V-necked pullover and school-cropped hair. Mary swallowed hard as he threw himself into her arms. She lowered her face to his and breathed in deeply the smell of his hair and neck, the aroma that had made her drunk with love when she had lowered him into his cot; it was complicated now by a redolence of football boots and pencils.

She laughed with the joy of seeing him and in return he seemed shy, not quite able to look at her, not sure if he should go on kissing her in the headmaster's study; but she sensed in his averted smile the movement of the low exhilaration in his heart. He held on hard to her arm.

Then Louisa peered round the door and Mary was almost overcome. She knelt down on the carpet the better to embrace her — her beautiful inward girl, with her big, puzzled eyes and delicate engagement with the untrusted world. She kissed her eyelids and her hair and her forearms, bare beneath the short-sleeved shirt and grey pinafore dress. She hugged her round the hips and laid her own face on Louisa's chest, then gathered Richard also into her embrace. She could not satisfy her need to touch them.

'Now then,' she said, standing up, 'that's enough of that nonsense. We're going out to lunch. The headmaster says we don't have to be back till half-past two. I'm afraid that means you'll miss Latin, so if you'd like me to get you back earlier, then — '

'No fear,' said Richard.

They drove to the local town, in whose market square was a hotel called the Swan. At the back was a dining room where Mary had reserved a table, though there were only half a dozen other people; she asked the waiter for Coca-Cola for the children and a dry martini for herself, though this turned out to be half an inch of warm vermouth in a wine glass with a maraschino cherry on a toothpick.

'Tell me everything,' she said. 'What's going on?'

She had forgotten how bad at conversation children were; they could not give any general picture of their lives or their progress in work or sport or art or anything at all. They both wanted the cocktail cherry from Mary's drink and found it difficult to think of anything else until she had summoned the waiter back and asked for two more cherries.

'What was Granny's funeral like?' said Louisa.

'Yes, why couldn't we come? It's not fair,' said Richard.

'It wasn't an occasion for children. There weren't any others there. It was sad, it was very sad.' That was all there was to it, but she thought she should put a better gloss on it. 'We sang some lovely hymns and there was a very nice speech saying what a wonderful person she was and I think Granny would have been very proud and happy.'

'Did you cry, Mummy?' said Richard.

'Don't be silly,' said Louisa. 'Grown-ups don't cry.'

'Well, they do sometimes, darling, but anyway, I didn't. I wanted to look after Grandpa. And afterwards we all went back and had a nice lunch and everyone was very kind. And although it's very sad that Granny's dead, it's natural and proper. And she was quite old, and we all said goodbye nicely and we'll all meet again one day.'

'I never got to say goodbye properly,' said Louisa. 'I wish I'd just been able to say goodbye.'

'Well, Granny said goodbye to you. She sent you her love. She particularly asked me.'

Richard said, 'I wanted to see the coffin.'

The waiter brought egg mayonnaise, grapefruit cocktail and pâté with thin, curled-up toast; Mary always ordered a variety of things on the grounds that the children would like one of them and she could eat what they didn't want. She asked the waiter to leave the food in the middle of the table. He looked puzzled, but did as she asked; he was a youth of about eighteen with a black bow tie and a white drip-dry shirt.

'They've got some lovely-looking puddings,' she said. 'Meringues and cakes and fruit salads.'

She ate some of the pâté, which had been rejected by the children. 'Washington's looking lovely,' she said. 'All the trees on Connecticut Avenue and the Mall going up to Capitol Hill. It's a beautiful time of year. And soon it'll be Christmas and we'll all be together.'

'Christmas is not for years,' said Louisa. 'And when will we see Daddy?'

'Well, you'll definitely see him at Christmas. And maybe he'll be over on business before then. It's possible.'

'Richard was crying in the boot room the other day.'

'Can I have some more Coca-Cola?'

'What's the magic word?'

361

'Can I have some more too?'

'More what?'

'More, please.'

The waiter asked if he should clear the plates. Mary nodded. 'Why were you crying, darling?'

'I wasn't.'

'You liar. You were.'

'Ssh. Why were you sad?'

Richard sighed and stuck out his lower lip. 'Nothing. It was just . . . Payne and Radford.'

'Who are Payne and Radford?'

'They're boys in his class.'

'Shut up, Louisa, you don't even know.'

'Ssh,' said Mary. 'Were they being horrid to you?'

Richard mumbled something and looked down. Mary was appalled. Something had happened to him; some light had gone out in him. To think that he of all children, with his physical ebullience, could somehow have given off the sense of weakness — the smell of it — that had drawn boys in to bully him . . .

The waiter arrived with roast chicken, a delicacy almost unknown to the children, expensive and modern, with its lean meat and golden colours. She had ordered steak and kidney pie as a reserve, but it was not necessary.

'What about you, Louisa? Are you having fun?'

'I don't like it. I miss my friends in Washington. The girls here said I had an American accent.'

'I don't think you have,' said Mary. 'I think you've lost it completely.'

'I have now. I did it on purpose.'

'And do you see lots of each other?'

'Not really,' said Louisa. 'We're in different classes and different dormitories.'

'But in playtime.'

They looked at one another with the old lag expression she had noticed in Brittany: a shrugging grimace. There was no tenderness between them; both appeared so intent on survival that they had overlooked the fact that they were there as a comfort to one another.

Mary looked away quickly. The two demands of motherhood she found hardest to manage were the illness of either child (always fatal until proved otherwise) and the spectacle of them being unkind or indifferent to one another. She was happy that Louisa and Richard looked well and ate hungrily from the desserts that the waiter slid off the trolley, but she became aware that they had moved away from her. She could no longer rearrange their lives and set them right by the sheer force of her benevolence; her cajoling smile was too far away to influence the world in which they lived, with its demands and codes and techniques of self-protection.

She lit a cigarette to go with the dusty hotel coffee while the children went off to play in the garden. Louisa's gentleness was being layered over by a kind of hostile reserve; for a moment Mary had a picture of what she might be like when she was a grown-up, and it was not the ravishing creature she had known as a small child but a marked, suspicious woman. She would still love her unreservedly, but she wanted her love to be a prized addition to a glorious life, not a consolation.

Back at the school, she gave them the presents she had brought from America: for Louisa, a View-Master with a circular reel of 3-D photographs and a book called *Eloise*, about a girl who lived in the Plaza hotel in New York; for Richard, a coonskin Davy Crockett hat and a Lionel train with a boat-loader freight wagon. She hugged them tight, one at a time, as they stood beside the car; she fought hard to control herself as they turned away and walked meekly up the steps, clutching their toys. She wished that they would hold hands as they had done before, when they came home and jabbered about their first day at school in Washington. Just a hand on the shoulder would do, Mary thought, as she watched them slowly mount the steps.

When she got back to London she would have to see what she could do for her father. Her company alone seemed to bring him little consolation, but she knew that it would be worse for him alone. She pressed the starter button on the Rover's walnut dash. Then, before going to sleep, she would call Charlie, to see that he was safely home and make him promise not to smoke in bed.

She breathed in deeply, dry-eyed, feeling the air catch in her chest. Through the car window, she saw the children turn and wave, briefly, then vanish into the darkness of the school, going their separate ways.

18

Charlie did not tell Mary about the visit he had received, but the implications of it fermented slowly in his thoughts. It was not what the two men had said; it was what they had not said. It was not the stated object of their visit that swirled in the back of his cloudy mind, but some of the implications that lay behind it. There was something destabilizing, but perhaps appropriate, in the thought that the heavy-footed agents of public secrecy could precipitate such intimately private suspicions.

He worked late in the new Embassy building, where he had been given a corner office overlooking Massachusetts Avenue. Mary saw little of him for a week or so and she saw nothing at all of Frank, who was accompanying Nixon on his final frantic swing. Then, as polling day approached, she and Dolores began to prepare for an election night party. The TV repairman was called in to improve the snowy picture; cases of gin, bourbon and scotch were delivered from the commissary at the Embassy, followed by Californian wine, beer and cartons of potato chips from the Spanish-owned grocery on Woodley Road. Since Eisenhower's administration had granted citizenship to her family, Dolores was herself a passionate Republican, but she was even-handed in her decoration: she pinned photographs of both candidates above the fireplace — Kennedy, airbrushed, narrow-eyed; Nixon, candid, purposeful — and looped a string of miniature paper flags along the mantel beneath them. She took a map of the United States from Charlie's small study at the back of the house and stuck it, in place of the landscape, on the wall between the windows with two boxes of coloured map pins underneath. Knowing the party was expected to last into the small hours, Dolores also volunteered to make a pot of Puerto Rican chili; Mary cooked chicken fricassée to an ancient recipe of her mother's for those whose constitutions might not be robust enough to take the searing meat-and-bean mixture on top of the electoral excitement.

In the kitchen Mary listened to the radio while she shredded vegetables for coleslaw. It was playing 'Mack the Knife' by Bobby Darin, as it had been, she remembered, when she prepared for the wedding anniversary party they had had eleven months before. In those days she had moved with light, automatic purpose; if she was disappointed by her husband or worried for his health, the doubts were not sufficiently developed to trouble her serene preparations. She spooned mayonnaise from a jar over the strips of cabbage and carrot in the deep mixing bowl. She was now so besieged by worry, so surrounded on all sides by clamorous uncertainty, that she could not raise her eyes from her emotional redoubt. She went through the day from one item of physical routine to the next, concentrating on whether she should add onions to the coleslaw (she did not like them

366

but the guests probably would), if her pink cardigan really went with the navy slacks she had put on that morning and on whether she had time to dash out and buy stamps for her letters to Richard and Louisa.

Katy Renshaw had wanted to recreate the spring weekend on Chesapeake Bay, but had found that neither Edward nor Charlie, nor anyone else in Washington, was able to leave the city on election night and so had reluctantly agreed to come to the van der Lindens instead. Sal, her sister, was also coming to DC and would be joining them for the party, in the unconcealed hope that Frank, for whom she had developed a lingering weakness on the lake and in the woodland cabin, would be among the guests.

Frank had persuaded his managing editor that there was no need for him to be with Nixon in Los Angeles for the result; however, there was now some disagreement over whether he should be in New York or whether, in view of his forthcoming posting to Washington, he would be better off in the capital. He promised to telephone as soon as he knew, and this uncertainty increased Mary's feeling of anxiety.

The news on the radio reported fine weather for voting in the South, along the Pacific Coast and on the Eastern seaboard, but rain in the Midwest was chilling into light snow in the foothills of the Rockies. It was thought that bad weather in Detroit and Chicago might keep some voters at home, but the chances of a November day being uniformly fine across the country were always negligible and the parties

367

were still confident of the heaviest vote in the history of democracy.

Mary had finished her preparations downstairs and was washing her hair in the bath when Charlie returned from work. He kissed her wet face, cleared a space for himself on the chair, draping her clothes over the radiator, and sat down.

'Are you all right, darling?' she said.

'What? Yes. All right. Benton's been off sick and it's been a busy day. Added to which, if Kennedy wins, the bastards want me to go to Moscow.'

'Moscow? Why?' Mary was appalled.

'Our people there will want a briefing on the new President and I'm supposed to know all about him. It'll help them deal with the Russians. Also, the Embassy here will come out looking good. The Americans will like the fact we've been so quick off the mark and they'll want to know how the Russians have responded.' He shrugged. 'It might help.'

'How long will you have to go for?'

'Just for about a week. I'll have to go to London first.'

Mary wondered how soon after the election Frank's Washington job would begin and how often she could see him in a week.

'Would you come with me to London?' said Charlie in a rush. 'I hate to ask, but you know what I feel about flying and . . . You know.'

Mary splashed some water on her face to cover her expression. She said, 'Are you telling me everything? This is not some favour for

368

Duncan Trench, is it? It's not something sinister?'

'No, it's not. I'm not allowed to do anything operational for Trench's people. That's an unbreakable rule. Sometimes people pass on information and I don't see why not. We're on the same side. But no, this is a very official trip. That's the whole point of it, really. To show willing. Openly.'

'But it's only if Kennedy wins?'

'Yes. If Nixon wins, they'll send David Chepstow.'

'Can you pass me that towel?' said Mary, climbing out of the bath. 'I feel suddenly very Republican. Nixon's not such a bad man, is he?'

'No one is beyond redemption.'

They went through into the bedroom.

'I asked Trench, by the way,' said Charlie. 'He said he'd drop in later.'

'I wish you hadn't. I don't like him.'

'He's been good to me,' said Charlie.

'Good to you? In what way?'

Charlie lit a cigarette and sat down on the bed while Mary dressed. 'There are a few things I've never told you,' he said. 'About work, and . . . related matters.'

Mary pulled a satin slip over her head and looked at Charlie, waiting for him to continue.

'I found myself in some difficulties. I suppose what it comes down to is that I was being blackmailed, though it was never put that crudely. I made some mistakes when we were in Japan and various people tried to profit from them.'

369

'Who?'

'The FBI, ultimately. I couldn't get them off my back, so I went to see Trench one day because his people have contact with them.'

'But what did they want from you?'

'Information. Always information. Usually about people I'd met in Moscow who might be visiting. Russians. If they're genuine or not. Also Americans I'd met. Their own people. They want to know about their weaknesses, if they might be susceptible and so on. Trouble was, I could never remember anyone's name. I was completely useless to them really. But that didn't get them off my back.'

'And what did Trench do?'

'I think he read the riot act. He told them to leave me alone.'

'And has it worked?'

'Yes, it has. I used to have these meetings with a man called O'Brien.'

'And that's over now?'

'Yes.'

'And what did Trench want in return?'

Charlie sighed. 'The occasional chat. 'Keeping in touch', he calls it. All this stuff is so unbelievably petty. It just wears you down. These constant niggling calls.'

Mary did not want to hear any more about Charlie's entanglements because she did not feel secure in the area of secrecy and disclosure, but she felt it would look suspicious if she did not ask for some details. Also, she was curious.

She said, 'These things that people knew about you. What were they? Girls, money?'

Charlie sighed. 'They were things like that. They were things that . . . I suppose what I mean is that I no longer mind if they're revealed. Nothing really matters any more. They've lost their power over me. If I were to lose my job because of some financial irregularity in the past, I wouldn't really care. And the other thing . . . I don't know.'

'What was the other thing?'

Mary was now dressed. She stood in the middle of the bedroom, looking at Charlie sprawled on the bed, as she had seen him so often before; but something in his manner made her stop.

This was neither the despondent slump of Charlie half-drunk, nor the amiable informality of the man whose lack of self-importance she had loved for so long: this was the languor of someone with nothing left to lose.

'Something of which', he sighed, 'I suppose I no longer feel uniquely culpable.'

Before Mary could digest his phrase, he rose from the bed. 'Let's have a stiff one, shall we, before these bores arrive?'

★　★　★

Two hours later, seen from outside, Number 1064 was blazing like a cruise ship in the backwaters of the Potomac. The occasional noise of cheering, laughter or dance music seeped through the closed windows to where Frank stood listening beneath the lamp on the opposite side of the street.

371

He had called to say that he was coming on the first shuttle he could make from New York. He had taken a taxi from the airport, but had stopped it a hundred yards or so short of the house so that he could walk the last part. He did not know why.

He could see figures move in front of the uncurtained windows, hands raising glasses and cigarettes, heads occasionally thrown back. He pictured the van der Lindens' friends inside, the Embassy people and journalists to whom such parties were an extension of work, churning round the gossip of promotion, appointment and divorce. At least tonight they had a subject for their hungry speculations, a real drama at which to marvel and enthuse.

And in among them was the woman he had first sighted in this same place at a moment he had known at once to be that to which all his life had been, with whatever Pacific loops and Indo-Chinese diversions, gradually leading him. He strained his eyes to make out her shape through the glass. She was there, inside, within his grasp.

Then, standing beneath the lamp, he knew why it was that he had decided to walk the last part of his journey. When he had asked Mary what she wanted from him, she had told him that he had to prove to her that there was a world outside time. As the wind came down the street, he turned up the collar on his coat and shivered. He could not do it.

She was there, inside, like a captive bird in her glass cage, but everything was breakable.

Knowing that his life depended on it, he had managed his passion for her not only with honesty, but, it seemed to him, with skill; he did not see how he could have done it better. He knew that when he had made love to her she had on occasions felt the same transcendence he had and that not only would she remember it until the day she died, but that it would change her view of dying.

Yet it was going to break. It was not he who wished to fracture it; he would give his life, without hesitation, to preserve what he had found with her: but when he walked across the street he would restart time's linear, destructive rush, and there was nothing he could do to prevent it.

★ ★ ★

Mary, unusually for her, had drunk too much. Charlie had poured her two large scotches with his own, and she had drunk them rapidly to quell her unease about what he had said: 'No longer . . . uniquely culpable': it was vague, but it was unsettling. She had drunk a glass of wine to celebrate Frank's phone call from La Guardia, and then, in the rush of arrival and the astonishment of the early poll predictions, had unthinkingly sipped her way through two or three more.

CBS had enlisted the help of a computer that belonged to IBM, into which had been fed the finest and most foolproof sample of early votes, cross-indexed and cross-slotted to take in every minute variation of human diversity, mathematical error and political history. It predicted, with solemn certainty, a victory for Richard Nixon by 459 electoral college votes to 78 for Kennedy.

The guests were divided in their preferences; many of the diplomats and journalists claimed to be impartial; yet even among Republicans there was a feeling that Kennedy would at least be an interesting president. There was disappointment in the room that the result was apparently going to be one-sided; people felt cheated of an all-night party, and this swung the waverers to the Kennedy cause. They cheered as the first results started coming in from Connecticut and showed the Democrats' East Coast machine to be living up to its reputation; Senator Bailey, with whom Frank had waited in the bedroom of Kennedy's Biltmore suite, had delivered the vote. Within an hour the tide of industrial city numbers had forced the computer to alter its prediction: it now foretold 51 per cent of the popular vote for Kennedy. Mockery of the poor machine rang through the laughter.

Mary laughed, too, not knowing why she did so. If Kennedy won, she would have to go to London; if Nixon won, she might at least find an excuse to go back to New York. She found her politics incline to the Republican, watching the screen intently as Eisenhower exhorted his troops to keep fighting to the last minute.

So Mary van der Linden stood in the sitting room, her dark hair alive in the electric glow of the table lamp behind her. She did not hear the front-door bell ring and was not aware that

Frank was in the doorway, looking across at her. He smiled, reflexively rubbed his chin with his hand to make sure it was still passably smooth and, clasping the drink that Dolores had pressed into his hand on arrival, made his way through the crowd to greet his hostess.

She retained the self-possession that had daunted him, as she turned and kissed him briefly on the cheek, not blushing or giving any indication of surprise.

'Frank,' she said, 'do you remember Lauren Williams and her husband Vernon? I think you met them last time you were here. We've been on holiday together since then, in France.'

'Oh boy,' said Lauren. 'Did we ever! What a place that turned out to be. We were the first people there since the Revolution!'

Frank smiled politely. 'How's the count going?'

'It's going to be close,' said Vernon Williams gravely. 'I think maybe Kennedy's shot his bolt. The Midwest's a landslide for Nixon. It's hard to see where Kennedy's extra votes are going to come from.'

Dolores took Mary aside to ask when she should serve the chili con carne and Mary noticed Katy's sister Sal sidling up to Frank. She watched his face to see if he would remember and, to her irritation, he seemed to do so with some enthusiasm.

Charlie was at his post behind the drinks table, approaching the moment of chemical equilibrium at which the world could still seem to him a glorious place. Next to him stood Katy

375

Renshaw, uncomplaining as he squeezed her round the waist, Kelly Eberstadt, a bony, intelligent-looking woman with orange beads over a black dress, and Duncan Trench, smoking a cigar and assuring anyone who would listen that either candidate was all right as far as he was concerned.

Frank slipped out of the room to use the telephone in the hall, as Mary and Dolores came back from the kitchen, bearing trays of food. The traffic through the narrow space was such that both women had to check their progress; Mary took a pace back so that she was almost standing on Frank's feet.

'So what's the second edition headline?' he was saying.

He held the telephone in his left hand, while with his right he surreptitiously caressed the back of Mary's thigh and then her hip, as she stood for a moment, her hands occupied, trapped in the noise and smoke of people pushing past.

''Kennedy Holds Commanding Lead'. Sounds all right. I'll come into the office in half an hour. I'll call a cab now.'

The blockage of people eased and Frank replaced the receiver. An argument was taking place in the sitting room between an Irish diplomat, who was saying that Nixon should concede and Duncan Trench, who pointed out that Kennedy had nothing left he could rely on winning and was still short of the necessary number of votes in the electoral college.

'The industrial north-east and the Old South

— we knew he'd win those. But what else is there?'

'California, for Christ's sake. Haven't you been listening?'

'It's far too soon to say,' said Trench crossly.

'Would you like some chili, Duncan?' said Mary. 'Or some chicken fricassée?'

'What, what? No thanks.'

'It's on the table if you change your mind.'

'Mary.' Frank took her wrist gently as she moved off. 'I have to go to the office to make sure everything's all right for the final edition, which goes at three. I could come back if you think the party'll still be going on.'

'Oh, I imagine so,' said Mary brightly. 'Looks as though it'll go on all night. The television just said the tide was starting to turn.'

'I hope not,' said Frank.

'Why? Do you want Kennedy to win?'

'I don't want the wrong headline. You know, another 'Dewey Wins' fiasco.'

'Who did you vote for?'

He was standing very close to her in the crowd; she could smell a faint aroma of toothpaste and bourbon on his breath as he leaned towards her and looked hard into her eyes. 'That's my secret. See you later.'

The cherry-and-white taxi was waiting outside. Within fifteen minutes Frank was going up in the elevator to his newspaper's office on L Street, near the junction of 21st. There were a dozen people clustered round the television set, with cups of coffee, a few bottles of Michelob and some packs of potato chips balanced on the typewriters and littered across the desks.

Frank had already written eight articles for the next day's edition, though five of them were in the B-matter pile — a ten-page alternate section on the winning candidate, giving details of everything he had done or said since infancy, except in the matter of his love affairs, on which the paper was silent. He had also contributed to an editorial that welcomed Nixon (or Kennedy) and pointed out that although it had been a close race, the paper had always believed that Kennedy (or Nixon) would ultimately prevail.

Frank took a beer from the fridge and joined the group in front of the television, which reported that Kennedy was only two votes short of victory in the electoral college.

'Where's Cordell?' he said.

'He's at Joe Alsop's,' said Maria, the office manager. 'He's written his piece and he's not coming back. That kid in Illinois called. Said it's in the bag for Kennedy.'

'Hmm,' said Frank. 'Depends how many Daley can make up in Chicago. What's happening in California? Has Scott called?'

'Yup. He's says it's stacking up for Kennedy.'

'So it's all over then?'

'Yeah, provided Scotty's right. They're not that far into the count yet. And, Frank, you need to call Bill Stevens in New York.'

Frank dialled the number. 'Hey, Bill. How's it going?'

'Pretty good. I'm fighting off Bob Levine who wants to go with 'Kennedy Elected'.'

'How long can you wait?'

378

'Forty-five. What's happening there?'

'Everyone's watching TV. Anything from Ike?'

'No. Red's still hanging on there. Says Ike's fuming at Nixon for screwing up. And at Kennedy for buying votes.'

'Sounds nice. You need any more from me?'

'Any more from you, Frank, and you'll have written the whole goddam paper. We just need to hear from Scotty one more time.'

'Why isn't he in LA?'

'Because he's one perverse sonofabitch. He thinks he can read the poll quicker there. He knows someone. Also he's pissed that we asked Julie Pereira to cover Nixon when you pulled out and — '

'I did not pull out, Bill, I — '

'Okay, okay, Frank, I need this line now. Call back in one hour.'

Frank smiled as he replaced the receiver. He had never heard Bill Stevens enjoying himself so much. He took another beer from the fridge and helped answer the phones; he too began to feel elated by the process that was taking place. He liked the idea that the spreadeagled states, for once, made up one country; that the young man in San Diego punched the same ballot as the old woman in Sioux Falls, South Dakota. He had felt this about his country when he went to train at Fort Benning in Georgia, where, for the first time in his life, he heard a New England accent. In the Pacific jungles he had experienced the federal unity with painful keenness, when his life depended on the speed of reaction shown by men from Detroit, Maine or Alabama. In

379

peacetime he tended to forget about these places.

He had voted for Kennedy in the end, even though he distrusted him. People said he roused their Democratic ardour less than Adlai Stevenson, that he was too cold, too rich and too dispassionate. Frank felt all this to be true, but thought he saw in him also some gambler's fire, which appealed to him. He felt that Kennedy, through his experience in war and his chronic illness, was familiar with extreme choices and would not fail to risk everything if he believed that that was the only way in the Russian troubles that lay ahead. Nixon, he believed, for all that he admired his mastery of detail and pitied him his awkwardness in the world, was a coward. Now that victory for Kennedy was so near, Frank found his journalist's indifference begin to give way to the thrust of elation.

An hour later he again called Bill Stevens, who told him they were going with the front-page headline 'Kennedy Elected'.

Maria opened a bottle of Four Roses and the dozen people in the office, whatever they had voted, drank to the new young president out of paper cups from the water dispenser. Then the telephone rang again.

It was the kid from Illinois saying the state was now too close to call.

Frank hung up. 'Illinois,' he said. 'You know it was in the bag? Guess what. It's out of the bag.'

'Shall I call New York?' said Maria.

'It's too late,' said Frank, as the telephone went again.

A young sub-editor on the other side of the office reached it first. He listened and nodded without saying anything. Eventually he put his hand across the mouthpiece and spoke to the room, 'It's Scott from San Francisco. California's now running neck and neck.'

'I'm leaving,' said Frank. He scribbled the telephone number at 1064 on a piece of paper and handed it to Maria. 'This is where I'll be if anyone needs me.'

There were three cabs on permanent call outside and Frank took one back to the van der Lindens' party, which had degenerated in his absence. There seemed, despite the lateness of the hour, to be more people there than before. In among the crowd Frank saw Charlie slumped on a sofa, raging incoherently at the television screen. The woman with the orange beads, whose name he had not caught, was standing beneath the stairs passionately kissing a man that Frank was fairly certain was not her husband. Duncan Trench and the Irish diplomat stood in exactly the same positions as before, though both seemed to have blurred with the passage of the hours, becoming dishevelled and inconsequential, as though each was struggling to remember why Trench was still jabbing his finger against the Irishman's chest. The sitting room was filled with half-eaten plates of food and packed ashtrays, but from behind Charlie's improvised bar Dolores was still doggedly pouring quantities of liquor over ice she shovelled from a plastic garbage pail beneath the table.

As Frank accepted a tumbler of bourbon, it

occurred to him that he too was drunk, a state which did not excite in him Trench-like aggression, or despair like Charlie's, but made him wonder where his hostess might be.

He walked through to the kitchen. There was no one in there among the débris, but as he turned to leave, the door on to the backyard opened and Mary came inside.

'I was just getting some fresh air,' she said.

'You OK? Feeling a little . . . ' He raised his eyebrows.

She smiled. 'Mmm. I don't know how it happened.'

'Liquor is how it normally happens.'

'And you?'

'Me too. It's been a long night. And we still don't have a president. I think I'd better step outside as well.'

Mary stood aside to let him pass.

'No,' he said, taking her elbow. 'I think you need to sober up some more.'

They walked down to the end of the grass, where they could see the rusty children's swing dangling in the darkness. Mary felt her heels sink into the lawn; her step was a little uncertain. They turned and looked back towards the house, where the kitchen window was orange and steaming.

Frank sighed. 'A big night for America,' he said.

'Yes.' Mary looked across the fence, over the trees and into the darkness of the rudderless capital. 'Are you excited?' she said.

'Yes.'

'I feel the world has stopped.'

Frank took her head delicately between his large hands. 'Your beautiful hair,' he said. He touched her lips, her very three-dimensional lips, with the tip of his tongue.

'When will we know?' she said.

'Tomorrow. Some time. That's today now, I guess.'

They stood for a moment, her body pressed in against his. When she closed her eyes the earth turned too fast, and she opened them again to see his eyes so close to hers in the darkness that she could make out the sharp lashes and the marks of the faded freckles beneath them.

'I love you,' he said.

'Too much.'

She leaned against the frame of the swing and felt his hands on her hips as she had felt them in the press of the hallway some hours before. That had been a prefiguring, a shadow of this moment, but she did not know if this one was more real. His hands went slowly up her thighs, lifting the skirt with practised care. She sighed again, but kept her eyes open for fear of the spinning world; and she liked to see his struggle to contain his desires beneath civilized movements; she liked the sense of her power over him of which it was evidence. He stood up tall and kissed her on the mouth at the same time that his hand slid in between her legs, so that her gasp was stifled in his mouth. She squirmed in his grip, but he would not release his mouth or hand and her movements intensified the pleasure of captivity.

'Not here,' she said, pulling back her head at last.

'It's too late.'

He sat on the child's swing and guided her hand to his belt, then to his lap; then he took her face once more in his hands and pushed back the hair behind her ears. 'Go on,' he whispered into one of them. 'The world's stopped after all. Go on.'

★　★　★

Dolores removed the smoking cigarette from Charlie's hand as she slid his arm from her shoulder and dropped him on to his bed. She pulled off his shoes and rolled him over on his side. He seemed to be asleep already. Dolores went over to the window to draw the curtains. She paused for a moment to look out over the backyard, and at the end of the grass, next to the children's swing, she could make out two figures joined in some desperate embrace; but it was too dark to see who they were before, with a swish of cotton interlined material, they were gone.

★　★　★

Mary went back to the party, while Frank smoked a cigarette on the swing. He let it rock a little back and forth beneath his weight. The sense of exhausted gratification lasted only for a minute; by the time she had straightened her clothes and begun to walk away, he wanted more of Mary, to be buried in her body always:

384

nothing else would do.

He carefully checked his belt, fly and shirt, ran a hand across his hair and straightened his tie. Back in the house, he went to the children's bathroom on the upstairs landing and in the bright light above the mirror, above the plastic tooth mugs and Donald Duck brushes, scrutinized himself more carefully for signs of the adultery. Down in the hall he called another cab and, while he waited, lent a hand with clearing up the wreckage of the sitting room. There were still a dozen or so revellers, listening to Frank Sinatra, drinking coffee, or, in a belated attempt at moderation, beer.

The front-door bell rang. 'Cab for Renzo?'

He kissed his hostess politely farewell on the cheek and shook hands with Edward Renshaw, who was also on the point of leaving.

'Good party,' said Frank.

'Absolutely,' said Edward. 'A pity there's still no outcome. 'That each man holds his loved one near/The nation sleeps but cannot breathe/Its weak heart failing in the night'.'

'Sure,' said Frank, as he walked up the lit path of Number 1064. 'And young Lochinvar is come out of the west. Or Boston, at least.'

Halfway back to his hotel, he told the cab driver to stop.

'Go to the White House, will you?'

Frank paid the driver and stood outside, looking into the lit windows, where he pictured the anxious staff pacing the corridors while the elderly leader slept away his final night of heirless power. The army officer who had been his commander-in-chief, the fatherly golfer who had swung his leg quite naturally over the side of the Jeep, changed into a suit (without ever looking quite at home in it) and strolled into the White House . . . It was curious, he thought, that this ordinary soldier, rather than his brilliant or ambitious aides, the scholars, sharks and specialists, should have had the imperial glory, that in his round and dimpled face America had chosen to see itself embodied. Presumably he didn't give a damn who followed him; secretly, he probably would have voted for Kennedy out of sheer irritation at the inauthentic, Godley-esque presence who had been beneath his feet for eight years.

Turning from the lit cupola, Frank began to walk through the cold and vacant streets of the capital. A feeling of despair enshrouded him. He had grown up with Eisenhower, then in the last months of the presidency his own sense of what was possible had drastically expanded. With the old guy went the limited dreams whose nourishment had once been enough. He went slowly up Pennsylvania Avenue to the west, a reverse presidential procession, towards the river; and on the bridge he paused and looked down for a long time into the water.

He thought of Roxanne, and Tilly, his Annamite girl, of whether they hated him or, perhaps worse, just shrugged at his memory. He felt alone.

Trucks and taxis occasionally went past, but he barely heard them. He could not seal Mary to himself; no flagrant act could force a union; no words could defeat the centrifugal force of love — away, always away, back into smaller particles, back into the darkness where he had dared to find it.

He felt a hand on his shoulder and looked up to see a grey-faced bum, a weary grandfather of the streets, asking him for money. Frank roused himself and felt in his pocket for a bill.

'Know who won the election, pal?' he said.

The man looked at him madly and backed away, muttering.

'It doesn't matter,' said Frank.

He handed him a dollar and walked into Georgetown as the sun was starting to come up behind him, edging the dormant buildings with hopeless light.

Back at the hotel he slept for two hours in his room, then turned on the television to discover that Nixon had conceded. He slept again, awoke, took a shower, shaved and put on clean clothes. It was ten o'clock when he walked out on to M Street to find some breakfast; he bought a copy of his own paper from a vending machine on the corner. It was a late extra edition that must have gone to press at about six, he calculated; the headline on the front page said, 'Kennedy Apparent Victor, but Losing Votes in Two Key States'. He pushed open the door of a diner and breathed the fug of bacon, boiling American coffee and fresh cigarettes.

19

Mary hugged her father on the threshold of the family house. He looked gratifyingly the same, not physically reduced by grief, as he held his daughter tightly to his chest for a moment or two, then released her so that he could also welcome Charlie, who was waiting on the step.

When she and Charlie were installed in her old bedroom at the top of the house, Mary went down to see what needed doing. Her father's domestic arrangements had not fallen apart as she had feared they might; once she had settled the men in front of the sitting-room fire with some coffee, she went out to the shops to stock up with what she and her father would need for the next week or so while Charlie was in Moscow.

She was relieved to be out of the house. It was the familiar smell that was intolerable, the odour of antiques polish, cut flowers, woodsmoke from the fire and something peculiar to the fabric of the house itself. This was the aroma of her childhood; for forty years it had been the smell of love and permanence. She did not know how her father could live with it; that, or the unchanged creaks and rattles that failed to register the crucial change in the human weight that sounded them, or was no longer there.

When she returned with half a dozen bags of groceries, she heard laughter from the sitting room, and blessed the part of Charlie that had always responded to her father, resolutely understanding what he called the point of him, even siding with him in pretend alliance against Mary. She joined them before lunch, pulling her chair up closer to the fire, stifling a yawn as she fought off waves of fatigue brought on by the sleepless flight.

'Keeping you up, are we?' said James, in a decades-old response to her yawn.

Mary completed the catechism. 'No. You're keeping me awake.'

'Charlie's been telling me about this Moscow visit. He's obviously a useful asset, knowing both sides, as it were.'

'That's right,' said Mary.

'Didn't you want to go too? See old friends and so on?'

Mary laughed. 'Daddy, I was only there for about five minutes. I was living with you most of the time. Don't you remember? When Louisa was ill. Anyway, it's difficult, getting people in and out.'

'It's exceedingly fraught,' said Charlie. 'They won't let me go alone, which is why I have to wait until Friday, when there's a group of building inspectors going. Things are very strained, what with the U-2 business and the collapse of the Summit and so on.'

James nodded. 'I can imagine you'd have to be careful. What exactly are your colleagues worried about?'

Charlie sighed. 'That I might be compromised in some way. They try to set you up with women, or drug your drink so you don't know what's happening. Then they take photographs. You're followed everywhere, every step, and everything you say is recorded. You're not allowed to travel alone outside the city, you have to be accompanied at all times. Even in Moscow they don't really like you to be on your own. I'm being put up by an old friend from the Embassy.'

'But you wouldn't actually . . . vanish, would you? As a diplomat of all people? Surely you have immunity and so on.'

'Of course. Though the Soviet definition of what you're allowed to do is so tight that if they chose to enforce it, pretty well any foreigner could be arrested. You have to be wary.'

And, presumably, sober, Mary thought to herself with a squeeze of anxiety.

'The worst thing,' said Charlie, 'is that there are no real records of anything. There are no telephone directories in Moscow. If someone disappears, the authorities can deny that there ever was such a person. If they had a listing in the phonebook their family could point to it as evidence that they really did exist. And there are no maps.'

'How do you know where you are?'

'You get to know the streets. The CIA have made a map and I believe we now have copies. That's the only one there is.'

That night at dinner, Charlie seemed preoccupied, joining in the conversation less than usual. He drank only a glass or two of wine, though Mary knew how much whisky he had earlier consumed upstairs. It was not surprising, she

390

told herself. Both of them were tired, and Charlie was nerving himself both for the flight to Moscow and for whatever was waiting at the other end.

* * *

The night before he was due to leave, Charlie awoke from a drugged sleep with a feeling that he was being stifled. He struggled to breathe as he climbed out of bed and made his way across the room to the window; he held hard to the sill as he looked through the parted curtains and down to the street lamp below. It took him some moments to recall where he was. Mary's home in London. But why? And was he truly there or would he wake to find himself in Moscow?

The weight of barbiturate tugged at him, dragging him back towards unconsciousness, but he did not want to go there, for fear of what he might find. There was sleep, there was unknowing; there were dreams and there were cities; all of them were separate realities, and in none of them could he locate himself.

He felt fear begin to sweep away the sedative power of the drug. He did not know if he was awake or dead, but he seemed to be waking up further, going up through levels of awareness that would make the ordinary sensation of living look like sleep.

His hand on the window frame was visible in the bright city darkness, but he did not recognize its shape; the fingers were not his. The flesh appeared transparent; the skin gave up the secret of what lay beneath, the wiring of the nerves and arteries.

Charlie breathed in deeply. He turned from the window and walked into the room. The wooden boards beneath his feet were for a moment reassuring; they were cold, familiar, and pressed as they should on to his skin, tree on flesh, hard on soft.

He sat on the edge of the bed and held his face in his hands. This, too, felt good, for a moment: the bone beneath the cheek on the strong palm. Then the thought that these two disparate things were part of the same body dismayed him; they were separate yet joined; one yet two. And his mind also was not one mind, but many; and he was not one man, one steady consciousness through which the world was mediated, but a plain, an open road for any reality that chose him for its own.

He slid to the floor and held on to the foot of the bed. He squeezed the wood beneath his hands. He wanted to call out to Mary, but was too frightened of the sound he might make. The noise that emerged might not be his own voice; it might turn out to be that of a stranger. He was frightened that Mary would hear his voice, but would not recognize it; that she would wake and run for help, calling for someone to turn out the intruder from her room.

One part of his mind told him he must let go of the bed, find the new pills Weissman had prescribed and take two, preferably with whisky. Yet he was scared that when they dropped him into unconsciousness he might find there a worse reality.

He watched the luminous hands of the travelling alarm clock, but could not make sense of the minutes. He hauled himself across the floor to his open suitcase and found the pills; from the frilled pocket at the back of the case he slid a bottle of Wild Turkey and unscrewed the cap. The rough spirit gave him immediate relief, enough at least to enable him to crawl back to the bed.

He climbed in with infinite care, terrified that he might wake his sleeping wife and that she would not know him.

★   ★   ★

In the morning, James drove them to London Airport in his slow Rover. Mary, at Charlie's insistence, went in the front with her father, while he sat stunned in the back, staring at the London streets that slid past his glazed eyes like painted cut-outs on a stage. He had told her nothing of what had happened to him in the night.

Mary was so used to seeing him depart unwillingly on flights that she did not see anything unusual in his demeanour. Her father, apparently sensing some heaviness in the atmosphere, switched on the car radio, on which the Light Programme was playing *Housewives' Choice*. He and Mary talked inconsequentially above the music.

'Could I borrow the car next week to go up to

Norfolk?' she said. 'It's the end of term and I can surprise the children by picking them up myself, rather than have you meet them at Liverpool Street.'

Charlie's head sank lower as the car travelled through the western suburbs; there was hardly any traffic on the Bath Road as they neared the airport. With frictionless despatch, the car was parked, the bag unloaded and the three of them were in the departure lounge, ready to check in.

'Mr van der Linden? My name's Sheila Millward.' A young woman in a dark suit was shaking Charlie's hand. 'I'm from the Foreign Office. I've been sent to introduce you to your travelling companions. There's a building inspector and three contractors.'

'Thank you,' said Charlie meekly, as she took him over to a group of four men carrying briefcases and heavy winter overcoats across their arms.

Mary stood with her father, watching as Miss Millward ushered Charlie through the procedures. They were almost two hours early, as instructed, and there was no one else checking in for Moscow. When his suitcase had been swallowed by the clunking conveyor, Charlie turned to face them, his head hung low, his body passive.

Mary swallowed and forced herself to smile. Miss Millward stood back tactfully to allow him to make his farewells. Charlie shook hands with James, then turned to Mary. She hugged him tightly and she smiled again, dry-eyed and encouraging, as she stood back.

'I love you,' Charlie muttered; or if those were not his words, Mary thought, they were something very like it.

He went with his group to the departure doors; he did not turn back as he vanished from sight.

★ ★ ★

In Regent's Park Mary gave herself to comforting her father. What he needed more than anything else, it seemed to her, was someone to listen to him. Occasionally she forced him to talk about her mother, but it became clear to her that it was too soon for any sort of catharsis. He was evidently still hoping that time would show it to have been a macabre mistake and that Elizabeth would walk back through the front door and explain. Instead, Mary listened to him talk about the minutiae of daily life, some of which — those, presumably that Elizabeth had taken care of, such as housekeeping — seemed to surprise and distress him.

At night she liked being in her childhood room because it gave her some sense of continuity when every other element of her life seemed fractured. Frank in New York, Charlie in Moscow, Richard and Louisa in their draughty school and her mother . . . All had gone from her. She pulled the blankets and eiderdown over her shoulders and forced herself to think of better days, of sailing on the lake, of dancing in the Renshaws' wooden cabin with the flush of wine and fire in her cheeks, swirling in the warmth of friendship and . . .

The telephone rang on the landing below with brutal urgency, and Mary was jerked from her half-sleep with a pounding heart. No matter how often experience told her they were wrong numbers or foreign inquiries, night-time calls meant only panic to her.

She went down the cold stairs in her nightdress to see her father, in his dressing-gown, hair dishevelled, lifting the receiver. He nodded a few times and she tried to read his grave face. Richard had fallen from a window; Louisa had . . .

'It's for you,' said James. 'It's someone from the Foreign Office.'

'Hello?'

'Mrs van der Linden? I'm sorry to telephone you so late. My name's Anthony Malbrook. I'm afraid we have a problem in Moscow. Your husband has had some sort of collapse and we need you to go and bring him home. It's a matter of some urgency.'

'Collapse? What sort of collapse? Is he all right?'

'Medically, I understand, he's not in any danger, though he needs expert treatment. However, his presence is a potential embarrassment. Our people are anxious that he should be got home as quickly as possible.'

'My God. Poor Charlie. Are you sure he's all right?'

'There's no flight tomorrow, but there's one on Wednesday. We'll need to get you a visa.'

'Do you promise me he's all right?'

'All I can tell you, Mrs van der Linden, is what I've been told by our people there, which is that medically there is no immediate danger, but that diplomatically it's vital he be taken home. I'll telephone if I have any more news and to give you details of your travelling arrangements.'

When Malbrook had rung off, Mary thought of more questions she wanted to ask him, but he had left no number. James laid his hand on her shoulder.

'He's not well,' she said.

'I thought he looked pale.'

'No, it's . . . He's really not at all well. He hasn't been for a long time. They want me to go and get him.'

'Well, that's good. Then you can bring him back to London and we'll have him properly looked after. You can all come and stay with me until he's better.'

'Yes . . . yes, he'd like that.'

* * *

The following day Mary rang Frank in his apartment at eight o'clock New York time to tell him what had happened. He gave her the telephone number and address of his newspaper's correspondent, Deke Sheppard, in Moscow.

'He's a good man. If you need help of any kind or just someone to talk to, give him a call.'

'I'm sure it'll be fine. I've got return tickets for

the two of us for Friday evening. I'll be there less than two days.'

'Be careful, Mary.'

'Of course. What were you doing when I rang?'

'I was eating a bagel and reading the paper.'

'Is everything all right there?'

'Everything's just fine. It's all just the same.'

'And you can see the New Jersey shoreline? And over Little Italy?'

'Let me see, I'll just walk across to the window. Yup, Jersey's still there. The Bronx is up, the Battery's down. Be good, Mary. For Christ's sake be careful.'

On Wednesday Anthony Malbrook, a tall man with wiry, grey-flecked hair, called in person at the Regent's Park house at eight in the morning to collect Mary in a black Riley. On the way through Hammersmith and Hounslow, he gave her instructions.

'You'll be met at the airport in Moscow by one of the embassy staff. It's a first secretary called Michael Winterburn. He's seen a photograph of you, so he knows what you look like. On no account must you talk to anyone else. Do you understand? Nobody. If for some reason Winterburn doesn't turn up, you wait for an hour, then ring this number.' He passed her a card and some money. 'Here are some dollars.'

'I'm not very good with public phones. Press Button A and all that.'

'I'm sure Winterburn'll be there.'

'But how is he? Charlie, I mean. Have you heard any more from Moscow?'

398

'Not since last night. There was a disaster with accommodation. He was due to stay with the Andersons — I think you knew them in Tokyo. But on Monday night they had to get out of their house in a hurry. There was a bugging scare of some kind. Then all the children arrived back for the holidays and they couldn't find him a bed. So they had to put him in the Hotel Ukraina. Do you know it?'

'By sight. But what exactly happened to him?'

'I understand that he collapsed at the Embassy, at a meeting. He was treated by the medical staff but he became difficult. There was some sort of scene in the lobby and then he refused to move from his hotel room. I'm afraid I really don't know the details, but I'm sure they'll fill you in at the other end.'

Mary nodded dumbly.

'You do understand, don't you?' said Malbrook. 'We don't really like you to travel alone, but there's no choice. Once you're at the other end, no taxis, no lifts. Just wait for Winterburn.'

'I understand. Oh, my God,' said Mary. 'I've just remembered something.'

The car was pulling up alongside the departures building.

'I was meant to be driving up to Norfolk to collect my children from school today. Will you telephone my father and ask him to ring the school for me? Explain what's happened. They'll have to put them on the train.'

'You could telephone from inside the building.'

'I'll try. But would you mind doing it as well to make sure?'

'Very well.'

Malbrook waited while Mary checked in her suitcase, then escorted her to the passengers-only point, where she showed her boarding pass. She walked forwards, stopped and turned.

Malbrook had pulled out a cigarette, on which he was inhaling with greedy relief. He raised a hand in farewell as Mary turned again and moved off towards the gate.

★ ★ ★

The plane was no more than half full, and Mary was able to sit by a window. It was a dark December day; the clouds were low and heavy over London. She watched the white lights at the wing-tip blinking as the plane trembled on the runway before surging forward and heaving itself up into the gloom, causing fragments of foamy cloud to break and billow past the perspex at her cheek. After a few minutes, the Comet stopped rocking and steadied itself above the grey cumulus; the stewardess leaned over with a tray of drinks.

In her anxiety Mary had forgotten to bring a book. She had finished the newspaper in the departure lounge and was now reduced to examining her passport. This is all I am, she thought: a monochrome snap and a handful of dates. She had envisaged herself as someone in a situation of unprecedented complication, of mortal delicacy, but in fact when it came to 'Special peculiarities, *signes particuliers*', the verdict (the verdict of the eternal crash-examiners, the verdict of the uninterested, error-prone posterity that followed death) was: 'NONE'.

She closed her eyes and tried to sleep, but could not free her mind of the picture of Charlie unconscious on the great wooden staircase of the embassy or vomiting in the upstairs dining-room beneath the portrait of George V, which many puzzled Russian visitors, to the Ambassador's delight, assumed to be a painting of the last tsar.

Two stewards came down the aisle with the heated dining trolley bearing salvers of liver and bacon or cod in parsley sauce and a large dish of peas and carrots from which they spooned a pile on to Mary's plate.

'Would you care for some coffee, madam?'

Mary smiled, thinking of Charlie: liver with milky coffee . . . My God.

'Just a glass of water, thank you.'

After lunch she pulled her feet up beneath her and folded her coat behind her back as she tried to make herself comfortable across two seats. It was already growing dark outside, as the plane curtailed the day, powering itself eastward over the darkening earth, above the enslaved lands of Eastern Europe.

Mary felt aware of the Western world she trailed with her: Macy's underwear against her skin; stockings from a 99-cent slot machine at Idlewild airport in New York (a kindly woman had helped her with the coins and provided the nickel and four pennies of which she was short); two sweaters from Lord and Taylor, and the coat itself, the warmest she had, from B. Altman's last spring sale. Would the immigration officials notice the label with distaste? Would she be arrested for flaunting illicit merchandise on the impoverished streets?

Her recollection of her brief stays in Moscow when Charlie had been posted there were unreliable. She had moved little outside the diplomatic vacuum on her visits; she had been so passionate to see her husband and so distraught to leave her ailing daughter, even in Elizabeth's medical care, that she had noticed little about the mechanics of life in the Soviet capital. A maid cooked for them in the two-room apartment in Sadova Samotechnaya; Charlie brought back food and liquor from the commissary at the Embassy, where it had been delivered fresh from Stockmann's in Helsinki. Mary had had no need to battle with the streets.

Yet, as the plane began its long descent, she felt now that she was going into the heart of enemy darkness. This was the place against which the vast and vigilant United States, by open politics and secret manoeuvre, fought with all its might; the people she knew in Washington, with their intellects and energies, their masters and doctorates and their billions of dollars, were bent to one overwhelming task, to protect the world from whatever fate was being concocted for it here, by men of no morality, men beyond reasoning, motivated only by a desire to impose their brutal system on yet more countries as they pushed both west and east; men whose missiles were more powerful, arms more numerous than the West's and whose satellites were already

402

orbiting the earth when poor America's had crumbled on the launch pad.

The captain thanked them for flying with him, and Mary shook out her coat as she stood up. She put on a pair of socks that Charlie had left behind in London and slipped her feet into a wool-lined pair of her mother's old boots. They were slightly too large for her, but with the extra socks they were warm enough.

She descended the wobbling steps that had been wheeled up to the fuselage, and on the final tread breathed in and dropped her weight on to Russian earth. She wrapped the coat round her against the wind as the passengers were escorted into the arrivals building, where bulbs of low wattage shed grudging light in the grey corridor.

Mary's case was among the first to be wheeled in from the plane, and her relief was tempered by a spasm of anxiety; she was no longer protected by the procedures of travelling or the programmatic politeness of the airline staff. Once through the door, she was on her own.

The official in his glass box examined her passport at length, snapping the pages between his blunt, orange-tipped fingers. He glanced back and forth at Mary's face; she saw him linger on the US Immigration stamps (unaware, perhaps, of how bad-temperedly they too had been granted) and on the American visa with its magnanimous 'INDEFINITELY' beneath the free-soaring eagle. He smacked a spare page with his Soviet frank and shoved the passport back. Mary replaced it in her purse and stepped through the gap.

The few people on the ill-lit concourse were manifestly Russian, bulkily dressed in cheap clothes, pale, downward-looking. Mary stood still and put down her case. The lack of any commerce gave the area a functional feeling; there was no pretence that the people were anything more than freight in transit. She looked at her watch; the plane was no more than a few minutes late and she had not been delayed unduly since landing.

She began to go through her pockets, looking for the card that Malbrook had given her, hoping for once that she would be able to make the telephone work, when she felt a hand lightly take her elbow and looked round to see a man in a striped shirt and patterned tie beneath a heavy overcoat. He introduced himself as Michael Winterburn, and Mary recognized the embassy way of speaking: cultured, reassuring, lightly ironic — a little wry sanity, it suggested of itself, in a mad foreign world.

He took her suitcase and let her through the doors to the parking lot, where he opened a Volga saloon and put her bag in the boot.

'Hop in,' he said. 'Jolly good of you to come at such short notice.'

'How is he?'

'He's all right, I think. The medic went to see him this morning and he's looking forward to seeing you. Sorry it's so cold. The ruddy heater doesn't work properly.'

Mary rubbed her hands between her clenched thighs to warm them; she had forgotten to bring gloves. She was surprised that no British wives had made the trip out to welcome her; in her experience they were always swift to gather round and help. Their absence worried her; she felt that Charlie must have done something to place himself beyond the normal considerations of form and politeness that were so important to diplomatic life.

The Volga left the airport compound and headed through the light snow towards the city; there were few other vehicles on the road and only sparse lights in the dark countryside around them.

After a few minutes, Winterburn said, 'When we get there, I'll book you into the Ukraina, then I'll pretty much leave you to it. As you know, the return flight is the day after tomorrow, and all we ask is that you keep a close eye on your husband. The Ambassador would like you to ring me tomorrow to let me know everything's all right, and again on Friday before you leave. I'll come and collect you in the afternoon.'

'I see,' said Mary. 'So I just stay in the hotel room.'

'Well . . . It's a little unfortunate that he's in a hotel in the first place. As you know, there was a disaster at the Andersons', where he was meant to stay. However, because the school holidays are starting they're chock-a-block with children and there was just no room — no room at the inn. Luckily these building chaps were coming out so they've been able to stick together. We've also put one of our fellows in a room on the same corridor, just to keep an eye

405

open, so everything's fine.'

'But what exactly happened?' said Mary. 'Why couldn't he come back on his own?'

'He just refused to move. He was in a pretty shocking state. It's a breakdown of some kind, I'm afraid. You were the only way we could get him out. And we really don't want the press getting to hear about it. Relations are pretty strained with them anyway. It's a big security risk for us. He's a loose cannon. It's bad enough having Burgess and people here.'

'Poor Charlie.'

'Anyway, the Ukraina's a bit of a dump, I'm afraid. One of Stalin's whoppers. Inconvenient, too. But there are lots of us in the diplomatic blocks opposite. Is that where you lived when you were here?'

'No, we were in Sadova Samotechnaya.'

'Ah, Sad Sam. So you know the ropes, anyway.'

'I don't remember much. I was only here for a few weeks, off and on.'

Winterburn slowed the car down as they came into the outskirts of the city and stopped at a junction. 'You do know that if you go out you'll be followed?'

'Yes. I don't expect to go out much.'

'No. But if you have to. Don't be alarmed. They'll have seen your visa and they'll be interested in why you're here. Just be careful, that's all. And, of course, I need hardly remind you, I'm sure, that the hotel room will be bugged. So. Discretion.'

They moved forwards again.

'And was Charlie any . . . any use? Before he fell ill?'

'Oh yes. The ambassador was delighted to see him. For weeks on end, we just get bundles of old copies of *The Times* here. Hardly know what's going on outside at all. We were all fascinated to hear about the election and Kennedy and so forth. And apparently he'd seen the permanent under secretary in London, too, so that was worth while. *Vaut le voyage*, as you might say.'

'So he hasn't destroyed his career or anything like that?'

'No, well . . . ' Winterburn did not seem sure on this point. 'I'm sure you know as well as I do, the service is tolerant about personal difficulties. There are strains and stresses in the job. The problem here is one of security, that was the alarm.'

'But in the long term, do you — '

'It's really not for me to say, Mrs van der Linden. Now, I'm just going to pull in here. Bit of a monstrosity, isn't it?'

They mounted the steps to the doors of the Ukraina. It was a building of gross imperial intent, in which considerations of design or beauty had been sacrificed to a display of skyscraping power, constructed by the slave labour of defeated Germans to the glory of the Soviet Union, one of seven Stalin monuments that lowered over the city. Mary grasped the wooden handle, on top of which was a small carved brass fir cone, and heaved. There were further doors, only one of which functioned,

407

before they found themselves in a gloomy, endless space, like a deserted ballroom in a power cut. They crossed the dun marbled floor, observed by two unsmiling men in bulky, ill-fitting leather jackets. There was a barber's shop, closed for the night, and a news stand, also closed, but no sign of activity; it might have passed for an outsize hospital, barracks or factory floor until Winterburn located a desk at which to register. He spoke Russian to a large woman in a uniform jacket beneath which, Mary could not help noticing, her enormous breasts sagged unsupported. She produced a key and handed it without speaking to Winterburn, who thanked her with a diplomatic smile.

'*Otchen spasibo*. I'll just take you to the lifts,' he said to Mary, 'then I'll leave you to it. Here are some roubles, though I don't suppose you'll need them. There's nothing to buy. The number's on the key. It's on the sixth floor. Do call if you need anything, won't you?'

As Winterburn walked off into the gloom, Mary pressed the button for the elevator. While she waited, she looked down. On the marble floor at her feet was a cockroach lying on its back; its legs thrashed impotently as it tried to right itself. Everyone she knew in New York was obsessed by what they called ''roaches' (they felt unable to utter the first part of the insect's name) but she had never actually seen one before.

She pressed the call button again and pushed at the struggling creature with the toe of her mother's boot, trying to help it over.

She wanted this interlude, whatever it was going to contain, to be over. She wanted to wrap Charlie in her arms.

After ten minutes the lift had still not come. Mary was aware of the two men watching her from the other side of the lobby; they did not lift their heavy stares, even for an instant. Another woman was waiting a few feet away; Mary turned and made a shrugging, interrogative gesture; the woman shrugged back, but seemed unsurprised by the wait.

After fifteen minutes the doors shuddered and clanked open. Two men pushed past, leaving the lift empty; Mary stepped in and pressed the number six; the other woman wanted eight. The inside of the lift smelled of pickled cabbage, sweat and urine, a special Moscow compound she remembered. After the ascent, Mary stepped out with relief and found herself on a dim landing with corridors leading both ways. At a desk sat an old woman in a black shawl, and Mary showed her the number on the key; in response, she raised a finger and pointed down a long, underlit passageway; then she stuck the same finger in the dial of an ancient telephone on the desk.

Mary walked uncertainly down the corridor, peering at the room numbers on the doors. Eventually, she came to it: 698. She raised her hand to knock, then paused: no etiquette guide that she knew had covered this situation. She rapped lightly with her knuckle. When there was no answer, she tried to slip the key into the lock, but her fingers were trembling too much. She dropped the key, and as she bent to pick it up, she saw the old woman standing at her desk, staring at her down the endless corridor.

The key rattled at the narrow indentation; finally, by holding it with both hands, Mary was able to sink it in the lock and turn it. She pushed the door open and dragged her case in behind her. The room was in darkness. She closed the door after her and searched the wall for a switch. As she moved forward in the half-light, out of the narrow hallway and into the room, she could see a round table in front of her, and she thought she could make out a figure on the other side of it. Her left hand touched a switch, which moved sideways in its plate; it worked a shaded lamp suspended from the ceiling, in whose glow she saw Charlie slumped at the table with his back to the window, apparently unconscious. 'Darling?' she said, going round and putting her hand on his shoulder. She put her arms round him and gently shook him; she tried to lift him up. He groaned a little and opened his eyes, which even in this light she could see were shot with blood, drugged, absent. He had not shaved for days and his chin spiked her hands as she supported his face and kissed him.

She held him in her arms, wrapping him up in her love as she knelt by his chair. He was coming round; he opened his eyes more fully and seemed to want to smile at her. He appeared to know who she was. 'My darling,' she said, 'oh, you poor thing.' She felt a responding pressure from his arms; he tried to speak, but could not;

then he rose with difficulty from the chair, tottered back for a moment and fell forward into her arms, where she held him for a long time, murmuring words of consolation, 'Mummy's here, it's all right, darling, it's all right', as she stroked him. Eventually she sat him down again and found the switches of two table lamps that lit the room as fully as their bulbs allowed, and showed as much as Mary wished to see.

The table was covered with a thick-piled crimson cloth with bobbles dangling from the edge; on it were two empty bottles of vodka and three plates used as ashtrays. There was also an opened tin of something, part-eaten, with a fork sticking out of it. Mary looked at the label; since she spoke no Russian, the words meant nothing to her, but it smelled like something that in the West you would feed to a cat.

She remembered the first time she and Charlie had met. The image went off in her mind like a flash-gun: Charlie, aged twenty-nine, lean, bright-eyed, at a party in London, talking to a group of people with delighted amusement but some frustration that he could not form the words quickly enough to catch the flight of his fantasy. There had been a young woman hanging on his arm, a potted palm or tree of some kind behind him, and a plaster pillar against which he occasionally leant his hand. But he had stopped when Mary approached to be introduced; his good manners prevailed over his exuberance and he brought her into the group of people, smoothing her stranger's path. She had loved him almost at once.

Mary moved with swift, unquestioning certainty. First, she went through the double doors in the bedroom and turned on the light there. The bed was unmade; Charlie's clothes lay about the room, but there were some clean ones in the open case. Through a further door was a bathroom, where she tried the water in the tub; the hot ran reasonably warm, and she searched for the plug. She would wash him, shave him, change his clothes: she would begin the long road back at once. After she had looked for five minutes, she remembered that this was another dull, recurring fact of life in Moscow: no bath plugs.

She got him through and undressed him; he made no resistance, and after she had given him a kind of standing blanket bath, shaved him, nicking him twice with the razor, which was no more than he usually cut himself, she dressed him in pyjamas and put him into bed.

'Has anyone been to see you today?' she said.

'A couple of bloody Embassy wives. I told them to bugger off.'

'I see. Well, I'm just going to tidy up a bit.'

In the main room there was a sofa with overstuffed plush upholstery; on the wall above were two cheap paintings of huddled trees, Soviet imitations, presumably, of nineteenth-century Russian landscapes. Near the entrance was a glass-fronted cabinet with a selection of plates, cutlery and vodka glasses, as though it was expected that guests would wish to entertain and dine quite lavishly, even though there was no room service and no food to be bought in the shops.

Mary looked up to the cornice, neatly cut from a plaster mould, with no sign of where the microphones were concealed; the light fitting was also scarless, and although the wooden cover in front of the radiator was loose, and could be moved, there were no visible wires behind it. The hatched parquet floor had a sheen so viscous-looking, like fly-paper, that she was surprised the rubber soles of her boots did not stick to it as she walked.

She emptied the ashtrays down the lavatory and washed the glasses in the sink; the plumbing in the bathroom was exposed, with chunky soil pipes running candidly across the tiled floor, while hot and cold water supplies had been spliced in around them, spaghetti-fashion. The holder with the roll of paper was on the opposite side of the room to the lavatory itself, a short but inconvenient walk away. In the bedroom, where Charlie had closed his eyes, she could find nowhere to hang his clothes, or hers, but piled them up more neatly in their cases.

She located a switch for a third table lamp in the sitting room, by whose light she noticed something that she had not seen before: a large envelope addressed to her. Inside was a further sealed envelope addressed to 'Doctor treating Mr van der Linden in London' and a note to herself from the doctor at the embassy, whose name, as far as she could decipher from his prescriptive scrawl, was Dixon Keslake. It told her that he had left a bottle of blue pills on top of

413

the cabinet in the bathroom and that she should ensure Charlie had three a day, but no more, and no other pills. She was to keep the bottle in her possession. He would call the next day to see how Charlie was; meanwhile she should allow him to drink as little alcohol as possible and try to make him eat. The doctor tried at the end to sound reassuring, though there were too many underlinings and phrases such as 'in no circumstances' for his conclusion to have an uplifting effect.

Mary went back into the bedroom, sat down on the edge of the bed and took Charlie's hand. She thought of how she had lain awake in Frank's bed on the first night in New York after they had made love. The practicalities of what she had fallen into and the vocabulary for them — 'affair', 'infidelity' — had seemed to her banal and inadequate; she had always believed that the adventure of marriage was incomparably more interesting than the petty indulgence of betrayal. She drew back the curtain on the window and looked down towards the Moscow River beyond the great bronze figure of Shevchenko, the Ukrainian poet braced rhetorically against the darkness below; then she turned back to the bed, where Charlie was beginning to stir. She would shortly discover the depth of her belief.

Charlie got out of bed and went through into the sitting room, in search of cigarettes and drink. Mary had a pack of Winston in her purse and pushed them over to him as they sat on either side of the table.

'Darling,' she said. 'Tell me. Tell me what happened.'

Charlie managed to light a cigarette. His voice was thin, devoid of expression. 'I don't want to live any more. I could stay alive for you or the children. I could do it. But I want you to set me free.'

Mary was too shocked to say more than, 'But we need you. There's so much for you still to do.' Fearing that this sounded onerous, she added, 'So much joy. So much pleasure for you.'

Charlie lowered his head into his arms. 'I know it all. I've seen too much.' He was mumbling into his hands; then he raised his tear-stained face. 'And now my brain's attacking me. The night before I left London, I woke up and I was hallucinating. I was in an unreal world . . . Of fear and panic. I can't come back. I can't come back into your world.'

Mary could not for the moment find the words to argue against the weakly voiced power of his despair.

'You forget the things I've seen,' he was saying. 'Those men in the river in Italy . . . All those corpses . . . The end, the only end of it all . . . Whether it's now or later, like your mother . . . The awful insignificance . . . You have to pit a fantasy against it. A self-deceit. And I have no more energy to invent it. You do it.' He stood up, apparently gaining strength. 'You make the fantasy, you create the belief that there is something you can make last or live or seem worthwhile. You're good at it. I've tried. Believe me, Mary, I have tried.' He slumped down again at the table.

Mary breathed in deeply. A tremor of self-consciousness came to her: this is my life, it seemed to be reminding her; this is the man I chose to spend it with, in what he regards, rightly perhaps, as a delusion, a convenient pretence that there can be value without permanence.

But he is my life, she thought, and I have no other, and I must save him if for no better reason than that I must save myself.

She crossed to his chair, knelt down beside him and dredged the depths of herself for the most charged, vital and persuasive memories of their shared life together. She recalled to him his insane joy at Louisa's birth; how he had rushed out to telephone his father. She described Richard's double-footed leap across the floor of their Tokyo flat, because a mere walk could not contain his appetite for living; she began an inventory of the children's most ridiculous words and phrases, mistakes she knew had made him subside, momentarily at least, with the burden of love.

She gripped his wrist with both her hands, her brow flexed in concentration as she provoked the flow of images, in a free-associated rush, knowing that among them there might be moments of such poignancy and joy that their inexplicable light would find a way into the dark logic of his despair.

When he tried to speak, she put her hand across his mouth for fear that the decisive example might not yet have come back to her, might still be on the edge of her memory. She talked of flats and houses, villas down dirt tracks and rented farmhouses where they had created characters from people they had met, where friends they loved as much for their forgiven weaknesses as for their admired strengths had held back the hours with talk; she recalled to him Louisa's blinking face when she emerged from water after swimming and her gurgling laughter; the day when they had sat and watched a school prize-giving, when Mary had known that he would have traded every honour, every degree and advancement he had ever received if his only son might once be mentioned in the junior school spelling prize; that every cell in his body was clamouring in desire for it; and she described the furtive movement of his hand to track away the tear that had rolled out from his clamped eye and exploding heart when it had been so.

'And the men you cared for in Africa and Italy, the families you wrote to,' she said. 'You managed that, my love, you rose above their loss and everything it meant. So did thousands of others like you. That's why we loved you, you wonderful generation of men, that you were strong enough to do that, to see what you saw, to go through all that, the death of friends, the death of people dear to you — to all of us, for God's sake — and would not let it shake your view that the victory was to the meek, the good, the modest. The men who never bragged or talked about it but just went quietly about their business afterwards. For our children, for gentle people like my father and like you. You fought that battle against the despair that might have followed and you won it. Once and for all time you won it. You can't throw back that victory now.'

She talked until she felt her throat begin to burn. Then she threw back her head to catch her breath, and as she did so her eye was caught by the plaster of the light-fitting in the ceiling above them. She thought of the concealed microphone, the invisible wires that tracked back to a large spool of slowly turning Soviet tape, so that everything she had said — her reasons for living and her reasons for wanting her husband to live — had been recorded and preserved for later scrutiny.

★   ★   ★

She held Charlie tightly in her arms that night in bed, and felt his resistance to living decontract as the blue pill did its gentle work. In the morning, she left him asleep and went downstairs in search of food and drink. As she left the room, the door opposite opened, and a fair-haired young man in a Western suit, clearly the Embassy's look-out, called a cheerful 'good morning'. She had another wait of fifteen minutes for the lift, so by the time she returned to the room, the coffee was cold and Charlie had no appetite for the bread and jam.

He remained in bed, staring ahead of him without speaking. Mary continued to talk to him as she set about tidying the room; her conversation was much lighter in tone than on the night before, though she made sure that it all looked to the future, to the plans she had for them and for the children. She had inherited a small amount of money from her mother; she did not mention that she had spent a little of it on her hotel bill in New York; she somewhat exaggerated to Charlie how much was left and how far it would go in helping to solve their financial difficulties.

In the middle of the morning a chambermaid with a metal bucket and a mop paid them a brief visit, seldom allowing her sullen gaze to stray from Charlie's prone figure on the bed. At noon Mary went downstairs again to bring up some food to the room, but again Charlie refused to eat it. She looked out of the window at the dim light over the city and wished the day would pass more quickly; there was nothing for her to do but sit in silence with him. The friendly wives who might have kept her company had clearly been deterred by Charlie's manner; she longed to go outside, but did not want to leave Charlie on his own. In the early afternoon there was another knock at the door, and this time it was Dixon Keslake, the Embassy doctor.

An ascetic-looking man with horn-rimmed glasses and an English pinstripe suit, he sat on the edge of the bed and checked Charlie's blood pressure. As the cuff inflated, he said, 'How did he sleep?'

'Quite well, I think,' said Mary. Charlie nodded dumb assent.

'You can leave us for a moment or two, Mrs

van der Linden,' said the doctor. 'If you'd just like to wait in the other room.'

Mary looked out of the window. The day seemed to be closing down already, ebbing away before it had really dawned. The bedroom door opened a few minutes later and the doctor emerged.

'Well, everything appears to be all right,' he said. 'He's obviously pretty stunned from the medication, but that's to be expected.'

'Yes, but what exactly is the matter with him? He was almost . . . suicidal last night.'

Keslake coughed as he put his stethoscope back in his bag. 'It's difficult to be certain. He's had, or is having, some sort of breakdown. I suspect that some of his symptoms may be caused by excessive alcohol. A kind of delirium. But it's impossible to be sure. I also think that the unhealthy atmosphere of Moscow has contributed. He feels hunted. I think he feels unsafe and will be an awful lot better when you get him home. That's not unusual, even among healthy people. The Moscow Twitch.'

'How long before he's back to normal?'

'I'm not sure he'll ever be exactly the same. He'll need psychiatric treatment to begin with, perhaps as an in-patient. Then he'll need to be treated for alcoholism. There may be liver damage as well. To be honest, Mrs van der Linden, I doubt whether he will ever resume the life he had in Washington. But will that be a loss? After all, it did him no good. It drove him to this . . . condition.'

Mary bit her lip. 'And what can I do now?'

'You must try to make him eat something. Soup at the very least. If he won't eat the food here, and I can't say I blame him, you must go and buy something. Go to one of the hard-currency shops, get something he really likes. Tempt him.'

'I can't remember where the nearest foreigners' shop is.'

Dr Keslake took her to the window and pointed. 'Walk along beside the river, then cross there at Borodinsky Bridge. Look. You can just see the bridge there, then that takes you up to Arbat Street, past that giant building, the one that looks like this hotel, which is the Ministry of Foreign Affairs.' In the absence of any maps, he gave her detailed directions. 'You do have some dollars, do you?' he said.

Mary nodded. 'Yes. But is it safe to leave him?'

'I've given him a little injection which will make him sleep for a couple of hours at least. Take the blue pills with you. I've confiscated all his others.'

'And what about . . . You know. The Russians.'

Dr Keslake smiled. 'I don't think anyone's going to come calling, and we've got our chap across the corridor. I think your poor husband has already compromised himself, Mrs van der Linden. There's nothing more that any third party could do. The priority is not to allow the gentlemen of the press to get wind of it. Relations are a little strained at the moment. And do remember the microphones, won't you? I'm sure Mike Winterburn mentioned them.'

Mary nodded and Keslake held out his hand. 'I'll call again at midday tomorrow to make sure you're all right to travel. I'll bring something nice to eat from the commissary. Try not to worry. Your husband is very unwell, but we reached him before it was too late. It will need a lot of care and a lot of patience, but we are in time.'

When she was sure Charlie was peacefully asleep, Mary left a note explaining that she would be back shortly, took her coat and scarf and walked down the passageway to the lift. In a mere five minutes she was down in the crepuscular lobby of the Ukraina, and a few moments later she was out in the cold world beyond.

It was snowing lightly, but the temperature did not seem much worse than on a severe winter's day in England; then, as she descended to the river embankment, out of the shelter of the huge building, she felt the cut of the wind. She wrapped her scarf round her head and ears, then quickly thrust her freezing fingers back into her coat pockets.

Her thoughts were on the moment: how long Charlie might sleep, what food she might find to tempt him, the route to the shop described by Keslake; but as she neared the bottom of the Borodinsky Bridge she felt a shudder going down her spine that was more than the wind driving through the woollen coat. Someone was following her.

She could hear no footsteps, she could see no figure from the corner of her eye, which was as far as she dared to turn her head; yet she was aware that eyes were on her, assessing her.

On the bridge she paused and looked down for a long time into the water.

Paralysed by self-consciousness, she listened for steps or breathing. They had warned her it would happen. She looked back towards the Ukraina, its awful bulk, with the upper floors stepped in a little as they reached the triumphalist peak. She tried to figure out which was Charlie's room; to see behind which lit window her life might be for ever changing.

She moved on briskly, almost trotting in her need to keep warm, as she passed the Ministry of External Affairs on her right. She could bring herself to do no more than glance at the hundreds of identical windows, behind which the machine of state Communism — its officials working on Romania or Hungary, making their plans for Poland and Czechoslovakia — was clanking in the dusk, as she hurried past and entered the elegant stretch of Arbat Street. She looked into the shop windows, thinking there might be something she could buy with the roubles Winterburn had given her that would save her a longer walk. It was difficult to tell what each shop was meant to have, since none had advertising or trade names, only a generic identification that she could not read. One room was more brightly lit than the others, and she could see a woman in a white apron, which suggested to her the possibility of food. She went in and looked round; the woman scowled at her from behind a counter, following Mary's gaze as it travelled down the long wooden shelves, from floor to ceiling, on every wall, that held nothing. By the till was a single jar of pickled cucumbers, and Mary backed out, smiling her apologies, into the street.

The light was almost gone from the day, drained down into the cold paving slabs beneath the soles of her mother's boots. The sensation of being followed returned at once, and with it came again a sense of objectivity about herself. She remembered standing in the bathroom of her New York hotel room, rolling on mascara before she took the subway down to Frank's apartment on that eventful afternoon. She had gazed at herself in the mirror and struggled for self-awareness: her brown eyes had stared back, candid and amoral, indicating only careless human atoms in their agitated moment.

Now, beneath the totalitarian gaze of her unknown pursuer, her muscles braced and locked against the cold, her sense of her self was restored to her: mother, daughter, wife — a person grafted by a million social fibres to the lives of those around her. Her nature and her temperament, the energy of love that she had poured into making not just the flesh of her children but their expectations and their apprehension of the world with all its bitter joy and contradictions — all these aspects of what she was became clear again to her.

She stood outside herself: she walked beside her KGB pursuer, her ardent shadow, and together they looked at the figure that she made. Small Western woman, wearing American clothes; alone; foolishly without gloves; of young middle age; mother and wife; deeply preoccupied. She felt a sudden, lifting movement in her soul, a tide of pure compassion for her plight. To be able to look at herself for a moment with the same disinterested scrutiny that she would give another human being was a liberation from the tunnel of her passion. For a few moments she walked without feeling the ground beneath her feet; she saw herself in a true perspective, as though God loved her.

★ ★ ★

At the end of Arbat Street she went past the Praga hotel, where she remembered dining with Charlie and some friends one night. She had eaten sturgeon, a mixture of insipid flesh and sharp bones, served in a circle with its pointed snout forced through its tail. She was now on what she remembered as the inner ring road, one of two concentric routes about the city, yet she also seemed to be heading towards the Kremlin. This was wrong, she knew; but which way was she supposed to go?

As she paused again, the relief she had been feeling gave way to fear. As she had seen herself for what she was, her duties had become clear. There was no longer any question in her mind what she would have to do: she would rededicate herself to her husband's well-being, and to that of her children. It was clear and it was good. Yet this future scared her because it had a simple consequence: the end of America. It would entail a life in which she would have to forsake the only feeling that had made her able to transcend the limits of her existence.

She had walked on, lost in her returning troubles, afraid to admit she no longer knew where she was going. Her hands were now so cold that she began to think about frostbite; it had happened once to someone they knew, a journalist, who had lost part of his ear. She must find gloves, she thought, and since she could not remember where the hard-currency shop was supposed to be the only answer was to go to GUM, the big department store behind Red Square. Everyone knew GUM; and although she would have to wait and although they would be of poor quality, there was at least a chance that they would have some.

Navigating by the Kremlin's castle walls, she had looped behind Red Square and found herself in a narrow passage that ran off Nikolskaya Street. It was hard to make her way when she could not read the street signs; the elementary Greek her father had taught her at the age of twelve was some help with the Cyrillic letters, but she was beginning to feel tired as well as deeply uneasy about the persistence of her follower. What if he should take her and bundle her into a car?

The daylight was nearly finished in the street; the last of the ochre, powder-blue and pistachio colours on the nineteenth-century stucco was fading to black. Down alleyways Mary glimpsed secretive courtyards; there were outsize tin drainpipes to deal with snow from the roofs, and their huge mouths were stuck with icicles; the half-basement windows were furred with grime and soot. Her cheeks were burning and her eyes were watering in the wind when she at last caught sight of the welcome, blocksized bulk of GUM.

Inside it was warm, heavy with the airless press of unwashed bodies. Unable to ask for what she wanted, Mary searched back and forth, retraced her steps, went upstairs, down, and up again, in such a rapid and apparently random manner that it occurred to her that she might well lose her shadow. There were no gloves to be had, however; not for roubles or dollars or for any number of hours standing in a line. 'Nyet,' said the woman behind the counter when Mary eventually reached it and pointed to the gloved hands of the next customer. 'Nyet'; and even she knew what that meant. There was nothing in the food department with which she could tempt Charlie; he did not care for pickled cabbage or rye bread. It occurred to her that she might ask the Praga hotel if they would let her take away a meal of chicken and rice, but it would be cold by the time she got it back to the Ukraina. She was reluctant to leave the aromatic fug of the big store, where at least the feeling had returned to her fingers, but she could not risk leaving Charlie for too long.

There were footsteps behind her again on the street. Be careful, Mary . . . For Christ's sake, be careful. Frank's words came back to her, and brought with them an idea. She could go and see his colleague in Sadova Samotechnaya; he might let her have some food and might also lend her some gloves. Sad Sam was easy to find, she remembered. It was on the outer ring, and all you needed to do was go up Petrovka Street, past the Bolshoi on your left, keep going straight for about ten minutes and you were there. It would be easier to call at the British Embassy on the other side of the river, but she did not want to go there; she did not want to be another 'loose cannon', or whatever the pompous term was they had used about Charlie. They did not know what glories had been his, what death-defying fire he had had. 'Then, blow me down, the little wife turns up on our doorstep without even a pair of gloves. Can you imagine?' She could hear the cultured, ironic tones of Michael Winterburn as he relished the anecdote. In any event, she wanted to see someone who knew Frank, an American who would give her American drinks and to whom she could say Frank's name as often as she liked under the guise of making polite conversation about the only thing they had in common.

She easily found the Metropol hotel, with its art nouveau façade and lobby full of KGB prostitutes, and, close by, the start of Petrovka Street. She felt vindicated, as though this proved her plan was sound. But she was very cold and, as the large blocks of Petrovka went slowly past, she became convinced that the footsteps were coming closer.

Thoughts of Frank, and of Charlie, began to fade from her mind; she had no energy left for anything but her own survival. Periodically she took her hands from her coat pockets and blew on them, but the warming effect of her breath was lost to the cold of the air. Sad Sam was more than ten minutes up Petrovka; it was much more, she discovered, when at last she came to a junction, but discovered it was only the inner, not the outer, ring road.

Mary's courage began to fail. She saw no taxis and would in any case have been too frightened to get into one. The cold had frozen her ability to think; even her mental energy was now required to keep her warm, as she pushed on blindly, increasingly fearful of the tap on the shoulder, the strong arm around her waist as the black Volga drew up alongside, leaking fumes from its exhaust, its doors held open from inside.

At the junction of the outer ring, she faltered. Was it left or right? This she could not afford to get wrong. She needed one last effort, and she prayed for the energy to make it. Then, on the other side of the road, and to her right, she saw the drab but familiar view they had had from the front window of their apartment. She hurried on and turned up the narrow street to Sadova Samotechnaya, shivering with relief. She stopped at the the guard post and gave the uniformed policeman the name of the paper and its correspondent. After two telephone calls, he gestured her through, watching her back with heavy eyes as he reached again for the receiver.

Mary pushed open the door at the corner of the block and found herself in a small wooden entrance box; another door led into a dingy hall with a stone floor and a caged elevator. A woman of about her age was coming down the stairs; she

429

turned out to be English and, in response to Mary's request, directed her to the fourth floor.

She knew better by now than to wait for the lift and ran up the tenement steps instead, arriving breathless and close to collapse. The door was opened by a plump American in spectacles with a cigarette between his fingers and a pen clenched between his teeth.

'Mr Sheppard?'

'Yep.'

'My name's Mary van der Linden. I'm a friend of a colleague of yours, Frank Renzo.' She paused. 'It's a bit of a long story.'

★   ★   ★

'Come on in,' said Deke Sheppard. 'Take your boots off. Here are some slippers.'

He left her in a small, untidy sitting room with piles of books and newspapers on the floor; Mary found a radiator and put her frozen hands against its ribs.

'Right,' said Sheppard, coming back into the room. 'I've told my secretary to hold any calls — not that anyone gets through much on the Moscow phone system. It's good to have a visitor. You from London?'

Mary explained her situation, and Sheppard nodded sympathetically. She did not explain the nature of Charlie's illness, but stressed that he must be made to eat and wondered if perhaps she could buy some food from him.

Sheppard smiled. 'Keep your dollars. You're a friend of Frank's, that's good enough for me.

Come and take a look in the kitchen, see if there's anything that takes your fancy.'

In a primitive square room, he opened various store cupboards. 'I get all this stuff from the Embassy, but I eat out most days. Tell me about that sonofabitch Renzo. What trouble's he in now? I heard they're sending him to Washington.' Sheppard had a big, phlegmy laugh.

Frank was coming to live in her home town at the moment she was leaving: the reminder came at a bad moment for Mary, and she struggled for a moment to compose herself among the cans of beans and jars of American preserves.

'He's doing fine. Now I suppose what I'd really like is some soup, but the trouble is, it'll be cold by the time I get it back.'

'Listen, lady, this is the twentieth century. Even here in Moscow. Ever hear of a vacuum flask? What's he like? Campbell's cream of chicken?'

'Are you sure?'

'Sure I'm sure. Now where's that can opener?'

They chatted about Frank while Sheppard made up what he called a Marshall Aid package: a flask of hot chicken soup, some sesame-seed bagels with Skippy peanut butter, a small box of Oreo cookies, two cans of tuna in oil with a spare can opener thrown in, some butter wrapped in greaseproof paper, a half loaf of wholewheat bread, a tub of imported coleslaw, some Stolichnaya vodka, a packet of Fritos corn chips, some local cherry jam, half a dozen tangerines and a large glass jar of Beluga caviar.

'Some guy gave it to me. They're always giving

431

it to me, hoping I'll write something nice about them, I guess. I hate the goddam stuff. Brings me out in hives. Now if you don't mind my saying so, you need some gloves. I have a couple of ladies' pairs I keep spare.'

Mary calculated that she had been gone more than two hours and that she needed to get back. As Sheppard burrowed into a drawer in a chest in the small entrance hall, she explained, while trying to minimize how foolish she sounded, her fear of getting into a taxi.

'Don't worry, I understand. Kind of unsettles you having these big goons following you around. I'll run you back myself. It's ten minutes round the ring and I need some air anyway.'

He overcame Mary's protests and forced a large rabbit-skin hat over his thin hair. 'This is my minus ten hat. I have a minus twenty as well. But we Muscovites don't get to put the flaps down till minus fifteen.' He gave her a big smile, full of America. 'We consider it what you Britishers would call 'unsporting'.'

He took her out to the courtyard and opened the doors of a muddy blue Volvo. With what seemed to Mary like miraculous speed after the rigours of her walk, they drove round the north-western rim of the city, past the zoo and the American Embassy, and crossed the river at the Borodinsky Bridge.

Mary thanked her saviour warmly, but her spirits fell as she found herself once more on the wide steps leading up to the Ukraina; she turned at the heavy doors, clasping her bag of supplies, and saw Deke Sheppard waving to her as he prepared to depart.

Back inside the murk, she crossed the expanse of the lobby and braced herself for the elevator wait. After a mere ten minutes she was clanking skyward, then making her way once more down the passageway beneath the sour gaze of the beshawled crone at her desk.

It seemed to Mary that she had already made this short walk an infinite number of times; its details had acquired the power of the eternal: Hell might be this reeking grey corridor, with its straight lines that converged to a never-realized vanishing point.

Once more as she fitted the key to the lock and opened the door she feared for what she would find inside. It was dark. When she had located the light switch, she placed the bag of food on the table and went into the bedroom. Charlie was lying down, curled up beneath the blankets, though something in his attitude made Mary think he was not asleep. She touched him on the shoulder and he slowly raised himself on to an elbow.

He smiled. It was the first time she had seen him smile since she had been in Moscow. She kissed him and told him she had brought some food. The smile left his face, but she said that after all the trouble she had been to, she expected him to try. She left him to get dressed while she laid out some plates and cutlery from the glass-fronted cabinet on the thick pile cloth with its curious dangling bobbles.

Charlie reached for the vodka bottle when he came into the sitting room, but Mary put her hand on his. 'You must eat first. You can have one drink afterwards if you've eaten.'

Meekly he spooned some of the soup to his lips. He grimaced at the taste, but managed to swallow it. Mary also began to eat; she had had nothing since arriving twenty-four hours earlier and found Deke Sheppard's picnic a feast of urgent flavours.

She watched Charlie spoon some caviar uncertainly on to a slice of bread.

What does it mean to love a man? she thought. Does it mean you take his weaknesses, his shaking hands, transparent failings, and subsume them in yourself, where you can heal, and make them strong, and give them back to him restored? It means that at some point you give up the idea of yourself as a person capable of infinite expansion. It means that if an impossible choice is to be made between his life and yours, you choose his. And it means that you cannot repine for this hard moment, because he is grafted on to you; that what you do for him you do also for yourself and for some separate entity that is greater than the sum of both, because the dangerous enterprise of your joined life is more dramatic, more arresting and more exciting than any alternative could ever be.

She could no more abandon him than she could turn away from the crying of her child. 'I love you,' she said.

Charlie's eyes filled with tears above the food he was struggling for her sake to eat. He swallowed and coughed. He said, 'You're more than I deserve.'

434

She said, 'I don't know what all this means. 'Breakdown'. What's that? But you will be well again. I'll make sure of that.'

'Will you stay with me?'

'Now?'

'No. Always.'

Mary looked round the room, at its sticky floor, botched carpentry and Soviet-approved paintings. She saw the wooden radiator cage, half-detached from the wall, and she thought of the wires that ran back into the plaster of the monstrous building, up to a listening station on the twenty-somethingth floor, where two bored men with nicotine fingers and raw faces watched the slowly turning spools and listened like recording angels to the answer she must give.

Her voice was very quiet in her throat. 'Yes,' she said. 'Of course I will.'

Charlie lowered his head to the table and began to weep in huge convulsions.

'Of course I will,' said Mary. 'And in return, you must promise me to live. I lost my fiancé in that war and I've never looked back, I've never compared you to one another. I loved you for yourself, because with your laughter and your stories you made life glorious. My darling, you invented it — a way of living it at least.'

She stood up, flushed with the daring of the moment. 'I won't let you join him among the dead. You owe it to him and to me and to all those thousands of young men not to give in.'

Charlie ceased his sobbing long enough to say, 'I know.'

Mary walked round the table and knelt by

him. She laid her head on his shoulder as she had done so many times when first they were together; and he, remembering, stroked back the thick, almost-black hair from her forehead with his faltering hand.

20

The next day, Dr Keslake called and certified Charlie fit to travel.

'Thank you,' said Mary. 'I think I'm supposed to let the Ambassador . . . '

'Don't worry,' said Keslake. 'I'll fix all that.'

After lunch on the remains of Deke Sheppard's largesse, Mary packed their cases and at two o'clock Michael Winterburn called to take them to the airport. Mary looked up one final time at the slabbed mass of the Ukraina behind them, the slave monument of one totalitarian order to another, its spiral point lost in greying snow; she closed her eyes as they climbed into the car and turned towards the West.

Winterburn could barely contain his relief as he sped them to the airport, chattering about Embassy matters, hoping insincerely that they would come back soon. Charlie made a weary grimace at Mary from the back seat, suggesting an imminent return was unlikely, and she stifled a laugh; it was their first moment of pleasure together since she had been in Moscow and she thought it was a good augury for what lay ahead.

At the airport, Winterburn helped them with their cases and watched through a glass screen until they had negotiated the line at passport control; it was as though he feared some last-minute hitch would throw Charlie back into his orbit, another Cold War bomb waiting to explode. When they walked across the runway to the plane and climbed the steps, Mary looked back into the terminal building where she thought she saw Winterburn's anxious face pressed against the glass. He would not relax until he saw them airborne, she thought: he would not uncork his celebratory bottle until the aircraft was fifty miles west of Berlin.

With the hours winding back in their favour, they were home in Regent's Park in time to see Richard and Louisa before bed. In front of the fire in the sitting room, Mary hugged them to her and did not doubt for a moment the justice of what she had decided in that distant hotel room. This was her life, these backs and ribs that she crushed in her embrace, the bloom of their cheeks against hers, the smell of Richard's fragrant neck and Louisa's just-washed hair.

In the morning she took Charlie to see a former colleague of her mother's, who read the letter from Dr Keslake and referred him to a hospital in Edgware that he recommended for its sensitive handling of such matters. Charlie was allowed to go home and pack his bag before being admitted the next day.

After a week he was allowed home on condition that he attend as an outpatient three times a week for half a day; they prescribed a regime of sedatives and psychotherapy while they awaited definitive analysis of the liver. Charlie went into Whitehall to speak to the people in Personnel, who said he should take as long as he needed to recover; Charlie's accumulated reputation was worth something and he drew heavily on its credit. They would wait for the medical situation to clarify, but if necessary they would not ask him to return to Washington; they would deem that posting complete and would bring forward his next due spell at home, to be commenced when he was fit.

Mary then took Louisa and Richard to see a school in Primrose Hill, where it was agreed that they should begin in January. Reunited with his parents and removed from the school in Norfolk, Richard began to regain his ebullience; Louisa's eyes remained wary, but her mouth started to lose the suspicious, downward turn it had acquired since she had been taken from Washington. Mary could register the tiniest changes in their skin, or the shine of their eyes, and was gladdened by what she saw. Louisa took Mary's old room at the top of the house, Richard the one next to it that had been earmarked for a sibling never born. Mary and Charlie occupied the spare room on the floor below, and the house slowly filled with noises of playing, quarrelling and entreaty that it had never known before, certainly not in Mary's soft-footed and solitary childhood.

One day when everyone was out, Mary telephoned Frank in New York. He was not at his office, so she left a message with the secretary in the newsroom to say that she and Charlie had returned safely from Moscow; the secretary told her that Frank was shuttling back and forth a good deal from Washington and so could not say for sure when he would next be in. He was 'familiarizing' himself with the White House, she said, in preparation for Senator Kennedy's inauguration, and Mary wondered if that familiarity would extend to the girls with Bermuda shorts and Shetland sweaters, the girls called Fiddle and Faddle and Squidge.

The only way to be sure of reaching him was by post; so on the next occasion she could contrive to be alone, she wrote to him, a letter of blind despair from her prison of family goodwill.

Louisa practised 'Silent Night' on the piano and Richard memorized the verses of 'While Shepherds Watched Their Flocks', with schoolboy variations. Charlie went dutifully to Edgware, and found that the little he drank at night made him nauseous; perhaps, indeed, that was the function of the pills. By day he was stunned by drugs; at night he dreamed in stormy visions like a painter in a Victorian asylum: he found himself in Dien Bien Phu, on the road where the fighter-bombers laid their napalm trails. He was with the T'ai tribesmen as they bayoneted the scorched Vietminh survivors; then he dreamed he was strolling on the Boulevard St Germain with the studious Captain Rigaud, his Montaigne's *Essais* still beneath his arm, and that the boulevard opened up at the Raspail junction into an elevated highway to the clouds, taking Rigaud to heaven.

Most of all he dreamed of the cold, candle-lit restaurant in Florence where he had dined off spaghetti parmigiana and occasional black-market mushrooms in the dank autumn of 1943. He looked at the grain of the wooden table and pictured in it the English streets where his letters of condolence to grieving parents had not been delivered. One night he dreamed that his beloved company was reunited, the dead men living, the prisoners returned, the wounded whole again, and that when the order came to occupy the forward part of the salient, he refused; that, to the fury of the officer commanding the battalion, he took his men back to the beach at Anzio, embarked them on various pleasure craft and went sailing in the bay.

On the morning of Christmas Day the children brought down their stockings to their parents' room and opened them on the bed. Over the years a polite gratitude had edged into their sense of pure marvel at the bearded overnight visitor, but their pleasure in acquisition was undimmed. They went *en famille* to the church in Primrose Hill, brazenly, Mary thought, toughly confronting the fact that the last time they had been there was for her mother's funeral. The vicar greeted them with a particular smile, that sympathized but also congratulated them on accepting that all things had their place in God's calendar — the death, the Birth — and it was proper to submit themselves humbly to the great mysteries of Being.

Mary felt it was a fraud, that some essential error had been made, and it was only until she could sort it out that she was prepared to go along with this hypocritical contrivance. She shuddered beneath the vicar's compassionate, congratulatory look and pulled her hand from his encouraging squeeze.

441

Her father opened some wine he had been saving to drink with the turkey, and Charlie made a jug of dry martinis, though he did not drink one himself. Mary could not understand her mother's oven, which seemed to work either at full temperature or not at all; but by a sequence of brief yet intense irradiations over several hours the turkey was at last sufficiently cooked to be eaten without danger. It was late in the afternoon by the time they finally went through to the sitting room for charades, port, tangerines and other rituals that made all of them in their different ways feel that normality, if not restored — if not indeed recapturable — was at least capable of being imitated.

James looked at his daughter with gratitude, knowing what efforts she had made for him; Charlie gazed at her with stunned incredulity, still not able to replay, even in his stormy dreams, what had passed between them in the room at the Hotel Ukraina. Louisa and Richard extracted promises that they would never be sent away again, and Richard climbed on his mother's knee, where he laid his head against her bosom, as he had when he was a baby.

Mary felt its comforting weight, heavy like ripe fruit, and barely allowed her glance to go through the undrawn curtain, where the top left-hand window pane gave directly on to the diminished traffic of the London flightpath; though once, as she stroked Richard's hair, she did see the wing-tip lights of an ascending plane, heading west, blinking like a solitary star in the festive sky.

★ ★ ★

After the holidays the French government exploded an atomic device in the Sahara Desert; the next day Charlie's superiors wrote to say that in view of medical reports which suggested that it might be three months before he worked again, they would not be asking him to return to Washington. They suggested that his wife might like to go and tidy up their affairs, as they were anxious to have use of Number 1064 and of his office in the new Embassy building.

'I suppose we could just get the stuff shipped back,' Charlie said. 'If you don't want to go.'

'Well, it's a bit of a nuisance, isn't it?' said Mary. 'But all the children's things are there, and of course I'd like to say goodbye to everyone in Washington.'

'How long do you think it would take?'

'I don't know. Perhaps a week.'

'On second thoughts,' said Charlie, 'why don't you take as long as you like? You deserve a break.'

She looked at him quickly to see if he was implying more than he said, but his expression showed only a mildly generous concern.

She bought the children's uniforms and prepared the Regent's Park house for her absence, laying in quantities of food and explaining to her father, as well as she could, how the oven worked. Richard and Louisa made her promise to leave nothing behind in her packing; she was not to assume they had 'grown out' of anything, as she too often did, giving their

443

treasured possessions away to charity.

On the morning of her departure her father said goodbye before he took the children out, as promised, to the West End. Mary, her suitcase packed and ready by the front door, stood with Charlie in the sitting room as they waited for the ordered taxi.

'Say goodbye to the Renshaws,' said Charlie. 'Tell Eddie I found those lines from Emily Dickinson we couldn't remember that night. Wait. I'll write them down.' As he took a pen and paper from the desk, he read out what he wrote: ''If 'All is possible' with him/ As he besides concedes/ He will refund us finally/ Our confiscated Gods — '.'

Mary took the piece of paper.

'Got your passport? Say goodbye to Dolores. Have you got some money to give her? And say goodbye to Benton for me.' He smiled. 'Hope she doesn't 'goof' or 'flip' when she hears I'm not coming back.'

The taxi driver rang the bell and Charlie told him they would be with him in a moment. He nodded and returned to his ticking cab.

Charlie, pale and diminished, kissed Mary on the cheek as she stood on the threshold.

'And you?' he said.

She smiled. 'Me what?'

'Will you be coming back?'

★　★　★

Squeezed into the washroom of the aircraft, 30,000 feet above the Atlantic, Mary shook her wet hands above the basin and searched for a paper towel. The plane was rocking on the high thermals, yet it drove onward undeterred on its hell-bent westward course, reeling in the hours. There was nothing she could do about it now. Above the basin was a mirror, illuminated by flickering strips along its edge. Mary looked at her face, unsteady in the turbulence, and in the no man's land above the ocean her earthly resolutions had no gravity. She said softly, 'I'm coming for you, my love. Don't worry, I'm coming'; and in the glass, her eyes reflected only the glaring light of her need.

At Number 1064 Dolores was waiting to greet her. 'There's a lot of messages for you, Mrs van der Linden.'

Upstairs, curled on the bed, Mary started dialling. The first call she made was to New York; the requests of other friends and colleagues could be made to fit in. She heard Frank's voice against the background clatter of typewriters and telephones.

'I should have time Wednesday and Friday,' he said. 'Can you make that?'

She calculated rapidly. It would mean she would have to squeeze her Washington appointments into one day, but perhaps she could come back afterwards.

'It's a little crazy here,' said Frank. 'Then I may have to go to DC.'

'I don't want to be in New York if you're coming here.'

Frank sounded tense. 'I know. We just have to keep in touch. I'll do everything I can.'

'I've come all this way to see you.' This was no time, she thought, for flirtation.

'I know.'

'I've got to see you, Frank.'

'Christ, sweetheart, I know. You can just come here, if you like. And then, I don't know. Look, I'll call tomorrow morning at ten. You be there.'

'I will.' She paused for a moment, then thought no better of it. 'I love you,' she said.

She slept badly, waking at London hours, but had fallen asleep again by the time Frank called.

'I'll meet you at one at O'Reilly's saloon, Wednesday,' he said.

'What happens if you can't make it? You need somewhere to leave a message. I'll take a room in my old hotel. Then at least you'll know where I am.'

'OK. I gotta run now.'

With the appointment made, Mary relaxed a little. She prepared some coffee downstairs and brought it back up to bed, where she began to work through the list of callers Dolores had left. Katy Renshaw offered to fix lunch the following day, Tuesday, for as many of the old group as she could. Next, she called a young man at the Embassy who had registered an interest in buying the Kaiser Manhattan and arranged for him to come and see it that evening. Benton said she could stop by the office any time to go through Charlie's things.

Mary went out on to the street. It was cold, and the forecast was discouraging; she needed to get any necessary driving over quickly before the streets became impassable. If there was freezing rain, as the met men predicted, the only way to get up a slope was to grind the edge of the wheel against the sidewalk for grip. The Kaiser Manhattan responded to some sentimental blandishments and a full choke; Mary moved the column shift into first and moved off cautiously. The Chinese couple opposite would be relieved, she thought, to be rid of the van der Lindens' noisy parties. Number 1082 was unoccupied; the French journalist who had lived there had been sent home, according to Dolores: the reason that no one had ever heard of his magazine was that it was a front for unacceptable activities.

The new Embassy building was fully occupied and had a security system that kept Mary waiting in the glass-fronted lobby for ten minutes before Benton arrived to take her upstairs. In Charlie's office the two women went through his papers and belongings, deciding what could be thrown away and what needed to be shipped back to London.

'Mr. Renshaw already went through most of the papers,' said Benton. 'He took some away and put these ones aside for you to look at.'

'Yes, yes . . . ' Mary could not concentrate, and she felt that Benton's gaze was disapproving.

'How is Mr van der Linden?'

'He's much better, thank you. I think he was . . . over-tired. Strained.'

'Sure.' Benton removed an empty vodka bottle from the desk drawer and dropped it into the trash. 'Mr Renshaw said to call when you came by.'

'Yes. I'd love to see him.'

A few minutes later, Edward Renshaw came into the room and took Mary in his arms. 'Mary, I'm so sorry to hear about all your troubles. Is there anything more we can do to help you here? Are you seeing Katy tomorrow? What can I do?'

Mary was touched by his concern. 'I don't know, Eddie. Turn back the clock. Take us back to your cabin in the woods. We were happy there, weren't we?'

Edward smiled. 'How is the old bugger? Not too downhearted?'

'Not too bad. He told me to give you this. It's part of a poem.'

'Yes, I remember now,' said Edward, glancing through it. 'Keep in touch, Mary, won't you? We'll probably be back in London next year.'

When Edward left, and when she and Benton had finished their sorting, Mary took a package from her shopping bag and held it out.

'Charlie asked me to give you this. It's just a little token. He didn't have time to . . . ' She found herself trailing off beneath Benton's stern look, as though she had guessed that Charlie had made no such request and that the silk scarf she unwrapped was the best Mary could do at the airport.

'Thank you, Mrs van der Linden. Please give your husband my best wishes for a speedy recovery. I had a great regard for him.'

'Thank you, I — '

'We all did here.'

'He's certainly always — '

'We thought very highly of him as a man.'

'Thank you.' Mary looked down.

'Perhaps your husband might also care to know that I'm getting married in the fall.'

Outside, on Massachusetts Avenue, Mary had a powerful sense of her old life. It had all been so simple. Tomorrow, if everything had not gone wrong, she would be at one of Kelly Eberstadt's mornings for the wives of the Asian embassies, where they laughed at the ambitions of their husbands, or at Katy Renshaw's bake sale for the church, or Lauren's book-reading group that was an excuse for a four-course lunch with Californian 'champagne'. The next day she would go to the cinema way up on Connecticut, where she would sometimes slip off alone in the afternoon to watch one of those French films that left her with a sense of the sweetness and density of life.

She swung the car to the left and headed for Georgetown: a few minutes later she parked on Dumbarton Street and walked down the hill. Through the windows of the neat houses she saw bookshelves that were laden with the knowledge their owners had purposefully ingested: the Rise of Napoleon, the Fall of Hitler; Congressional records and confessional memoirs. The shelves passed no judgement on the grist — on Gramsci's *Prison Notebooks* as against the speeches of Mussolini — provided it was milled and turned into mental food for the Republic. To show that these people were not mere grinders of statistic and policy, there was even fiction among the alleged facts — Twain, Mark, up near Truman, Harry S; and Wilson, Edmund leaning into Wilson, Woodrow; it could be only a matter

449

of time, Mary thought, before the recollections of Salinger, Pierre squeezed in against the slender volumes of Salinger, J.D.

In Fiorello's she remembered how their life had been when they arrived in Washington, and with what delight she had set about furnishing and decorating Number 1064. Happy girl, as her mother had doubtless said.

★   ★   ★

She sold the Kaiser Manhattan that night to a bachelor defence specialist, who relished its lumpy, louche appearance and seemed not to notice the dent in the fender or to mind that it had rolled so many hard miles. 'My girlfriend's going to love this,' he said, making Mary feel unconscionably old. There was a message from Dolores to say that Frank had called, but when she telephoned his apartment there was no reply.

On Tuesday morning, with Dolores's help, she sorted out what needed to be shipped, what could be sent to the thrift shop and what could be thrown out. She had to take a cab to Katy's house in Chevy Chase and she asked for him to come back at three to take her to Union Station.

'How's the book going, Mary?' said Lauren.

'Oh, that . . . I haven't really had much time.'

They parted with warm embraces and lingering endearments, though in the eyes of Katy, Lauren and Kelly there was an identical look of puzzled concern as the driver stowed the bag in the trunk and Mary's slight figure climbed into the back of the cab. All three watched intently as the car moved off gingerly in heavy rain that was on the verge of freezing.

★ ★ ★

As her train approached New York, Mary inhaled and braced herself. It was a reflexive response to the approach of the city, to the skyline that sometimes looked half-charred — pocked and glowing like scorched wireless valves or the honeycombed filaments of broken gas fires. Coming over the Queensboro Bridge from the big airports, shooting out of the Midtown Tunnel up the ramp of 41st Street, even crawling in the easy way beneath the Styx into Penn Station, you needed to prepare a little; it was not a city to which you would want to cede the early points.

The street of Mary's hotel was high and narrow, between Broadway and Seventh Avenue, and lived in a grey light. The commercial deliveries on either side meant that the traffic was permanently blocked and no car made it through without sounding its horn at least once. There was a slow construction project going on, where steel girders were hoisted and locked in place by acrobats in hard hats with wrenches dangling from their leather pouches. She walked from Penn Station with her light suitcase and stepped round the earthbound workmen who were looping steel hawsers on to long timbers, like railways sleepers, and knocking the half-hitch into place with hammers. Further up the sidewalk was blocked by wooden hoardings that surrounded the labouring crane.

It was not much of a street, it was more of a thoroughfare, she thought, or would have been if it had been passable. The hotel itself was between a Chinese laundry and a locksmith; opposite were a few tawdry clothes shops and a narrow deli selling pale buns and pink sodas. Yet once she had registered and found her room, Mary felt at home again among the fancy whitewood furniture and the crimson carpets with their shampoo whorls.

She hung up her dresses, checked that there were no messages, then called home in London. She spoke to her father, who told her he was just expecting Charlie back from Edgware. When she had sent all her words of love and encouragement, she looked at her watch and worked out how many hours she had to endure before she saw Frank at one the next day. She had kept three of Charlie's sleeping pills when she cleared the bathroom cabinet at Number 1064 and packed them, along with the Donald Duck toothbrushes from the children's bathroom, in her own spongebag. The best way to pass the hours was to be unconscious, she thought: she took a white pill, like her husband, though, unlike Charlie, she washed it down with a glass of water from the faucet. It was only nine o'clock when, having set the alarm against some European coma, she climbed into bed.

In the morning she waited in the hotel, not daring to leave in case Frank should call to change the arrangement. It was not until half-past twelve that she went down on to the street. She was five minutes early at O'Reilly's, a

452

bar on Fifteenth Street near Third Avenue, close to Frank's office but not so close that they would see too many of his colleagues. She walked round Union Square to pass the time, and as the buildings of New York revolved about her, she felt a dread that he would not be there, or that the missing weeks would have fatally changed him. At five-past one, she pushed open the saloon door.

He was sitting at the bar, holding a newspaper cautiously open, at arm's length, as though ready to snap it shut at any moment should its contents disappoint him. He glanced up as she entered the warm room, then slid off the stool. She crossed the bare floorboards and put her arms round him; she kissed him briefly and settled on the stool next to his.

Nothing had changed. She looked at his face, the eyes with their splinters of hazel, the soft smile. Her dread vanished. She did not need to ask him what he thought or felt because she could see in his face, in his entire demeanour, that everything was the same, that no real time had passed for him since he had said goodbye to her on the night of the election.

Seeing this, she took his hand on top of the bar and kept looking into his face; there was no need to say anything. He looked back and she could see that he also felt profoundly comforted. When, after a minute or so, neither of them had spoken, Frank said, 'Well, I don't know where to begin.'

'I suppose you could get me a drink.'

'Okay. Now tell me about Moscow.'

'I didn't care for it at all.'

He smiled. 'I heard bad things about that place.'

'Communism is not a complete success. Not entirely. I think the West could yet win this war.'

'It's doing a good job of losing at the moment. And Charlie?'

'Charlie. He . . . He'll be fine.'

'Is he coming back to America?'

'No.'

Frank looked down at the bar.

Mary said. 'We don't need to talk about this now.'

'I guess not. You back in your old hotel?'

'Yes. It's like home.'

'You want to get something to eat?'

'Not really.' She sighed. 'I just want to look at you.'

'Sure thing. Can I look back?'

'You can.'

She heard the snare-drum rattle of the swizzle stick against the glass, but his eyes did not leave hers.

'So. You gonna live in London?'

The tone of the conversation was still light. 'I guess so.' She was still able to smile. 'But maybe not.' It was not she who said it; someone else said these things when she was with him.

'Where does that leave me?'

'I suppose it leaves you in Washington, Frank.'

'When you going back?'

'Saturday evening. From Washington.'

'Could you change that?'

'What do you mean?'

'I mean, call the airline and get them to reroute you from New York. I'd be free Saturday.'

'I see. I thought you meant . . . '

'What did you think?'

'I thought you meant . . . Cancel it.'

'Is that what you'd like?'

Mary let her eyes leave his face for the first time. She looked down and bit her lip. 'Yes,' she said, 'that's what I'd like.'

'But you can't do it, can you?'

'I . . . I'm not sure that I can.'

'It's a moral thing, isn't it?' he said. 'After all this, it comes down to a question of right and wrong.'

'Can we talk about something else? What'll we do on Saturday?'

'I always thought we'd find a better way of dealing with this. What I feel about you. I thought we'd find a higher plane, whatever you want to call it.'

'But I couldn't find the words for that better way.'

'Me neither. But morality, I mean . . . ' He threw his arms apart. 'The simple goddam right or wrong, it seems . . . I don't know.'

'It seems like a blunt instrument.'

'Yeah.' He breathed in deeply. 'Though I guess the good thing is that you can understand it. A kid could follow it. It all makes sense.'

'Frank, I don't think I can take this conversation right now. I'm going to make a fool of myself if we carry on. I'm going to cry or something. There are people watching. Can we please talk about something else?'

After the pleasure of seeing that everything was the same for Frank, Mary had briefly convinced herself that the near future consequently held for her only sweetness and delight. As the conversation had progressed, however, she began to see that it was not that clear; it did not follow that because the most important thing in her life was secure, the rest would serenely flow: rather the opposite, in fact.

At that moment she glimpsed the magnitude of what was actually awaiting her.

She said, 'I don't think I'm going to be able to manage this.'

'Look,' said Frank, 'I got a lot of things on the next coupla days, but I'm sure I can make some time. What do you say we make a date for lunch on Friday? I'm going to Minneapolis tomorrow, but I should be back Friday morning. Then I'll be free later in the day. Then, what the hell, your plane's not till Saturday evening, right? We got all the time in the world.'

'Don't you have to get back to work?'

'Well, right now I do. But I'll call you later.'

'What about this evening?'

'I have a job. I can't get out of it.'

'What time will it finish?'

'Late.'

'I don't care how late it is. Call me. Come to my hotel. Don't even call. Just come.'

She sat up in the chair in her hotel room that night, trying hard to stay awake, assailed by wave after wave of displaced sleep — last night's, tomorrow night's, the sleep of the hours that had gone missing over Greenland and Labrador. She was scared that if she slept she would not hear the telephone ring up from Reception. She glared at the silent instrument, then felt her heavy eyelids falling once again. Across the room was her open suitcase, whose contents struck her as pathetic: the carefully chosen clothes, the new shoes she thought he'd like, the wicked self-delusion of the whole enterprise. Back in London her darling children slept their innocent, restoring sleep, while here in the decadent jungle she was howling like some alley cat in the darkness.

God forgive me, she thought, God help me. I didn't make myself like this; I didn't ask to know this awful passion.

When at last the telephone sounded on the nightstand, she did not know if she should answer. But it was him. He came upstairs and made love to her. Although she joined in avidly, wretchedly, she hated it because it confirmed that she was lost; she was desperate and out of human control.

★ ★ ★

Frank left at six in the morning to catch his plane to Minneapolis. He felt shocked and exhausted by the night before. Christ, he thought, as he buckled his seat belt, I had myself down as a man not easily thrown, but now I'm in some area I can't handle. I don't know where I am. I have no bearing, no maps — it's like Guadalcanal.

He felt a miniature smile at the comparison.

The stewardess leaned over with a tray of breakfast and smiled back dutifully, thinking that he, like all the other early business travellers, was flirting with her.

However much he resented the minutes of absence from Mary, it was almost a relief to be away, to see bright snowy air beneath him. Escape, escape, there was always that thing in a city man, he thought. The first time he had managed was during the Depression when, like so many others of his age, he had ridden a freight train from the railroad yards of South Chicago. He had gone with his brother Louis, out east past the Studebaker plant at South Bend, where the men were on strike. There were clear skies all the way to Cleveland, and he and Louis had thought nothing of the hardship or the stench of fellow travellers in the boxcars. Louis was without a job; Frank had just left an insurance office on La Salle Street, where the winter sun never broke through the grey canyons. The idea was to get as far as Buffalo, then maybe cross the border into Canada and start again in Toronto. They liked the sound of Toronto — the Italian cadence of the name — and refused to believe that it was settled by Scottish Puritans. But they were turned back at the border and, after a month in Detroit, slipped back into Chicago, took a streetcar from the station and began once more the forlorn search for work.

The next escape had been in France, where, after a period of rest and recreation, his unit was despatched in 1945. He had never been to

Europe before and found the unscarred part of France more beautiful than any landscape he had seen outside the Art Institute on Michigan Avenue. They travelled through the small towns of Belgium in triumph, throwing candy bars from the roof of train cars to the children waiting by the track. As they came to Aachen, they saw the rubble of a real front and their exhilaration stalled. They relieved another unit, dug in just short of the Rhine, and from his foxhole Frank could see the twin towers of Cologne cathedral. Billy Foy was next to him and they clutched one another's arms in wonder at the sight. Two days later they pulled out, crossed the river and ran through an area the artillery had flattened, yet even in the rubble there were courtyards with flowering fruit trees and a sense among the young men as they leaped over piles of German bodies that nothing now could halt their progress. They ran into enemy patrols and, down below them by a river, a company of German infantry. Even as they surrounded them and cut them off, Frank was aware of the beauty of the meadows, of the sheep grazing on the side of the hill as they ran through them, firing.

They navigated, it seemed to him, by church steeples in the moonlight. One night they were so far ahead of the supplies that they ran out of ammunition; they lay on a hillside with German cannon going off all round them. Wexler and Douglas had assembled a mortar, but there was nothing to fire from it, so they took it apart, stood up the face plate, like a waffle-iron, and took cover behind it. In the morning, with new supplies, they resumed their progress through the cobbled streets and flowering orchards of the German villages.

If only, as Billy said, they had not had to kill so many people on their way.

Frank looked out of the window as the plane began its descent toward the Twin Cities. The most exhilarating means of escape had been Mary; it was through her that he had finally seen a way to transcend what he had become and to leave behind the wounds the public world had laid on him. How truly did she feel the same?

In Minneapolis he stayed in the hotel where he had met Charlie. He called Mary and spoke to her in her room; she sounded feminine, her voice light and almost girlish, yet frighteningly composed, as she always did on the telephone.

That night Frank lay down on his bed and gazed up at the ceiling. It was Mary's choice, he thought. He could not be the instrument of so much destruction. Her future was hers to decide, and so, it followed, was his.

★   ★   ★

Mary woke late on Thursday to find Frank gone. She looked round the dishevelled hotel room, at the scene of the crime, abandoned clothes, and she longed, suddenly, for respectability.

Towards one o'clock she went outside into the city, with no particular goal in mind. She had to watch her step in the narrow streets, where push-boys were wheeling handtrucks full of dresses, sport coats, skirts and blouses that swayed from their metal rails as they guided them to the delivery trucks that stood with their engines running at the kerb as the disgorged bolts of material were replaced by finished garments. The freed workers of the sweat-shops pushed into cafeterias and lunch counters or clustered round the pitchmen at the junction of Broadway. On the street corner, they gazed up longingly at the winter sun, obliquely visible through the gaps of the looming skyscrapers, checked their wristwatches and reluctantly chucked away their cigarette butts before heading back into the workrooms where no light shone.

On Seventh Avenue, out of habit, Mary took a cab downtown to the Village and walked round Washington Square. The temperature was only a little above freezing and she dug into the pockets of her coat to find the gloves that Deke Sheppard had given her. She looked from the south side, between the wintry trees and through the triumphal arch up Fifth Avenue to the distant Empire State Building, a mile or more away, but clearly outlined in the sparkling air.

She would stay here; she would make this her home. When Frank came back, she would tell him what she had decided. Somehow, she would make an arrangement with the children and with Charlie; she would divide herself between the two countries, and if the children continued to live, as they should, in her parents' house, they would be safely wrapped in the love of family that had once been hers.

It was done, it was decided, and she passed the day, somehow, a sandwich, a long sleep in her room, a movie in the small cinema next to the Plaza, a cocktail in the Warwick on Sixth Avenue, and home to an early night. She switched her airline departure from Washington to New York; she thought it would be tempting providence to cancel the return completely. She called Dolores to make sure the men from the shipping company had been, but she could not bring herself to telephone London.

It was quiet when she awoke in the morning: no dumpster truck resounding, no rain pattering on the condenser, but a soft ethereal quietness. She released the white roller blind to see snow rising up the shaft between the buildings, floating upwards, falling and rebounding like popcorn on the hot air of the ventilation shafts below. She climbed back into bed to watch it. Frank telephoned from the airport at Minneapolis and asked her to meet him at one o'clock in the bar of a hotel called the Ambassador on East 68th Street, just off Madison.

She tried to read a book, she tried to read a newspaper, but found it impossible to concentrate. She took a long bath and dressed in a navy skirt and a beige cashmere sweater, what she had worn on her first lunch date with him, fussing and straightening the hems; she made up carefully, as for a performance. She had brought her mother's old fur-lined boots in case of such weather and, although they spoiled the appearance of casual chic she had wanted, there was no alternative on the snowbound streets.

She arrived punctually at one at the Ambassador, whose lobby was like a viable small town, with a hairdresser's at one end, through whose window Mary could see an elderly woman with orange hair reading *Life* magazine. In front of her was a newspaper kiosk with piles of the *Times* and the *Wall Street Journal* stacked on the floor beneath lead weights. The circulated air was warm and heavy; she hesitated for a moment as her eye was caught by the white flutter of a letter tumbling down the glass-fronted mail chute beside the elevator.

She found the bar, which was decorated like a gentleman's club with wood panelling and leather armchairs. This time Frank was not there. Mary took a seat at a table, where a white-jacketed waiter leaned over her with an empty tray.

'Yes . . . A tomato juice, please.'

She was beset by questions. What if, when she said that she was leaving her family to live with him, Frank should say no? Did it make any difference that they would first of all be in Washington, and who knew where after that? Was it New York itself that she really cared for? Was her decision motivated by something unworthy? That one she could answer: it was love, there was no doubt about that; it was an unstoppable force: it was, in its own way, a moral force.

What would her mother have said about this awful decision?

463

She had a clear vision of her mother's loved face. She would be appalled. Or would she? The one thing dead people were sure to be was understanding: they would, like Troilus floating high above the world of fallen Troy, break into eerie laughter. From their perspective, there was no mortal urgency; *tout comprendre, c'est tout pardonner*, after all, but it was more than that: to know everything is to laugh at it. It was in any case her mother who had once explained to her how the jealous Titans had so resented humanity's perfection that they had sundered the human soul and left each lost half for ever searching for the other. That, she had told the fourteen-year-old Mary, was the Greeks' explanation of the love instinct, of its awful power.

She sipped the drink, keeping her eyes on the door into the lobby. Each time a shadow came across it, she tensed forward in her chair. The minutes were passing.

Perhaps the reason she had made this decision was out of simple self-protection: she could not face the pain of separation from Frank. It was not a moral choice, or even one of balanced judgement, it was simply cowardice. She did not know. In the long term perhaps the separation from her family would be worse. That too she did not know. It was impossible to analyse these things, and that was how in the end she had made her choice: out of instinct, because estimation and judgement had failed her.

'Would you care for another drink, ma'am?'

It was nearly half-past one.

'No . . . Yes, yes, please.'

464

Clearly, he had been delayed. But why had he not got word to her? Surely he could have called the Ambassador and had them pass a message to the lady on her own in the bar? She began to dislike all the men who came into the room, smacking their shoulders, knocking the snow off their shoes, congratulating themselves on the nugatory achievement of having survived a minor snowfall on the streets of New York before they gorged themselves on giant sandwiches and burgers from the bar. She hated them because they were not Frank.

By the time she left, at ten to two, she was close to tears of frustration. She had kept a level head, she felt; she had kept calm through a great deal in the last few months, but there was something in his failure to appear that seemed unforgivably cruel. She went back to her own hotel, despondently, in order to sit by the telephone.

★   ★   ★

It was six in the evening and she was again dozing when it rang. He was at La Guardia. Snow had closed the airport at Minneapolis; he had rented a car and driven across the state to Green Bay, Wisconsin. He had talked himself on to a small propeller plane to Chicago, where the runways were clear.

'My darling,' she said. 'I . . . I was afraid. But I shouldn't have worried, should I?'

'Do you want to come down to my apartment?'

465

'Yes. Call me when you're back. I don't want to be too quick for you . . . '

One last time, she sprung the chrome catch of the yellow cab on Seventh Avenue and headed south.

She had one thought as the snowflakes rose and churned beneath the rushing street lights: Charlie. Everything she had said to him in Moscow still held true; nothing had been insincere. Yet here she was a world apart: there were different skies, altered gravitational fields; the polar forces were switched and reinvented.

Charlie, even in his confused state, had been very delicate. She remembered his words when he had first hinted that he knew something was going on. 'I no longer felt . . . uniquely culpable.' It was beautifully phrased: she could leave it or take it. How little, she thought with a wistful squeeze of regret, how little she had cared about his own affair to which this was a tactful admission. And then, when she had left London a few days ago, he had again been meticulous; he had simply asked a question: 'And will you be coming back?'

Perhaps all those years of inventing lines of poetry had paid off; if he had been coarser or plainer in his words, there might have been no way back. Perhaps verbal nicety was more than just decorative or pedantic. Perhaps it had kept a life available to her.

★ ★ ★

466

After dinner they returned to Frank's apartment. Mary had said nothing of any decision she had reached; she could not bring herself to break the shimmering pleasure of the night. Frank put on a record and passed her a drink; they could see the snow whirling outside the window, as it fell to the streets so far below. Mary moved closer to Frank on the couch and he wrapped his arm around her.

When they lay in bed later there seemed to be no sounds at all from the city, not even the comforting rumble of distant automobiles and of their tyres throwing up slush.

Frank was lying on his back, crying silently, determined that Mary should not know. The thing about crying when you lay on your back, he thought — something he had forgotten since the last occasion, when he heard of his father's death during his time at army training camp — was that the water rolled into your ears.

He remembered the drill sergeant, who was always screaming at the wretched Godley, and how he had once turned to him, when, after a day-long cross-country hike with weighted packs, they had been required for no obvious reason to scrub the floor of the barracks. 'Be a man, Renzo,' the sergeant shouted, with his face up against Frank's, brandishing a scrubbing brush beneath his nose. 'Don't be a wop. Be a man.'

In the morning Frank did what he had done so many times before: went to the bakery and bought bagels for breakfast, then bought a newspaper. 'So many times . . . ' Who am I kidding? he thought. What did he really mean? Twelve? Thirteen? Eighteen at best.

Mary did not want to leave the sanctuary of the apartment; when Frank suggested they go out later, she said it was too cold.

'What time's your flight?' he said.

'At seven. So I suppose I need to be there at about five.'

'Sure.'

'But, Frank . . .'

'Yes?'

'If you'd like me to stay, I will.'

She was still sitting on the couch, but now dressed, composed, her hands folded in front of her knees.

Frank breathed in. 'That's not a decision I can make for you, sweetheart. I'll support you, but you have to decide alone.'

'I know,' said Mary calmly. 'But I wanted to have some idea before I decided whether it would be . . . welcome to you.'

Frank felt the tears coming at him again and he sucked the air in over his teeth. Be a man, Renzo. He heard the mocking Southern voice.

'I want to stay, Frank. I've decided. I decided while you were away. I'm not going to tell you all the agony of the choice. I'm being true to something beyond myself. This is my only life and I believe that I'm doing the right thing. I think we would be happy.'

'You're an extraordinary woman, Mary. You surprise me more and more.'

Mary sat motionless, as though she did not

dare to move, in case it affected the outcome of his thoughts.

Frank said, 'If you go, that'll be an end of something in me. Some hope, or some desire. Some thought that I could be more than I am. It'll close over. It'll die. But I'll still . . . I'll still be a man. I'll still be someone. I'll be someone who knew something great. Once in his life.'

'Oh my God, Frank.' Mary's voice was shocked; it had gone quiet. 'It sounds as though . . . ' She trailed away.

He turned to face her. 'Mary, I think you should go home.'

Mary let out a moan of grief and went to him. He felt detached from her, as he looked down at the top of her head, thrust against his shirt; he held her there, tightly, because he knew if he saw her face he would weaken and change. Her body was quite still in his arms: she was not crying.

Frank could think of no consolation to offer because the thoughts were too awful to find words. Death would cure her; death would also solve his woe; but he could not say such things.

Eventually he managed to say something, a shadow of what he meant. 'The way you make people love you, the way you made me love you . . . That's something your mother left to you, I guess. It's a legacy from her, from the happiness she gave you. The way you've inspired me with a sense of what life could be. That's no mean gift. No one else has done that. No one I've ever met could possibly do that. It's something you inherited. A gift of love.'

Mary pulled back her face from his chest. 'It's

not much of a legacy, is it? The ability to make people miserable. A talent for despair.'

He could think of no reply.

She said, 'I won't beg you, my love. I'm too old, too proud. And I'm too unhappy. But I swear to you that I have thought about this and I know in some deep, deep place inside me, somewhere that I can't explain, that it's right. And I know another thing. A simple, simple thing. That we'd be happy. It's a kind of miracle, Frank. That we've come from so far apart, different worlds. Across the sea. But only I could give you the happiness that you deserve. The life that could be yours.'

Frank went to the kitchen, poured coffee that he did not want, made as though to wash some cups, did things to keep his hands moving. Then he sat on the stool he had used on the first night Mary came to his apartment, to keep himself away from her.

'I won't do it,' he said.

'Are you being a coward, Frank? Is it that you don't dare?'

'Maybe it is. You can believe that if it helps you. I want to go out. I want to get out of this apartment.'

'Can I come?'

'Of course. I have only a few hours left of you. I'm not taking my eyes from your face.'

They were early for lunch in the local bar, where the young waitress was still setting the salt and pepper on the tables.

'Sure it's okay,' she said. 'What can I get you?'

The bar began to fill, and somehow they went

470

through the process of lunch as though they were normal people. A menu came and went; they placed an order and drank without knowing it from the glasses on the table.

A nervous exhilaration came over them because they knew they had almost no time left. At the next table was a man in his thirties with a boy of about eight, possibly a son to whom a divorce settlement gave him weekend access. The man tried to cheer the boy along, talking of the ball game they would see later and the big dessert he was going to order him. The boy was no good at conversation and between times the man kept sneaking glances at the newspaper on his lap.

Frank and Mary, with no reason to hold back, said things of riskless rhetorical candour.

Mary told him what her mother had explained about the Titans and concluded, 'You are the other half of my soul. I can't bear that I wasted all those years before I met you.'

'I wasn't ready for you. It couldn't have happened a day before it did. My life was leading to that point.'

'Was it the Caesar salad for you, sir?' said the waitress, leaning over them.

'My life is over,' he said. 'It dies when you board that plane.'

'I want you to tell me everything because I'll never have the chance to talk to you again.'

'In thirty minutes, sweetheart?'

'Don't look at your watch. Just don't look.'

'Nothing in my life was of any consequence before I met you.'

471

'Would you care for any desserts?'

'One thing we need to agree. I need to know this, Mary, to stop me from going insane. If you go, you go. There's no coming back. Get in that taxi and it's over. I can't take any more. I'm a strong man, but I can't take any more of this. Is that a deal?'

'It's a deal. And no writing afterwards. No telephone calls. A complete break.'

'Swear to me, swear to God.'

'Shake my hand on it.'

'OK. Now tell me everything you need to say.'

Mary's good humour faltered for a moment. 'All I can think to say is that I love you.' She sniffed noisily.

'OK, OK,' he said, frantic not to let the scene degenerate. 'I'll tell you . . . I'll tell you . . . '

'Just tell me how much you love me. Tell me.'

'I love you with all my heart . . . I love you so much that my life is worthless without you, that — '

'Then let me stay, my darling. Let me stay.'

'Can I get you folks the check now?'

Mary looked up from the table for the first time and saw that the place was almost empty; their waitress was now eating her own lunch at the bar.

It was dark when they emerged; it had stopped snowing and Grove Street was almost empty. They went one last time across to Frank's building, and, up in the apartment, he called for a taxi to take her to the airport.

Now that it was coming he wanted it to be over; yet he could not bear to take his eyes away

472

from her face. If he looked hard enough, he thought, he might imprint its image permanently on his retina, so she would not really be gone, but would be a veil or mist through which he would see the rest of his life.

They managed to remain calm, even humorous as the minutes passed. Then there was a silence.

Frank said, 'I will think of you every day. All the time. If ever you should think of me and wonder what I'm doing, I'm thinking of you. That's all I'll be doing. Nothing else.'

She smiled. 'I believe you.'

'How can you smile at me at a time like this?'

'It's my happy temperament, Frank. I'm famous for it.'

The telephone rang. It was the taxi.

'I'll come down with you. I'll carry your case. Have you got your ticket? Passport?'

Mary stood inside the front door of the apartment. 'Remember the deal? This is your last chance. Once I'm gone . . . '

He could not speak, so leaned down and grabbed the suitcase and walked along the corridor towards the elevator. She smiled at him wanly as they waited.

Downstairs they crossed the marble lobby.

'How ya doin', Frank?' said Giovanni, the Super, coming out of his office.

The cab was waiting by the kerb. The driver threw Mary's bag into the trunk.

'Idlewild Airport,' said Frank. 'Have you got money?'

Mary nodded. She looked up into his face,

473

scraping it with her eyes. 'Goodbye, Frank.'

He held her once, wordlessly, then released her. She did not look out of the cab window as the vehicle moved off, indicating as it swung out slowly on to Christopher Street. Frank stood, shivering, watching the tail lights as the car slowed down in the slush, made a slow, deliberate right into Waverly Place, and disappeared.

★　★　★

Back in his apartment, Frank felt reasonably calm. He was certain he had come to the right decision, certain that Mary would, in the course of the years, come to think so too. He wished that he had had a photograph. Maybe he could break the deal just once to write and ask for one. He wished that he had had a little more time. But what they had done together, the time they had had, surely that was enough; surely, he thought, lighting a cigarette, prowling across the room, that had a density and richness off which he could live for ever.

The difficulty lay in passing the future days. Whatever hours remained in his life would be filled by other things, by other people; not by her.

The task began now. There was an an evening to dispose of, to bury. He picked up the newspaper and began to flick through it, scanning two pages at once. He turned on the television, which was showing an old ball game, and forced himself to watch it. The third baseman stepped to the plate. There was one out and two men on base. It was a good-looking game. He might call Bob Levine later, maybe look in at the Five Spot.

He had been watching the game for twenty minutes; he had killed off almost an hour of his life already.

He went through to the kitchen and poured himself a bourbon, threw in some ice, took a deep pull and poured up to the brim again. He did not really know what he was feeling.

The game wore on. He sneaked a look at his watch. It was six-fifteen. Checked in, baggage away. She was almost gone.

He went through to the bathroom and washed the traces of newspaper ink off his hands. He ran his damp fingers through his hair and looked at himself in the mirror above the basin. The face had gazed back from worse places than this: scraps of mirror hanging from a jungle tree, shared toilets in freezing tenements. He smiled stiffly. He felt all right.

He went into the bedroom to find a towel to dry his hands. Among the shambles of the unmade bed, he found one. Beside it, wrapped up in twisted sheets, his hand touched something soft. He pulled it out. It was one of her sweaters.

He held it up, then laid it against his cheek. His hands were shaking. What kind of human being am I? he thought. I had a chance to get outside the limits of my life. She stood on my doorstep; she gave me one last chance. Oh, Jesus Christ. Jesus Christ.

Oh, Mary. He looked at his watch. It was

twenty-past six. He had forty minutes. He ran from the apartment, grabbing his coat in the hall; he sprinted down the corridor to the elevator and jabbed the call button repeatedly with his finger.

Down on Christopher Street he looked frantically back and forth, then ran up to Sixth Avenue. A yellow light was coming towards him. He leaped into the road and waved his arm. The driver swerved over, the front end of the car bucking as the braking tyres fought to grip the road beneath the slush.

'Idlewild. Here's twenty bucks. Twenty more if you make it in less than thirty minutes. Go on!'

The driver, an elderly white man with a greasy-necked plaid jacket, said, 'OK, pal. Don't push me.'

He swung the cab in a leisurely circle to the right, up West Ninth Street.

'Which way you wanna go?'

'I don't know. You're the fucking driver. The fastest way.'

'You sure don't wanna miss that plane, do ya?'

The cab crawled across town, gripped by the red lights of Manhattan at every junction, like an honoured visitor to whom the island was fastidiously reluctant to say farewell. The cars tailed back beneath the East River: people from Queens coming in for Saturday night, Frank thought, but why so many going out? In the line for tolls, they funnelled into the slowest chute, the cabin manned by some kid on his first experience of handling currency, the drivers placidly searching pockets, rear seats, trunks and trailers for the right change.

Frank was struggling hard to hold himself in check.

'I have to make that goddam plane,' he said. 'I just have to.'

'You told me, pal. I'm doing my best. I didn't ask all these cars to park their asses in front of me.'

They were on the Van Wyck Expressway at last, the boulevard the City had cut through Queens to speed the traffic to the waiting planes.

'What the fuck is going on?' said Frank.

'Beats me, bud. Maybe there's a game on.'

'Change lanes. Get on the inside. Push through. Know any shortcuts?'

'Relax, will ya?'

'Where you from? Aren't you from Queens?'

'No, I'm from the Bronx.'

'Aren't you supposed to know the fucking city?'

'Listen, bud, you go on like this and I'm gonna put you down, twenty bucks or no twenty bucks.'

'Forty. Move it.'

The gantries overhead showed white directions on their placid green rectangles: suburbs you would never want to visit, rows of nothing in the flightpath, magnets for the idling traffic.

'I never seen it like this before,' said the driver. 'Friday evening, yes. Friday, it's bad. People goin' to Long Island. But Saturday. Beats me. It's ten to seven. We ain't gonna make it. Face it, feller, we ain't gonna make it.'

Frank looked down at his watch in the darkness of the car's interior; the luminous minute hand was sweeping to the upright. The cab was moving at five miles an hour, then stopping; then jerking forwards for a few yards, then stopping again. They were not even getting signs to Idlewild; the airport directions were all still for La Guardia.

Frank no longer looked from the window of the taxi; he gazed only at the face of his watch, and when the minute hand touched twelve he lowered his head into his arms and held it for a long time, silently, rocking himself in the darkness.

At fifteen minutes past, he said, 'How far are we away?'

'At this rate, I guess another twenty minutes.'

'All right. Pull over. Go up this ramp. Stop the car as soon as you can.'

The driver swung through from the outside lane, where he had been stuck, cut across two lanes of resentful traffic, off the freeway and up on to a raised road that looped back over a bridge.

'Keep going,' said Frank. 'Take that small turn there. Down to the right.'

They were on a narrow road that was leading towards a group of houses.

'Pull over right here.'

The cab stopped and Frank opened the door. He stood up and looked down at the solid lights of Van Wyck beneath them; then he walked a few paces towards the row of framehouses, pinched, shivering and indifferent in the winter night.

By the road was a ditch and he knelt down, lifting a handful of leaves made damp by the snow. He let them fall from his hands, then picked up more and rubbed them into the back of his neck. He looked up at the lightless sky and then walked back, uncertainly, to the car.

As he stood beside it, he felt a cry coming up from inside him, not a sob but something like a shout of strangled, raging grief, and as it came out of his lungs, he bellowed and howled, trying to free himself of what was welling up inside him, and he began to hammer at the roof of the taxi with his fists, again and again, so the soft metal bent beneath the impact.

The driver came round. 'What the hell you doin' to my car? Are you some kind of crazy?' He pushed Frank in the chest. 'Get out of here, will ya?'

The driver climbed back into the cab, turned round and drove off towards the ramp that would take him back to the expressway. Frank felt his knees give way beneath him and he buried his face in the damp leaves to muffle the noise of his howls.

21

Mary was too shocked by the speed of events to feel much as the taxi made its way through the streets of the East Village. Each light seemed to yield its green obediently as they approached, so it was not until the East River that the car slowed down out of top gear. She turned her head around to see the last of that monstrous skyline which always reminded her of Dresden, with only the strongest buildings left standing. They moved rapidly onward to the Tunnel at First and 41st . . . At last! She had found her new prime number, her escape from the grid.

There seemed to be hardly any traffic at all on the way to Idlewild.

'Where is everyone?' she said. She was hoping for an accident, some terrible pile-up of cars, of slewed and jack-knifed trailer-trucks across the highway, that would make it impossible to complete the journey.

'I guess it's the game,' said the driver, a young man in a leather jacket. 'Enjoying the ride? It's a new car. I only had it three weeks. Where ya headed?'

'London. England.'

'Which airline?'

'BOAC.'

'OK, you're right by the main entrance in the arrival building there.'

Mary looked up at the modest framehouses on

the embankment above the expressway and she envied the people who lived there for the tranquillity of their lives. She was frightened by the thought of how long it was going to take her to digest what was happening to her.

The green and white signs above the road began to flash their terminal messages: La Guardia, then International Airport. Her throat was dry. She could barely believe the speed with which they were completing the journey. The driver was delighted when his headlights picked out the upright rectangle of the new Arrival building; the site itself was full of half-finished work, notably the TWA terminal, a white bird-like structure through whose skeletal wings tall girders rose into the night. There were hardly any cars on the slip roads or at the front of the building; it was more like an airfield than an international airport.

Mary was on the kerb, and the driver hauled out her suitcase while she fumbled for the right money to pay him. She hoped he would suddenly stop and say something like, 'It's all right, lady. It's a practical joke. I have to take you back now.'

He said nothing after he had thanked her, but climbed back into the yellow car and switched on his light. Mary went through the plate-glass doors to the check-in. Her hand was shaking a little, perhaps from exertion, as she hauled her bag on to the scale. The woman behind the desk politely checked the ticket, and again Mary hoped she would tell her it was the wrong day or the wrong place, but she merely smiled and wished her a pleasant flight as she handed back the passport.

She went, as instructed, to the escalator at the end of the hall and up to the first floor. There was an atmosphere of calm and opulence: all the women wore hats; the men were dressed in suits and ties. The polished floor was barely used, and the ashtrays in their upturned metal cones were empty. It was still only six o'clock and her flight was not due to leave for another hour. She didn't know what to do to make the time pass, so she went along to the BOAC lounge. Inside there was a feeling of studied luxury, as though they wished to put the facts of flying as far away as possible. There was a smell of leather from the seats; the woodwork was in teak and the end wall was covered in blue and magenta leather squares. She sat at a vacant table — all the tables seemed to be vacant — and ordered a vodka and tonic, something she never normally drank.

She tried to think of Louisa and Richard, but she could not concentrate. They were young and what they felt could not touch her at this moment. It was a disease of being the age she was that had made her feel that her deepest experiences of love — for her mother, for Frank, for her children, for Charlie — were in some way presentiments of dying. She could not tolerate the experience of loving as desperately as she did; she would rather they were all dead, so she would have nothing left to suffer. She knew it was not rational: Louisa and Richard never gave a thought to their mortality; even her mother as she neared the end had been curiously indifferent to it.

She smoked a cigarette and ordered another drink. She gazed at the décor. She had the time to take in every detail.

She could not think clearly about the events of the last year; the memory of them rushed at her from different angles, impossible to hold, though one thing did strike her in the confusion. Her private decision to take a room in New York had been influenced by her impetuous need to escape from Duncan Trench's importunings; Charlie's first suspicions of her behaviour had been suggested to him by agents of the FBI, while her own moment of emotional clarity in Moscow had been precipitated by the haunting presence of the state's unseen watchers. What strange days, she thought. And then poor Billy Foy, used up and thrown away . . .

She drained the drink down to the ice. The alcohol was doing something to weaken her resolve. She was finding it very difficult to keep herself calm in this formal, well-behaved environment.

She began to believe that she had made a mistake. She should have stayed with Frank. She had had one chance, and out of some confused motive — pride and fear as much as anything — she had let it slip. At half-past six there came an announcement over the tannoy system.

Her flight had been delayed for an hour.

It was this news that fractured her resolve. She knew she could not wait that long. She stood up and went out into the hallway to look for a telephone. There was a booth halfway down, next to a news stand. Somehow she was going to have to make those coins work for once, those nickels, dimes and pennies.

She knew Frank's number by heart, but she pulled out the book of matches — the original one on which he had first written it. She did not want to make a mistake at this stage; she didn't want to beg a stranger to come out to the airport for her.

Her hands were shaking so hard she couldn't fit the nickel in the slot. She clamped the receiver between her shoulder and her ear and used both hands to steady the coin. She drove it home with her thumb and dialled.

As she listened to the connection being made, Mary sensed two or three people waiting in line behind her. She heard the telephone ringing in Frank's apartment.

She had not cried once — at least, not that she could recall — since this chain of terrible events had begun. Now she felt something filling up inside her, a great reservoir on which the lid was beginning to lift.

No one answered the telephone. Hearing the impatient clucking of the people behind her, she slowly redialled, showering coins on the polished floor. A man in a felt hat picked them up and put them back into her hand with a gracious smile; his act of kindness almost broke her self-control.

There was no doubt that this time she had dialled correctly. There was still no answer, but she did not dare to hang up in case Frank was running down the corridor from the elevator, dashing into the room and lunging for the phone, grabbing it the very moment it stopped ringing.

So, to fool the people behind her, Mary began to speak, as though he had really answered.

'Hello, Frank,' she said. 'How are you? I'm fine, I'm fine . . . '

At that point tears at last erupted from her eyes and began to wash down her cheeks. Her voice died in her throat. Now she faced a different problem: she could not turn around and let the people see her disarray. She had to pretend to make another call. She rotated the dial again, affecting, through blinded eyes, to read another number from the book of matches. She stamped her foot in mock impatience, shook her head and dialled again.

Eventually she had regained enough control to swivel quickly from the telephone. She could not see to replace the receiver in its cradle, so left it dangling on its flex, as she rushed into the news vendor, where she closely examined the long rows of magazines on the shelves.

For ten or fifteen minutes she stood in front of the display with tears of death running down her face on to her coat. She had no handkerchief with which to staunch them, so kept turning round to avoid inquiring stares. To kill more time, she thought she should buy presents for Richard and Louisa, and grabbed a doll, a tinny statue of the Empire State Building and made her way to the till with lowered eyes. She gave over a ten dollar bill but could not see to pick up the change. She waved a generous hand behind

485

her to the protesting storekeeper and went to the ladies' washroom, where she found a cubicle and sat down heavily behind a locked door. Her body was heaving and shaking in her arms. She could not stop it.

She heard her flight being called, and made her way unsteadily to the gate, her face streaked black with run mascara.

On the plane she found herself sitting next to a young man. She was by the window and she turned her head away from him to stare at the retreating baggage truck. The perspex was cold against her forehead.

The plane taxied to the end of the runway, and she felt it brace, then rush towards the night. She did not know she had so many tears inside her. They were not like the two bilious little pearls she had squeezed from her reluctant eyes in her parents' rose garden as her mother lay dying — though she supposed they were related to that day. They were a river, a torrent, that ran and washed down her face, drenching the collar and the front of her sweater. The rims of her eyes were like fire.

The young man, embarrassed, offered her a handkerchief, which she took wordlessly. She could not stop crying. They were in the air, heading for Europe, and she could not stop crying.

She felt time begin its linear rush, the big plane gobbling up the hours in its howling craw, and she wept and wept and wept.

She thought of Frank, she thought of him below her on the ground. She did not know what he was doing then, but she formed a picture in her mind. Once, when she and Charlie were coming from Boston, the plane had flown around the southern tip of Manhattan. She did not think it likely her BOAC plane was doing so that night, but, because of the weather, it just might be. There obviously was a flightpath there, she thought, because she could see the planes from Frank's window.

Her idea of what Frank was doing was quite clear.

He was back in his apartment. He had put on a favourite record and it was playing softly at the other end of the room. There were the bass and drums, the piano hitting its rhythm and the trumpet snaking out above them.

He poured himself a drink and went over to the big window that overlooked the Jersey shore, holding the glass in his hand. He gazed for a long time into the night, and up there he saw the wing-lights of her plane as it turned towards the East; he watched intently as the small light went flashing on, off, on, off in the black snow clouds; and he raised his glass to it, he drank to it in a gesture of love and forgiveness, as in the uprushing hours it blinked once more, then vanished, swallowed by the dark.

We do hope that you have enjoyed reading
this large print book.

Did you know that all of our titles
are available for purchase?

We publish a wide range of high quality
large print books including:
Romances, Mysteries, Classics
General Fiction
Non Fiction and Westerns

Special interest titles available in
large print are:
The Little Oxford Dictionary
Music Book
Song Book
Hymn Book
Service Book

Also available from us courtesy of Oxford
University Press:
Young Readers' Dictionary
(large print edition)
Young Readers' Thesaurus
(large print edition)

For further information or a free
brochure, please contact us at:
Ulverscroft Large Print Books Ltd.,
The Green, Bradgate Road, Anstey,
Leicester, LE7 7FU, England.
Tel: (00 44) 0116 236 4325
Fax: (00 44) 0116 234 0205